Corpus Stylistics in *Heart of Darkness* and its Italian Translations

Corpus and Discourse

Series editors:
Wolfgang Teubert, University of Birmingham, and Michaela Mahlberg,
University of Birmingham

Editorial Board:
Paul Baker (Lancaster), Frantisek Čermák (Prague), Susan Conrad (Portland),
Dominique Maingueneau (Paris XII), Christian Mair (Freiburg),
Alan Partington (Bologna), Elena Tognini-Bonelli (Siena and TWC),
Ruth Wodak (Lancaster), Feng Zhiwei (Beijing).

Corpus linguistics provides the methodology to extract meaning from texts. Taking as its starting point the fact that language is not a mirror of reality but lets us share what we know, believe and think about reality, it focuses on language as a social phenomenon, and makes visible the attitudes and beliefs expressed by the members of a discourse community.

Consisting of both spoken and written language, discourse always has historical, social, functional, and regional dimensions. Discourse can be monolingual or multilingual, interconnected by translations. Discourse is where language and social studies meet.

The *Corpus and Discourse* series consists of two strands. The first, *Research in Corpus and Discourse*, features innovative contributions to various aspects of corpus linguistics and a wide range of applications, from language technology via the teaching of a second language to a history of mentalities. The second strand, *Studies in Corpus and Discourse*, is comprised of key texts bridging the gap between social studies and linguistics. Although equally academically rigorous, this strand will be aimed at a wider audience of academics and postgraduate students working in both disciplines.

Research in Corpus and Discourse
Conversation in Context
A Corpus-driven Approach
With a preface by Michael McCarthy
Christoph Rühlemann

Corpus-Based Approaches to English Language Teaching
Edited by Mari Carmen Campoy, Begona Bellés-Fortuno and
Mª Lluïsa Gea-Valor

Sadness Expressions in English and Chinese
Corpus Linguistic Contrastive Semantic Analysis
Ruihua Zhang

Working with Spanish Corpora
Edited by Giovanni Parodi

Studies in Corpus and Discourse

Corpus Linguistics in Literary Analysis
Jane Austen and Her Contemporaries
Bettina Fischer-Starcke

English Collocation Studies
The OSTI Report
John Sinclair, Susan Jones and Robert Daley
Edited by Ramesh Krishnamurthy
With an introduction by Wolfgang Teubert

Text, Discourse, and Corpora. Theory and Analysis
Michael Hoey, Michaela Mahlberg, Michael Stubbs and Wolfgang Teubert
With an introduction by John Sinclair

Web As Corpus
Theory and Practice
Maristella Gatto

Corpus Stylistics in *Heart of Darkness* and its Italian Translations

Lorenzo Mastropierro

BLOOMSBURY ACADEMIC
LONDON • NEW YORK • OXFORD • NEW DELHI • SYDNEY

BLOOMSBURY ACADEMIC
Bloomsbury Publishing Plc
50 Bedford Square, London, WC1B 3DP, UK
1385 Broadway, New York, NY 10018, USA

BLOOMSBURY, BLOOMSBURY ACADEMIC and the Diana logo are
trademarks of Bloomsbury Publishing Plc

First published 2018
Paperback edition first published 2019

A catalogue record for this book is available from the British Library.

Library of Congress Cataloging-in-Publication Data
Names: Mastropierro, Lorenzo, author.
Title: Corpus stylistics in Heart of Darkness and its
Italian translations / Lorenzo Mastropierro.
Description: New York : Bloomsbury Academic, 2017. |
Series: Corpus and discourse | Includes bibliographical references and index.
Identifiers: LCCN 2017010077 | ISBN 9781350013544 (hardcover) |
ISBN 9781350013551 (epdf) | ISBN 9781350013568 (epub)
Subjects: LCSH: Discourse analysis, Literary. | Translating and interpreting–Methodology. |
Literary style. | Conrad, Joseph, 1857–1924–Literary style. |
Conrad, Joseph, 1857–1924–Language and
languages. | BISAC: LANGUAGE ARTS & DISCIPLINES /
Linguistics / General. | FICTION / Literary.
Classification: LCC P302.5 .M383 2017 | DDC 813/.912–dc23
LC record available at https://lccn.loc.gov/2017010077

ISBN: HB: 978-1-3500-1354-4
PB: 978-1-3501-1256-8
ePDF: 978-1-3500-1355-1
ePub: 978-1-3500-1356-8

Series: Corpus and Discourse

Typeset by Newgen Knowledge Works Pvt. Ltd., Chennai, India

To find out more about our authors and books visit
www.bloomsbury.com and sign up for our newsletters.

A Tonia e Giovanni.
Grazie di tutto.

Contents

Illustrations

Figures

Tables

Acknowledgements

Many friends and colleagues have assisted me along the way to the publication of this book. I would like to thank Peter Stockwell, Dan McIntyre, Wolfgang Teubert and Florent Perek for commenting on previous versions of the manuscript or parts of it. I am especially indebted to Michaela Mahlberg, who has supported me in so many respects. Very special thanks also go to Gavin Brookes for his invaluable feedback and to Maristella Gatto for believing in me from the very beginning of this journey. Finally, my deepest gratitude goes to Emma Zimmerman and my family, for their constant and unconditional support.

Introduction

This book presents a corpus analysis of Joseph Conrad's ([1902] 1994) *Heart of Darkness* (*HoD*) and four of its Italian translations, combining corpus stylistics and descriptive translation studies. Corpus stylistics is the application of corpus methods to the study of literature by relating linguistic description to literary interpretation (Mahlberg 2013). Descriptive translation studies is concerned with the empirical examination of the product, the process and the function of translation (Toury 1995). Sharing a number of fundamental assumptions, these two disciplines are particularly apt to be combined. First, they both adopt an empirical approach to investigate language. Second, they consider language to be a social phenomenon. Translating, as well as writing and reading literature, is a highly contextualized activity, related to linguistic and extralinguistic aspects alike. Both corpus stylistics and descriptive translation studies seek to account for the extralinguistic factors in the examination of the linguistic ones. Finally, the two disciplines hinge on comparison. Corpus stylistics defines and describes style on the basis of the identification of a difference between a sample and a norm, a text and a reference corpus (Halliday 1971, Fowler 1966, Leech and Short 2007). Similarly, descriptive translation studies rests on the comparison of the source text (ST) and the target text (TT) as the primary method of analysis (Bassnett 2007, Munday 2008).

There are several advantages in adopting a corpus approach in the study of literature and its translation. Computer technologies allow the researcher to analyse texts on a scale and level of statistical detail that would be unachievable for the human analyst alone. Novels can be as short as *HoD*, which is about a hundred pages, and still it would be impossible to parallel the computational abilities of the computer with standard reading. The data offered by the calculator can help with the stylistic analysis, as numerical evidence is used to substantiate claims about style (Leech and Short 2007: 38). However, it is not only a matter of sheer computing. Corpus methods offer new and unprecedented ways to study and compare texts. They add new descriptive tools to the stylistician's toolkit and make possible types of analysis that were not previously achievable. With new methods come new research questions.

This book has three overarching aims. The first aim is to carry out a corpus stylistic study of *HoD*, focusing on the role of textual patterns as building blocks of the fictional world. I argue that literary themes are related to the way the fictional world is linguistically constructed. Examining the linguistic construction of the fictional world allows me to study how textual patterns contribute to the text's themes. The analysis concentrates mainly on lexical and semantic patterns, through the examination of semantic preferences and semantic prosodies. Semantic preferences and prosodies play a key part in conveying meaning in texts (Sinclair 1991, 2004), and their role in literature has been proved to be similarly meaningful (Louw 1993, Fischer-Starke 2010, Munday 2011). Moreover, semantic preferences and prosodies are not strictly defined on the basis of frequency cut-off points, that is, there is no frequency threshold for a word to be part of a semantic preference and/or prosody. This is important because *HoD* is a short text, especially compared to the amount of words that corpus linguistics usually deals with. Semantic preferences and prosodies are not affected by the size of *HoD*, as they can account for the cumulative effect of words that do not occur frequently in the text. In contrast, the identification of frequency-based patterns (such as collocational or colligational patterns) can be affected by the size of the text/corpus, given that these patterns are usually defined in statistical terms.

The second aim of this book is to compare four Italian versions of *HoD*, concentrating on the effect of translation on the relation between textual patterns and the fictional world. I show that this relation is affected by the linguistic alterations resulting from translating, independent of whether the alterations are conscious translation strategies or unconscious changes. Modifications in the patterns of the original result in discrepancies in the representation of the fictional world between the ST and the TTs. This study argues that these discrepancies are not only limited to the linguistic level, but are also concerned with the interpretational level. Specific aspects of *HoD*'s fictional world are strictly related to its major themes; therefore, the changes in the patterns can also affect the interpretation of these themes.

Finally, the third aim is to establish a methodological synergy between corpus stylistics and translation studies, outlining a framework with broader applicability beyond the specific analysis of Conrad and its Italian translations. Nevertheless, the present study is mainly focused on Conrad and *HoD*, as this text and its translations represent an ideal case study to explore the relationships between textual patterns, fictional worlds and literary themes.

There are many reasons behind the decision to focus on Joseph Conrad and *HoD*. First, Conrad is an author who, from a stylistic point of view, has a lot to offer. With his writing, Conrad aims 'to make [the reader] hear, to make [him/her] feel – it is, before all, to make [him/her] *see*' (Conrad 1950: ix, emphasis in the original). As he puts it in his literary manifesto, the renowned preface to *The Nigger of the Narcissus* (Conrad [1897] 1950), Conrad believes that a writer should be 'devot[ed] to the perfect blending of form and substance' (Conrad 1950: ix) and should have a 'never-discouraged care for the shape and ring of sentences' (Conrad 1950: ix). He is very aware of the importance of the linguistic form in his literary aesthetic, knowing that it can assist in the development of his artistic aims. Conrad is well-known for going to considerable effort to pursue *le mot juste* (Knowles 2009b: 34). This attention to prose form as a means through which to convey his artistic intentions makes Conrad an exemplary subject for a study such as the present one. Second, Conrad and especially *HoD* occupy a central position in the English literary canon, and their popularity is reflected in over a century of sustained interest. This is very useful for a corpus stylistic analysis because it means that there is an abundance of evidence of how both readers and critics have responded to Conrad's novels. The study can therefore be informed by, and interact with, this critical background. This also applies to the translations. Conrad's popularity is by no means tied to national boundaries, but is instead widespread all over the world. The critical discussion of his works has been equally lively in Italy (Ciompi 2005), and *HoD* in particular is the novel with the largest number of Italian translations in Conrad's oeuvre (Curreli 2009: 149), with over twenty versions since the first one in 1924. As such, *HoD* is a valuable text for the study of literary translation. An additional benefit to studying Conrad is that the vast majority of his texts are readily available on the internet, free from copyright restrictions. This means that the process of retrieving texts in the appropriate digital format and building reference corpora is greatly facilitated.

This book is structured as follows. Chapter 1 sets the theoretical ground for the interdisciplinary dialogue between corpus stylistics and translation studies. It introduces the study of style with corpus methods, both in literature and in translation, and illustrates the specific approach that this work adopts. Chapter 2 defines the two major themes of *HoD* that are analysed: 'Africa and its representation' and 'race and racism'. To do so, the chapter outlines the critical reception of *HoD* and emphasizes the themes that seem to be the most relevant to contemporary criticism. Chapter 3 sets out the methodology of the project and discusses the practical implication of using a corpus stylistic approach to study literary translations. This chapter also details the research questions of this book, explaining how each one is addressed by the methodology. Chapter 4 starts the analysis, using keywords to establish a link between the lexical level of *HoD* and the two major themes identified in Chapter 2. By grouping the keywords into 'fictional world signals' and 'thematic signals', this chapter identifies categories of relevant items that are analysed in detail in the following chapters. Chapter 5 focuses on the first group of keywords, related to 'Africa and its representation'. This chapter carries out a quantitative and qualitative analysis of the fictional representation of the African jungle, both in the ST and in the TTs. It discusses the role that lexico-semantic patterns play in building up the representation of the jungle and examines the effect of translation on how the jungle is depicted in the TTs. Chapter 6 concentrates on the second group of keywords, which is linked to the theme 'race and racism'. This chapter uses a similar approach to the previous one, this time applied to the study of the fictional representation of the African natives. The way the African characters are linguistically constructed in both the ST and the TTs is examined and compared, and the discrepancies identified are analysed in terms of the effect they have on how the theme 'race and racism' is interpreted. Chapter 7 approaches the texts from a different perspective to the previous chapters, as it aims to compare the translations as whole texts, rather than focusing on specific linguistic features within the texts. This is done by employing principal component analysis, a statistical method that offers a measure of the general degree of difference between the texts. Chapter 8 discusses the central findings of this book, highlighting its contributions to the field, as well as outlining some further avenues for future research.

Overall, this book aims to make an innovative contribution to the application of corpus stylistics to the study of literary translation. By examining the relation between textual patterns, the fictional world and central literary themes, it contributes to a more nuanced understanding of the interaction between form and meaning in literature, and how translation affects the interplay of the two. In doing so, this book seeks to demonstrate the potential of interdisciplinary research, by triangulating corpus methods, stylistics and translation studies. The present study also aims to participate in the critical discussion of Conrad and *HoD*. My focus on central themes allows me to contribute to key areas of

Conradian studies, offering a linguistic perspective on fundamental aspects of *HoD*. Fredrick R. Karl (in Purssell 2009: 83) has claimed that Conrad is a writer 'about whom very little remains to be said'. Ultimately, I seek to challenge this narrow viewpoint by demonstrating how an interdisciplinary approach to Conrad's *HoD* foregrounds previously overlooked textual features that in turn provide fresh insight into such a popular and iconic text.

A Corpus Stylistic Approach to the Study of Literary Translation

1.1 Introduction

This book examines the relationship between lexico-semantic patterns and fictional worlds in *HoD* and four of its Italian translations. The approach used is that of stylistics, while corpus linguistics provides the tools for the analysis. This chapter deals with the interaction between the two, and their application in translation studies. Section 1.2 introduces stylistics, emphasizing in particular its focus on both linguistic description and literary appreciation, and its comparative nature. Section 1.3 discusses the interface between stylistics and corpus methods, reviewing the overall development of the field. Section 1.4 provides an overview of recent developments in corpus stylistics, with particular attention to studies that share features with this book. Section 1.5 brings translation studies into the picture, outlining the approach that this book adopts to study translation. Analysing style in translation often involves the comparison of the ST with the TT; in Section 1.6, I argue that corpus stylistics can enhance this comparative perspective and support the analysis with empirical data. Sections 1.5 and 1.6 also stress that a (corpus) stylistic approach to the study of translation is not necessarily tied to linguistic description only, but is able to account for extra-textual factors too, for example, manipulative effects. Section 1.7 introduces the notion of translation manipulation, how it is discussed in translation studies literature, and how it is used here. Finally, Section 1.8 closes the chapter with some concluding remarks.

1.2 Stylistics and the comparison of style

Stylistics is the linguistic study of style in language (Leech and Short 2007; Lambrou and Stockwell 2007; Simpson 2004). It is applied both to literary and non-literary texts (cf. Jeffries and McIntyre 2010), although it is predominantly concerned with the former, as in the case of this book. Stylistics rests upon the idea that there is no reason to 'separate the literary from the overall linguistic' (Jakobson 1960: 377), as the distinction between literary and non-literary language does not necessarily stand up (Carter 2004). Linguistic models and techniques can be applied to analyse literature, enhancing our understanding of literary texts. The aim of stylistics is to link linguistic description to literary appreciation. As Leech and Short (2007: 11) put it, we study the style of Conrad because we assume it can tell us something about him as a literary artist. This understanding of stylistics as combining linguistic description and literary appreciation has been advocated by Spitzer (1962), who proposes the 'philological circle' as a means to explain the interaction between the two. Linguistic analysis and critical interpretation are linked to each other in a cyclical motion; there is no priority given on either but rather mutual collaboration. One motivates and informs the other. The text is considered at the same time a sample of language in use and a literary work, and is analysed as such.

Stylistics is, by definition, a multidisciplinary field, as it encompasses perspectives from literary studies and linguistics alike. Because of its tendency to unite two disciplines that have been traditionally considered separate, stylistics has been criticized by both linguists and literary critics. Stubbs (2005: 5) explains that linguists are often sceptical towards stylistics, as they are uninterested in investigating individual texts. On the contrary, they tend to study regularities across language, in order to develop general theories. On the other hand, literary scholars can find stylistic analysis flawed by circularity and arbitrariness (Fish 1979, 1980), especially when claims on literary style are based on a few specifically selected linguistic examples. Despite the scepticism, stylistics develops its main strength exactly from the interaction of these two diverse yet strongly linked disciplines. Far from being the only focus of the analysis, the linguistic description complements the critical interpretation. Studying the linguistic form helps to explain why we perceive the text in a given way and offers an observable justification for our readerly experience, which might otherwise remain unexplained. Even if this just confirmed existing interpretations with empirical data, it would be a positive outcome nevertheless. As Stubbs (2005: 6) makes clear, the confirmation of what we already know would still give us confidence that the stylistic method is reliable, because it matches the findings of other broadly established approaches. From the other direction, when literary appreciation informs linguistic scrutiny, the analysis acknowledges the 'literariness' (Carter 2004) of the text, so that each formal feature is studied in the context of the artistic effects conveyed by the text.

Another characteristic feature of stylistics is that it is 'essentially comparative in nature' (Halliday 1971: 341). Investigating the style of a text often entails identifying features that characterize that text when compared with others. For instance, Senn (1980) recognizes in Conrad's narrative an adjectival style. This implies that Conrad's use of adjectives is perceived as different from that of other writers. If every other author used adjectives in the way Conrad does, then this feature would not be characteristic anymore. Therefore, in order to classify Conrad's use of adjectives as a stylistic feature of his novels, we need to compare them with other novels by other authors and recognize a difference in their adjectival use. In other words, 'usage in one text is significant only by comparison with usage outside it' (Fowler 1966: 22).

Comparison in stylistics can be established on a number of different levels. Leech and Short (2007) identify three principal ones. First, a textual example can be compared to a general set of texts, which represent a heterogeneous sample of language (e.g. comparing Conrad's novels with other general purpose texts). Second, a textual example can be compared to a set of texts written by the same author or of the same genre (e.g. comparing *HoD* with the rest of Conrad's novels). Third, a textual example can be compared to the whole text from which it is taken (e.g. comparing the first chapter of *HoD* with the remaining ones). These different comparisons relate to three types of deviation from a perceived norm: primary deviation, secondary deviation and internal deviation (Leech and Short 2007: 44). 'Primary deviation' is a deviation from general language; 'secondary deviation' is a deviation from authorial or genre-specific norms; 'internal deviation' is a deviation from the norms of the text itself (Leech 1985: 45–8). This book focuses mainly on secondary deviations, comparing *HoD* against Conrad's other novels and against other literary texts from the same period.

Comparison is equally fundamental in translation studies, given that most of the questions the discipline deals with – from the strategies employed by the translator to the different statuses of the ST and TT in their respective cultures – are analysable mainly through comparing translations against originals, or vice versa. 'More broadly', Bassnett (2007: 19) explains, the comparison of the original and the translated text 'will expose the relationship between the two cultural systems in which those texts are embedded'. In terms of stylistic analysis, it is only through the comparison of the ST with the TT that differences in style can be discovered: '[a]ny alteration, muffling, exaggeration, blurring, or other distortion of authorial voice will remain hidden until and unless some element of the TT reveals the mediation or until the TT is compared to its ST' (Munday 2008: 14).

Comparing texts is at the basis of the analyses that follow and, more generally, comparison takes centre stage in this book: it is not only an intrinsic part of the stylistic analysis, but is also fundamental in studying translation. Given that comparison can be greatly enhanced by corpus methods and tools, it is not surprising that the use of corpus approaches has become an established practice in stylistic analysis.

1.3 Corpus stylistics

In their second edition of *Style in Fiction*, Leech and Short (2007: 286) acknowledge that stylistics has experienced a 'corpus turn' in recent years, with a growth in the number of studies applying corpus methods to the analysis of literature. This growth has been fostered by the increasing availability of texts in electronic format and user-friendly software for text analysis, making it possible for more and more researchers to benefit from the advantages that the application of corpus methods in stylistics entails. In particular, there are two main areas in which these advantages are most striking: providing quantitative data and bringing new analytical techniques.

As explained in the previous section, stylistics is essentially comparative in nature (Halliday 1971). Comparison is necessary to prove that a linguistic feature characterizes one text against the background of standard usage. There must be a difference in the consistency and tendency of occurrence compared to a norm in order to define that feature as typical of a given author or text. Consistency and tendency are best examined in terms of frequency (Leech and Short 2007: 34), and frequency can be accurately described quantitatively. According to Halliday (1971: 343), all instances of recognizable style, whether of an individual writer, of a single book or of an entire genre, have distinctive features that can be analysed in terms of relative frequency. For example, Senn (1980: 21) specifically identifies adjectival series – sequences of two, three or more adjectives – as characteristic of Conrad's adjectival style. In *HoD*, there are about 170 two-part adjectival series, 22 three-part, 10 four-part, 2 five-part and 1 eight-part series (Senn 1980: 22). This quantification provides us with an idea of the proportion of series in *HoD*. However, if we want to claim that adjectival series are a linguistic feature that characterizes *HoD*'s style, we need to be able to compare the frequency of series in *HoD* with their frequency in other works by Conrad or books written by other authors. A significantly higher frequency in *HoD* compared to other novels would allow us to claim that adjectival series are typical of *HoD* and represent one of its characteristic linguistic features. Quantitative description is therefore essential to any claim about style: '[t]he more I, as a critic, wish to substantiate what I say about style, the more I will need to point to the linguistic evidence of texts; and linguistic evidence, to be firm, must be couched in terms of numerical frequency' (Leech and Short 2007: 38). A corpus approach to the study of style enhances the quantitative description of the text and provides numerical data to a level of statistical precision and sophistication that would be impossible for the researcher to achieve manually. Computers retrieve quantitative figures faster and more accurately than any human reading. This makes it possible to analyse exhaustively large amount of texts, such as very long novels or even the whole oeuvre of an author, in a way that would not be feasible to do otherwise.

However, there is no such thing as the completely objective measurement of style, as numbers alone cannot tell us whether a linguistic feature is stylistically relevant. By comparing frequencies we can establish whether a feature is 'deviant' – that is, whether or not a difference exists 'between the normal frequency of [that] feature, and its frequency in the text or corpus' we are using for comparison (Leech and Short 2007: 39) – but we cannot be sure if it has stylistic relevance, namely 'foregrounding'. A linguistic feature is foregrounded if it has 'value in the game' (Halliday 1971: 344), if it 'relates to the meaning of the text as a whole' (Halliday 1971: 339) and is used for a specific literary end (Leech and Short 2007: 40). Foregrounded features do not simply 'stand out' as distinctive, but are also usually considered to possess literary–aesthetic importance, which makes them 'highly interpretable' (Jeffries and McIntyre 2010: 31). It would therefore be too simplistic to say that quantification alone is enough to identify stylistic features, as not all deviant features have stylistic significance. A linguistic feature can occur unusually frequently and yet not contribute in any way to the style of a text. However, although not all deviant features are foregrounded, all foregrounded features are instances of statistical deviance (Leech and Short 2007: 41). In a search for stylistic significance, one can start from those linguistic features that a frequency comparison highlights as deviant, as they are more likely to be foregrounded, compared to non-deviant features. In this respect, the quantitative dimension that corpus methods bring to stylistic analysis facilitates the identification of likely candidates of fore-grounded features.

The second major advantage that corpus methods bring to stylistics is the introduction of new analytical techniques. The use of the computer not only provides quantitative assistance for the stylistic analysis, but also enriches it with new practices and descriptive categories. Besides making the search for stylistic features faster, more precise and more reliable, corpus methods expand altogether the range of features identifiable. Mahlberg (2013: 18) explains that the innovations that have come about in corpus linguistics have in turn extended the stylistician's toolkit. Borrowing models and concepts from the cognate field of corpus linguistics, the stylistician can apply descriptive categories to the study of style that are typical of a corpus approach and cannot be studied otherwise.

Consider 'keywords' and 'semantic prosody', for instance, two concepts that are largely employed in this book. Keywords are words that occur unusually frequently in one text/corpus compared to a norm, represented by another text or corpus (more on keywords in Chapter 3). They are retrieved automatically by the computer, which compares word frequencies across the two texts/corpora, and are most typically seen as signalling the 'aboutness' (Scott 2016a) of a text. Some of the keywords that the computer retrieves can be evidence for what one might already think a text is about. However, some others can elude the reader's intuition and reveal features that might be difficult to notice without the help of the computer. Culpeper (2009), for example, uses keyword analysis on the character-talk from Shakespeare's *Romeo and Juliet*, comparing individual characters dialogues to identify which words are specific to each of the protagonists. He shows that keywords not only confirm what we already expected about the characters of the play (for instance, 'that Romeo is all about love', Culpeper 2009: 53), but they also point out less intuitively recognisable aspects, such as some grammatical features of Juliet's talk (*if, yet, or, would, be*) that, at first, might not seem relevant, but that actually distinguish stylistically Juliet as a character experiencing anxieties (Culpeper 2009: 53).

Semantic prosody is similarly hidden from the reader's intuition, but can be successfully unveiled with the help of corpus tools. Semantic, or discourse, prosody is described as the tendency of a unit to occur with words or phrases that express writer/speaker attitudes (Stubbs 2002: 65; McEnery and Hardie 2012: 135; cf. also Chapter 3). For example, the lemma CAUSE tends to occur with words for unpleasant events, such as *problems, death, concern,* and *damage* (Stubbs 2002: 65). These words embed CAUSE with attitudinal meaning, giving it a negative or 'unpleasant' semantic prosody. In some respects, the notion of semantic prosody is related to that of connotation, the main difference being that semantic prosodies are not accessible to intuition but can be discovered only with the help of corpus methods (Louw 1993: 159). Despite their elusiveness, Louw (1993) shows that semantic prosodies can play an important role in establishing irony and, more generally, he claims that their study should be at the heart of stylistic analysis (Louw 1993: 173). Departing from or adhering to an established semantic prosody has an effect on the reader, who will have their prior knowledge about the use of an item challenged or not, respectively. Louw (1993: 161) gives the example of how Philip Larkin makes use of the negative semantic prosody of *utterly* to convey a negative meaning in the final line of his poem 'First Sight'. Whereas Lodge, in his novel *Small World*, departs from the established negative semantic prosody of the item *bent on* to create an ironic effect. Semantic prosodies are therefore an important addition to the stylistician's toolkit; their study, and that of keywords, has been made possible thanks to the integration of corpus approaches into stylistic analysis, offering perspectives that traditional stylistics alone could hardly obtain.

The contributions of corpus linguistics to stylistics make 'corpus stylistics', the corpus-assisted study of literary style, an advantageous approach to study literary texts and their translations. Corpus stylistics enables the investigation of stylistic features throughout and across multiple texts, reducing selectivity resulting from 'cherry-picking' only selected extracts. This means that I can investigate the linguistic features that contribute to establishing *HoD*'s major themes throughout the whole novel and its translations. Even though *HoD* is a short text, a similar analysis would have been barely possible without the aid of a computer. Moreover, corpus stylistics enhances empiricism with its quantitative dimension and improves textual comparison, a fundamental aspect of both stylistic and translation studies research. Texts and linguistic features are more easily and accurately compared with the help of the computer, which also provides numerical data to substantiate claims about style and differences of style in translation. Finally, corpus stylistics widens the range of phenomena that can be looked at. Some of these phenomena are notoriously invisible to the naked eye. Semantic prosodies, for instance, can develop from the use of individual words, whose cumulative effect is noticeable only if they are taken into account all together. In the following chapters I show that, although 'inaccessible to human intuition' (Louw 1993: 157), semantic prosodies play a major part in the process of building up the fictional world in *HoD*.

The advantages that a corpus approach brings to stylistics are not limited to the technical side of the analysis, though. Corpus stylistics is concerned with interpretation as much as it is with description: in corpus stylistic analysis the qualitative perspective is as important as the quantitative one. Quantification alone cannot explain a style; rather, it can support the process of interpretation. In other words, quantification and description are never the goal of the study, but a means to formulate or test our intuition-based interpretations (Ho 2011: 10). Mahlberg (2013: 5) successfully captures the balance between the quantitative and qualitative sides of the discipline in her understanding of corpus stylistics: 'the application of corpus methods to the analysis of literary texts by relating linguistic description with literary appreciation'. Mahlberg (2013) emphasizes that corpus stylistics is not simply corpus linguistics applied to literary texts. The linguistic description that comes about through corpus methods should inform – and, at the same time, be informed by – the literary appreciation of the text. Mahlberg (2013: 12) draws on Spitzer's (1962) 'philological circle' to explain this cyclical and intertwined relation with her 'corpus stylistic circle'. Our reading of the literary text is nuanced by the linguistic description that the corpus approach provides. At the same time, the study of stylistic features is informed by our critical interpretation. (Corpus) linguistic description and literary appreciation complement each other and work together to produce a better understanding of the text.

1.4 Corpus stylistics at work

The use of the computer to study literary language has produced a wide range of research avenues, quite diverse in terms of scope and methods. They differ, among other aspects, on which type of analysis, quantitative or qualitative, is emphasized or on the number of texts taken into account: a corpus of several texts or just an individual novel, for example. Given this variety, this section does not aim to offer an overview of the field as a whole. Rather, I discuss research that touches upon the notions outlined in the previous sections, as well as illustrate examples of quantitative and qualitative approaches, in view of the triangulation of stylistic and computational perspectives that the following chapters present. Section 1.4.1 focuses on more quantitative approaches to corpus stylistics, such as computational stylistics and stylometry. Section 1.4.2 discusses instead more qualitative approaches, concentrating specifically on the use of corpus methods to study patterns in literary texts.

1.4.1 Quantitative approaches to corpus stylistics

The use of computers to assist the analysis of literary texts predates the term 'corpus stylistics' itself. Computer-assisted methods have been extensively used in the fields of computational stylistics and stylometry long before corpus stylistics was established as a field in its own right. For example, Burrows (1987) already used computational techniques to study Jane Austen's language and the idiolects of her characters at the end of the 1980s. More recent but similar in scope is Craig's (2008) examination of different styles in the dialogues of fifty of William Shakespeare's characters by looking at the frequency patterns of the fifty most frequent words in these dialogues. Computational methods have not only been used to analyse the writing of specific authors, but also to explore style variation across fiction. Egbert (2012) builds on Biber's (1988) original multi-dimensional analysis and applies it to a large corpus of British and American nineteenth-century fiction. Whereas Biber (1988) examines the distribution of sixty-seven linguistic features across different registers to analyse language variation in speech and writing, Egbert (2012) focuses on literary style and stylistic variation across one hundred texts by ten different writers. He takes into consideration the degree of co-occurrence of fifty-nine linguistic variables to determine stylistic tendencies between 'thought presentation vs. description' (Dimension 1), 'abstract exposition vs. concrete action' (Dimension 2) and 'dialogue vs. narrative' (Dimension 3). The resulting variation in these dimensions across the texts proves to be accurate in distinguishing the writing style of the novels, both at a between-author and at a within-author level.

Authorship attribution is another area of study in which computational methods are frequently applied to literary texts. Generally speaking, a range of different statistical measures and techniques are applied to texts whose authorship is disputed in order to provide an 'informed guess' on who the author may be. For instance, Binongo and Smith (1999) use principal component analysis to attribute the authorship of Shakespeare's *Pericles*, the first two acts of which were argued to be written by George Wilkins rather than by Shakespeare himself. Segarra et al. (2016) use word adjacency networks to investigate the authorship of the *Henry VI* plays. Hoover (2002) employs cluster analysis to investigate whether word sequences are more effective than individual words in disambiguating texts by different authors and grouping together texts by the same writer. These methods have also been used to study Conrad, more precisely his works written collaboratively with Ford Madox Ford. Rybicki et al. (2014) apply 'Rolling Delta', an implementation of Burrow's (2002a) 'Delta' authorship attribution algorithm, to *The Inheritors*, *Romance* and *The Nature of a Crime*. Rybicki et al. (2014) are able to show which parts of each text display a higher or lower agreement with the style of either Conrad or Ford (represented by their respective, single-authored, works). In this way, they signal the authorship of the passages.

These studies are characterized by a strong emphasis on the quantitative approach, making use of advanced computational and statistical techniques. While employing computational methods, this book tends instead towards the qualitative side of stylistic analysis. In Chapter 7, I use principal component analysis to compare *HoD* and its translations as whole texts, but the results of this technique are triangulated with the findings of the more qualitative investigations in Chapters 5 and 6 (see Chapter 3 for more details). As explained by Mahlberg (2013: 178), the use of technically less complex computational and corpus methods in corpus stylistics puts special emphasis on the qualitative aspects of the analysis.

It was mentioned before that 'corpus stylistics' is an umbrella term that covers a wide range of methods and approaches, but in this book it is used to distinguish it from the computational approach discussed in this section. In the next section, I discuss relevant corpus stylistic research.

1.4.2 Corpus stylistics and the study of textual patterns

This book discusses lexico-semantic patterns in *HoD* and its Italian translations because patterns are a constituent element of all language registers and play a fundamental role in the conveyance of meaning. 'Patterns' in language can be defined as any repetition of words, sounds, rhythms or structures (Hunston 2010: 152). It is repetition that gives meaning to patterns, a meaning that goes beyond that of the single occurrence of that given word, sound, structure and so on. Sinclair (1991, 2004), with his 'lexical item' model (discussed in detail in Chapter 3), has shown that meaning, rather than being associated with individual elements, is conveyed by patterns: meaning affects structure and structure affects meaning (Sinclair 1991: 496). Of course, this equally applies to the language of literature, where patterns have been seen to develop many different functions.

Stubbs (2005: 15), for instance, argues that looking at patterns, rather than single words, is more effective if one wants to understand the complaints about repetitiveness that many critics have directed at *HoD*. If we looked at the relative proportion of different words over the total number of running words in *HoD* compared to other novels, we would find that *HoD* does not stand out as a particularly 'repetitive' text. Youmans's (1990) figures of lexical variation across different writers show that this proportion in *HoD* is within the norm, when compared with texts such as *Middlemarch* by George Eliot or *Oliver Twist* by Charles Dickens. According to Stubbs (2005: 15–16), the impression of repetitiveness is more likely to arise from the repetition of lexico-grammatical patterns, rather than of individual words: long strings of adjectives and nouns, 'abstract noun + adjective with a negative prefix' constructions, or repetitions of words with negative prefixes and suffixes.

Similarly, Starcke (2006) focuses on patterns in her analysis of Jane Austen's *Persuasion*. She shows that particularly frequent word sequences develop semantic and grammatical patterns that can shed light on the characters related to them. For example, Anne is frequently the agent of 'psychological' word sequences such as *she could not* (Starcke 2006: 102). These sequences are used to indicate the character's inner life and, in this respect, they reflect that thoughts and perceptions are the focus of the novel. This approach is extended by Fischer-Starcke (2010), who looks at how semantic and syntactic patterns encode literary meanings in Jane Austen's novels, and in *Northanger Abbey* in particular. An important point that Fischer-Starcke (2010: 196) makes is that patterns can be inherently connected. Just as words and structures relate to each other to create patterns across texts, so too may one pattern link to another and together create a larger unit. Because corpus stylistics makes it possible to analyse longer stretches of text in linguistic detail, it can reveal links between different parts of the text, links that may have gone unnoticed if the focus was on selected extracts only (Fischer-Starcke 2010: 197).

The identification of patterns with a corpus approach is not only a matter of being able to search across large amounts of language at once, highlighting features not visible through the analysis of limited extracts. A major advantage comes about with the sorting capability of the software, which displays language in a way that is convenient for the detection of repeated patterns, that is, concordances. Concordances show the instances of the word or phrase we are searching for in the corpus in a layout that aligns these instances vertically (Sinclair 2003: xiii). Concordances allow the corpus to be read 'vertically' (Tognini-Bonelli 2001: 3), scanning for repeated patterns across several texts at the same time in a way that would not be possible reading a text 'horizontally'.

On the left in Figure 1.1 there is a sample of concordance lines for *seemed* in *HoD*. *Seemed* is at the centre of every line, within a portion of the context in which it occurs. According to Stubbs (2005), the lemma SEEM contributes to the feeling of vagueness in the text: in *HoD*, things *seem* something, instead of just *being*. With just a quick look, we can flick through the concordance lines vertically to check who/what seemed what, identifying patterns in the use of this word. This is more difficult to achieve if we read line by line 'horizontally'. The extract on the right of Figure 1.1, for example, includes just the first two occurrences of *seemed*; this format does not facilitate the identification of patterns as a concordance does.

Sinclair (1991: 42) maintains that the quality of evidence concordances offer is 'superior to any other method'. It is not surprising that they are recurrently used in corpus stylistics. Mahlberg and Smith (2010) make extensive use of concordances to study Jane Austen's *Pride and Prejudice*, focusing on the concordance lines of *civility* and *eyes*. Concordance lines foreground strikingly verbatim repetition of the same words, allowing them to effectively identify lexical patterns such as LIFT *her eyes*. This construction is used to reveal the character's inner feelings without stating them directly: *lifted up her eyes in amazement, unable to lift up her eyes* or *dared not to lift up her eyes* are all expressions of the character's emotional state conveyed in terms of body language.

Another important function of patterns in literature – especially for the aims of this book – is that of acting as building blocks of fictional worlds. Patterns can be associated with individual elements of a literary text, such as characters,

mind with its hint of danger that seemed, in the starred darkness
, red gleams that wavered, that seemed to sink and rise from
as buried. And for a moment it seemed to me as if I also were
'Towson's Inquiry,' etc., etc. He seemed to think himself
mute spell of the wilderness--that seemed to draw him to its
to 'nurse up my strength' seemed altogether beside the
believe them at first--the thing seemed so impossible. The fact
when actually confronting him I seemed to come to my senses,
confounded for a moment. It seemed to me I had never
he quite overwhelmed me. He seemed to be trying to make up
of this modest and clear flame. It seemed to have consumed all
a piece of, but so small that it seemed done more for the looks
vigorous draws at his pipe, it seemed to retreat and advance
was only a savage sight, while I seemed at one bound to have
of the fecund and mysterious life seemed to look at her, pensive,
, with closed eyelids--a head that seemed to sleep at the top of
near enough to be spoken to seemed at once to have leaped
appealing fixity of her gaze, that seemed to watch for more

When I woke up shortly after midnight his warning came to my mind with its hint of danger that seemed, in the starred darkness, real enough to make me get up for the purpose of having a look round. On the hill a big fire burned, illuminating fitfully a crooked corner of the station-house. One of the agents with a picket of a few of our blacks, armed for the purpose, was keeping guard over the ivory; but deep within the forest, red gleams that wavered, that seemed to sink and rise from the ground amongst confused columnar shapes of intense blackness, showed the exact position of the camp where Mr. Kurtz's adorers were keeping their uneasy vigil.

Figure 1.1 *Vertical reading (left) vs. horizontal reading (right)*

settings or even its atmosphere (cf. Chapter 4). Occurrence after occurrence, patterns can produce a contextualising effect, contributing to establishing the fictional world. Mahlberg and McIntyre (2011) show how keywords can be seen as world-building elements that construct the setting of Ian Fleming's *Casino Royale*. Mahlberg (2012a, 2013) illustrates instead how 'clusters', repeated sequences of words, can externalize features of both the fictional world and of the characters in it. She retrieves and classifies 5-word clusters on the basis of formal features in a corpus of Dickens's novels. The resulting cluster categories ('labels', 'speech clusters', 'body part clusters', '*as if* clusters' and 'time and place clusters') are then related to specific functions. For example, 'label' clusters are shown to contribute to the identification of characters and themes, '*as if* clusters' signal the author's or narrator's comments and interpretation, and 'time and place clusters' define the 'when' and 'where' of the fictional world (Mahlberg 2013: 40).

The importance of patterns as building blocks of characterization is also discussed in Mahlberg and Smith (2012), Mahlberg (2012b) and Hori (2004). Using the web tool *CLiC* (http://clic.bham.ac.uk/), Mahlberg and Smith (2012) analyse patterns in suspended quotations and argue that they contribute significantly to shaping characters in Dickens's *Hard Times*. Particular attention is put on the patterns of *pause* (*after a pause, after a short pause, after a moment's pause*), which are shown to be overused in suspensions compared to their use outside suspensions. These *pause* patterns add up to the description of the characters' body language and, at the same time, create an actual pause in their speech, in this way enacting a twofold function in which style and narration are related. Mahlberg (2012) and Hori (2004) demonstrate how given patterns can be related to specific characters. Mahlberg (2012b) looks at body language clusters linked to Tulkinghorn and Bucket in Dickens's *Bleak House*. Hori (2004) looks instead at collocational patterns in Dickens's language and illustrates how different recurrent collocations distinguish characters, not only in their speech, but also in non-dialogues used to describe their specific appearance, behaviour or actions.

The role of formal patterning in the process of characterization is in line with a cognitive stylistic understanding of the phenomenon. According to Culpeper's (2002a) model, the impression of characters in the reader's mind is the result of the interaction of two elements: the reader's prior knowledge of people in the real world and actual textual cues in the pages of the book. The reader picks 'characterisation cues from linguistic triggers' (McIntyre 2014: 152) and processes them together with their prior world knowledge in order to produce their understanding of a given character. Mahlberg (2013, 2012a, 2012b) has shown that linguistic patterns occurring consistently throughout a text can be part of the bottom-up textual information, that is, the linguistic triggers that, together with prior knowledge, shape the impression of a character in the reader's mind.

In addition to their function as building blocks of fictional worlds, and also as a result of that, patterns can contribute to major themes in literary texts. This idea takes centre stage in this book, as the lexico-semantic patterns identified are analysed in terms of their contribution to some of the major themes in *HoD*. The role of patterns in the process of theme construction in *HoD* has been briefly discussed by Stubbs (2005). He argues that repeated phrasal patterning and recurrent lexical fields not only contribute to the feeling of repetitiveness in Conrad's short novel, but also convey the theme of uncertainty that characterizes both Marlow's narration and the whole text. Stubbs (2005: 19) refers specifically to the 'mist/haze' semantic field, to the *as if/as though* constructions, and to the 'preposition + *the* + noun + *of* + determiner + noun' phrases (*in the midst of the incomprehensible, into the gloomy circle of some inferno, into the heart of the darkness*, etc.), explaining that their frequent occurrences blur the boundaries between appearance and reality, certainty and uncertainty. However, Stubbs (2005) only hints at the function of these patterns and at the role they may play in the interpretation of the short novel. Being the focus of the analysis, I show in depth how specific lexico-semantic patterns that build up fictional entities also participate in the process of theme construction. I also discuss the part these patterns can have in shaping the readerly experience, paying particular attention to the relation between linguistic features and established literary readings.

It is important to note that the identification of patterns in itself does not constitute a stylistic analysis. Patterns do not necessarily represent a stylistic feature, as much as frequency does not always indicate a style. It is 'foregrounding' that makes a feature stylistically relevant, and a foregrounded feature can be recognized as such mainly through qualitative analysis. This stresses once more the importance of balancing the quantitative and qualitative perspective in a corpus stylistic study, so that the linguistic description of patterns is related to the interpretation of the text. Mahlberg (2012: 93) maintains that, in the corpus-assisted analysis of literary texts, quantitative data might need to be dealt with differently compared to what is usually done with larger amounts of language. This is because corpus stylistics necessitates detailed qualitative inspection to complement a quantitative breakdown, as the stylistic relevance of quantitative data cannot be assessed on the basis of statistical significance alone.

In this section, I discussed some studies that show how the computer can be used to analyse literature, mainly focusing on corpus stylistic approaches to the identification and examination of patterns in literary texts. The aid of the computer makes it easier to spot these patterns, but also provides new ways to study their functions. This of course applies to the stylistic study of translation too. The following sections introduce translation to the discussion, explaining the role comparison plays in its analysis and why corpus methods are an effective way to compare different translated texts.

1.5 Linguistic and cultural approaches in translation studies

In Section 1.2, I argued that comparing texts represents a fundamental aspect of much research in translation studies, and that comparison takes centre stage in this book. It is important, therefore, to define the basis on which this comparison is established. What approach do we adopt to analyse and compare translations? Traditionally, there have been two main approaches through which the study of translation has been carried out: linguistic approaches and cultural approaches.

This book argues for the use of corpus stylistic models and methodologies to study literary translation. It analyses linguistic features across texts as the primary basis for the comparison of four Italian versions of *HoD*. As such, this book illustrates a linguistic approach to the study of translation. 'Linguistic approach' (or 'approaches') is an umbrella term that denotes 'theoretical models that represent translation and/or interpreting as a (primarily) linguistic process and are therefore informed mainly by linguistic theory' (Saldanha 2008: 148). More practically, the term is also used to refer to studies that make use of linguistic paradigms, methodologies and concepts to explain translation and its workings. Because of the emphasis they give to the textual level, linguistic approaches have been criticized for being naively restrictive and unable to account for the extra-textual factors involved in translation, similarly to the way stylistics has been accused of being too 'cold' and 'scientific' in its analysis of literary texts (McIntyre 2012: 1). This critique has been largely influenced by the proponents of cultural approaches to translation (cf. Snell-Hornby 1988, Venuti 1996, Arrojo 1998, Hermans 2014b), who have been very sceptical towards linguistically oriented models, especially the early ones such as Nida's (1964) and Catford's (1965). 'Cultural approaches', grounded in cultural studies and theories, emerged during the so-called cultural turn in translation studies in the early 1990s (Bassnett and Lefevere 1990) and have been traditionally seen in opposition to linguistic approaches. However, as Kenny (2001) explains, this opposition is unnecessary, as the criticisms that cultural approaches have addressed to linguistic ones are largely based on a narrow view of linguistics, which overlooks the contribution that linguists such as J. R. Firth have brought to the field.

One of the main criticisms traditionally addressed at linguistics-inspired approaches was that they tended to consider translation as 'mere repetition or neutral recovery of meaning' (Arrojo 1998: 45). According to Arrojo (1998: 28), essentialist (including linguistic) approaches tend to conceive meaning as an immobile essence that can be objectively recovered from the text and transferred across languages, almost loss-free. This assumption builds on a dualistic understanding of the relation between form and meaning. Dualism accepts that form and meaning are two separate entities and that form is mainly one of the possible variants in which a meaning can be expressed (Leech and Short 2007: 13). On these premises, Arrojo (1998) objects that linguistic approaches assume that it is possible to shift meaning across different languages, but also cultures, as if meaning 'trascend[ed] its form, circumstances and history, and [. . .] could be forever kept and protected from difference and change' (Arrojo 1998: 28). However, Arrojo's (1998) objection to the separation of form and meaning was and is shared by several linguists. Firth (1957), whose ideas are at the basis of corpus linguistics, strongly believed that meaning is strictly linked to linguistic form and extralinguistic situation. He in fact rejected the dualistic perspective. More recently, Sinclair (1991: 7) likewise maintained that '[t]here is ultimately no distinction between form and meaning', as he proved so through the corpus analysis of real-world texts. These ideas have had an important impact not only on linguistic approaches, but also on translation studies in general, as they contributed to a change in orientation, from a conceptual, decontextualized understanding of meaning to a situational perspective, in which meaning is closely related to usage (Baker 1993: 237). Therefore, a linguistic approach to translation would not necessarily consider meaning as a neutral essence that transcends form; on the contrary, form and context of situation are essential for the transfer of meaning, as a correspondence in meaning between two expressions also relies on a correspondence between uses.

Another common criticism that proponents of cultural approaches have addressed to linguistic approaches was that the latter often fail to account for the circumstances in which translation takes place, given their focus on textual – as opposed to extra-textual – factors. Linguistics-oriented approaches were regarded to have the 'worrisome tendency' to study translation merely as 'a set of systematic operations autonomous from the cultural and social formations in which they are executed' (Venuti 1996: 108). Linguistics was deemed unable to 'serve as a proper basis' (Hermans 2014a: 10) for the study of something as socioculturally bound as, for example, literary texts. Yet, many linguists have recognized the connection existing between language and its context of occurrence. Once again, Firth (1957) was one of the first to maintain that language is a social phenomenon very much linked to the outside world, and since then linguistics has moved forward as to encompass the analysis of texts in context as instantiation of discourses and representation of ideologies. This is particularly evident in the field of critical discourse analysis (CDA), which combines linguistic frameworks such as Halliday and Matthiessen's (2004) systemic functional grammar to the work of critical theorists, in particular Foucault and Bourdieu. CDA builds on the notion that language is not only socially influenced, but also influences directly social relationships; as such, in CDA the relation between language and culture is central. Drawing on these developments in linguistics, many translation scholars have successfully explored issues that were considered out of range for a linguistic approach, such as ideology (Munday 2008) and translators' discursive presence (Bosseaux 2004). Finally, as Saldanha (2008: 152) points out, the adoption of a linguistic approach that aims at rigour in textual analysis does not necessarily mean disregarding extra-textual factors or ignoring the fact that language is a social phenomenon with direct implications in the outside world.

Despite its influence in translation studies, the tension between linguistic and cultural approaches has often resulted from miscommunication between the two sides. Kenny (2001: 57) suggests that the proponents of culturally oriented perspectives have tended to consider linguistics as a 'monolith fashioned along Chomskyan lines', failing to recognize that linguistics was also developing in other directions. These developments, such as those by Firth and his successors, have proved the criticisms levelled at linguistic approaches to be inaccurate, showing that the two views can have shared interests and aims. However, instead of highlighting these similarities, the debate has focused on the differences between the approaches. Intersections do exist though, as shown by the many linguistically driven studies that have similar preoccupations for the relation between form and meaning and the sociocultural nature of translation as those of more culturally oriented approaches. By building on these similarities and by adopting a (corpus) stylistic approach, I wish to contribute to the view that linguistic approaches are not necessarily in direct opposition to cultural ones; that linguistics does not lead only to a prescriptive and abstract view of translation; finally, that the analysis of textual features can shed some light on extra-textual factors as well.

Another aspect that characterizes the approach adopted in this book is its orientation towards the ST. The comparison of the TTs is based on the findings of the stylistic analysis of the ST, and it aims to show whether differences exist between the original and the translations, as opposed to analyse stylistically the TTs in their own right. In this respect, this approach can be considered ST-oriented. An 'ST-oriented' analysis is generally based on close textual comparison, and relies on this comparison to provide answers to the research questions (Saldanha 2014: 101). It may be argued that a focus on textual comparison leads to the assumption that any striking stylistic feature in the TT is a reproduction of – or attempt to reproduce – a corresponding striking feature in the ST. However, as I suggested earlier, an approach grounded on textual comparison is not necessarily oblivious to extra-textual factors. As Saldanha (2014: 101) explains, not all the answers can be found through textual comparison, as translating often involves other external parameters: 'the mediator's interpretation of the original; the purpose of the mediation – bearing in mind that the purpose the translation is intended to serve may differ from that of the original; and the audience for the translation' (Saldanha 2014: 101). These parameters are central in the present book, especially the mediator's interpretation of the original (see Chapter 6). Ultimately, even though ST-oriented, the approach adopted here aims to explore both the linguistic and the non-linguistic aspects that are involved in translation.

1.6 Corpora and translation

Corpus linguistics and descriptive translation studies, as theorized by Holmes (1972) and Toury ([1985] 2014), share a number of underlying tenets (Laviosa 2002). First, both approach their object of study from an empirical perspective and examine real-life language samples, rather than using intuition-based assumptions. Second, both assert that generalizations of empirical findings need to be based on the study of large amount of data, as opposed to individual instances only. Finally, both disciplines aim to describe probabilistic rules of behaviour in the analysis of their object of study, rather than formulating prescriptive assertions (Laviosa 2002: 16). This common ground has enabled a methodological interaction between the two fields and today 'corpus-based translation studies', as some scholars dubbed this multidisciplinary area (Kenny 2001, Laviosa 2002, Kruger et al. 2011, Oakes and Ji 2012), is a lively research avenue, with its own dedicated publications and international conferences. Similarly to what happened with the 'corpus turn' in stylistics (Leech and Short 2007: 286), the 'corpus turn' in translation studies provided both more efficient ways to answer relevant questions and suggested new questions altogether. Shifting Tymoczko's (1998: 1) famous words from 1998 to the present, corpus-based translation studies and the corpus turn have helped translation studies to 'remain vital and move forward'.

This section discusses the use of corpus methods to study translation. Section 1.6.1 outlines the interaction between the two disciplines and the wide variety of approaches and models that it has generated. Section 1.6.2 introduces the specific paradigm that this book adopts, illustrating some relevant studies in the field. Section 1.6.3 focuses instead on more computational methods to the study of translation, while Section 1.6.4 discusses the difference between the analysis of the translator's style and that of the author's style in translation.

1.6.1 Corpus linguistic approaches to the study of translation

Since its early days, corpus-based translation studies has been a heterogeneous and diverse field, encompassing a range of different strands, approaches and aims. It has had a major role in the development of existing fields as well as con-tributing to the rise of new research areas. For example, the use of corpus tools and methods has taken centre stage in the latest developments in contrastive linguistic studies, offering unprecedented perspectives on the similarities and differences of languages in use and enabling inter-language research on the fre-quency distribution of linguistic features across languages (e.g. Johansson 2003, Granger et al. 2003, Lavid et al. 2009). Similarly, corpus methods have also been integrated in the existing area of translator training. Baker (1999: 287–8) argues that the use of corpus resources has been particularly useful in the cases where translation students are learning in a foreign language environment and can-not rely on their mother tongue intuition to decide whether something sounds natural in the target language or not. In these situations, corpora can provide data to check and compare the equivalence of patterns in the working languages.

An application that has flourished thanks to the contribution of corpus-based translation studies and in which corpus methods are extensively employed is the comparison between translated language and non-translated language, so as to identify the distinctive features that characterize translation as a language variety in its own right. Baker (1993) is usually seen as the forerunner of this paradigm, which aims to understand 'what translation is and how it works' (Baker 1993: 243). Corpora of translated texts are compared to corpora of non-translated texts to emphasize the similarities and differences between them. Baker (2004), for example, examines the frequency and distribution of a range of 3-word, 4-word and 5-word fixed and semi-fixed phrases across translated and non-translated English texts. This application of corpus-based translation studies has led to considerable research in the area of 'translation universals', that is, those linguistic features that typically occur in translated texts as the result of the mediation between two languages, independent of the pair of languages involved (see Baker 1993, Laviosa 2002, Olohan 2004 and Laviosa 2008 for a critical appraisal). Øverås (1998), for instance, uses corpus methods to investigate Blum-Kulka's (1986) 'explicitation hypothesis'. According to this hypothesis, the level of cohesive explicitness tends to increase in the TT, regardless of the languages involved in the translation practice. In order to prove this, Øverås (1998) looks at the frequency of additions and specifications as examples of cohesive explicitness in a corpus of 20 Norwegian novels and their English translations, as well as 20 English novels and their Norwegian translations. Øverås (1998: 16) is able to confirm Blum-Kulka's (1986) hypothesis, providing quantitative evidence to support it.

Grabowski (2013) adopts principal component analysis and cluster analysis to investigate the universal of levelling out in a corpus of literary Polish. In particular, multivariate analyses are used to measure the variation between translated and non-translated texts, in order to verify whether translations are more similar to each other compared to original texts and translated texts (Grabowski 2013: 265). His results confirm the levelling out hypothesis, although Grabowski (2013: 275) calls for more quantitative and qualitative research that could replicate the study in more varied language registers or in a larger corpus of translated Polish. A different application to the study of universals is that proposed by Redelinghuys and Kruger (2015), who look at explicitation, simplification and normalization as an indication of translator expertise. They hypothesize the existence of differences in the occurrence of these phenomena across the writing of inexperienced translators, experienced translators and non-translated writing. Their findings support the idea that differences exist between translated and non-translated language, at the same time providing evidence that the frequency and distribution of universals vary depending on the level of expertise of the translator. However, explanations for these phenomena remain speculative (Redelinghuys and Kruger 2015), as there is no means to test why these features appear with different frequency in different texts. The overall speculative nature of translation universals has often been pointed out, since it is difficult to assess whether these phenomena are actually universal or simply contextual, occurring in language-specific contexts. Ulrych and Anselmi (2008) discuss exactly this, aiming at developing a distinction between language-specific and universal features of mediated discourse. They indeed advocate this distinction, especially as far as English is concerned: given its role as a lingua franca, English is particularly receptive to hybridism and, as such, varies and changes through usage by nonnative speakers and interaction with other languages via translation (Ulrych and Anselmi 2008: 270).

The focus on universals exemplifies a strand in corpus-based translation studies that aims to study translation as a language variety. This strand is complemented by another one that instead investigates specific text-pairs as individual instances of the translation phenomenon. These two parallel (and sometimes intersecting) strands reflect, in general terms, a corpus linguistic and a corpus stylistic approach. The corpus linguistic strand, as exemplified by the research on translation universals, looks for regularities across whole corpora, in order to develop generalizable theories that can be applied to the translated language. The corpus stylistic strand, on the other hand, focuses on individual texts, rather than general corpora. Comparison is usually established at the level of ST vs. TT, instead of non-translated language vs. translated language, and the resulting findings are interpreted in order to mirror the specific context of production of each individual translated text. This approach follows a widespread awareness in corpus-based translation studies that linguistic description and comparison alone are not always enough (cf. Section 1.5). Context-specific phenomena need to be addressed alongside linguistic-specific ones: translation is hardly separable from the sociocultural background in which it takes place. This book adopts a corpus stylistic approach, discussed in the next section.

1.6.2 Corpus stylistics and translation studies

A corpus stylistic approach takes into account both linguistic and extralinguistic factors and aims to contextualize the translation phenomenon under analysis. This implies the necessity of combining perspectives and methods from different disciplines (Saldanha 2009: 6), so as to avoid the emphasis on the text that the use of corpus tools necessarily entails. In this respect, this strand tries to achieve multidisciplinarity in a similar way to how corpus stylistics aims at multidisciplinarity when analysing literary texts. It is not coincidence that, especially in the ambit of literary translation, corpus-based translation studies has looked at corpus stylistics in order to integrate in its approach an attention to qualitative as well as quantitative analysis and an interest for the critical interpretation of the text.

The corpus stylistic strand is exemplified, among others, by the work of Bosseaux (2004, 2006) and Winters (2005, 2007, 2010). Bosseaux (2004, 2006) analyses the French translations of Virginia Woolf's *The Waves*,[1] focusing on the rendition of *you* in Bosseaux (2006) and on deixis, modality and transitivity in Bosseaux (2004). The aim is to show that the alteration of these features in translation not only affects the linguistic surface of the novel, but also its overall framework. In one of the passages examined in Bosseaux (2004), for example, the translation and repetition of *I* and *must* in relation to the character Bernard vary in the two TTs. These changes alter the way Bernard comes across, as the depiction of his mind style is affected by the translators' choices. Bosseaux (2004: 272) is therefore able to use the data provided by the computer to study narratological aspects of the TTs. Likewise, the difference in the translation of *you* (Bosseaux 2006), which in French can be rendered with the informal *tu* (second person singular) or *vous* (second person plural and formal second person singular), affects the formality of some characters and the overall register of the text. One of the translators renders the novel more formal, while the other conveys more intimacy and familiarity. Again, Bosseaux (2006: 609) shows that 'microtextual shifts have consequences on the macrostructure and point of view of the novel'.

A similar point is raised by Winters (2005, 2007, 2010), who analyses point of view, speech and thought presentation and modal particles in two German translations of F. Scott Fitzgerald's *The Beautiful and Damned*. In particular, Winters (2007) focuses on the repetition and variation of speech-act report verbs in two different TTs. She identifies the most frequent speech-act report verbs in the original and then compares the frequency and variation of their translation in the two German versions. Matching the quantitative data with the qualitative analysis of textual extracts, Winters (2007: 424) engages with the relation between translator's choice and adherence to a perceived language norm. She shows how the difference in translating these verbs can be interpreted in terms of whether or not the translators conform to the convention of avoiding repetition when possible. Another particularly revealing case is that of the modal particle *wohl* (Winters 2010), as it demonstrates clearly how linguistic alterations affect the overall reading of the text. Modal particles do not exist in English. The addition of the modal particle *whol* by the German translators introduces an element of insecurity to the characters (Winters 2010: 182), which is absent in the original. Even though this choice is moved by (target) linguistic constraints, Winters (2010) argues that it may reveal something about the translator's attitude towards the text in terms of their own perception of the character as being insecure.

Mahlberg (2007b) shows that readers' perceptions of characters can be distorted in translation, when the translators fail to reproduce what can initially look like unimportant linguistic features. This is the case of the cluster *his hands* [. . .] *pockets* in Charles Dickens's *Bleak House* and its German translation. Mahlberg (2007b: 130) reports that the translator only picks up the physical activity related to the cluster, but the contextualization of this action within the behaviour of the character is less clear than in the English original. Consequently, the characters in the German text lose part of their characterization tied to the contextual meaning of putting their hands into their pockets.

Clusters in translation are also studied by Čermáková (2015), who focuses on their repetition as a potential signal of stylistic relevance. Her investigation of John Irving's *A Widow for One Year* and its Czech and Finnish translations looks at the repetition of two 10-word and 12-word clusters in the ST and in the TTs. She finds that the alteration of the verbatim form of the clusters affects the stylistic effect their repetition creates in the original. This is particularly true in the case of the cluster *a sound like someone trying not to make a sound*. This cluster is not only repeated verbatim many times, but also plays with the repetition of the word *sound*. Čermáková (2015) reports that *sound* is also a keyword, related to one of the main themes of the novel. In this way, Čermáková (2015) manages to link cluster and keyword analyses, showing how different linguistic features and patterns are interconnected to create literary effects.

Keyword analysis is also used in Mastropierro and Mahlberg (2017) as a starting point to study cohesive networks in H. P. Lovecraft's *At the Mountains of Madness* and in one of its Italian translations. The study focuses on how cohesive networks, based on the repetition of the thematically relevant keywords *peaks*, *mountains* and *foothills*, contribute to the establishment of the short novel's fictional world. Mastropierro and Mahlberg (2017) show that the use of different target language words to translate the ST keywords results in cohesive patterns that are different from those in the original. They suggest that these alterations can trigger different associations in the mind of the target reader, therefore affecting how the fictional world is perceived. The same text is also employed to investigate Lovecraft's use of adverbs in Mastropierro (2015). Mastropierro (2015) relates the frequency and distribution of *-ly* adverbs in *At the Mountains of Madness* with topical or climactic turns in the plot, showing how this idiosyncratic linguistic feature has stylistic relevance. Mastropierro (2015) then illustrates how this stylistic feature is dealt with in two Italian translations, which preserve it to different extents. He argues that, when the frequent repetition of these adverbs is avoided in favour of the TT fluency, the stylistic effect is affected, as well as its potential to emphasise climactic turns in the story.

Li et al. (2011) adopt a less quantitative approach, using more basic corpus methods and emphasizing instead the extralinguistic context of production. Li et al. (2011) use type/token ratio and sentence length to compare two English translations of Cao Xueqin's *Hongloumeng*, relying on a comprehensive apparatus of contextual information to interpret the statistical data. They look at the translators' mother tongue, their second language, where they lived and studied, the position they held and their mode of translation (Li et al. 2011: 5), together with the translators' comments on their version and their translation philosophy. In this way, they hypothesize that, for example, one of the translations uses a wider range of vocabulary because its translator opted for a more faithful rendition that aims to 'introduce the Chinese literature and culture to the English-speaking world' (Li et al. 2011: 9). As a result, a wide range of words is employed in order to translate literally all the cultural references and allusions. The other translator uses instead longer sentences, probably because of his mother tongue, English, which tends to have much longer sentences than Chinese, which on the contrary displays more paratactic structures (Li et al. 2011: 11).

The corpus stylistic strand proves that a linguistic approach to the study of translation does not necessarily lead to view the translated text as 'a set of systematic operations autonomous from the cultural and social formations in which they are executed' (Venuti 1996: 108). On the contrary, the integration of corpus stylistics in corpus-based translation studies has given greater relevance to the link between 'micro-linguistic events' and 'macro-social structures' (Saldanha 2009: 6), between textual features, interpretation and reception. Finally, a corpus stylistic approach emphasizes how text, context and translation interact.

1.6.3 Computational approaches

Despite its corpus stylistic approach, this book also uses more quantitative methods to compare the Italian translations of *HoD*. These methods have been extensively used in corpus-based translation studies, similarly to the way they have been used early on in stylistic analysis (cf. Section 1.4.1). An example of such an application is McKenna et al.'s (1999) study of Beckett's Trilogy (*Molloy, Malone Dies* and *The Unnameable*) and in its French translation. They use principal component analysis to compare the frequency patterns of the most frequent words in the STs and in their TTs, segmented in twenty sections each. They find that, although the texts' most frequent words change from English to French, it is still possible to identify similarities in the patterns across the sections. This result is interpreted as evidence of the maintenance of 'stylistic overtones' (McKenna et al. 1999: 169) across translation, that is, the reproduction of an equivalent textual style that resists the inter-language shift. A similar result is reported by Rybicki (2006) in his comparison of character idiolects in Henryk Sienkiewicz's Trilogy (*Ogniem i Mieczem, Potop* and *Pan Wolodyjowski*) and its two English translations. Rybicki (2006) builds on Burrows (1987) and, analysing various character configurations (major characters, recurring characters, characters participating in the public/political/love plot and female characters), discusses whether equivalent idiolects are preserved in the character dialogues in the TTs. His analysis shows that idiolects are indeed transferred from the STs to the TTs, despite the translational and inter-language shift.

Pagano et al. (2016) use multivariate cluster analysis to investigate the retranslation hypothesis (Berman 1990), according to which retranslations tend to be more source-oriented than first translations. To do so, they study an extract of 213 words from Katherine Mansfield's *Bliss* and ten of its translations, five in Spanish and five in Portuguese. Based on sixty-eight systemic functional linguistic variables (e.g. clause type, process type, theme, etc.), they cluster the extracts on a plot and show that the variation between them is not always related to whether the extracts are first or successive translations; a finding interpreted as suggesting that the retranslation hypothesis in not always true. Vandevoorde et al. (2016) employ computational methods to measure semantic difference between originals and translations. Their approach builds on and expands the semantic mirroring technique, a procedure that retrieves semantic fields on the basis of back-and-forth translation of semantically related items. With their 'extended mirroring analysis' (Vandevoorde 2016: 134), they investigate the Dutch semantic field of inceptiveness in a sample from the Dutch Parallel

Corpus, a 10-million-word parallel and comparable corpus comprising five text types and four translation directions. The study points to differences between the two compared fields of inceptiveness (in the source and target texts), which differ in terms of fine-grained sense distinctions.

Computational methods have also been used to study translators' authorship, in the same way as they have been employed to investigate original writers' authorship. Burrows (2002b), for example, applies his measure of stylistic difference, 'Delta procedure' (Burrows 2002a), to the comparison of fifteen English translations of Juvenal's 'Tenth Satire' with corpora of original writings. The goal is to test the reliability of Delta in identifying the relation between the translations and the original texts by the same author. Hung et al. (2010) use principal component analysis and cluster analysis to support a hypothesis about the attribution of twenty-four Buddhist sutras to the same translator or group of translators, given that they were traditionally considered to be translated by different translators. Finally, Rybicki and Heydel's (2013) study focuses on collaborative translation. Here, multivariate analysis is adopted to attribute the specific contribution of each of the two different translators who collaboratively translated in Polish Virginia Woolf's *Night and Day*. In particular, they apply cluster analysis to Delta-normalized word frequencies (Burrows 2002a), showing that this method can recognize precisely where the shift between the two translators takes place in the text. When comparing different works by the same translators, Rybicki and Heydel (2013) argue that the original author's signal seems to prevail over that of the translator, that is, there is a greater likeliness between two translated texts by the same author than between two translated texts by the same translator. For example, the two sections of Woolf's *Night and Day* by different translators are more similar to each other than each translator-specific section with other translations by the same translator. They conclude that this finding opens new avenues for the study of translation as a textual genre in its own right, where translational agency can be seen as authorial: 'stylometry may help to define the "filter" that shows the translator's multifaceted identity as an artist' (Rybicki and Heydel 2013: 716).

1.6.4 Translator's style and author's style in translation

Before concluding this section, it is important to mention that there is another approach to corpus-based translation studies that, even though it employs corpus stylistic methods, focuses instead on the style of the translator, as distinguished from that of the original author. Baker (2000) has proposed a methodology to identify and investigate translator style, structured on two key points: (i) the study of translator style is TT-oriented, mainly based on the analysis of TTs without considering the corresponding STs; (ii) translator style is represented by the characteristic features of the translator's language, which are not a response to the ST style. In this respect, Baker (2000) sees translators as possessing linguistic 'thumb-prints' or 'fingerprints' in their own right, independent from the original author's linguistic features. If one wants to demonstrate that translation is not only a reproductive activity, but a creative one as well, then it is important – Baker (2000: 262) claims – that we explore not only authors', but also translators' style.

Baker's (2000) methodology has been followed and developed further by Saldanha (2011a), who offers a revised definition of translator style based on four key points: translator style is (i) recognizable across a range of TTs by the same translator, (ii) distinguishable from that of other translators, (iii) coherent in its patterns of choice and (iv) has a discernible function (Saldanha 2011a: 30). Again, the emphasis is mainly on the TT, free from the influence of the original's style. This approach is exemplified in Saldanha (2011b), where the styles of two translators are compared on the basis of their use of foreign words. The two corpora used include the English translations by Margaret Jull Costa and by Peter Bush, respectively. Their comparison reveals different trends in dealing with culture-specific items, which are typical of the translators, rather than responses to ST features, and reflective of the way they see themselves in their role of intercultural mediators (Saldanha 2011b: 257).

Wang and Li (2012) focus instead on Baker's (2000) notion of translator fingerprints, examining two Chinese translations of James Joyce's *Ulysses*. In order to identify typical features of each translation, they use keyword analysis to compare one TT with the other. Specifically, they examine the preferences of each translator for particular verbs and Chinese emotional particles. They also compare the frequency of post-positional adverbial clauses across the two TTs, considered as a rhetorical effect that weakens the importance of the dependant clause. Wang and Li (2012) conclude that the differences between the two translations confirm the existence of translator fingerprints. However, instead of arguing for the independence of the translator's style, they claim that it is a result of both the influence of the translator's first language and of the source language (Wang and Li 2012: 91).

A similar position is taken by Huang and Chu (2014) and Huang (2015). Huang (2015) distinguishes between 'S-type' translator style and 'T-type' translator style: the former is the result of the strategies adopted to cope with specific features of the ST, while the latter refers to the idiosyncrasies of the translators themselves. He theorizes a parallel methodology that encompasses the analysis of both S-type and T-type stylistic features (Huang 2015: 54), in order not to ignore entirely the role that the ST plays in the translation process. This methodology is shown in Huang and Chu (2014), where both S-type and T-type perspectives are considered. In this study, Huang and Chu (2014) analyse a corpus of English translations of contemporary Chinese novels. They identify a characteristic feature of one of the translators, that is, the preference for the use of indirect speech with the third person and the past tense to deal with the Chinese omission of personal pronoun subjects and lack of tense markers. They suggest verifying whether this S-type feature (a strategy used to cope with an aspect of the ST) occurs consistently in all the translations by the same translator, so as to confirm whether it is also a T-type feature, that is, an idiosyncrasy of the translator themselves (Huang and Chu 2014: 138).

The approach to the relation between ST and TT adopted by the aforementioned studies is more TT-oriented compared to that adopted in this book. As I explained in Section 1.5, this book is mainly ST-oriented. In this respect, the features of the TTs identified are analysed in terms of their relation to ST features, rather than as characteristic of the translators' style. The point of departure will always be the style of the original author, so the TTs are examined in order to see to what extent the author's style is maintained, and what effects discrepancies in style have on the reception of the TT.

1.7 Investigating manipulation

Translation is a complex social phenomenon, imbued with cultural, ideological and political implications. These implications are reflected in, and reflect, the choices translators make, and even the choices they do not make. As mediators between different cultures and societies, translators can act as 'crucial agents for social change' (Tymoczko 2010: 3), and not seldom their decision-making power has been used to perform acts of resistance and activism such as supporting language movements, shifting cultural values and gender struggles (Tymoczko 2010: 229). In the specific context of literature, translation has been equally seen as playing 'a most active' role (Even-Zohar 1990: 46) in any literary system. Translating literature can establish affiliation and construct identities, challenge societal norms as well as reinforcing them, and contribute to literary innovation or fixation alike (Even-Zohar 1990). In the final analysis, translation influences the context in which it is produced and, at the same time, is influenced by it.

According to Lefevere (1992), the influential role of translation in literary systems is due to its potential to substitute the original: '[translation] is able to project the image of an author and/or a (series of) work(s) in another culture' (Lefevere 1992: 9), replacing the ST for those who have no knowledge of the source language. This projection, 'rewriting' in Lefevere's (1992) own words, is far from a neutral reproduction: '[a]ll rewritings, whatever their intention, reflect a certain ideology and a poetics and as such manipulate literature to function in a given society in a given way' (Lefevere 1992: vii). There are two mechanisms in control of this manipulative process, one operating outside the literary system, the other inside of it. From the outside, the process is controlled by the 'patronage' (Lefevere 1992: 11), that is, those powers – both individuals and institutions – which 'can further or hinder the reading, writing, and rewriting of literature' (Lefevere 1992: 15). Sovereigns, presidents, royal courts, social classes, religious institutions, political parties, publishers and the media are all examples of patronage. From the inside, the manipulative process is put into practice by the 'professionals' (Lefevere 1992: 14), for example, critics, reviewers, translators, teachers, scholars and anyone who works directly with literature and its products. Being mainly concerned with the ideological side of literature, patronage acts through the professionals to ensure that the ideology of a literary text is aligned with their own agenda. The professionals rewrite works of literature to make sure that their ideology is deemed acceptable to the norms and conventions of the context of production. Through this system, patronage and professionals can manipulate translation and its reception in the target culture. These ideas underpin what in translation studies is generally referred to as the 'manipulation school' (Hermans 1999: 8), a paradigm which assumes that '[f]rom the point of view of the target literature, all translation implies a degree of manipulation of the source text for a certain purpose' (Hermans 2014a: 11).

Although ideological agendas cannot be comprehensively pictured by looking at linguistic alterations alone, the analysis of textual discrepancies between the ST and the TT and the stylistic choices in the TT have the potential to reveal signals of the translators' manipulative presence (Munday 2008: 14). As discussed in Section 1.6.2, changes at the linguistic level of a text can affect its interpretational level and these changes can be motivated by the translator's agenda. A corpus stylistic approach to the comparison of ST and TT can therefore point to potential manipulations, in cases in which the choice of the translator cannot be explained on the basis of ST features alone. But how do we recognize a choice that is not motivated by features of the ST as manipulative?

The answer to this question rests on the definition of manipulation. However, despite the centrality of the issue in the discipline, translation manipulation remains an 'underexplored phenomenon' and, as a result, lacks a 'comprehensive and unequivocal definition' (Dukāte 2009: 15–16). More precisely, manipulation has been discussed in so many different terms that it is difficult to pinpoint the concept precisely. For instance, Venuti (2008: 1) talks about the 'translator's own manipulation of the translating language' in reference to the domesticating strategy dominant in the Anglo-American publishing system aimed at producing TTs that read as fluently as possible. Nonetheless, there is no definition of manipulation and it is not clear whether or not all the linguistic choices of the translator are manipulative. Other scholars provide examples of manipulative phenomena in real translational contexts, examining them either stylistically (Munday 2008) or socioculturally (Tymoczko 2010). But most of these examples occur in circumstances in which the balance between the two cultures/languages involved is clearly uneven, for example in postcolonial or undemocratic contexts. One may ask whether manipulation also occurs in more ordinary contexts, especially if we consider that the theorists of manipulation (Hermans 2014b, Lefevere 1992) claim that all translations imply a certain degree of manipulation. As Díaz-Cintas (2013: 282) remarks, manipulation is definitely not 'the sole property of totalitarian, undemocratic regimes'.

Dukāte (2009) has attempted a systematization of the phenomenon, aiming to categorize the different types of manipulation discussed in the literature. She distinguishes two main different types of manipulation: 'text-external' (Dukāte 2009: 90) and 'text-internal' (Dukāte 2009: 101) manipulation. The former is the manipulation that proceeds outside the text. For example, the choice of what not to translate or what to omit completely from the TT can be a form of text-external manipulation. The latter includes all forms of manipulation contained in the text, for instance the manipulative effects resulting from the alteration of the linguistic features of the ST for a given purpose. Text-internal manipulation is what the literature in translation studies generally refers to with the term 'manipulation'. Both of these can be further divided into manipulation as improvement, manipulation as handling and manipulation as distortion (Dukāte 2009: 89). Finally, all these types of manipulation can either be conscious or unconscious. Despite this meticulous classification, Dukāte (2009: 112) explains that, in the end, 'everything anybody does or does not do is manipulation'. In other words, her answer on whether translation is manipulation is that it 'depends on the evaluator's vantage point and his/her understanding of the manipulation and expectations of translation' (Dukāte 2009: 130). Thus, it seems that manipulation is a concept that resists constrictive definitions.

In spite of its indeterminacy, it is still possible to recognize some characteristics that are usually associated with a shared understanding of manipulation, specifically as it is conceived by the 'manipulation school' (Hermans 1999: 8). Even though the ideas of the 'manipulation school' are said to be applicable to all kinds of translation (Schjoldager 1994: 70), this paradigm is mainly concerned with studying manipulation in the context of literary translation, as opposed to other types of translation. Literature is more prone to being manipulated and to manipulate because of its cultural and ideological implications (Dukāte 2009: 151). Within the context of literature, manipulation is seen as affecting all instances of translation (Hermans 2014a: 11), although to different degrees. Yet, regardless of the extent, manipulation is mostly considered a negative phenomenon, rather than a positive one: it is a distortion of the ST's truth, which is misrepresented (Dukāte 2009: 75), rather than an improvement in the TT. Most importantly, manipulation is considered to be motivated: there is always a specific purpose behind it. Usually, this motivation is due to cultural, political or ideological considerations (Dukāte 2009: 46). Translation can be inspired by ideology, or constrained by it, depending whether the translation is in agreement with or in opposition to the dominant ideology (Lefevere 1992: 8). Nevertheless, ideology always takes centre stage in manipulative phenomena. Overall, these general characteristics can act as guidelines to indicate whether a TT stylistic choice that does not seem to be motivated by ST features can be considered as manipulation or not. They might not be comprehensively representative of the whole phenomenon, but they still reflect a widespread and shared understanding of the concept in translation studies.

Despite its recognition as a matter of fact in translation, manipulation has rarely been investigated from a linguistic perspective (Munday 2008 being one of the few exceptions). This is also due to the fact that manipulation has been traditionally seen as a concept related to cultural approaches and therefore difficult to explore from a linguistic perspective. Yet, as shown in Section 1.5, linguistic approaches have been successfully applied to the study of ideology, and CDA-based research has proved that discourses and ideological stances can also be investigated from a linguistic point of view. Corpus methods in particular have made an enormous contribution to the study of the relation between language and ideology, helping CDA to overcome its own disciplinary limits. Corpus linguistics can provide a 'pattern map' (Baker et al. 2008: 295) of the text(s) analysed, a quantitative overview of the data that helps in identifying what to focus on, while at the same time reducing 'cherry-picking' practices. This quantitative dimension contributes to the empiricism of the analysis and its reliability, because it offers sound indicators of frequency of the specific phenomena examined (Baker et al. 2008: 296). The benefits of this methodological interaction have been extensively demonstrated by several studies, which have used corpus methods to investigate linguistically discursive constructions and representations (Gabrielatos and Baker 2008), ideological stances (Orpin 2005), and underlying discourses (MacDonald and Hunter 2013). These and many other studies have shown that a (corpus) linguistic approach is appropriate to explore the relationship between ideology and language. As such, it is equally suitable to investigate manipulative effects in translation as, according to the very proponents of the 'manipulation school', manipulation is largely an ideology-motivated phenomenon. This book therefore aims to provide a linguistic perspective on manipulation, through the stylistic analysis and textual comparison of *HoD* and its Italian translations. In particular, I investigate whether the discrepancies between ST and TTs produce effects that, in line with the understanding of manipulation here discussed, can be considered manipulative.

1.8 Conclusion

This chapter traced a discussion that connects stylistics to literary criticism and to translation. The common denominator of this discussion has been the corpus approach. Being comparative in nature, stylistics benefits greatly from the adoption of corpus methods, which expand the stylistician's toolkit and enable new perspectives on the study of literary texts. This does not mean that corpus stylistics focuses only on the description of linguistic features. On the contrary, it uses innovations from corpus linguistics to trigger a more comprehensive understanding of literary texts. The study of translation too is essentially comparative, as it is based on the comparison of an ST to a TT. Translation studies has equally found in the use of the computer a way to enhance empiricism and objectivity, which are at the heart of the descriptive approach to the discipline. But despite the emphasis on the linguistic level that this method entails, extra-linguistic aspects can still take centre stage in the analysis. A linguistic approach to the study of literary translation is not oblivious to the (manipulative) effects that translating can have on the reception and interpretation of the text, because textual and extratextual levels are strictly related. Alterations in the lexical level can affect the interpretational level, while TT stylistic choices not motivated by ST features can indicate the translator's intervention. Finally, through the corpus-assisted analysis of *HoD* and its Italian translations, this book makes a contribution to the methodological dialogue between stylistics, corpus linguistics and translation studies.

Africa and Africans in Joseph Conrad's
Heart of Darkness

2.1 Introduction

Linguistic patterns in literary texts can serve two functions: they can produce stylistic effects and function as triggers for literary themes. Wales (2011) argues that the goal of stylistics is to analyse both functions. Stylistics should show how a text works 'not simply to describe the formal features of texts for their own sake, but in order to show their functional significance for the interpretation of the text; or in order to relate literary effects or themes to linguistic "triggers" where these are felt to be relevant' (Wales 2011: 400). While the relation between patterns and artistic effect is an extensively explored topic in stylistics, the stylistic examination of themes is an area that is 'awaiting development' (Leech and Short 2007: 304). This book is equally concerned with both of these aspects: it offers a study of lexico-semantic patterns as formal constituents of Conrad's style and as triggers of fictional themes in *HoD*.

Mahlberg (2007a) explains that there are two main ways to start a corpus stylistic study and select items for closer examination: either taking suggestions from literary insights and arguments from literary criticism or checking the frequency information of the words in the text and picking those whose frequencies appear noteworthy (Mahlberg 2007a: 22). This study opts for the first way, because it fits better the object of the analysis and the aims of the book. A frequency-based selection can dismiss low-frequency items that can nevertheless play an important role in the process of theme construction (cf. Section 3.4.2.1). Themes are more likely to emerge from the interaction of different linguistic features, as the result of the cumulative effect of several items which may or may not occur very frequently. Because the frequency of these items might not be very high, the selection of what to study based on frequency cut-off points risks ignoring their contribution. On the other hand, suggestions from literary insights would not be tied to formal criteria, but would instead account for the way the text is read and interpreted by critics. Moreover, taking suggestions from literary criticism allows me to discuss aspects of the short novel that are central in the scholarly debate, in accordance with the purpose of making a significant contribution to the critical study of *HoD*.

Literary criticism thus plays a particularly significant role in this study, especially in its inception, as it can indicate established and widespread perspectives on the themes of *HoD*. A review of the reception of the novel brings forward the themes that are generally considered 'major' by literary critics, foregrounding aspects of the text that can be analyzed in order to study such themes. The purpose of this chapter is to provide an overview of the reception of *HoD*, so as to emphasize some of those themes that have received the most critical attention. In other words, I 'take suggestions' (cf. Mahlberg 2007a: 22) from literary criticism as a starting point for analysing the relation between patterns and themes. Two major themes emerge from this discussion: 'Africa and its representation' and 'race and racism'. I argue that the postcolonial approach to Conrad has emphasized the importance of the imperialist context in the interpretation of his novels. In the specific case of *HoD*, this emphasis has given new prominence to the way Africa and Africans are depicted, as their fictional representation has been seen to reflect ideologies and attitudes. The following section introduces briefly Conrad's canonical position in English literature, while Section 2.3 discusses the postcolonial approach to Conrad criticism as one of the most dominant approaches to his texts. The themes 'Africa and its representation' and 'race and racism' are presented in Section 2.4 and Section 2.5, respectively. Finally, Section 2.6 offers some concluding remarks.

Before moving on, though, it is important to provide a working definition of 'theme', to explain how the term is used in this book. As van Peer (2002: 254) points out, this term is not easy to pin down, given the several – and sometimes opposite – perspectives from which it has been discussed and the terminological confusion deriving from the use of numerous synonyms or quasi-synonyms. Cuddon (1979: 695) simply defines 'themes' as the central ideas of literary texts that can be stated either directly or indirectly. More relevant to the present study, Childs and Fowler's (2006: 239) definition stresses the recurrence of a theme: the theme is something that 'run[s] through a work, linking features which are un- or otherwise related'. Another aspect of the concept of theme that is important to my use of the term is pointed out by van Peer (2002: 256), who argues that 'a theme is not "given" in the text', but rather is ' "extracted" or "derived" from the text's semantic material'. This explains why different themes may be proposed by readers of the same text (van Peer 2002: 256). The subjectivity of themes is also recognized by Wales (2011: 393), who states that themes are inferred from 'our interpretation of [a literary work's] plot, imagery, and symbolism, etc.' These are the two aspects that are most important for the use of the term in this book: recurrence and subjectivity. For all practical purposes, I therefore use 'theme' to refer to an element or matter that recurs through a literary text and that emerges from subjective interpretation, in this specific case, that of the literary scholars. In this respect, 'theme' is different from the 'aboutness' (Scott 2016a) of a text; *HoD* is not, strictly speaking, 'about' Africa or racism. However, 'Africa and its representation' and 'race and racism' can be seen as subjects that emerge from the recurrence of certain events, images and symbols, which have been interpreted by the literary community as thematically relevant.

2.2 Conrad and the literary canon

Since the publication of his first novels, Conrad has been the object of widespread literary attention. At the beginning of his writing career, his work was already highly considered and, despite some criticism, literary scholars generally acknowledged that Conrad would leave a mark in the history of literature. In the first full-length study dedicated to his work, Curle (1914: 1) claimed that 'Conrad's work actually does mark a new epoch'. A few years later, Waugh (1919: 267) foresaw that 'Conrad's reputation appears to be absolutely assured'. Early reviewers of his books shared the same positive considerations (cf. Simmons 2009 or Peters 2008), recognizing in Conrad an innovative strength and an originality in style and themes that distinguished him from his contemporaries. This overall approbation continued to grow after his death (1924) and the definitive consolidation of his literary fame came in the 1940s. Leavis's ([1948] 1973) *The Great Tradition* is widely regarded as establishing Conrad's work in the canon. Leavis (1973: 1) included Conrad among the greatest English novelists, together with Jane Austen, George Eliot and Henry James, and, by doing so, helped to foreground Conrad as a writer worthy of scholarly attention (Niland 2009). This strong interest in Conrad matched the increasing professionalization of academic criticism of the 1940s. This process underpinned the re-evaluation of Conrad's work and resulted in the publication of numerous serious scholarly studies that finally established Conrad's 'modern' reputation

(Knowles 2009a). From then on, Conrad's work has been firmly located within the literary canon and today critical interest in his novels is livelier than ever.

In more than a century of uninterrupted criticism, Conrad's oeuvre has been discussed in many different ways and from diverse perspectives. According to Ciompi (2005), Conrad has been read from a political, psychoanalytical, semiotic, deconstructionist, metafictional and imperialist point of view, among the others. Thus, although his position in the canon has remained unaltered throughout recent decades, critics have focused on different aspects of his work, and have interpreted them differently, depending on the historical and sociocultural period in which they have been writing. In this wide array of differing paradigms, one of the most important and influential perspectives on Conrad's narrative has been the postcolonial approach.

2.3 The postcolonial approach in Conrad criticism

An important moment in the history of Conrad criticism is the aftermath of the Second World War. Before that, during the interwar years, Conrad's literary fame goes through a period of 'faltering popularity' (Knowles 2009b: 68), in which his work is perceived as 'out of touch' (Knowles 2009b: 68) with the new generation of readers, distant from the emerging concerns of the time. According to Knowles (2009b: 68), for instance, Conrad 'exclude[s] modern women (and women readers); he depreciate[s] intellect in a scientific age; and he ignore[s] complicated sexual involvements and social reforms'. However, after the Second World War, Conrad's work is increasingly seen to align with the current generational mood. He is considered modern and prophetic for having foreseen the catastrophic effects of supremacist policies. The analysis of his work assists in thinking critically about the destructive results of the extremist nationalalistic ideologies which were manifested in the war. In particular, it is Conrad's multilanguage, multicultural background – his being a writer who transcends national boundaries – that makes his work seem suitable for theoretical readings aimed at criticising aggressive nationalistic ideologies (Niland 2009: 78).

This new interpretative trend reaches its apex in the period that witnesses the breaking apart of the British Empire. In this context, Conrad's involvement with the imperial and colonial question acquires a new meaning. In the early phases of his reception, this involvement was mostly seen as a secondary aspect of Conrad's narrative: it was mainly the settings of his novels that contributed to the exotic feeling that Conrad's work was considered to have. Conrad was in fact often paralleled to Robert Louis Stevenson because of his Malaysian and seafaring settings (Simmons 2009: 60). However, with the rise of postcolonial perspectives, Conrad's engagement with imperialist issues takes centre stage in any interpretation of his work. Said (1994) argues that Conrad's narrative is so embedded in the imperialist ideologies of its time that it would be impossible to disentangle the two without missing Conrad's argument: '[w]ithout Empire, [. . .], there is no European novel as we know it' (Said 1994: 69). The postcolonial approach has thus established itself as one of the most widespread and discussed approaches in Conrad criticism today.

Edward Said plays a fundamental role in establishing this postcolonial perspective, being a forerunner in applying this approach to literature and, in particular, to Conrad's writing (Niland 2009: 79). Said's (1994) interest in Conrad is focused on issues of imperialism and postcolonialism. The study of Conrad is simply unthinkable without considering these questions. In Said's (2009) view, Conrad's work can be read as both imperialist and anti-imperialist at the same time. On the one hand, Said (1994) recognizes an awareness of the disastrous consequences of cultural imposition in Conrad's work; on the other, an inability to conceive alternatives to this imposition, a different course for this process. Although progressive in some respects, Conrad's work is nevertheless embedded in the ideologies of its own time. As a result, Conrad overlooks the fact that, under the surface of what seemed exoticism to him, India, Africa and South America had their own independent histories and cultures, which the imperialists subsequently trampled (Said 1994: xvii). Said (1994) finds this perspective perfectly reflected in Marlow and Kurtz:

> They (and of course Conrad) are ahead of their time in understanding that what they call 'the darkness' has an autonomy of its own, and can reinvade and reclaim what imperialism had taken for *its* own. But Marlow and Kurtz are also creatures of their time and cannot take the next step, which would be to recognize that what they saw, disablingly and disparagingly, as a non-European 'darkness' was in fact a non-European world *resisting* imperialism so as one day to regain sovereignty and independence, and not, as Conrad reductively says, to reestablish the darkness. (Said 1994: 30, emphasis in the original)

In the end, Said (1994) suggests that there is no real alternative to imperialism in Conrad. Conrad's acute critique of the imperialist enterprise condemns its atrocities, but it does not go as far as to conclude that imperialism itself has to cease so that the colonized could live their lives free from European dominance: '[a]s a creature of his time, Conrad could not grant the natives their freedom, despite his severe critique of the imperialism that enslaved them' (Said 1994: 30).

Another major contribution to postcolonial readings comes from novelist and critic Chinua Achebe. Achebe is a particularly influential figure because, by accusing Conrad of being a 'thoroughgoing racist' (Achebe 1990: 11) during a 1975 public lecture at the University of Massachusetts, he generates a persistent debate that has consolidated further the importance of the colonial and imperialist context of Conrad's writings. In contrast to Said (1994), Achebe (1990) argues that Conrad implicitly and explicitly conforms to the imperialistic ideology, and that this is evident in the way he depicts Africa and Africans in *HoD*. Africa is seen as a 'place of negation' (Achebe 1990: 3), the antithesis of what Europe should symbolize, the wilderness in its natural form, without control or ties. It is exactly what contemporary readers expect and Conrad simply acts as 'purveyor of comforting myths' (Achebe 1990: 5), giving them precisely what they want to be shown. Similarly, Africans are wild and unbound, so distant from the Europeans that they seem almost inhuman. Achebe (1990) in fact claims that Conrad conceals every aspect of their humanity, depriving them of language and identity.

Achebe (1990) is aware of the fact that the attitude towards Africa and Africans in *HoD* could be Marlow's, rather than Conrad's. He recognizes the different layers of narration in the text, and the distinction between the author (Conrad), the first narrator (the unnamed man on the yawl Nellie) and Marlow (whose account is reported by the first narrator). However, Achebe (1990: 9) sees these literary figures merely as 'layers of insulation'. Despite this narrative artifice, Achebe (1990: 10) does not recognize in the text any alternative framework of reference for the reader to judge Marlow's actions and opinions differently from Conrad's. Conrad would have been able to offer this alternative set of references, if he had considered it necessary, but he did not: 'Marlow seems to me to enjoy Conrad's complete confidence' (Achebe 1990: 10). Conrad's responsibility for Marlow's attitude thus leads Achebe to believe that it was Conrad himself who had a problem with black people, an intimate and maybe unconscious antipathy (Achebe 1990: 13). Even admitting the influence of the dominating prejudices of the time, Achebe (1990) still recognizes the attitude towards black people in the text as Conrad's. For example, he attributes to Conrad an 'inordinate love' (Achebe 1990: 13) for the word *nigger* and an obsession with blackness.

In spite of the wide range of approaches from which *HoD* has been studied, Achebe (1990) complains that the assumed racism of the short novel has been ignored. Ultimately, he wonders 'whether a novel which celebrates this dehumanization, which depersonalizes a portion of the human race, can be called a great work of art. [His] answer is: No, it cannot' (Achebe 1990: 12).

The postcolonial approach to Conrad criticism is relevant to this study for several reasons. First of all, because this reading of Conrad's work is one of the most widespread and discussed today. Interpretations such as Said's (1994) and Achebe's (1990) have shaped the critical reception of *HoD* so deeply that it is almost impossible to ignore postcolonial and imperialist issues when studying the short novel. This means that focusing on these aspects allows this book to contribute to current critical debates. Moreover, given its enormous influence on contemporary criticism, the attention to postcolonial issues enables me to examine the effect of dominant readings on the translation practice. Said (1994) argues that Conrad's texts can be read both as espousing and as opposing the imperialist enterprise, whereas Achebe's (1990) controversial accusation has split critics between those who agree with him and those who do not. Thus, these issues are clearly debatable and where the translator stands in this debate can be reflected in their translation. Even-Zohar (1990: 51) defines translation as 'an activity dependant on the relations within a certain cultural system', the shape of which is not defined once and for all by its ST. Different translations of the same original can therefore differ depending on how the translation/translator relates to their cultural system. According to Lefevere (2014: 238), this relation is inescapable, as no translator can ever escape from the dominant ideology/poetics in the target context of production. It is always possible to see a given translation as belonging to a given sociocultural context. Through the comparison of the TTs, I investigate the extent to which the postcolonial reading – as one of the most influential approaches to the text – is reflected in the linguistic choices of the Italian translators. This is in line with Lefevere's ([1985] 2014) understanding of the study of literature, which should

> explain how both the writing and rewriting of literature are subject to certain constraints, and how the interaction of writing and rewriting is ultimately responsible, not just for the canonization of specific authors or specific works and the rejection of others, but also for the evolution of a given literature. (Lefevere 2014: 219)

In other words, my analysis can shed some light on the potential ways the Italian versions of *HoD* have been filtered by the mediating role of the translators. Finally, the fact that the postcolonial approach has emerged in the second half of the twentieth century means that the early Italian translation of *HoD* has been produced in a period in which these questions were not at the forefront of critical attention. This provides a more diachronic perspective, as it is possible to compare the early TT with the contemporary TTs and study whether the latter have been influenced by their context of production in a way that the former could not have been.

As mentioned in Section 2.1, this book focuses on two themes that have emerged as particularly prominent from a postcolonial approach to *HoD*: 'Africa and its representation' and 'race and racism'. Each of these themes are discussed in Section 2.4 and Section 2.5, respectively.

2.4 Africa and its representation

The 'where' of literature has recently played an increasingly central role in literary criticism, especially in the context of modernism (Brooker and Thacker 2005b, Thacker 2005). The relationship between literature and geography is bidirectional: literature contributes to the understanding of social, geographical places through fictional representation; at the same time, social spaces help to shape literary forms and styles. Thacker (2005: 63) terms the outcome of this interaction 'textual space' – the resulting interplay 'between spatial forms and social space in written text'. The study of textual spaces goes beyond describing how a given place is represented in the text, but accounts also for how this depiction is culturally and socially constructed. Ultimately, textual spaces connect fictional to real places, but also sociocultural questions to literary forms and styles. As a result of this interaction, textual spaces have the power to shape the perception of spaces and places both inside and outside literature.

Jarosz (1992: 106) states that, through the use of metaphors and symbolism, the written representation of places has the same potential, although figurative, to construct, shape and destroy spaces in the same way that historical, material, social and ecological forces have. Africa has been persistently associated with a series of metaphors; one of the most dominant is Africa as the 'dark continent'. Jarosz (1992) argues that this enduring metaphor has played a significant role in defining the perception of the continent. The 'dark continent' metaphor has not only influenced how literature, travel accounts, news reports and academic writing represent Africa, but it has also affected, in a derogative manner, the sociocultural perception of Africa itself. The persistence of this metaphor has moved Africa's geographical and cultural variety into the background, putting in its place a homogenising 'other'. Africa acts as a blank space, deprived of differences, and functioning as a mere term of comparison for Western notions and values. The perpetuation of this symbolism in the last hundred years has confirmed and even legitimated domination discourses such as imperialism, sexism and racism (Jarosz 1992).

Likewise, Hegglund (2005: 44) identifies two other persistent and related metaphors through which Africa has been depicted in the twentieth century: as a realm of timeless myths and as part of the historical process of globalization. In line with Jarosz (1992), Hegglund (2005) argues that the mythical 'image-Africa' has triumphed over the historically contextualized and real Africa. The image-Africa has homogenized the real Africa, substituting its varied culture with a timeless place out of history, which keeps resisting modernity and civilization. Given this assumed resistance to modernity and civilization, Africa is also seen as the place where globalization should take place. The continent therefore emerges as the object of study for explorers and colonists, who impose a Western filter on all non-Western places and things. The effect of this dual metaphor is, again, uprooting Africa from its sociocultural and historical background, and replacing it with an ahistorical and ageographical image, an empty container into which any number of symbols can be projected (Hegglund 2005: 48).

Within the aims of the postcolonial approach, the way Conrad depicts Africa plays a major role in the interpretation of his novels. Conrad's textual spaces are seen to be in dialogue with issues of power and domination typical of the twentieth century, and his fictional representation of Africa is studied as a reflection of ideologies and attitudes towards both the continent and the colonial enterprise in general. GoGwilt (2005) recognizes the key role of Africa and its representation in *HoD*, arguing that the way the continent is formulated is 'a touchstone for the modernist rupture' with the enlightened European history and geography (GoGwilt 2005: 66). Hampson (2005: 56) proposes a contrastive approach that compares Congo in *HoD* with Congo described in Conrad's personal records of his journey in the African continent. Hampson (2005) emphasizes the discrepancies between the fictional representation of the journey along the Congo River in the short novel and the logs reported in Conrad's records, and uses these differences to foreground the author's intention to depict Africa in a metaphorical way. Overall, since its publication, *HoD* has helped to shape the representation and reception of Africa, by virtue of its fame and critical acclaim. This is true not only in literary contexts, but also in wider popular culture. A postcolonial approach to *HoD* thus foregrounds the relation between the text and the imperialist context, emphasizing the way Africa is fictionally constructed. Analysing the textual representation of Africa in *HoD* makes it possible to establish a link between linguistic features of the text and one of the major themes I seek to discuss: 'Africa and its representation'.

2.5 Race and racism

By accusing *HoD* of racism, Achebe (1990) has had an enormous impact on academic criticism. His reading has 'significantly altered the landscape of Conrad scholarship' (Purssell 2009: 86), challenging the canonized status that, more than twenty-five years before, Leavis ([1948] 1973) had granted Conrad. Engaging with *HoD* today necessarily demands an engagement with what Achebe (1990) has said about it (Allington 2006: 132), whereas before his public lecture the issue was virtually non-existent.

From *HoD*'s early reception right through to the 1950s and 1960s, there were barely any references to racial issues in Conrad's short novel. On the contrary, Conrad was praised for 'neither dehumanis[ing] nor europeanis[ing]' (Curle 1914: 122) his non-European characters, who are portrayed with 'curious fidelity and insight', and placed in a 'world of their own, hidden from our understanding – the world of savage fears and beliefs' (Curle 1914: 122). Referring to *HoD* specifically, Curle (1914) appreciates Conrad's representation of 'the whole sadness and dark unrest of savage minds – I mean the minds of real, untutored savages' (Curle 1914: 122). Similar responses to Conrad's work can be found in a number of contemporaneous reviews, criticisms, advertisements and biographies (cf. Peters 2008), none of which make any reference to racial issues. Randall (1925, in Peters 2008), for example, praises Conrad's ability to portray faithfully different races and nationalities, without any kind of subjective imbalance: 'to those who know them, the Malays, Chinese, Indians, Negroes and Arabs are as convincing as the Englishmen' (Randall 1925, in Peters 2008: 115).

In comparison to the early reader, today's readers cannot help but engage with ideas of race and racism, for almost every critical edition of the novel deals with these issues, or at least mentions them. As Allington (2006: 133) observes, readers are 'obliged, in reading *Heart of Darkness*, to take a stand on a matter of controversy that, in the Sixties, simply did not exist – namely, whether or not it is a racist book'. Likewise, today's critics cannot ignore this controversy. In fact, the critical debate surrounding *HoD* and racism has been ongoing for the past four decades, and has generated a vast amount of research on the topic.

Within this debate, few critics have shared Achebe's (1990) accusations as directly and passionately as him. Almost every discussion of *HoD* that has followed Achebe's (1990) lecture, however, has acknowledged the pertinence of the issue of racism. Brantlinger (1985), for example, recognizes the powerful criticism of imperialism and racism that *HoD* offers but, at the same time, admits that such a criticism is 'characterized as both imperialist and racist' (Brantlinger 1985: 365). Lawtoo (2012) adopts a similar twofold position. He admits that ' "racism", as Achebe recognised, is clearly part of [Marlow's] rhetoric' (Latwoo 2012: 249). At the same time, he suggests that perhaps Marlow is simply attempting to establish a connection with his white listeners through the use of the same racist rhetoric that dominated Conrad's time. In other words, Marlow is merely providing his listeners with what they expect. Coats (2013: 645) recognizes in the use of scientific racist discourse (such as the reference to phrenology in *HoD*) one of the aspects that most disturbs Conrad's readers. Although scientific racist discourse is often accompanied by its critique, its inclusion can nevertheless signal 'more than a set of passing references to contemporary cultural life' (Coats 2013: 645). Miller, too, acknowledges the use of racist stereotypes and clichés in *HoD*:

> I want to believe, as many other critics do believe, that Conrad was not a racist and that he was in *Heart of Darkness* attacking the racist side of imperialism, partly by embodying it ironically in Marlow. Nevertheless, the novel employs many racist stereotypes as well as racist clichés from journalism and popular literature of the time. (Miller 2012: 30)

Miller's (2012) quotation is a relevant one because it suggests that the issue of race and racism is taken into account even when the critic does not want to agree with Achebe (1990). Zins (1982), for instance, claims that Conrad was an anti-imperialist and anti-racist precursor, and that *HoD* manifests his progressive thoughts. Zins (1982: 121) reads the short novel as a direct denunciation of colonialism in Africa, and argues that Achebe (1990) is 'definitely doing injustice to Conrad' (Zins 1982: 122) by accusing him of being racist and directing antipathy towards black people. But, even though 'in its deepest sense, contrary to Achebe's opinion, the story is antiracist' (Zins 1982: 147), Zins (1982) still concedes that Conrad did not entirely escape the ideological conventions of the imperialist tradition, and uses them to stereotype the Africans (Zins 1982: 125). A similar concession is put forward by Watts (1990). He is very keen to emphasize the importance of the sociocultural context in the interpretative process, claiming that subordinating *HoD* to present-day value systems and criticising the text for failing to encompass them may be itself an exercise of ideological and temporal imperialism (Watts 1990: xxvi). According to Watts (1990), *HoD* can be seen as a progressive and anti-imperialist text when framed in its native context. Nevertheless, some of Marlow's attitudes towards the Africans remain patronising and misguided (Watts 1990: xxi).

Ultimately, Achebe (1990) has not deprived *HoD* of its canonical status, or completely won over public and critical opinion, but he has been successful in making the academic community acutely aware of potential issues of race and racism in the text. This lively debate has consequentially drawn great attention to the way in which the African natives are represented in the text. Most – if not all – of the critics discussed in this section make reference to how Africans are depicted in order to support or discredit the hypothesis that *HoD* is a racist text. Therefore, analysing the fictional representation of the African natives enables me to link the linguistic level of the text to the theme 'race and racism'.

2.6 Conclusion

This chapter looked at Conrad's established position in the literary canon and argued that, although his canonical status remains unchanged, critics prioritized different aspects in their reading, depending on the historical and socio-cultural context in which their interpretations took place. Aspects such as the representation of Africa and of Africans were of little interest to early readers of *HoD*, while today they are dominant, given the development of postcolonial approaches to literature. The postcolonial approach gives great importance to the imperialist context in Conrad's novels, stressing the relevance of its representation as a reflection of ideological stances and attitudes. This discussion led to the identification of two major themes in *HoD*, which are central in critical debates today: 'Africa and its representation' and 'race and racism'. Given their centrality, this book focuses on each of these themes in detail.

There are several reasons why focusing on these themes is a well-grounded choice for the analysis that is carried out in the next chapters. First, they represent central themes in the current critical debate. They do not only emerge from one of the most discussed approaches to the text, but are also concerned with very controversial and influential issues. By examining these two themes in particular, this book aims to contribute to a current and important discussion in Conrad criticism. Second, 'Africa and its representation' and 'race and racism' lend themselves to a discussion of linguistic features. Both can be investigated through the analysis of the textual representations of two aspects of the fictional world, that is, Africa and Africans. As explained in Sections 1.5 and 1.7, the linguistic analysis of textual representations can also shed light on ideologies and stances beyond lexical choices. Finally, the discussion above showed that these themes are debated and disputed, especially the issue of racism. There is no unanimous critical agreement about whether *HoD* is a racist text or not. Within the aim of the present research, such conflicting stances can be likely signals of discrepancies among the TTs, as different positions on controversial matters can result in different ways to deal with given features in the ST. In other words, the translators may have approached the translation differently according to whether or not they agree with Achebe (1990), and whether or not they read *HoD* as imbued with racist implications.

Texts, Corpora, Methods

3.1 Introduction

This chapter introduces the texts, the corpora and the methods employed in this book. From a more general point of view, this chapter also discusses how corpus stylistics can be applied to the study of literary translation, so as to develop a methodological framework that could be further employed in other studies. Section 3.2 starts by stating the research questions, while Section 3.3 presents the ST and the TTs under investigation and introduces the two reference corpora used. Section 3.4 is the core of the chapter, which discusses the analytical steps that are employed to answer the research questions. The discussion is both methodological and theoretical as it does not only concern the actual procedures to be used in the analysis chapters, but also addresses the implications of applying such methods to the study of translation. Finally, Section 3.5 closes the chapter with some concluding remarks.

3.2 The research questions

This book discusses the role of linguistic patterns as building blocks of the fictional world and triggers of major themes, both in literature and in translation. It seeks to explore the effects that textual patterns can have on the interpretation of the text and how this interpretation can change as a consequence of translation. This discussion arises from the corpus study of *HoD* and four of its Italian translations, examining how the lexical level of the texts contributes to literary meaning through repeated lexico-semantic patterning. Specifically, the present study answers the following four research questions, into which the overall contribution of this book has been broken down:

RQ1)   Which sets of text-specific words relate to the themes 'Africa and its
       representation' and 'race and racism' in *HoD*?

RQ2)   What are the linguistic patterns of these words and how do they
       contribute to the development of these themes?

RQ3)   What are the effects of translation on the linguistic patterns and on the
       way they convey themes in the Italian versions?

RQ4)   How do the TTs compare to each other when examined as whole texts,
       in terms of their overall degree of similarity/difference, as opposed to
       the way they compare to each other when only the identified linguistic
       patterns are taken into account?

RQ1 deals with a key issue in corpus stylistic research, that is, how to relate linguistic scrutiny and literary appreciation. Corpus stylistics approaches a literary text through the examination of its linguistic form. Therefore, it is of primary importance that the given aspect of the text one wants to focus on (e.g. a theme, a character, the setting, a particular literary effect, a well-known interpretation, etc.) is approachable from a linguistic point of view. By answering the first research question, I identify *HoD*-specific words that are related to the two major themes selected, in this way providing a starting point to study further how the two themes are linguistically instantiated.

Building on the first research question, RQ2 deals with studying the textual patterns of the words identified with RQ1. Conrad is renowned for his characteristic narrative voice (Senn 1980), the result of a constant stylistic effort that would enable him to 'make [his readers] hear, to make [them] feel – it is, before all, to make [them] *see*' (Conrad 1950: ix–x, emphasis in the original). By establishing the relation between the two major themes and the lexical level of *HoD*, I identify the exact linguistic techniques Conrad uses to 'make us feel, to make us see' his fictional world. Specifically, this question explores the stylistic features that contribute to constructing the fictional representation of Africa and the fictional representation of Africans.

With the third research question, the Italian translations are brought into play. This question is concerned with the effects of translation on the interpretation and reception of literature. Translation can reflect the translators' personal interpretation and/or bias, which in turn can affect the TT's reception in the target culture (cf. Section 1.7). By answering RQ3, I explore the effects of the translational shift on the stylistic features previously identified. The fictional representations of Africa and of the African natives are compared in the TTs and the ST. The comparison aims to show how alterations at the textual (linguistic) level can affect the overall extra-textual (interpretational) level of the TTs, sometimes with manipulative effects on the text reception.

The purpose of the fourth question is to add a wider perspective to the comparison of the translations. The analysis of the TTs, as addressed by the third research question, focuses on comparing the effects of translation on the specific linguistic patterns identified through the second research question. In contrast, RQ4 aims to look at the TTs as whole texts, so as to examine whether their overall degree of similarity and difference differs from what emerged when the comparison was based on the specific linguistic features only.

In addition, by addressing these four research questions, this book aims to make two complementary contributions. The first is offering an original contribution to the study of *HoD*, providing new perspectives on the short novel that cannot be obtained without a corpus-assisted method. The second involves building up a methodology for the study of literature in translation in general. This book seeks to develop a method that can be extracted from the specific study of *HoD* and its Italian translations and applied successfully to other works of literature and their translations.

3.3 Texts and corpora

The raw material for any corpus stylistic research is digital texts. These texts can either be studied individually, or gathered together to form a 'corpus', that is, a collection of digitized texts selected with explicit criteria and for linguistic purposes so as to be representative of the aspect/variety of language one wants to study (for other definitions see Stubbs 2002, Tognini-Bonelli 2001). The research presented in this book makes use of both individual texts and corpora, the former as the object of the analysis, the latter as representative norms against which the object of the analysis is compared. Specifically, this research uses five individual texts, *HoD* and its four Italian translations, and two reference corpora, the general reference corpus (RC) and the Conrad corpus (CC). The following sections introduce and describe each text and corpus, illustrating the criteria with which each has been selected and compiled, and explicating the aims for which they are employed.

3.3.1 *Heart of Darkness*

Choosing the object of the analysis is never a straightforward decision, especially in corpus studies, where the selection is influenced by many external factors and has numerous methodological implications. Hence, the choice of *HoD* is not fortuitous, but rather motivated by various methodological and practical factors.

As mentioned in the Introduction, there are many reasons behind the decision to concentrate on *HoD*. The first is its popularity; Conrad is one of the most well-known authors in British and world literature and has been considered as part of the literary canon for decades (cf. Chapter 2). As a result, he has been extensively studied. The critical and academic interest in his works has been continuous since he started writing and *HoD* in particular has taken centre stage in an innumerable amount of studies. This century-long interest is beneficial in many respects. First, it provides plenty of material with which to inform a corpus stylistic analysis. This book investigates the linguistic instantiation of major themes in *HoD*. I argued in Chapter 2 that the review of the literature can offer an informed picture of the themes mostly discussed by literary critics, emphasizing those aspects of the texts that are central in the critical debate. Having a wide range of critical studies from which to take suggestions is therefore an important advantage. Second, the abundance of critical material spread over many decades is fundamental to contextualize the text's reception at different stages. This diachronic perspective is important in order to frame the TTs within the critical milieu in which they have been produced. Translations respond to the sociocultural environments in which they are born. Having a wide range of critical readings for each time period facilitates the search for the potential influences of the context of production on the TTs. Finally, Conrad's popularity is also mirrored in the large number of languages his texts have been translated into. *HoD* is the first work by Conrad that arrived in Italy in book format and since then it has become Conrad's most translated work in Italy (Curreli 2009: 149), with twenty different versions spanning from the first 1924 book translation to the latest editions of the 2000s. This allows me to select translations of different periods and analyse the potential effects that the ever-changing reception of the original has had on them.

The other main reason to choose *HoD* is purely practical, namely, the availability of texts in digital format. One of the greatest limitations of corpus studies is that the range of potential analyses is influenced by the actual availability of digitized texts (Fischer-Starcke 2010: 30). The programs for linguistic analysis work only with digitized texts, so their availability is a critical factor to take into account when choosing what to study. Of course, texts that are not already available can be digitized for the purpose. However, this process is often very demanding and time-consuming (cf. Section 3.3.3), or simply not possible at all due to copyright constraints. Hence it is not surprising that the choice of what to study is also based on what is already available in electronic format, with all the limitations that this entails. These limitations have been acknowledged by Fischer-Starcke (2010: 29), who admits that the original idea of including in her Gothic reference corpus all of the texts mentioned in Austen's *Northanger Abbey* was abandoned because these texts are not all available in electronic form. Similarly, Mahlberg (2013: 3) explains that the free availability of electronic texts is one of the three reasons for her choice to concentrate on Dickens.

The vast majority of Conrad's works, including *HoD*, is available for free from the website Project Gutenberg (www.gutenberg.org). As far as the translations are concerned, the large number of Italian versions is equally mirrored in the wide availability of many different e-book editions. These e-books provide a sufficient assortment of translations that do not need to be converted, being available already in digital form. This means that all the texts needed for this research are readily available in electronic format, except for the 1924 TT, which has been manually digitized (cf. Section 3.3.3). The digital version of *HoD* used in the present study has been retrieved from Project Gutenberg. The file has been edited to remove the index, introduction, chapter headings, Project Gutenberg licence notes and any other element that was not written by the author and/or makes no part of the body of the short novel. The resulting text counts 38,759 words.

3.3.2 The reference corpora

The term 'reference corpus' here refers to a corpus designed and compiled to be representative of a specific language variety so that it can be used as the basis for comparison. This study employs two reference corpora to be compared with *HoD*: RC and CC. These reference corpora are used in the keyword analysis (cf. Section 3.4.1 for more details) to identify words that are typical of *HoD*, that is, words with a deviant frequency. In addition, RC and CC are also used in Chapters 5 and 6 to compare the frequency and usage of other relevant items, whether they are keywords or not, in order to provide an idea of how these items are used in *HoD* specifically, compared with the other novels by Conrad (CC) or other fictional texts from the same period (RC).

RC aims to represent the English fictional written language contemporary to Conrad. Comparing *HoD* against RC provides information about the differences between *HoD*-specific language and the more general literary language used in that period. RC is composed of forty-two texts by twenty-one British authors, each author represented by two works, for a total of 4,177,872 words (see Appendix 1 for the list of texts used). These novels, short novels and collections of short stories were written between 1887 and 1922, in this way matching the years in which Conrad wrote his works: Conrad published his first work, *Almayer's Folly*, in 1895 – although he started writing it some years before – and his last novel, *Suspance*, was published posthumously in 1925. All the texts included in RC have been retrieved from Project Gutenberg. It is worth mentioning that RC has no internal balance between the texts. Although each author equally contributes to the corpus with two works, these have different lengths and therefore influence the data differently. This issue can be easily dealt with by compiling the corpus using separate text files for each work, instead of a single one containing all the works together. By doing so, it is possible to spot whether one text – or a minority of them – is individually affecting the outcomes of the analysis.

CC contains most of Conrad's fictional works, so that comparing *HoD* against CC shows the differences between *HoD*-specific language and Conrad's general fictional language. CC counts 1,724,568 words and includes all the fictional works by Conrad available on the Project Gutenberg website except *HoD*, for a total of twenty-three works: eighteen novels and short novels and five collections of short stories (see Appendix 1 for the list of texts used). Conrad's collaborations with Ford Madox Ford and his autobiographical writings have been excluded, for this corpus is designed to study Conrad's fictional style, rather than his general written language. CC, as well as RC, have been manually checked to delete what does not constitute Conrad's fictional language: indexes, introductions, prefaces, notes, chapter headings, appendices, Project Gutenberg licence notes and any other writing extraneous to the very body of his work.

RC and CC are the main reference corpora used throughout this book. In addition to these, in Chapter 6 I also use a secondary reference corpus, itTenTen (Jakubíček et al. 2013). Available as a preloaded corpus on the *Sketch Engine* platform (Kilgarriff et al. 2014), itTenTen is a large Italian corpus (3 billion words) built with texts collected from across the internet, inclusive of a wide range of text types and registers. itTenTen is employed to provide additional corpus evidence for the study of the potential racist implications of the items related to the theme 'race and racism' (cf. Chapter 6).

3.3.3 The translations

This study makes use of four different Italian translations. Three of them are contemporary translations, whereas the fourth is an early translation, dated 1924. The texts of the three contemporary translations have been obtained from their e-book versions, available on various online e-book stores. The files have been converted into txt format and edited so as to delete their introductions, prefaces, indexes, notes and chapter headings, in line with the editing of the ST and reference corpora. The Bur edition of *HoD*, *Cuore di Tenebra* (henceforth Translation B), was published in e-book format in 2010, but the translation was originally written by Giorgio Spina in 1989. It is composed of 37,715 words. The Garzanti edition of *HoD*, *Cuore di Tenebra* (henceforth Translation G), was published in e-book format in 2011 and originally translated by Luisa Saraval in 1990; this text is composed of 38,493 words. The Mondadori edition of *HoD*, *Cuore di Tenebra* (henceforth Translation M), counts 36,442 words; it was published in e-book format in 2010, while it was originally translated by Rossella Bernascone in 1990.

The early TT (henceforth Translation S) is the 1924 translation by Alberto Carlo Rossi, the first Italian book-translation of *HoD*. The edition used for the analysis was published in 1928 (40,556 words) by the publisher Sonzogno, which reprinted the original 1924 translation with only some minor, formal alterations (Curreli 2009: 189). Translation S is not available in digital form so, after receiving the permission from the current copyright holder, I created a digitized version of the text. To begin with, the book was scanned. Then, with the aid of an optical character recognition (OCR) software, the scanned pages were converted into a text file. This text went through a twofold process of checking. First, it was automatically checked with the help of *Microsoft Word* spell checker; second, I revised the text manually, in order to eliminate the remaining typos and misspellings. The OCR software, for example, is likely to confuse *l* with *I*, or *c* with *e*, especially when the scan of a page is not particularly clear. When the mistake of the OCR results in a non-existing word, *Microsoft Word* spell checker is able to spot it, facilitating the editing process. However, when the reading of the OCR does not produce what the spell checker sees as a mistake, for instance with *case/ease*, manual checking is required. This example gives an idea of the laboriousness of manually converting texts into electronic form: it is a long and complex process that involves repeated readings of the text, all of which require time-consuming precision. Table 3.1 provides details about the reference corpora and texts used in this book.

Table 3.1 *Texts and corpora*

Text	Translator	Publisher	Translated	Published	Words
HoD	/	Blackwood	/	1902	38,759
Translation S	A. C. Rossi	Sonzogno	1924	1928	40,566
Translation B	G. Spina	Bur	1989	2010	37,715
Translation G	L. Saraval	Garzanti	1990	2011	38,493
Translation M	R. Bernascone	Mondadori	1990	2010	36,442
RC	/	/	/	/	4,177,872
CC	/	/	/	/	1,724,568

3.4 Data analysis

Corpus analysis is the result of the interaction between four fundamental components: 'corpus creation', 'discovery', 'hypothesis formation' and 'testing and evaluation' (Laviosa 2002: 8). These components interact with and inform each other in order to assemble the methodology of the study. In this process, the data that the corpus provides plays a cardinal role. However, how the data is used in relation to the hypothesis formation can vary. Borrowing Laviosa's (2002) terms, the hypothesis formation does not necessarily have to be the consecutive step to the discovery (corpus creation > discovery > hypothesis formation > testing and evaluation), but can also precede the entire process (hypothesis formation > corpus creation > discovery > testing and evaluation). In the first case, the data resulting from the discovery is the starting point for the hypothesis formation, which is then tested and evaluated. In the second case, the hypothesis is formulated before the corpus creation and the discovery, and thus informs them. The data resulting from the discovery is used to test and evaluate the pre-existing hypothesis. These two different approaches to corpus analysis have been called, respectively, 'corpus-driven' and 'corpus-based' (Tognini-Bonelli 2001). Tognini-Bonelli (2001) defines 'corpus-based' as the approach that interrogates the corpus to testify and improve pre-existing hypotheses 'that have not themselves been formulated in the light of corpus data' (Tognini-Bonelli 2001: 65). Whereas a 'corpus-driven' approach (Tognini-Bonelli 2001: 84) aims at building hypotheses from scratch, completely free from theoretical premises, so as to reflect entirely the corpus evidence.

In practical terms, the distinction between the corpus-based and corpus-driven approaches has a mainly heuristic value, as the two approaches do not represent opposite paradigms but, more realistically, two extremes of the same cline. Their dichotomous opposition is in fact more theoretical than realistic. The main characteristic that distinguishes the corpus-driven from the corpus-based approach, that is, the theory-free paradigm, is 'a myth at best' (Gries 2010: 330), as achieving a complete detachment from any existing assumptions is virtually impossible. More realistically, the corpus-driven approach aims to keep theoretical premises at a minimum, so the difference between the two paradigms can be seen in terms of the degree to which they employ theoretical premises, rather than whether they use them or not. What is more, the two perspectives can be combined, as shown by Rayson (2008), who links elements of the corpus-based and the corpus-driven paradigms into his 'data-driven' approach (Rayson 2008: 543). Along these lines, this book does not comply with any of the two approaches in particular, but rather adopts a more flexible attitude. Corpus-based is of course the dominating approach, given that the review of the literary criticism in Chapter 2 provided me with indications and suggestions for the investigation of the data. However, this does not prevent the use of other methods or approaches that tend towards the -driven end of the corpus-based/corpus-driven continuum. Specifically, Chapter 7 uses principal component analysis to compare the TTs as whole texts, as opposed to the comparison based on selected stylistic patterns undertaken in Chapters 5 and 6. As such, the analysis in Chapter 7 is more corpus-driven than corpus-based, since the criteria for the comparison are not based on pre-existing premises, for example, derived from the literary criticism. On the contrary, the texts are compared purely on the basis of the frequency patterns of their most frequent words, so the findings reflect only the formal features of the texts, aiming to keep pre-existing hypotheses at a minimum.

The methodology of the present book is structured in four steps, as represented in Figure 3.1. I briefly introduce them here in order, so as to have a complete overview of the methodology; then I focus on each of them separately in the remaining sections of this chapter. The first step (Chapter 4)

Step 1	Identification of specific words related to major themes	Answer to RQ1
Step 2	Detailed analysis of word patterns	Answer to RQ2
Step 3	Comparison of patterns in translation	Answer to RQ3
Step 4	Comparison of the translations as whole texts	Answer to RQ4

Figure 3.1 *Methodology overview*

identifies groups of text-specific words that are related to the major themes discussed in Chapter 2. This step moves the focus of the analysis from the whole text to specific items, in order to narrow down the range of the investigation to individual items that are relevant to the purpose of this book. To do so, I carry out a keyword analysis, with the aim of emphasizing the link between the lexical level of *HoD* and its major themes. The selection of specific groups of keywords to analyse in detail is made adopting Mahlberg and McIntyre's (2011) model for keyword categorization. This particular model is chosen because it is specifically designed to be applied to literary texts and allows the researcher to focus on the recognition of themes rather than on the counting of keywords. This step of the methodology provides an answer to the first research question.

The second step examines in detail the lexico-semantic patterns of the words in the categories selected, in order to investigate their contribution as building blocks of the fictional world. In particular, Chapter 5 is concerned with the patterns that convey the fictional representation of the African jungle, while Chapter 6 deals with the patterns related to the fictional representation of the African natives. Quantitative and qualitative analyses are linked in these chapters, where the items are studied as units of meaning (Sinclair 1991, 2004) which develop specific local textual functions (Mahlberg 2007b, 2013). In this investigation, semantic preference and semantic prosody takes centre stage, as they play a fundamental role in constructing linguistically the jungle and the natives in *HoD*. This step provides an answer to the second research question.

The third step of the methodology explores the effects of translation on the lexico-semantic patterns identified in the original. This step is also carried out in Chapters 5 and 6: the TTs are compared to highlight the differences and similarities in the fictional representation of the African jungle and of the African natives. This comparison shows the consequences of textual alterations on the potential interpretation of *HoD* in the target context, with a special emphasis on the manipulative effects such alterations may create. This step provides an answer to the third research question.

In the last step of the methodology, principal component analysis is used to compare the TTs with each other and with the ST. Here the perspective on the texts' relation is shifted from the level of individual linguistic features to that of the whole texts. This step aims to compensate the previous comparison and to account for the TTs in their entirety. This procedure provides an answer to the fourth research question.

3.4.1 Lexis and themes

By its very nature, the corpus approach prioritizes the lexical level over the other levels of a text (Mahlberg 2005: 189, cf. also Chapter 1). This may be seen as a limitation, especially in the study of literary texts, as lexis is only one of the levels through which the 'literariness' (Carter 2004) of a text is conveyed. However, the focus on lexis does not mean that the analysis is limited to the lexical level, because through the examination of the words a text is made of we can examine grammatical, semantic and pragmatic patterns. Corpus stylistics is about relating the lexical description that the corpus approach prioritizes to higher levels of abstraction, up to stylistic effects and literary appreciation. In other words, the corpus stylistician uses the insights the corpus provides as a means towards a deeper understanding of the literary work. This emphasizes once more the importance of the link between linguistic analysis and critical interpretation, and one way to establish this link is by focusing on lexical choices that are stylistically relevant.

The search for relevance in lexical choices is benefitted by the fact that lexis is the level of linguistic form which allows for the greatest variability and the greatest freedom of choice (Fowler 1966: 16). The selection of one word instead of another is likely to convey a certain degree of meaningfulness. However, not every lexical choice forms part of the style of a text indiscriminately. Generally, to be considered a feature of style, a lexical choice has to be consistent: choices in isolation may be stylistically meaningful per se, but it is patterns of repeated choices that develop the style of a text as a whole (Leech and Short 2007: 34). Consistency and repetition in lexical choices are best examined in terms of their frequency in the text, so frequency can be a useful indicator of stylistic relevance (cf. Chapter 1). Following Leech and Short's (2007) notion of style as a function of frequency, a frequency deviance has the potential to convey literary relevance, considering that a linguistic feature must first be deviant in order to also be foregrounded (Leech and Short 2007: 41). Therefore, a convenient starting point towards the search for foregrounded features is comparing the actual frequency of a given lexical choice against its expected frequency, in order to establish whether or not the frequency of this lexical choice is deviant. This is not to say that all instances of deviance are stylistically significant, but rather that deviant features are likely candidates to convey literary relevance, as opposed to features with a normal frequency of occurrence.

In corpus linguistics, a common way to identify words whose frequency is unusually high (or low) in comparison with some norm is through keyword analysis. Within the aims of corpus stylistics, the use of keyword analysis has a twofold value: it enables an easy and automatic identification of deviant words and, at the same time, establishes a link between lexis and the content of the text. Keywords provide an effective way to characterize a text or a genre (Scott 2016a). Scott (2016a: online) explains that 'aboutness' keywords – items that indicate what a text is about – are one of the three typical categories of keywords. Similarly, Stubbs (2005: 11) recognizes that nouns from a keyword list can reflect the topics of a text. However, Stubbs (2005: 11) also argues that only superficial topics are emphasized with keyword analysis, while 'underlying themes' are not visible. In the case of *HoD*, for example, he explains that noun keywords such as *Kurtz* and *river* indicate only superficial topics, as opposed to inner themes. I argue instead that keywords can also be related to underlying themes. Although individual keywords alone cannot account for the totality of a theme in a literary text, I show that groups of keywords in *HoD* are linked to its major themes. This link is established through the patterns that the keywords create. The relation between keywords and fictional themes is also acknowledged by Mahlberg and McIntyre (2011: 207), who maintain that keywords have the potential to be both 'signals for the building of fictional worlds' and 'triggers for thematic concerns of the novel'. Toolan (2008: 112) raises the same point, explaining that keywords can be 'pointer to a text's themes and preoccupations'. Keyword analysis can therefore prompt a link between linguistic description and literary interpretation. Given its potential to relate lexis and content, keyword analysis is employed in this book to address the first research question: how to identify sets of text-specific words that relate to the themes 'Africa and its representation' and 'race and racism'.

From a quantitative point of view, carrying out a keyword analysis is useful in many respects. First, it is an efficient way to begin a study, because it substantially narrows down the data to analyse and facilitates the selection of fewer items to examine in detail. At the same time, the procedure circumvents the researcher's bias, as keywords are generated automatically by the computer, 'blindly', without considering meaning relations between them. Moreover, all keywords are statistically significant by definition, as they are the result of a calculation that reduces the risk that their deviant frequency is due to chance. In sum, keyword analysis allows the researcher to start the investigation with a controlled number of items that are statistically significant and automatically generated.

These advantages have been illustrated by numerous studies. For example, Culpeper (2002b: 14) explains that keyword analysis is particularly beneficial because it is an automated technique that, within minutes, emphasizes words that are good indicators of potentially relevant features of a text. He demonstrates this by looking at patterns in the characters' dialogues in Shakespeare's *Romeo and Juliet*, identifying both content and function words that characterize the style of the protagonists' talk. Toolan (2008) uses keywords in his analysis of narrative prospection and expectations. He assumes that some textual features create expectations for the progression of the narrative, and that these features must be prominent in order to be identified by the reader and create an expectation (Toolan 2008: 108). He therefore uses keyword analysis to specify foregrounded features of texts. He explains that keywords are particularly useful for his study, because they are both thematically relevant and unlikely to be ignored by the reader, by virtue of their recurrent frequencies. Čermáková and Fárová (2010) prove that keyword analysis can be similarly useful in the study of literary translation. They look at keywords in J. K. Rowling's *Harry Potter and the Philosopher's Stone* and its Finnish and Czech translations. They aim to investigate how some thematically relevant keywords (*wand, cloak, owl, eyes, door, wizard, broomstick, troll, broom* and *stone*) have been translated. Through qualitative analysis of text extracts, Čermáková and Fárová (2010: 183) compare the functions of the keywords in the ST and in the TTs, concluding that a keyword analysis could have helped the translators to identify more easily items that required special attention.

It is worth specifying that generating a keyword list does not constitute an analysis in itself. Despite the advantages of using this technique, it is the qualitative examination of keywords that points out their meaningfulness. This is particularly true in the context of corpus stylistics and the study of literary texts, where keywords have to be examined in light of the text content and its critical interpretation. O'Halloran (2007), for instance, focuses on the keyword *would* in James Joyce's 'Eveline'. This item has been recognized as a keyword in the same text by Stubbs (2002), but Stubbs's (2002) qualitative analysis of the function and patterns of *would* is limited. Stubbs (2002: 130) only states that *would* signals the fact that in the short story Eveline is thinking about hypothetical possibilities for her future, although in the end she fails to put them into practice. In contrast, O'Halloran (2007) investigates the way *would* is used both quantitatively and qualitatively, exploring its patterns in free indirect thoughts (e.g. *she would* [. . .] and *Frank would* [. . .]) using Hallidayan transitivity analysis (Halliday and Matthiessen 2004). O'Halloran (2007: 236) proves that Eveline's conscious hopes about her future leak subconscious doubts and signal in advance her final decision not to follow Frank.

The main purpose for adopting keyword analysis in this book is to identify *HoD*-specific words that relate to the major themes discussed in Chapter 2. As I aim to relate the lexical level of *HoD* to its themes, keywords are used as a starting point to identify patterns that act as building blocks of the fictional world and triggers of thematic concerns. To address this specific purpose, this book adds a further level of discrimination to the keyword analysis, a classification into categories that are likely to represent the themes of *HoD* better than individual keywords. The classification of keywords into sets and categories is not new in corpus linguistics. McEnery (2009) develops a model to identify moral panic in a corpus through the classification of its keywords. He identifies seven categories that would reflect a moral panic in a text or a corpus: 'object of offence', 'scapegoat', 'moral entrepreneur', 'consequence', 'corrective action', 'desired outcome' and 'moral panic rhetoric'. If the keywords resulting from the comparison of two corpora fit this categorization model, than this indicates that the corpus under analysis contains a moral panic (McEnery 2009: 96). Similarly, Gabrielatos and Baker (2008) adopt keyword analysis to explore discursive constructions around refugees, asylum seekers, immigrants and migrants (RASIM) in the UK press between 1996 and 2005. They argue that by grouping relevant keywords into specific topics and attitudes it is possible to identify the different discourses of RASIM between tabloids and broadsheets (Gabrielatos and Baker 2008: 10). A similar application is Bachmann's (2011) analysis of discourses on civil partnership in the UK Houses of Parliament. Bachmann (2011: 88) also divides keywords into thematic groups and then investigates their functions in context, demonstrating how this methodology allows him to emphasize which topics are predominant in the debates (Bachmann 2011: 100).

However, these models have been used to study language varieties other than literary language, and therefore may not work equally well for the analysis of *HoD*. The model adopted here is instead designed to work specifically with literary texts, namely, Mahlberg and McIntyre's (2011) model. Mahlberg and McIntyre's (2011) model offers a way of classifying relevant keywords into thematic categories which emphasize their role as building blocks of fictional worlds and themes. They propose two main categories: 'fictional world signal' keywords and 'thematic signal' keywords. In Chapter 4, I show how these sets suit perfectly the aims of this project and help to establish a link between the lexical level of *HoD* and its major themes.

3.4.2 From words to extended units of meaning

Firth (1957: 179) famously stated that 'you shall know a word by the company it keeps'. Words in fact do not exist in a void. On the contrary, they establish meaningful connections with the words that precede and follow them. Knowing these connections can be very useful for the stylistician: if we assume that stylistic features 'form [. . .] significant relationship[s] with other features of style, in an artistically coherent pattern of choice' (Leech and Short 2007: 40), then looking at the way words and linguistic items relate to each other can help us to understand how stylistic features create patterns in a text. The study of stylistic features should therefore go beyond the analysis of individual words and encompass the relationships that words establish in their context of occurrence.

More than anyone else, Sinclair (1991, 2004) has shown that focusing only on individual words is limiting, because the word in itself is not an independent unit. A more suitable unit of meaning is the 'lexical item' (Sinclair 1991, 2004), a functionally complete unit that overcomes the formal boundaries of the single word. The lexical item is defined by the sum of the lexical, grammatical, semantic and pragmatic relations the item establishes in its context of use. Sinclair (1991, 2004) proposes a model to study the lexical item as a unit of meaning, a model that revolves around the interaction between the 'core' item and four structural categories: 'collocation', 'colligation', 'semantic preference' and 'semantic prosody'. Meaning is likely to develop from the interaction between the structural categories and the core.

The first structural category develops on the lexical level and is called 'collocation'. Collocation (Sinclair 2004: 28) is defined as the tendency of two or more words to occur frequently together within a few words (usually four or five) of each other. It is a purely lexical relation based on probabilistic principles (Stubbs 2002: 64) which, although has a limited effect on the overall meaning of the unit, operates strong constraints at the level of lexical choice (Sinclair 2004: 28). This means that the selection of a word can be limited by its collocational patterns. Moving to a level higher than the lexical one, we find colligational relations. 'Colligation' (Sinclair 2004: 142) develops on the grammatical level and is defined as the tendency of grammatical phenomena (or lexis plus grammatical phenomena) to co-occur together. Colligation is a more abstract category than collocation, for its identification involves conceptualising words (immediately perceptible) as representing grammatical categories.

The next step of the model moves from individual words and grammatical categories to groups of semantically related words. This semantic interaction between the core and its context is termed 'semantic preference'. Sinclair (2004: 142) defines it as the tendency of an item to co-occur regularly with semantically related words, that is, words that form part of the same semantic field. Semantic preference also advances the model towards abstraction (Stubbs 2002: 88), as semantic fields have typical and frequent members, but remain mainly open-ended categories. The last structural category, 'semantic prosody', extends to the pragmatic relations of the unit of meaning and contributes to express the speaker's/writer's attitude. It is defined by Sinclair (2004) as the attitudinal tendency in the realm of pragmatics that unveils evaluative stances about the topic of the discourse. It is the most abstract structural category, because it is open to a wide variety of different realizations, since 'in pragmatic expressions the normal semantic values of the words are not necessarily relevant' (Sinclair 2004: 34). Nevertheless, semantic prosody plays a key role in the construction of the unit of meaning as it defines the function the unit is meant to have. All the other categories of the unit follow this functional choice and are interpreted accordingly.

Let us consider a practical example. Figure 3.2 shows thirty concordance lines of *reduce* from the British National Corpus (BNC), retrieved via the online tool *BNCweb* (http://corpora.lancs.ac.uk/BNCweb/) and sorted randomly. As explained in Section 1.4.2, concordance lines enable a 'vertical' reading of the corpus that facilitates the identification of repeated patterns. At the collocational level, *reduce* co-occurs frequently with *costs* (*reduce the costs, reduce its costs, reduce costs, reduce real payroll costs* and *reduce costs further*). *Costs* is in fact one of the strongest collocates of *reduce* in the BNC, together with *emission* and *risk*, in a span of 5:5 (5 words to the left and 5 words to the right of the core *reduce*). However, *costs* is not the only noun occurring at the right of *reduce*. This core also co-occurs frequently with other nouns or noun phrases, for example, *reduce the myth, reduce agricultural subsidies, reduce evaporation, reduce the total fat, reduce the deep-felt sense of dissatisfaction* and *reduce the heat*. This tendency is an instance of colligation: *reduce* colligates frequently with nouns and noun phrases in the R1 position (one slot to the right of the core).

Grouping together these nouns and noun phrases, it is possible to identify the semantic preference of the core *reduce* for words belonging to the semantic fields of business/economics (*costs, strategy, taxpayer, solicitors, debt, payroll, company,* etc.), medicine (*fat, diet, urine, surgical, operations, abdominal, cholesterol,* etc.) and environment/pollution (*evaporation, petrol, consumption, pollution, emissions,* etc.). In terms of prosody, one may think at first that *reduce* has a negative attitudinal meaning – reducing is bad, as opposed to increasing, which is usually good. However, the concordance lines show that *reduce* has instead an overall positive semantic prosody. This is mainly due to the fact that the objects of the verb *reduce* are things that are usually considered beneficial to reduce, such as *reduce the cost, reduce significantly its overall operational impact on the environment, reduce its outstanding debt, reduce the total fat, reduce petrol consumption,*

ayer by raising the revenue from users; deterrence — to	reduce	the cost to the taxpayer by reducing demand for a service;
the white man has felt compelled to tame the desert, to	reduce	its primeval vastness to human dimensions. In particular, l
ion of abstract and general relations. These two features	reduce	the myth to the level of 'theory' as far as
mmunication networks within the processor complex to	reduce	overhead in communication between the processors. Peak
Agriculture, Clayton Yeutter, urged the EC and Japan to	reduce	agricultural subsidies. At the end of October the Departm
ssues. The Bank has developed a strategy which aims to	reduce	significantly its overall operational impact on the environ
system to sustain, and that is why he took steps to	reduce	it. That has been welcomed everywhere except on the Op
ıber of the European Community. Fragmentation would	reduce	our influence to virtual nonexistence. And I also believe t
through the ages been obsessed with finding methods to	reduce	complex, individual human personalities to 'types'? In m
tice permanently.' Solicitors also fear the changes could	reduce	public access to legal aid and increase the likelihood of a
ver the next twelve months. DG is taking Luna boxes to	reduce	its costs — Omron is still seeking other OEMs. Omron
t result in lower costs. Learning effects may also help to	reduce	costs and thereby prices. These effects arise when expans
d be a form of national savings. The government would	reduce	its outstanding debt, freeing capital for private investment
ın there were behavioural remedies proposed in order to	reduce	the extent of the product tie. Following the report, althoug
will be obliged to water crops at dusk or dawn only to	reduce	evaporation. Watering gardens, washing cars and filling s
:ut the total calories down to 1,850. The simple changes	reduce	the total fat in the diet by quiet a large amount.
money that you pay to the government and, second, to	reduce	real payroll costs while raising employees' perceived inco
wanting to pass urine occurs. This approach attempts to	reduce	the frequency of passing urine and increase bladder capac
d with overdrive (product feature) which enables you to	reduce	petrol consumption on motorways' (customer benefit). Th
ximmental. However, breeders have been taking steps to	reduce	calving problems and also to breed longer, taller animals.
s which had taken place since 1979 had done nothing to	reduce	the deep-felt sense of dissatisfaction, and that in many est
ıpulsive overeaters or performing surgical Operations to	reduce	the abdominal apron or reduce the length of the intestines
raise the supply price (S), which in turn will	reduce	the MEI. This could follow if the capital goods producing
arts? How is each item of the Country Code intended to	reduce	conflict between locals and visitors? How may the use of
. She was also advised that she should continue to try to	reduce	weight and should not return to her work (which involved
, and some 5000 are already fitted in homes. It can	reduce	the amount of water needed to flush a lavatory by 40 per
ınalysis. Even if one thinks one's own company will not	reduce	costs further, it is dangerous to make the same assumptior
cally. Healthier eating will help control your weight and	reduce	your cholesterol levels, so the simple message is: Eat less
n control options which can be implemented speedily to	reduce	pollution emissions from traffic, industry and homes. Dec
the eel (if using). Bring to the boil,	reduce	the heat and simmer for 10 minutes. 3 Add the remaining

Figure 3.2 *Example of unit of meaning in the BNC:* Reduce

reduce conflict, reduce weight, reduce your cholesterol levels, reduce pollution emissions. As mentioned earlier, the pragmatic function of the lexical item dictates the other functional choices of the unit, as the semantic prosody and the core are the obligatory elements in Sinclair's (1991, 2004) model. In this case, the positive semantic prosody of *reduce* calls for collocates that can convey this positive evaluation. Hence, *reduce* often refers to things or conditions that are good to decrease because, for example, they are dangerous for one's health, business or the environment: among them, the most frequent are *costs*, *risk* and *emissions*. Grammatically speaking, these things and conditions are expressed with the use of nouns or noun phrases, hence the colligational tendency of *reduce* to co-occur with this particular grammatical class.

Sinclair's (1991, 2004) model shows that meaning is a shared contextual endeavour, rather than an intrinsic feature of individual words. In a similar fashion, style is also a shared contextual endeavour, the sum of artistically coherent patterns of choices (Leech and Short 2007: 40), rather than the result of single linguistic features. Both meaning and style thus share the fact that they emerge from the mutual interaction of linguistic features on different textual levels. This parallelism would make Sinclair's (1991, 2004) model a suitable approach to analyse textual items in search for stylistic features. However, in practice, this model has been designed to work with large amounts of data and to identify general patterns of the language. Yet the study of an individual literary text may not offer as much data, and the patterns emerging from its analysis do not necessarily apply to general usage. This book does not intend to identify wide-ranging patterning around the selected keywords that account for the behaviour of these words in general. Rather, what I am interested in is *HoD*-specific patterns that contribute to the literary meaning of this particular text. Moreover, Sinclair's (1991, 2004) unit of meaning is mainly based on a fixed core and the patterns around it, while in literary texts the same stylistic effect can be shared by multiple cores/items. I show that in *HoD* stylistic effects can be spread over more than one core, each contributing in a different but interrelated way to the same stylistic effect. Overall, the structure of the lexical item and the way it works in theory may not match the practical aims of the analysis of a short literary text.

To tackle the potential mismatch, a more flexible notion designed to work also with literary texts and to cope with their specific traits has been proposed by Mahlberg (2007b, 2013): 'local textual functions'. Local textual functions are 'textual' because they account for the function of items in texts, rather than in more generalized language contexts. They are 'local' because their description of functions is specific to the text(s) analysed, so do not necessarily have to work outside of it (Mahlberg 2007b: 121, 2013: 17). Moreover, local textual functions can be shared or similar across multiple units, accounting for the interaction of different lexical items towards the creation of the same meaning/effect. The combination of Sinclair's (1991, 2004) lexical item model and Mahlberg's (2007b, 2013) local textual function constitutes the groundwork for the second step of this book's methodology. This step is applied in Chapters 5 and 6 to examine the textual patterns that contribute to the themes 'Africa and its representation' and 'race and racism'. This combined application provides an answer to the second research question. In particular, Chapters 5 and 6 build on the findings of the keyword categorization in Chapter 4, by exploring how the fictional representation of the African jungle and the fictional representation of African natives are linguistically realized. The items forming part of the thematic categories are studied as units of meaning, with particular attention paid to their mutual inter-action in order to highlight shared and text-specific local textual functions. Chapters 5 and 6 focus especially on two interacting phenomena: semantic preferences/prosodies and the network they establish throughout the text via lexical cohesion.

3.4.2.1 *Semantic preference and prosody in literary texts and their translations*

Semantic preference and semantic prosody play a particularly important role in this study and, more generally, in corpus stylistic analysis. Their importance is due to the unity of effect they can establish across several items, overcoming the issues arising from working with smaller corpora and hence lower frequencies. The corpus stylistician often works with frequency ranges that are much lower than those which a corpus linguist is used to dealing with. *HoD*, for example, is in the range of a few dozen thousand words, as opposed to the multi-million (or even multi-billion) word corpora employed in corpus linguistic research. In principle, this is not a problem since frequency is always a relative parameter and its significance is based on comparison. However, in practice, low-frequency ranges affect the potential of frequency to highlight repeated patterns in texts. Setting a frequency threshold and limiting the analysis to phenomena whose occurrence is higher than the cut-off point (e.g. collocational or colligational phenomena) can leave out part of the picture.

Consider the study of collocation, for example. In their examination of col-locations in translation, Baroni and Bernardini (2003) and Bernardini (2007) advocate a frequency-based approach that accounts for the strength of relation-ship between collocates, through the use of significance testing statistics. A simi-lar frequency-based approach applied to the present study would be limiting. A word like *darkness*, for example, occurs only 25 times in *HoD*. We might be aware of its relevance in the text, because it is a keyword and because it is intuitively recognizable as related to the novel's main themes; as such, we might choose it for further investigation. However, with only 25 occurrences, it is unlikely that examinations based only on frequently repeated behaviours highlight anything relevant. In fact, if we look at the collocations of *darkness*, only seven collocates occur more than 3 times, and only eleven occur more than twice; among these eleven collocates, only two are content words. These occurrences would not pro-vide enough data to identify frequency-based collocational patterns that could be relevant to the aims of this study.

On the contrary, frequency cut-off points are less of a defining criterion in the analysis of semantic preference and semantic prosody, as both phenomena can be constructed by the cumulative contribution of words that co-occur with a core just once. In the case of *darkness*, all of the collocates that occur only once could still be relevant to the analysis. Although they would not contribute to collocational patterns, they would instead contribute to semantic fields. Moreover, semantic preference and prosody function over wider contexts, involving larger sets of words, and can be shared by different items: several units of meaning contributing together to the same semantic preference and/or prosody. The potential of semantic fields to account for items that, individually, would not have occurred frequently enough to 'stand out' is acknowledged by Rayson (2008), in his study of the Labour and Liberal Democratic parties' manifestoes for the UK 2001 general election. He shows that the identification of key semantic domains in short texts (the manifestos are around 30,000 words each) highlights aspects of the manifestoes that previous frequency-based keyword analyses ignored. Rayson (2008: 544) explains that the investigation of dominant semantic fields has been useful to 'group together lower frequency words and multiword expressions which would, by themselves, not be identified as key, and would otherwise be overlooked'.

Although semantic preference and semantic prosody are phenomena which have been extensively discussed (in particular by Partington 2004 and Bednarek 2008), previous research has mainly focused on the English language, while other languages and contrastive analyses have been neglected (Xiao and McEnery 2006: 108). Among the few exceptions, Xiao and McEnery's (2006) study of collocation, semantic prosody and near synonymy in English and Chinese shows the relevance of semantic preference and prosody in the context of translation. They focus on three sets of near synonyms in English: the *consequence* group, the *cause* group and the *price/cost* group. With quantitative data and qualitative analysis, they prove that even what is considered the Chinese equivalents of the English terms can have different semantic prosodies. Being aware of this difference is helpful for the translator and the language teacher alike (Xiao and McEnery 2006: 126). Similarly, Oster and van Lawick (2008) aim to raise awareness of the importance of semantic preferences and prosodies among translation students and professionals. Failing to reproduce semantic and pragmatic conventions can result in unintentionally imprecise translations. Oster and van Lawick (2008) discuss the example of the Spanish expression *tomarse algo a pecho* and the German equivalent *sich zu Herzen nehmen*, concluding that even though the two may share a similar meaning, they are not pragmatically equivalent (Oster and van Lawick 2008: 342): the Spanish version is sometimes used in negative or offensive utterances, while the German equivalent is not. Munday (2011) also examines semantic prosody in translation in his contrastive analysis of *loom large* and its Spanish dictionary correspondent, *cernerse*. Munday (2011) discusses Louw's (1993) understanding of prosodies, according to which they are inaccessible to the speaker/writer's conscious intuition. Although inaccessible to the speaker/writer, Munday (2011) argues that prosodies can be perceived by the reader, who is able to grasp the irony that results from the contradiction of an established prosody. Therefore, translators too may be aware of semantic prosody, or at least the effect it creates in the text (Munday 2011: 182–3).

This book contributes to the discussion of semantic preference and semantic prosody in translation. I look in detail at the effect of translation on these phenomena, comparing text extracts across several translations. I also consider whether alterations to semantic preferences and prosodies can affect the building of the fictional world and the major themes in *HoD*. In this way, I seek to contribute to a more nuanced understanding of these aspects of the unit of meaning in the specific context of literary translation.

3.4.2.2 *Lexical cohesion in literary texts and their translations*

Chapter 5 shows that different lexical items can share the same semantic preference and prosody across the text. The network these patterns establish contributes significantly to the cohesion of *HoD*. Cohesion therefore plays an important role in the understanding of how lexico-semantic patterns act as building blocks of the fictional world. Given the importance of this aspect, before moving to the third step of the methodology, it is worth discussing further the concept of cohesion, how it has been approached with corpus methods, and how it has been discussed in the context of translation.

'Cohesion' is the sum of meaning relations existing within a text. It occurs when the interpretation of a given textual element is dependent on the interpretation of another one, so that decoding one effectively involves decoding the other accordingly (Halliday and Hasan 1976: 4). For example, in the previous sentence, *another one* is interpreted in relation to *element*; as such, it establishes a cohesive link with it. This type of cohesive relation is defined as 'substitution' and involves the replacement of one item by another (Halliday and Hasan 1976: 88). Substitution is one of the four types of 'grammatical cohesion', together with 'reference', 'ellipsis' and 'conjunction'. In addition to the grammatical level, cohesion can also be realized at the lexical level, through the selection of vocabulary. In this case, we talk about 'lexical cohesion' (Halliday and Hasan 1976: 6).

In Halliday and Hasan's (1976) seminal model, there are two main lexical cohesive devices: 'reiteration' and 'collocation'. Reiteration is created when one item refers back to another one with which it shares a common referent. It can be realized through the repetition of the same word or with the use of a synonym, near synonym, superordinate or general word (Halliday and Hasan 1976: 278). Collocation – a different use of the term compared to its usual understanding in corpus linguistics (cf. Section 3.4.2) – is established by the association of words that regularly occur together and share any recognizable semantic relation (Halliday and Hasan 1976: 285). In contrast to reiteration, two items linked by collocation do not have to share the same referent. Collocation can in fact be created not only by synonyms, near synonyms and superordinates, but also by complementaries (*boy/girl, stand up/sit down*), antonyms (*wet/dry, like/hate*) or converses (*order/obey*), as long as a meaning association is recognizable. Collocation is therefore an umbrella term that covers any instance of cohesion resulting from the co-occurrence of words that are associated by various types of meaning relations (Halliday and Hasan 1976: 287).

Lexical cohesion – especially collocation – is always contextual, as a word establishes a cohesive link only if it occurs in the context of other related items. This makes lexical cohesion more difficult to estimate than grammatical cohesion, because its effect on the text is subtle (Halliday and Hasan 1976: 288). Potentially, any lexical item can or cannot establish a cohesive relation, but there is no way to know it just looking at the item by itself. On the contrary, with grammatical cohesion, it is relatively easier to say. Halliday and Hasan (1976: 288) explain that *he*, for example, clearly calls for a cohesive link, as its identity needs to be retrieved from somewhere. This does not necessarily happen with lexical cohesion, as a lexical item 'by itself carries no indication whether it is functioning cohesively or not' (Halliday and Hasan 1976: 288). An important part of the study of lexical cohesion is therefore the analysis of the textual environment in which words occur, in order to investigate whether or not a cohesive link is established with other associated words in the context. When Halliday and Hasan (1976) published their study, they claimed that the most important thing to do when analysing a text with respect to lexical cohesion is to use common sense and rely on our knowledge as speakers of the language and its vocabulary: '[w]e have a very clear idea of the relative frequency of words in our own language, and a ready insight [. . .] into what constitutes a significant pattern and what does not' (Halliday and Hassan 1976: 290). Today, besides our common sense and knowledge, we can also use corpus linguistics and its tools. Corpus methods provide more precise frequency figures and a better illustration of patterns in texts; hence they can contribute to an important degree to the study of lexical cohesion.

From a corpus linguistic perspective, lexical cohesion can be studied as the interactions of units of meaning and the cumulative effect these interactions create. Cheng (2009) illustrates this interaction in her analysis of lexical cohesion in a corpus of public speeches about the SARS outbreak in Hong Kong, showing that the semantic preferences and prosodies of related items can interact to create a cohesive discourse. Mahlberg (2009) also describes the interaction of units of meaning and their effect on cohesion, but she defines it in terms of interacting local textual functions. Warren (2009) looks instead at frequently occurring lexical words, arguing that they can function as 'source[s] of lexical chains' (Warren 2009: 50). Their repetition across the text – and the repetition of other similarly frequent and related words – establishes lexical cohesive links. Overall, the analysis of how textual patterns relate to each other in texts can add further detail to our understanding of lexical cohesion. Hoey (1991: 10) argues that 'the study of the greater part of cohesion is the study of lexis, and the study of cohesion in text is to a considerable degree the study of patterns of lexis in text'. Patterns of lexis are efficiently studied through corpus methods, which make it easier to identify repeated textual behaviours in large amount of data. Ultimately, the analysis of patterns of lexis is an effective way to approach lexical cohesion from a corpus perspective.

Given its contextual nature and interrelatedness, lexical cohesion is a complex issue to deal with in the translation practice. With grammatical cohesive devices (e.g. the pronoun *he*), the translator is automatically aware that they function cohesively and will therefore translate them accordingly: *he* clearly refers to another referent in the text. In contrast, lexical items do not always make explicit their cohesive function, so the translator needs to take into account the whole (con)text to decide how to deal with such items. For example, *love* does not have any cohesive function per se, but it functions cohesively if it occurs in the same context of words such as *affection, hate* or *husband*. In cases like this, the translator should not only be concerned with isolated phenomena, but should also 'trac[e] a *web of relationships*, the importance of individual items being determined by their relevance and function in the text' (Snell-Hornby 1988: 69, emphasis in the original). Sometimes the translator does not or cannot reproduce the same web of relationships existing in the ST. This can create misalignment with the lexical chains of the ST and affect the cohesion of the TT. To prevent this happening, Baker (2011) suggests:

> Whatever lexical and grammatical problems are encountered in translating a text and whatever strategies are used to resolve them, a good translator will make sure that, at the end of the day, the TT displays a sufficient level of lexical and other types of cohesion in its own right. Subtle changes – and sometimes major changes – are often unavoidable. But what the translator must always avoid is the extreme case of producing what appears to be a random collection of items which do not add up to recognizable lexical chains that make sense in a given context. (Baker 2011: 216)

This is particularly crucial in the context of literary translation, where lexical chains contribute to make the fictional world cohesive. Corpus methods can be useful in this respect, to identify lexical chains existing in texts, looking at frequent content words or thematically relevant items (cf. Mastropierro and Mahlberg 2017). With the help of a concordancer, it is possible to gather all the instances of a given item and examine how it is used in its context throughout the text. In Chapter 5, I show how a corpus approach can be used to identify and study such cohesive networks, both in the original and in translation.

Corpus methods have been employed to study cohesion in translation, but mainly grammatical cohesion in technical translation. For instance, Krein-Kühle (2002) analyses how the English demonstrative determiner/pronoun *this*, as a cohesive device, is translated into German technical texts. Trebits (2009) focuses instead on the use of conjunctions as a way to establish cohesive links in general English texts and EU English documents, pointing out the most frequently used cohesive devices of conjunctive cohesion in the EU translations. As for the study of lexical cohesion in literary translation, the area remains mainly unexplored. One exception is Øverås's (1998) investigation of cohesive devices in the translation of fiction from Norwegian into English (and vice versa). However, the main focus of this study is testing Blum-Kulka's (1986) 'explicitation hypothesis'. This book aims therefore to fill this gap, providing a corpus-assisted study of lexical cohesion in literary translation. Specifically, Chapter 5 shows that the interaction of units of meaning creates cohesion in the fictional representation of the African jungle. I demonstrate that semantic preference and semantic prosody are shared across several items, and this shared feature throughout *HoD* establishes a network of semantically related lexical chains. Comparing the TTs, I also illustrate the effect of translation on these lexical networks, and how their alteration affects the cohesion of the representation of the jungle in the Italian versions.

3.4.3 Units of meaning in translation

Sinclair's (1991, 2004) model considers meaning as being spread over a unit for-
mally larger than an individual word and resulting from the cumulative effects
of several linguistic levels. This model overcomes the rigid description of lexis
and grammar as separate phenomena, enabling us to see them as interacting
together with the pragmatic function that a given item enacts in its situational
context. By taking into account this wider context it is possible to study aspects
of language that exceed the formal boundaries of a text, unfolding their social
(in a Firthian sense) nature. Extensive corpus research (cf. Section 1.7) has demonstrated that analysing collocations, semantic preferences and prosodies is an
effective method to gain insights into the sociocultural implications of linguistic strategies. Translation is likewise concerned with sociocultural implications.
Besides being a process in which meanings and forms are shifted from one language to the other, translating also involves a situational, contextual and cultural displacement. As argued in Chapter 1, a linguistic approach to the study of
translation needs to be able to account for the double linguistic and extralinguistic nature of the translation phenomenon, and Sinclair's (1991, 2004) model can
provide this twofold perspective.

Comparing translations on the basis of the lexical item and its contextual
relations limits the risk of being too tied to word equivalence. The idea that
meaning is not restricted to the single word – but is, rather, the result of a
network of textual links – calls into question the very concept of translation
equivalence established at the word level. The shift from the individual word
to the lexical item as a unit of meaning leads to a similar move from a word-
to-word understanding to a lexical-item-to-lexical-item conceptualization of
equivalence. From a methodological point of view, the comparison of lexical
items across languages benefits greatly from the availability of corpus evidence,
which enables the researcher to compare formal patterning both in the source
and in the target language. Tognini-Bonelli (2001: 150) argues in favour of this
type of equivalence and suggests a series of progressive steps to identify and
evaluate comparability across languages adopting Sinclair's (2004) model and
a corpus approach.

The first step consists of identifying the formal patterns of a given source
language lexical item and assigning the related meaning/function to each of the
specific patterns, on the basis of source language corpus evidence. In the second
step, a prima facie translation is assigned to each meaning/function that item
enacts. Ideally, this step should be informed by translation corpora but, in the

absence of these, the prima facie translation is assigned with the help of reference books, together with the past experience of the translator. The third and final step replicates the first step but in the opposite direction, moving from a target language function, as represented by the prima facie translation, to its formal patterning realizations in the target language. Once the relation between the source language item and the target language item has been established, it is possible to investigate their equivalence, namely, whether the item develops the same function in both languages. Any area of non-correspondence would represent an issue for the translator, whose task 'is exactly that of bridging these gaps in the light of the linguistic and extra-linguistic constraints' (Tognini-Bonelli 2001: 150).

Tognini-Bonelli's (2001) method for the comparison of units of meaning in translation is based on Sinclair's (1991, 2004) model and, as such, raises the same issues described in the previous section when applied to the study of literary translation. For example, Tognini-Bonelli (2001) advocates the use of comparable corpora in the first and third steps as an 'absolute necessity to establish equivalence' (Tognini-Bonelli 2001: 154). However, the way a lexical item is built in *HoD* might not be matched in any other corpus, being characteristic of *HoD* alone. What this study seeks to investigate is how *HoD*'s specific themes are conveyed through *HoD*'s specific formal patterns, even though these patterns cannot be exemplified through external corpus evidence. It is therefore necessary to find an alternative model that would allow for such a comparison. In line with the analysis of the original, it makes sense to consider local textual functions as the currency for translation comparison, instead of units of meaning. The notion of local textual function is a more flexible concept that fits better the needs of a study like this one, which aims at investigating the translations of a specific literary text. The comparison of local textual functions grounds the third step of the methodology, through which the third research question is addressed, namely, what effects translation has on the lexico-semantic patterns which convey the major themes in the Italian versions. The patterns identified in *HoD* in relation to the fictional representation of the African jungle and the African natives are studied in the TTs as well. The aim is to investigate whether or not they establish the same local textual functions. If not, the analysis examines the consequence of the mismatch. In this respect, this procedure aims to identify those 'blank areas of no match' (Tognini-Bonelli 2001: 150) in which divergences develop, as divergences can signal a more patent intervention by the translator.

3.4.4 The bigger picture: Principal component analysis

As explained in the previous section, the third step of the methodology is concerned with the comparison of the translations. This comparison is based on the patterns identified in the original, which in turn emerge from the study of the items foregrounded by the keyword analysis. Therefore, even though indirectly, the comparison of the translations builds on the keyword analysis. However, keywords are only part of the picture: quantitatively speaking, the patterns they develop represent just a minimal portion of the texts. Keywords are the result of a frequency comparison, where only items with deviant frequencies are highlighted, whereas words occurring with similar frequency across different texts or corpora are ignored. The words overlooked by the keyword analysis are, consequentially, overlooked during the comparison of the TTs. The aim of the fourth step of the methodology is to take into account, as much as possible, this 'unused' part of the source and target texts and employ it to compare the translations. To do so, principal component analysis (PCA) is employed in the last part of this book.

PCA is a statistical procedure that, in corpus/computational linguistics and stylistics, is used to generate a measure of difference across texts or corpora. This measure is based on the performance of a given number of variables, usually the most frequent words (MFWs) in the texts. The frequency patterns of a pool of MFWs are compared across texts in order to see how overall similar or dissimilar these texts are when compared with each other. The basic principle behind this is that the 200 or 300 MFWs in any text, for example, are likely to account for the vast majority of the tokens in it. Therefore, even though what we are comparing is the frequency of common words used in all texts (i.e. weak discriminators), they are able to account for most of the variance across the texts and can discriminate between them more reliably than a smaller set of infrequent words, that is, strong discriminators (Burrows 2002b: 679).

In this book, PCA and keyword analysis work with different yet mutually compensating sets of words. Chapters 5 and 6 focus on low-frequency content words (resulting from the keyword analysis in Chapter 4); PCA in Chapter 7 uses mainly high-frequency function words. It is worth specifying that function words are not always excluded from a keyword analysis. Scott (2016a: online) explains that high-frequency function words can be keywords too, claiming that they may be indicators of the style of the text, rather than of what the text is about (cf. Chapter 4 for the three types of typical keywords). However, this does not affect the part PCA plays in this study, as function words are excluded from the keyword analysis. This is because the aim of this study is to explore the role of textual patterns as building blocks of the fictional world. Content words are more likely to relate to the fictional world than function words; therefore, I intentionally focus on content words and exclude function words from the keyword lists. As a result, function words are not accounted for in Chapters 5 and 6, while PCA in Chapter 7 shifts the focus and uses what has been put aside in the previous chapters.

To show how the two approaches differ in terms of the words they work with, consider Table 3.2, which lists the 50 MFWs in *HoD* sorted by frequency. The vast majority of these items are very common function words; as such, they are excluded from the keyword lists, supposing that they appeared in such lists. The

Table 3.2 *50 MFWs in* HoD

N	Word	Frequency	N	Word	Frequency
1	the	2,292	26	all	185
2	of	1,372	27	an	180
3	a	1,151	28	this	176
4	I	1,133	29	they	159
5	and	992	30	no	157
6	to	894	31	were	157
7	was	672	32	out	153
8	in	616	33	we	151
9	he	593	34	by	143
10	had	503	35	one	136
11	it	485	36	would	133
12	that	423	37	said	131
13	with	376	38	be	125
14	his	340	39	very	125
15	on	315	40	is	124
16	you	308	41	been	123
17	as	293	42	from	122
18	for	274	43	have	121
19	at	263	44	like	120
20	me	250	45	up	120
21	my	248	46	what	117
22	not	245	47	so	112
23	him	222	48	could	110
24	but	214	49	man	110
25	there	204	50	some	102

majority of them in fact does not make part of the keyword lists altogether. This means that almost all of the fifty MFWs in *HoD* are not taken into consideration for the analyses in Chapters 5 and 6. However, the sum of the frequencies of these fifty MFWs accounts for over 46 per cent of the total amount of tokens in *HoD*, even though they are only 0.9 per cent of the total number of types in the text. PCA works exactly on these principles: (i) it uses very frequent and very common MFWs that account for the majority of tokens in the text; (ii) it uses these MFWs to discriminate between texts in a more efficient way than using infrequent but very text-specific words.

PCA provides an alternative perspective to the relation between the TTs. PCA uses such a large portion of the total number of tokens in the texts that, statistically speaking, the analysis can be said to approximate comparison at the level of whole texts. One could object that, because function words appear in all texts independently from the author or genre, they are not particularly well-suited to differentiate one text from the other. However, words do not function as discrete entities (cf. Section 3.4.2); on the contrary, they develop their meaning through the sum of the relationships they establish with other words. Function words are the markers of these relationships and, as such, they are also the markers of everything these relationships entail (McKenna et al. 1999: 152). In conclusion, PCA is adopted as a technique to address the fourth research question, namely, to provide a picture of how the TTs relate to each other when looked at as whole texts, as opposed to the way they relate to each other when they are compared on the basis of specific linguistic patterns alone. The perspective that PCA offers is also useful for contextualising the analyses in Chapters 5 and 6 within a wider framework. The two methods – analysis of individual linguistic features and PCA – enable comparison on different but compensating levels: placing the findings one next to the other shows whether these multiple levels of analysis match in their depiction of the relationship between the TTs.

3.4.5 The software

The present work makes use of *WordSmith Tools* (Scott 2016b) and *R* (R Core Team 2016) as the main programs for the analysis, while *Intelligent Archive* (Craig 2015) is used to generate the input for *R*. *WordSmith Tools* is an extensively used software suite for linguistic analysis and the main tool of this study, as almost all the data used in this book have been retrieved using it. The version used is the sixth, which has three main tools: Concord, used to generate concordance lines for a specific search item; WordList, which generates frequency lists of words and clusters; and Keywords, for comparing two different word lists and generating keyword lists. These three applications provide additional features to develop a great variety of tasks, giving the researcher the freedom to set many parameters and options according to the needs of the study.

In Chapter 7, *R* is used, as *WordSmith Tools* does not have any function for carrying out multivariate analyses. *R* is a software environment for statistical computing and graphics. It offers innumerable functions and packages designed to carry out specific tasks, including multivariate analyses and, specifically, PCA. The package used to perform PCA is *FactoMineR*, developed by Le et al. (2008). In the same chapter, I also use *Intelligent Archive*. *Intelligent Archive* is an application developed at the University of Newcastle, Australia, specifically designed for preparing a set of data to be exported to an external spreadsheet or statistics program such as *R*. As stated on the application's webpage, while most of the text-processing programs focus on more linguistic outputs, such as concordance lines, *Intelligent Archive* is more statistical and only produces frequency word counts. Within the aims of this study, *Intelligent Archive* is used to create automatically parallel wordlists.

3.5 Conclusion

This chapter discussed the methodological framework that underpins the present book and described the steps that are carried out to answer the four research questions. Each step has been designed to add a new layer of scrutiny to the analysis, resulting in a progression: from the whole texts to specific linguistic features and then back from linguistic features to the whole texts (cf. Figure 3.1). The keyword analysis foregrounds words that are significantly more frequent than others, making them stand out in the text as a whole. Mahlberg and McIntyre's (2011) model of keyword categorization helps to recognize the major themes in these prominent words, so that a connection between lexis and content can be established. Then, these items are analysed in detail, as developing local textual functions in the process of themes construction. The outcome of this in-depth analysis becomes the starting point for the comparison of the TTs, taking into consideration linguistic as well as interpretational aspects. Finally, PCA goes back to the whole texts, establishing a comparison from a wider point of view and counterbalancing the local perspective that the previous comparisons provided.

Rather than delineating a linear procedure, these steps can be seen as forming a methodological circle, in which the last stage can feed in and go back where the first stage started. The analysis moves from the whole texts to individual features through the study of keywords and lexical items, then from individual features back to the whole texts through PCA, as shown in Figure 3.3. Although this book completes only one round of the circle, it is possible to start again, as findings of PCA on the relations between the texts can inform the analysis of specific lexical features. I show that the outcome of Chapters 5 and 6 and the outcome of Chapter 7 are compatible with each other, even though they are based on different levels of linguistic scrutiny. With this awareness, it would have been possible to start another cycle and explore how these different layers interact with each other. This approach aims to offer a more holistic picture of how literary texts and their translation work, where diverse linguistic levels are regarded as intertwined and affecting each other.

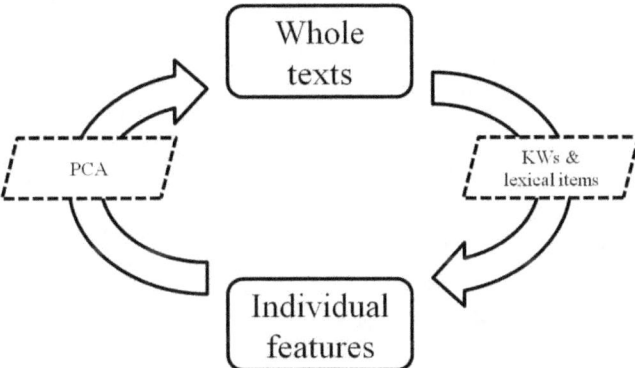

Figure 3.3 *The methodological circle*

From Lexis to Themes: The Keyword Analysis

4.1 Introduction

The first step of this study is to identify text-specific words that can be related to the representation of Africa and to the representation of the African natives in *HoD*. I argue that keyword analysis is an optimal way to do so, as this method offers several practical advantages. It makes it possible to start the investigation with a controlled number of items that are also statistically significant and automatically generated (cf. Section 3.4.1). Moreover, a keyword analysis can provide both a text-based and a reader-based perspective on *HoD*. On the one hand, keyword analysis is strictly text-based. This is because keywords are retrieved on the basis of textual features only, while the reader's understanding of the text does not play a major role in their identification. Keywords are characteristic items of a text, as their frequency is significantly higher or lower compared with the norm. They are generated blindly, only on the basis of their frequencies, without reflecting any 'meaning relationships between them' (Mahlberg and McIntyre 2011: 206). On the other hand, grouping keywords into thematic categories reflects a specific understanding of the text, rather than formal features. As such, categorising keywords offers a reader-based perspective. As this study aims to investigate the themes 'Africa and its representation' and 'race and racism', keywords are categorized in accordance with this aim. These two themes emerged from the review of the literary criticism in Chapter 2, which can be considered an informed, shared and consolidated understanding of the text. Finally, generating keywords and grouping them into thematic categories represents a way to link text-specific features to a reader-based understanding of the text, in this case, that of the critics. This link is in line with the 'philological circle' (Spitzer 1962) underpinning stylistic analyses, which seeks to relate linguistic description and literary appreciation (Chapter 1).

Section 4.2 describes the procedure to generate the two keyword lists used in this study. It also discusses methodological aspects of the keyword analysis, such as the selection of a reference corpus and the statistical cut-off point used to generate keywords. Then, comparing the two lists, it demonstrates the advantages of using multiple reference corpora. Section 4.3 concentrates on Mahlberg and McIntyre's (2011) model for the classification of keywords, arguing that this particular model fits the needs of the present study. Section 4.4 offers an overview of the keyword classification and describes some of the categories identified, while Section 4.5 explains which categories and keywords are selected to be studied in detail in the following chapters. It also introduces the resulting 'Africa words' and 'African words', and discusses the items they contain and the reasons behind their selection. Finally, Section 4.6 provides some conclusions and links to the chapters that follow.

4.2 Generating the keyword lists

In a keyword analysis, the choice of which reference corpus to use is a fundamental methodological decision. This decision can affect the outcome of the analysis, as using different reference corpora usually produces different sets of keywords. To minimize the effects deriving from the choise of any single reference corpus, and to make the analysis more reliable, multiple reference corpora can be used. In this book, two reference corpora are used to generate two keyword lists: the first using CC, the second using RC. As Fischer-Starcke (2010) explains, generating multiple sets of keywords by comparing a text to different reference corpora makes it possible to compare the resulting sets. Words that are shared among lists are more significant, as their status as a keyword does not depend on any individual reference corpus: being key in more than one set of data makes keywords better indicators of the distinctive aspects of a text. I can therefore compare the resulting keyword lists to identify words that are as specific to *HoD* as possible.

The first list (List 1) is generated by using CC as a reference corpus. CC is built to represent Conrad's language-internal norm, so that comparing *HoD* to CC points out those words that characterize *HoD* against Conrad's fictional language. The second list (List 2) is obtained by employing RC as a reference corpus. As RC seeks to represent the external norm of the literary language of the period, comparing *HoD* to RC emphasizes those items that characterize Conrad's short novel against general fictional language. Comparing the two keyword lists foregrounds items that are fundamentally typical of *HoD*. Only those words that are shared by both lists are selected, in this way minimising the risk that they could reflect Conrad's linguistic idiosyncrasies, rather than intrinsic features of *HoD*. At the same time, this comparison makes it more likely that the resulting keyword categories reflect themes that are *HoD*-specific, as opposed to themes that are generally central in Conrad's works.

The selection of the reference corpus is not the only procedural decision that has a major effect on the outcome of the analysis. Another criterion that affects significantly a keyword analysis is the statistical cut-off point for considering a word a keyword. As explained in Chapter 3, keywords are generated by comparing the frequency of each word in the wordlist of the text we are interested in with the frequency of the same word in the reference corpus wordlist. If the frequency of a given word in the text is 'unusually' high (or low) compared with its frequency in the reference corpus, then that word is considered a keyword. Programs such as *WordSmith Tools* use statistical tests – usually chi-square or log-likelihood – to check whether the difference in frequency is 'unusual'. The result of the statistical test is compared against a given cut-off point to determine whether the difference in frequency is statistically significant. However, this cut-off point is not fixed but can be set by the user of the software. The decision is up to the researcher and different cut-off points produce different sets of keywords.

Consider log-likelihood and *p*-value, which are used in this analysis to generate keywords. The *p*-value threshold represents the cut-off point that *WordSmith Tools* adopts to define a keyword. If the *p*-value resulting from the log-likelihood calculation is lower than the cut-off point, then that word is recognized as a keyword. A *p*-value of 0.05, for example, indicates a 95 per cent confidence that the outcome of the keyword analysis is not due to chance; a *p*-value of 0.01 indicates a 99 per cent confidence; a *p*-value of 0.0001 indicates a 99.99 per cent confidence; and so on. The lower one sets the *p*-value, the fewer keywords one obtains, since the frequency difference needs to be more striking to pass the cut-off point. Therefore, the selection of the *p*-value threshold has important implications for the analysis. However, there is no agreement over the 'right' cut-off point (Baker 2010: 26) and the selection of which threshold to use may depend on the needs of the study. Setting too high a *p*-value threshold usually generates too many keywords. McEnery (2009: 98) explains that, while it is indeed possible to analyse a large number of keywords, a smaller and more coherent subset is preferable (as a reference, Baker (2006: 127) considers 22 keywords a 'manageable' amount, although what is 'manageable' and what is not depends on the type of analysis). At the same time, too low a *p*-value cut-off point can exclude important words from the investigation, especially when the text under analysis is not particularly large. Baker (2010: 26) points out that the larger the texts or corpora we are examining, the larger the amount of keywords we are likely to obtain. Given that *HoD* is only approximately 39,000 words long, by setting a very low threshold we might run the risk of cutting out relevant words related to the representation of Africa and of the natives. As an example, comparing *HoD* with CC by setting a *p*-value of 0.0001 generates 88 keywords, while lowering the *p*-value to 0.0000001 (which is *WordSmith Tools* default setting), generates only 28 keywords, cutting out words such as *savages*, *darkness* and *niggers* which I show to be relevant for the analysis of the representation of the African jungle and the African natives. I therefore use as a cut-off point a *p*-value of 0.0001, which indicates 99.99 per cent confidence that the results of the keyword analysis are not due to chance. In this way, the analysis is not penalized by the fact that *HoD* is a short text. Setting a *p*-value of 0.0001 and a minimum frequency of 3 generates 88 keywords for List 1 (*HoD* vs. CC) and 183 keywords for List 2 (*HoD* vs. RC).

Once the two lists have been generated, all function words are deleted, so that only content keywords remain. There are two reasons behind this decision. First, excluding function words reduces further the number of keywords to consider in the analysis. This is particularly important, given that combining the two lists without removing function words would produce 271 keywords, which are too many to analyse in detail. Moreover, content words are more likely to reflect major themes. Even though function keywords have been shown to be equally indicative of stylistic features (Culpeper 2002b, 2009), this study aims specifically to establish a link between the lexical level of *HoD* and its thematic concerns. I argue that this link is better established by looking at content words rather than function words. Content words convey most of the semantic meaning of a text and are therefore a better starting point to relate lexis to themes, compared to grammatical items. Removing function words reduces the number of keywords to 76 in List 1 and to 163 in List 2. The two lists are reported in Table 4.1 and Table 4.2.

Comparing the two lists, it can be observed that the vast majority of the items in List 1 appear in List 2 as well. This suggests that what distinguishes *HoD* among Conrad's works also characterizes it against other fictional works of the same period. Besides proper names (which are text-specific in most of cases), keywords such as *ivory, river, darkness, forest, wilderness, niggers, station*

Table 4.1 *List 1 (HoD vs. CC; content words only)*

N	Keyword	N	Keyword	N	Keyword	N	Keyword
1	Kurtz	20	earth	39	intrusted	58	patches
2	manager	21	cipher	40	caravan	59	screech
3	pilgrims	22	staves	41	Fresleven	60	lots
4	station	23	pilot	42	etc	61	arrows
5	Kurtz's	24	steamer	43	wheel	62	work
6	ivory	25	brooding	44	rifle	63	administration
7	steamboat	26	see	45	surf	64	science
8	rivets	27	stream	46	banks	65	tin
9	river	28	savages	47	restraint	66	ominous
10	wilderness	29	waterway	48	cutters	67	chaps
11	snag	30	fossil	49	months	68	crawled
12	bush	31	nightmares	50	sometimes	69	introducing
13	shutter	32	woods	51	eloquence	70	kind
14	bank	33	grass	52	helmsman	71	mend
15	forest	34	wool	53	attack	72	hens
16	boiler	35	reaches	54	darkness	73	things
17	pole	36	manager's	55	invasion	74	agent
18	hippo	37	unsound	56	knights	75	niggers
19	stretcher	38	martini	57	shamefully	76	fog

and *steamboat* indicate the specific content of the short novel and distinguish it against other works both by Conrad and other writers. As suggested by Fischer-Starcke (2010: 66), the fact that these keywords appear in both lists maximizes their significance as characteristic features of *HoD*, bringing support to their examination as potential indicators of *HoD*-specific themes.

Looking at those words that do not appear in both tables is equally indicative of the advantages of using two reference corpora. For instance, if only List 1 had been considered, it would have seemed that *science* and *work* are typical of *HoD*. However, this would have been misleading. List 2 reveals that these words occur with a comparable frequency in other texts of the same period, suggesting that they are not as specific to *HoD* as it would have appeared if only one reference corpus was used. Focusing on the keywords that appear in List 2 but not in List 1, it can be seen that more than half of the words in List 2 are not shared by the other list. This means that if I had compared *HoD* with RC only, I would have had more than 60 keywords that are not as specific to *HoD* as I originally wanted, but rather represent lexical preferences or idiosyncrasies of Conrad's overall fictional language. Consider *sea* and *ships*, for example, which appear in

Table 4.2 *List 2 (*HoD *vs. RC; content words only)*

N	Keyword	N	Keyword	N	Keyword	N	Keyword
1	Kurtz	42	very	83	tin	124	murmur
2	manager	43	screech	84	swayed	125	yells
3	pilgrims	44	pole	85	rifle	126	villages
4	Kurtz's	45	black	86	aspect	127	nowhere
5	river	46	patches	87	ashore	128	absurd
6	ivory	47	trading	88	staves	129	imagine
7	steamboat	48	cutters	89	too	130	steam
8	station	49	nightmares	90	sometimes	131	tobacco
9	rivets	50	administration	91	yarns	132	row
10	wilderness	51	darkness	92	carriers	133	glitter
11	steamer	52	reaches	93	Russian	134	frightful
12	shutter	53	immensity	94	Europe	135	lank
13	forest	54	etc	95	below	136	months
14	snag	55	banks	96	devil	137	warlike
15	Marlow	56	agent	97	crawled	138	approach
16	bush	57	leaped	98	depths	139	bearers
17	earth	58	martini	99	desolation	140	canoes
18	coast	59	winchesters	100	immense	141	gleams
19	helmsman	60	Fresleven	101	fog	142	wool
20	deck	61	waterway	102	indistinct	143	cliff
21	bank	62	ships	103	feet	144	hanged
22	pilot	63	mud	104	intrusted	145	heard
23	shore	64	grass	105	fireman	146	cipher
24	boiler	65	brooding	106	fusillade	147	hut
25	stretcher	66	nigger	107	whites	148	continent
26	lot	67	riverside	108	rags	149	gloom
27	hippo	68	ominous	109	seemed	150	myself
28	seaman	69	fellows	110	sea	151	steamed
29	sombre	70	confounded	111	whisper	152	attack
30	trade	71	chap	112	pitiless	153	miles
31	savages	72	glance	113	overboard	154	sorrow
32	stream	73	impenetrable	114	mystery	155	fright
33	creek	74	abreast	115	introducing	156	arrows
34	surf	75	eloquence	116	shamefully	157	fringed
35	niggers	76	unsound	117	stillness	158	see
36	restraint	77	invasion	118	inconceivable	159	savagery
37	wheel	78	profound	119	lost	160	hammock
38	savage	79	lots	120	purpose	161	aft
39	chaps	80	swede	121	amazing	162	starched
40	fossil	81	afar	122	bends	163	cotton
41	company's	82	manager's	123	current		

List 2 but not in List 1. *HoD* is about a journey by water and these two keywords seem to reflect this topic. However, *HoD* is more specifically about navigation along a river. Seafaring and ships are certainly common topics in Conrad's fiction, but they do not single *HoD* out among Conrad's other novels. Therefore, *sea* and *ships* do not appear in List 1. Another example is provided by *creek* and *riverside*. More than *sea* and *ships*, these two keywords seem to refer precisely to the journey on the Congo River and as such appear to reflect specifically the content of *HoD*. Yet, keywords such as *waterway* or *bank* would reflect more characteristically this topic, because they are shared by both lists. Thus, comparing the two lists tells us that *waterway* and *bank* are better candidates to analyse in detail than *creek* and *riverside*.

4.3 The keyword classification model

The comparison of List 1 to List 2 produces a final list of 67 keywords. These keywords can be considered specific of *HoD* and so are used as the starting point for the creation of the categories. The final list of keyword is presented in Table 4.3.

Scott (2016a: online) explains that there are three types of words that usually make it into a keyword list. The first type is 'proper nouns'. In Table 4.3, this

Table 4.3 *Keywords shared by List 1 and List 2*

N	Keyword	N	Keyword	N	Keyword	N	Keyword
1	Kurtz	18	hippo	35	manager's	52	darkness
2	manager	19	stretcher	36	unsound	53	invasion
3	pilgrims	20	earth	37	martini	54	shamefully
4	station	21	cipher	38	intrusted	55	patches
5	Kurtz's	22	staves	39	Fresleven	56	screech
6	ivory	23	pilot	40	etc	57	lots
7	steamboat	24	steamer	41	wheel	58	arrows
8	rivets	25	brooding	42	rifle	59	administration
9	river	26	see	43	surf	60	tin
10	wilderness	27	stream	44	banks	61	ominous
11	snag	28	savages	45	restraint	62	chaps
12	bush	29	waterway	46	cutters	63	crawled
13	shutter	30	fossil	47	months	64	introducing
14	bank	31	nightmares	48	sometimes	65	agent
15	forest	32	grass	49	eloquence	66	niggers
16	boiler	33	wool	50	helmsman	67	fog
17	pole	34	reaches	51	attack		

type is represented by *Kurtz, Kurtz's* and *Fresleven*. The second type is 'about-ness keywords', that is, those words that give a good indication of the content of a text. This is the most relevant type of keyword for this study because these words enable me to establish a preliminary link between the lexical level of *HoD* and its themes. The vast majority of the entries in Table 4.3 belong to this type, for example, *bank, administration, river, ivory, pilgrims, station, darkness, nig-gers* and *wilderness*. The third type of keyword is represented by high-frequency words that may be indicators of style rather than of 'aboutness'. This type of key-word is underrepresented in Table 4.3, as function words have been removed from the two original lists. However, though not high-frequency, there are some words in the table that are more likely to be related to the style of the text rather than its content. For instance, keywords such as *etc* or *unsound* are certainly not signals of what *HoD* is about, but rather seem to indicate some of Conrad's styl-istic preferences, such as the use of negative prefixes (Stubbs 2005: 16) or the use of *etc* to shorten a dialogue line that goes uselessly on for too long.

Scott's (2016a: online) 'aboutness' keywords include exactly the type of key-words that are relevant to this study, namely, those that reflect the content of the text. However, this classification is too general for the aims of this work, for two related reasons: (i) not all 'aboutness' keywords can be related to *HoD*'s themes and (ii) the 'aboutness' category does not make any further distinction between the different aspects and levels within the content of a text.[1] Limiting the group-ing of keywords to this category would only result in a large and undifferenti-ated set of content words, too general to refer to specific aspects of the fictional world, such as the African jungle and the African natives. A further level of dis-crimination is therefore required. More complex models for the classification of keywords have been discussed in corpus linguistic literature (cf. Section 3.4.1), but they have not been designed to be applied to literary texts and may not work equally well with *HoD*. Thus, I opt for Mahlberg and McIntyre's (2011) model of keyword classification, which better fits the needs of this study.

Mahlberg and McIntyre's (2011: 207) model was originally designed to study keywords in Ian Fleming's *Casino Royale* as 'signals for the building of fic-tional worlds as well as triggers for thematic concerns of the novel'. Mahlberg and McIntyre (2011) classify keywords into two main categories: 'fictional world signals' and 'thematic signals'. Fictional world keywords are defined as 'world-building element[s]' (Mahlberg and McIntyre 2011: 209) that, with their concrete meaning, contribute to establishing the fictional environment of the novel. For example, *table* is classified as a fictional world keyword, because it has a concrete meaning that refers specifically to the fictional world of the novel: *table* is used repeatedly to refer to the gaming tables in the casino. In the case of *HoD*, *bush* and *station* are two examples of fictional world keywords, as they contribute to establish the fictional setting in which the short novel is set. Thematic signal keywords, on the other hand, are less concrete than fictional world keywords: they can be ambiguous, metaphorical or evaluative because of their polysemy. As such, they are open to wider interpretations (Mahlberg and McIntyre 2011: 209). These keywords can signal themes of the text and work in conjunction with other textual items – for example, other fictional world and/ or thematic signal keywords – in order to establish these themes. Mahlberg and McIntyre (2011: 209) identify *gambler* as a thematic signal keyword in *Casino Royale*. Besides its concrete meaning related to the casino setting, *gambler* can also be interpreted as referring to a 'risk-taker' attitude, embodied by James Bond. Together with other keywords, *gambler* can be seen as establishing the theme 'taking risks' (Mahlberg and McIntyre 2011: 209). In *HoD*, an example of a thematic signal keyword is *wilderness* since, in addition to its concrete meaning of 'wild land covered in vegetation', it can also be considered as the opposing force that resists the Western colonizers and be interpreted as signalling broadly the theme 'colonization and its consequences'. Fictional world signal and thematic signal keywords are the two main categories of the model. These two categories are further broken down into subcategories that group more specifically different aspects of the fictional world or diverse themes of the text. For instance, Mahlberg and McIntyre's (2011) fictional world category is divided into 'characters' and 'settings and props', each of which with its own subgroups. This system of subcategories allows me to pin down exactly the aspects of *HoD* I am interested in, and to populate the relative subgroups with keywords to be analysed in depth in the successive stages of the analysis.

As explained in Section 4.1, the value of grouping keywords for a corpus stylistic study also derives from the fact that these categories make it possible to account for critical interpretations. Categories are shaped in accordance with a subjective understanding of the text which, in the case of the present study, is represented by the established interpretations of the literary critics. By populating these categories, then, I create a link between the text-based features of *HoD* and their interpretation, although to different extents. Fictional world keywords are in fact more text-based than reader-based, in the sense that they reflect more closely lexically driven features of the text, rather than their subjective understanding by the reader. A character's name (*Kurtz*) or a descriptive reference to the novel's setting (*river*) are less open to interpretation than, say, a polysemous term such as *wilderness* or *darkness*. Thematic signal keywords are instead more reader-based than text-based, as they work on multiple levels of meaning and require more interpretative efforts.

However, this does not mean that only thematic signal keywords are able to account for the interpretation of *HoD*. Even though fictional world keywords refer to more concrete aspects of the text and are therefore less susceptible to subjective interpretations, they can equally have interpretative implications when contextualized. Consider *forest*, for example. At first, this keyword can appear neutral or concrete, as it clearly refers to the setting of *HoD*, the Congolese forest. As such, *forest* is classified as a fictional world signal keyword. Nonetheless, I want to argue that the fictional world plays a fundamental role as a trigger of thematic concerns in *HoD*: as explained in Chapter 2, the theme 'Africa and its representation' is related to the way the jungle is depicted in the short novel. *Forest*, then, participates in the building of the theme of Africa and, in conjunction with other fictional world keywords, accounts for a more reader-based aspect of the text. In the two following chapters, I illustrate how fictional world signal keywords are related to the two major themes that emerged from the discussion in Chapter 2. I provide evidence for the argument that keyword categories – fictional world signal and thematic signal – can be seen as lexically driven features of the text where both text-based and reader-based perspectives interact.

4.4 The keyword categories

To create the categories, each item in the final list of keywords (Table 4.3) is examined with the help of the concordancer. Words with related meanings are put together into the same group. Each successive keyword that does not fit into one of the existing groups leads to the creation of a new group, until the exhaustion of the items. In this process, the categories are reshaped and adjusted so as to obtain the best fit for the keywords, in line with the aim of the model that is establishing the categories themselves, rather than quantifying the keywords. Table 4.4 shows the resulting categories. All the keywords resulting from the comparison of List 1 and List 2 (Table 4.3) have been classified in the two main categories of the model, fictional world signal and thematic signal keywords, plus an extra 'Unclassified' group. This group collects those items that do not fit in any of the existing subcategories. This does not necessarily mean that these words are not significant, but simply that there are not enough keywords to create separate categories using them. If more keywords were taken into account,

Table 4.4 *'Fictional world signal' and 'thematic signal' keywords*

Category	Keywords
Fictional world signal	
Characters	
Names	Kurtz, Kurtz's, Fresleven
Equipment & tools	pole, stretcher, Martini, rivets, staves, wool, rifle, arrows, tin, hippo
Natives	savages, cutters, chaps, niggers, helmsman
Colonizers	manager, manager's, pilgrims, chaps, agent
Setting & props	
Places	Earth
Station	manager, manager's, pilgrims, chaps, administration, station, agent, ivory, fossil
Forest	bush, forest, hippo, grass
River	river, stream, waterway, reaches, surf, bank, banks, snag
Boat & sailing	steamboat, boiler, steamer, pilot, wheel, screech, crawled, shutter
Temporal indicators	months, sometimes
Atmosphere	
Negativity	brooding, nightmares, restraint, ominous, darkness
Thematic signal	wilderness, darkness, invasion, fog
Unclassified	etc, eloquence, lots, cipher, see, intrusted, attack, shamefully, introducing, unsound, patches

perhaps the items in the 'Unclassified' category might have formed further sub-categories of their own. As it is, they are not considered in this study.

The fictional world signal keywords are divided into four subcategories, representing fundamental aspects of the process of building up the fictional world. These subcategories are 'Characters', 'Setting & props', 'Temporal indicators' and 'Atmosphere'. It is interesting to notice that the 'Characters' subcategory is very different from that obtained by Mahlberg and McIntyre (2011), a difference that is indicative of specific aspects of *HoD*. First of all, the subgroup 'Names' contains two names only, *Kurtz* and *Fresleven*. Considering that the latter is a very minor character in the story, it can be said that 'Names' is not a very populated category in *HoD*. In contrast, Mahlberg and McIntyre (2011) have six names in the same subgroup, and they even specify that their 'Names' group only includes major characters (Mahlberg and McIntyre 2011: 211). In *HoD*, characters are rather referred to with common nouns, as indicated by the subgroups 'Natives' and 'Colonizers', which are more largely populated than 'Names'. This is not only the case for general groups of people (*savages, niggers, cutters* and *chaps* for the natives; *pilgrims* and *chaps* for the colonizers), but it happens also with specific characters that have more than a passing role in the story, such as the African helmsman of Marlow's steamboat or the manager of the station. The paucity of proper nouns and the abundance of common nouns in the 'Characters' subcategory confirm Stubbs's (2005: 8) observation about *HoD* that 'people are not named, but identified by their functions'. More generally, this relates to discussion about the text's vagueness, a feature that many critics have recognized. Leavis (1973: 180), for example, argues that Conrad makes a virtue out of not knowing what he means, Murfin (1989: 131) claims that *HoD* is a 'masterpiece of concealment', while O'Prey (1983: 23–4) recognizes a 'climate of doubt and vagueness' that surrounds and characterizes *HoD*.

This vagueness is paralleled in the 'Setting & props' and 'Temporal indicators' subcategories. Stubbs (2005: 8) argues that *HoD* is full of 'examples of this vagueness about places, times, and people', specifying that major places are never named and that the timescale of the story is similarly very vague. The 'Temporal indicators' subcategory includes two keywords: *months* and *sometimes. Months* occurs 17 times, but is preceded by a precise number (*nine months, six months, three months, two months*) only 4 times. The rest of the times, it occurs with a more abstract adjective – mainly *some months* (3 times), *few months* and *several months* (2 times) – or without any specification at all, as in *for months* (3 times) and *only months* and *months afterwards*. The frequent occurrence of *sometimes* (24 times) reinforces this sense of indefinite and unstated time that permeates the text. The insistent recurrence of *sometimes* is part of a larger stylistic feature: Stubbs (2005: 10) shows that more than 200 occurrences of *something, sometimes, somewhere, somehow* and *some*, together with other expressions of vagueness such as *kind of* and *sort of*, occur in *HoD*.

The 'Setting & props' subcategory mirrors the 'Characters' subcategory because it does not include any proper nouns. Proper place nouns are common in other keyword analyses of literary texts. For example, the 'Places' subgroup in Mahlberg and McIntyre's (2011) study includes *Royal-les-Eaux* and *Paris*, while Fischer-Starcke's (2009: 521) study of Austen's *Pride and Prejudice* identifies, among the others, *Meryton, Hertfordshire, Netherfield* and *Longbourn*. The absence of proper place nouns in *HoD*'s keywords is revealing, especially considering that proper names are generally regarded as one of the most frequent types of keywords in any text (Scott 2016a: online). Conversely, major places in *HoD* are mostly referred to with general common nouns, as exemplified by *station*, *forest* and *river*, three of the keywords with the highest keyness value that relate to the principal locations of the story.

The 'Atmosphere' subcategory is not included in Mahlberg and McIntyre's (2011) original classification and reflects a different aspect of the text compared to 'Characters', 'Setting & props' and 'Temporal indicators'. The items in 'Atmosphere' are not as concrete as those in the other fictional world signal subcategories, but equally shape the fictional world, although in a different way. Instead of relating to specific characters or places, words such as *brooding, nightmares, unsound, restraint, ominous* and *darkness* strengthen that negative and gloomy feeling, that dark atmosphere that lies heavily on *HoD* and characterizes it. They still contribute to building the fictional world, but emotionally rather than materially. Consider *brooding* and *ominous*, for example,whose concordance lines are shown in Figure 4.1 and Figure 4.2.

Followed by *over* 5 out of 9 times, *brooding* suggests the presence of a bleak aura, a negative atmosphere weighting down on the events and characters of the book. *Brooding* also occurs with other equally negative terms, especially *gloom* (5 times) and *sombre* (2 times). *Ominous* similarly participates in this effect, emphasizing the mysterious quality of everything in the story. *Voice* (line 7) and *murmur* (line 3) are *ominous*, as well as the *patience* (line 6) of the African forest and the appearance of the native woman that Marlow meets in one of the stations (line 4). Revealingly, in line 1 it is *atmosphere* that has something *ominous* about it.

1 monstrous town was still marked ominously on the sky, a brooding gloom in sunshine, a lurid glare under the stars.
2 out there in the luminous estuary, but behind him, within the brooding gloom. Between us there was, as I have already
3 gave to his black death-mask an inconceivably sombre, brooding, and menacing expression. The lustre of inquiring
4 , its exasperating torment, its black thoughts, its sombre and brooding ferocity? Well, I do. It takes a man all his inborn
5 farther back still seemed condensed into a mournful gloom, brooding motionless over the biggest, and the greatest,
6 go out suddenly, stricken to death by the touch of that gloom brooding over a crowd of men. Forthwith a change came
7 a peace. It was the stillness of an implacable force brooding over an inscrutable intention. It looked at you with
8 us without a stir, and like the wilderness itself, with an air of brooding over an inscrutable purpose. A whole minute
9 low shores in diaphanous folds. Only the gloom to the west, brooding over the upper reaches, became more sombre

Figure 4.1 *Concordance lines of* brooding

1 am not used to such ceremonies, and there was something ominous in the atmosphere. It was just as though I had
2 broken phrases came back to me, were heard again in their ominous and terrifying simplicity. I remembered his abject
3 Embalm it, maybe. But I had also heard another, and a very ominous, murmur on the deck below. My friends the
4 and superb, wild-eyed and magnificent; there was something ominous and stately in her deliberate progress. And in the
5 , however, in the light of later information, strikes me now as ominous. He began with the argument that we whites, from
6 The high stillness confronted these two figures with its ominous patience, waiting for the passing away of a
7 I had seen firing into a continent. It was the same kind of ominous voice; but these men could by no stretch of

Figure 4.2 *Concordance lines of* ominous

'Atmosphere' keywords can be considered halfway between the fictional world signal and the thematic signal keywords. On the one hand, as shown by the concordance lines, 'Atmosphere' keywords contribute to shaping the fictional world by describing aspects and defining details of the characters, places and events, not in a concrete sense, but rather through evoking atmosphere. In this respect, they act as fictional world keywords. On the other hand, their abstract nature enables them to convey wider or multiple meanings, and therefore reflect broader themes. Critics have argued that one of the aims of Conrad with *HoD* was to throw over the reader 'a brooding gloom', to convey a 'resonance and tenebrous atmosphere' (Guerard 1966: 44). Therefore, 'Atmosphere' keywords in *HoD* can also act as thematic signal keywords. It is not a case that *darkness* appears in both the 'Atmosphere' subcategory and in the thematic signal category: I discuss the textual patterns of *darkness* in detail in the next chapter, showing how these contribute to the theme 'Africa and its representation'.

Thematic signal keywords are not grouped into further categories, because they are fewer in number compared with the fictional world signal keywords. However, even if they were more numerous, it would still be difficult to group them into subcategories, as these words convey different meanings and work on multiple levels at the same time, as a result of their polysemy. As such, it would not be easy to pin them down into any specific group reflecting a given use. This seems to be an intrinsic characteristic of thematic signal keywords: their polysemy, Mahlberg and McIntyre (2011: 212) explain, 'is relevant to viewing words as thematic signals, which relates to the fact that polysemy is a concept strongly associated with literariness'. Similarly to my classification, Mahlberg and McIntyre's (2011: 210) keyword grouping identifies only 5 thematic signal keywords, with no further subdivision.

As mentioned earlier, *wilderness* can be seen as conveying different meanings. It has a concrete meaning of 'wild land covered in vegetation', but it can also be interpreted as the inner spirit of the African forest, the contrasting force that resists the colonization process. *Darkness* too works on multiple levels. Besides its concrete meaning of 'absence of light', this word has been interpreted in several different ways. *Darkness* can refer to the dark centre of the African forest, in the literal sense of 'heart of darkness', but it can also refer to the dark heart of the imperialistic enterprise. Both *wilderness* and *darkness* play a fundamental role in the representation of Africa and are discussed in detail in the next chapter.

The keyword *invasion* similarly develops a twofold meaning. First, *invasion* refers to the concrete presence of a given character or group of characters in a place where they should not be: for example, the presence of Kurtz in the depths of the wilderness is defined as *invasion*. At the same time, *invasion* can also be interpreted as referring to the entire colonial mission, and to the overall imposition of the Western culture forced on the non-Western world. In fact, in four out of five cases, it is the African natives or the wilderness itself that wait patiently for *the passing away of this fantastic invasion*. This is far from saying that this pattern alone conveys a hypothetical 'invasion' theme. However, in conjunction with other items (maybe other keywords), *invasion* may well be seen as contributing to the establishment of this theme.

This is equally valid for *fog* which, more than *invasion*, possesses a concrete meaning. However, *fog* does not refer to any specific place in particular (and consequently it is not simply a fictional world signal keyword), but its presence is spread out across the text. Watt (2006: 350) argues that mist and haze are persisting images in *HoD*, which express the fugitive and indefinite nature of the impressionist experience the text enacts. The haze that surrounds Marlow's story symbolizes the ambiguous quality of any individual experience: '*Heart of Darkness* embodies more thoroughly than any previous fiction the posture of uncertainty and doubt' (Watt 2006: 355). It can be said that the theme 'uncertainty of individual experience' (which is related to the theme 'vagueness' discussed earlier) is reinforced by the pervasive use of the fog/mist/haze image. Stubbs (2005) points out that *fog* and other semantically related words (*blurred, dusk, mist/misty, murky, shade, smoke, dark*, etc.) are used almost 150 times in the text: 'Marlow is often looking into a fog, uncertain of what he is seeing' (Stubbs 2005: 9).

4.5 The 'Africa words' and the 'African words'

The previous section offered an overview of the keyword categories, illustrating how they touch upon a wide range of different aspects of the fictional world and different themes. However, this study focuses on two specific aspects of the fictional world, which are related to the two major themes that emerged from the discussion in Chapter 2, 'Africa and its representation' and 'race and racism'. I argued that these two themes are strictly linked to the way Africa and the Africans are fictionally represented in the text. I therefore concentrate on categories and keywords that refer directly to the African forest and the natives. This focus results in two groups of words, which are then analysed in detail in the following chapters. The next sections introduce the two groups and explain the criteria behind their selection. Section 4.5.1 introduces the 'Africa words', while Section 4.5.2 presents the 'African words'.

4.5.1 The 'Africa words'

The obvious starting point for the discussion of the representation of the African forest is the 'Setting & props' subcategory, in particular the 'Forest' group. This group includes 4 keywords: *bush, forest, hippo* and *grass*. Among these, *forest* is immediately relevant: it occurs 23 times and it always refers directly to the aspect of the fictional world I aim to analyse. On the contrary, *bush, hippo* and *grass* are less relevant. *Hippo* occurs only 5 times and refers mainly to the hippo meat that a group of natives bring with them on Marlow's steamboat – this is the reason why *hippo* also appears in the 'Equipment & tools' subcategory. *Hippo* also refers once to an actual hippo living in the forest close to the station. *Bush* and *grass* occur more frequently (18 times each), but refer to partial aspects rather than to the African jungle as a whole. It can be said that *bush, grass* and *hippo* are 'props' of the setting 'Forest', rather than referring directly to it. Although they contribute to building up the fictional world, they do not reflect as specifically and comprehensively as *forest* the overall representation of the African forest.

Looking outside the 'Places' subcategory, there are three other words that develop a similar function as *forest* and are therefore included in the analysis. The first one is *jungle. Jungle* is used as a (near) synonym of *forest*, in the sense that it refers directly to the same physical place. However, *jungle* was not identified as a keyword. This might be a consequence of the fact that *jungle* is not very frequent (it occurs only 6 times), considering that the outcome of a keyword analysis depends on frequency figures. The *p*-value threshold used might have been too restrictive for the study of *HoD*. If the *p*-value cut-off point is increased from 0.0001 to 0.001, *jungle* becomes a keyword when comparing *HoD* to CC, while increasing it to 0.01, it becomes a keyword also when comparing *HoD* to RC. As a matter of fact, *jungle* is used over 7 times more frequently in *HoD* than in CC (normalized per 1,000 words) and almost 4 times more frequently than in RC. However, these differences are not statistically significant with a *p*-value as low as 0.0001. *Jungle* is equally taken into consideration because, aside from its frequency, this word is as relevant as *forest* for the study of the theme 'Africa and its representation'. *Forest* and *jungle* are used by Conrad with the exact same referent, and both describe the African forest in a concrete yet comprehensive way.

The remaining two words provide instead a less concrete and more meta-phorical perspective on the representation of the African jungle. The first one is *wilderness*. I argued in the previous section that *wilderness* is a polysemous word. In its concrete sense, this thematic signal keyword is used to refer to the jungle, but at the same time it also has a more abstract meaning, that is, the living soul of the African jungle that resists Western intrusion. Including *wilderness* in the 'Africa word' group makes it possible to develop the examination of the repre-sentation of the African jungle on two levels: the concrete representation and the metaphorical representation. This is equally valid for *darkness*. Although at first it might appear that *forest, jungle* and *wilderness* have a different referent from *darkness* and that the former are not directly connected to the latter, *darkness* plays an important role in the representation of the African jungle. Its relation with the jungle derives from its multiple meanings, which are mirrored in the variety of different – and sometimes contrasting – ways the darkness in *HoD* has been interpreted. Similarly to *wilderness, darkness* has a concrete and straight-forward interpretation which is directly related to the indomitable and wild heart of Africa. The very title of the short novel refers to the heart of darkness as the centre of the African continent, dark and mysterious. This link has been acknowledged by Goonetilleke (1999: 11) and O'Prey (1983: 12), who recognize the strong influence of Henry Morton Stanley's accounts of his travels in Africa – *Through the Dark Continent* and *In the Darkest Africa* – on Conrad's short novel. In line with this interpretation, *darkness* can be seen as directly relating with *forest* and *jungle*: though as a metaphorical expression, *darkness* refers to the same actual place alluded to by the other two words.

An alternative interpretation sees the darkness in *HoD* as an abstract notion rather than a metaphorical reference to a physical place. In this sense, the dark-ness can convey numerous figurative meanings at the same time. Watts (1990) describes this darkness as 'moral corruption, night, death, ignorance, and that encompassing obscurity of the pre-rational and pre-verbal which words seek to illuminate' (Watts 1990: xx–xxi), whereas O'Prey (1983) describes it as 'the unknown, [. . .] the subconscious; it is also a moral darkness, it is the evil which swallows up Kurtz and it is the spiritual emptiness he sees at the centre of exist-ence; but above all it is mystery itself, the mysteriousness of man's spiritual life' (O'Prey 1983: 18). This interpretation sees the darkness linked to a multitude of either overt or covert themes, ranging from the colonial enterprise and its exploiting actions to the withering of the heart because of greed and selfishness resulting from a Mephistophelian exchange of soul for achievements. In this sense, there would be no direct link with Africa, therefore the connection of *darkness* with *forest* and *jungle* may be feebler, or even non-existant. However, there are critics who put these two interpretations together. Goonetilleke (1999), for instance, interprets the darkness as both 'the centre of Africa' and, at the same time, 'the unknown, the evil in humanity, the hidden self and the negation at the back of all things' (Goonetilleke 1999: 39).

As a thematic signal keyword, *darkness* develops multiple meanings in *HoD*. Through this polysemy, it is possible to establish a connection between *darkness* and the African continent, as the idea of darkness is also used to refer metaphorically to the Congolese jungle. Including *darkness* in the analysis allows me to investigate whether there are parallelisms with the use of *forest*, *jungle* and *wilderness*, while strengthening the double perspective on the metaphorical and concrete representations of the African jungle. Finally, the four items selected for the study of the fictional representation of the African jungle are: *forest, jungle, wilderness* and *darkness*; henceforth referred to as the 'Africa words'.

4.5.2 The 'African words'

With respect to the fictional representation of the African natives, the selection of the items to analyse in detail starts from the 'Characters' subcategory, specifically from the 'Natives' group. Also in this case there are keywords that are not as relevant as others; thus, not all of the words in the group are taken into account. As for the representation of the African jungle, the aim of the analysis is to examine the general depiction of the Africans, rather than just a partial aspect of their representation. Therefore, terms that refer to the natives as generally as possible are preferred over words that refer only to a selection of them. As a result, only two out of five words are selected from the 'Native' group: *savages* and *niggers*. Although used in different contexts, these terms refer to the natives in general, and not to specific individuals. By contrast, *cutters* and *helmsman* refer to precise characters. *Cutters* occurs 4 times, always in the compound noun *wood-cutters*, and refers to a small group of Africans who helps Marlow in his journey through the wilderness. Similarly, *helmsman*, which occurs 7 times in total, refers to the African helmsman of Marlow's steamer, a precise individual. *Chaps* is discarded because it is not used for the Africans specifically, but is rather a superordinate word adopted for other groups of characters as well, for example, the colonizers (this is the reason why it also appears in the 'Colonizers' group).

Besides *niggers* and *savages*, seven other words are selected in order to study the fictional representation of the Africans. These are: *nigger, negro, savage, native, natives, black, blacks*. There are three interrelated reasons for this further inclusion. The first reason parallels the decision to include *jungle* in the 'Africa words'. *Nigger, negro, savages, native, black* and their plural forms are all words Conrad uses to refer specifically to the African natives. Even though their frequency of use in *HoD* is not statistically significant with the chosen parameters, this does not mean that they are not relevant for this analysis. As suggested in relation to *jungle*, the choice of a different cut-off point or different selection criteria could have resulted in their inclusion among the keywords. *Nigger, savage* and *black* are already keywords, but in List 2 only, while *savage* becomes a keyword in List 1 if the *p*-value threshold is increased from 0.0001 to 0.001. Finally, adding *nigger, negro, savage, native, natives, black* and *blacks* to the group ensures that all the general words employed in the text referring to the Africans are accounted for; in this way, the study of the representation of the natives is as comprehensive as possible.

The second reason for the inclusion of these terms is related to the first: the selection of a singular form leads to the selection of a plural form, and vice versa. Unlike the 'Africa words', both singulars and plurals are relevant in this case. While there is only one fictional entity to which the terms *forest, jungle, wilderness* and *darkness* can refer, there are multiple natives, therefore it is important to consider *nigger, savage, native* and *black* when they refer both to an individual and when they are used in the plural to refer to a group of people (except for *negro*, which occurs only in its singular form). One could object that a word such as *helmsman*, for example, has been discarded because it is used to identify an individual native, while here singular forms that equally refer to individuals are taken into account. The difference here is that, in the case of *helmsman*, the individual referred to is always the same character, whereas *nigger, savage* or any other of these terms are used indistinctively for multiple characters as a general noun.

The third reason to support the inclusion of these additional words is that this methodological decision is in line with a study by Kujawska-Lis (2008), which has very similar aims to this investigation. Kujawska-Lis (2008) compares two Polish translations of *HoD*, one preceding and the other following Achebe's (1990) public lecture. She investigates whether the contemporary translation differs from the early one as a consequence of the influence that Achebe (1990) had on the contemporary translator. In order to do so, Kujawska-Lis (2008) focuses on the lexical choices used to translate the ST items referring to the

African natives. In particular, she looks at the words *nigger, negro, black, savage, native, brute* and their Polish translations. Kujawska-Lis (2008) shows that the lexical choices of the contemporary TT maintain or even emphasize the potentially racist implications of the original. On the contrary, the early translator replaces the most derogatory terms with more neutral ones, tuning down the ST's potential racist implications. As a result, in the early translation, Marlow 'is decidedly less verbally aggressive and mentally superior to the Africans' compared to the Marlow in the contemporary TT, who is instead 'biased both linguistically and intellectually' (Kujawska-Lis 2008: 176). She argues that, as a consequence of these alterations, the two TTs can have a different influence on the TT reader, for the early TT tunes down the possibility to read the text in line with Achebe's (1990) evaluation, while the contemporary one opens the door to it. Thus, Kujawska-Lis's (1990) study supports the choice of these terms as an appropriate selection to analyse the effect of translation on the fictional representation of the Africans.

Based on these three reasons, the words selected to study the fictional representation of the African natives are: *nigger/niggers, negro, savage/savages, native/natives* and *black/blacks*; henceforth referred to as the 'African words'.

4.6 Conclusion

This chapter set the basis for the analysis in the following chapters, leading to the identification of relevant *HoD*-specific words that relate the lexical level of the text with the two major themes discussed in Chapter 2. In this way, this chapter addressed the first research question. The upcoming chapters examine in detail the words within the two groups: Chapter 5 focuses on the representation of the African jungle through the examination of the 'Africa words', while Chapter 6 concentrates on the representation of the African natives through the investigation of the 'African words'.

As I argued in Section 4.1, this keyword analysis and the resulting creation of the two groups reflect a twofold approach to the text: a text-based and a reader-based perspective. On the one hand, some items in the Africa and African groups are keywords, either in both lists (*forest, wilderness, darkness, savages, niggers*) or just in one list (*nigger, savage* and *black*). These words stand out on the basis of their significant frequency and, as such, they reflect specific features of *HoD* from a text-based perspective. On the other hand, there are words (*jungle, negro, native/natives* and *blacks*) that do not have a text-based significance (at least with the statistical criteria adopted here). However, they are still significant from a reader-based point of view, as they relate to the specific themes I intend to study. The resulting groups, 'Africa words' and 'African words', are therefore not restricted by formal criteria, but are combined with a more interpretative approach to the text, in order to encompass aspects of literary appreciation into the linguistic description, in line with the aims of stylistic research.

'A Place of Darkness': The Fictional Representation of the African Jungle

5.1 Introduction

This chapter examines how the African jungle is linguistically represented in *HoD* and its four Italian translations. The examination starts from the outcome of the keyword analysis and categorization (Chapter 4), in particular from the 'Africa words' (*forest, jungle, wilderness* and *darkness*). Section 5.2 begins by looking at *forest, wilderness* and *jungle* as units of meaning, showing how these items enact together a local textual function that contributes to build up this specific aspect of the fictional world. Section 5.2.2 explains that *darkness* is strictly related to *forest, wilderness* and *jungle*, sharing with them similar lexico-semantic patterns. I argue that the four items jointly establish a cohesive image of Africa throughout the whole text. Their shared patterns create a metaphorical representation of Africa as a 'place of darkness', a representation that is more figurative than concrete. Section 5.2.3 discusses the interpretative implications of this representation, linking them with the existing literary criticism. In addition to the 'place of darkness' representation, the analysis of the 'Africa words' also foregrounds a secondary tendency, that is, the depiction of the jungle as a personified entity. Section 5.3 discusses this tendency, explaining which linguistic features instantiate it and what stylistic effects they create.

From Section 5.4 on, the focus shifts to the TTs. Section 5.4.1 compares the TTs and discusses how the alterations introduced in translation affect the representation of the jungle as a 'place of darkness'. Section 5.4.2 shows that, although the lexico-semantic patterns identified in the original are maintained, some of the translators' alterations have an effect on the lexical cohesion of the text. Section 5.4.3 looks instead at the effects of such alterations on the personification of the jungle. Section 5.4.4 considers the potentially manipulative effects of these changes. Taking into account the understanding and definition of 'manipulation' in the translation studies literature, Section 5.4.4 discusses whether or not the alterations identified can be regarded as examples of manipulation. Finally, Section 5.5 provides a concluding discussion.

5.2 The African jungle as a 'place of darkness'

In this chapter, I discuss two tendencies in the linguistic construction of Africa in *HoD*. The main tendency involves representing the jungle as a dark, immense and closed place: this representation is labelled 'place of darkness'. In this section, I study this representation, showing the stylistic patterns that instantiate it and considering its interpretational implications.

5.2.1 *Forest, jungle* **and** *wilderness*

Forest, jungle and *wilderness* occur respectively 23, 6, and 22 times. They are all used to refer to the same aspect of the fictional world, namely, the African jungle, although in different ways. Whereas *forest* and *jungle* label the place concretely, *wilderness* is used both concretely and metaphorically (cf. Sections 4.4 and 4.5). However, the analysis of their concordance lines and of the words occurring with them in a span of 5:5 shows that *forest, jungle* and *wilderness* are functionally related. The three of them co-occur with the same semantic fields, that is, they share the same semantic preferences. Consider the concordance lines of *forest* in Figure 5.1.

First, *forest* is described as a place closed in its boundaries, unwelcoming to external intrusions. This is conveyed by words such as *fence* (line 5), *closed* (line 7), *surrounded* (lines 10 and 16) and *impenetrable* (line 17), together with the construction *the * of the forest*, where the wildcard position is occupied by terms for borders and edges: *border* (line 4), *edge* (lines 6, 11 and 19) and *limit* (line 23). I call this semantic field 'closedness'. Example (1) shows the entire sentence in line 7, to demonstrate how this aspect of the representation of the African forest is enacted in a longer extract. This passage not only emphasizes that the forest has borders, but also that once these borders have been crossed, it is difficult to get out.

1	that mysterious life of the wilderness that stirs in the forest, in the jungles, in the hearts of wild men. There's no
2	shoulder-blades. Then the whole population cleared into the forest, expecting all kinds of calamities to happen, while,
3	his short flipper of an arm for a gesture that took in the creek, the mud, the river–seemed to beckon
4	flitting indistinctly against the gloomy border of the forest, and near the river two bronze figures, leaning on tall
5	took these sticks to bed with them. Beyond the fence the forest stood up spectrally in the moonlight, and through that
6	that I leaped to my feet and looked back at the edge of the forest, as though I had expected an answer of some sort to
7	The reaches opened before us and closed behind, as if the forest had stepped leisurely across the water to bar the way
8	deck. A frightful clatter came out of that hulk, and the virgin forest on the other bank of the creek sent it back in a
9	stream. It was then well on in the afternoon, the face of the forest was gloomy, and a broad strip of shadow had already
10	there had been between, had disappeared. Of course the forest surrounded all that. The river-bank was clear, and on
11	persistently with his whole arm. Examining the edge of the forest above and below, I was almost certain I could see
12	without any perceptible movement of retreat, as if the forest that had ejected these beings so suddenly had drawn
13	by Jove! was in my nostrils, the high stillness of primeval forest was before my eyes; there were shiny patches on the
14	itself in the calm of the evening. The long shadows of the forest had slipped downhill while we talked, had gone far
15	were poured into the clearing by the dark-faced and pensive forest. The bushes shook, the grass swayed for a time,
16	Station. It was on a back water surrounded by scrub and forest, with a pretty border of smelly mud on one side, and
17	kings. An empty stream, a great silence, an impenetrable forest. The air was warm, thick, heavy, sluggish. There was
18	because on a certain occasion, when encamped in the forest, they had talked all night, or more probably Kurtz had
19	I was convinced, had driven him out to the edge of the forest, to the bush, towards the gleam of fires, the throb of
20	was keeping guard over the ivory; but deep within the forest, red gleams that wavered, that seemed to sink and
21	the trees, and the murmur of many voices issued from the forest. I had cut him off cleverly; but when actually
22	but as a rule Kurtz wandered alone, far in the depths of the forest. Very often coming to this station, I had to wait days
23	and was looking at the shore, sweeping the limit of the forest at each side and at the back of the house. The

Figure 5.1 *Concordance lines of* forest

(1) The reaches opened before us and closed behind, as if the forest had
     stepped leisurely across the water to bar the way for our return. We
     penetrated deeper and deeper into the heart of darkness.

The second dominant aspect in the description of *forest* is represented by the
semantic field 'darkness', which conveys the idea of the forest as a dark place,
both literally and figuratively. This field includes words such as *gloomy* (lines 4
and 9), *spectrally* (line 5), *shadows* (line 14) and *dark-faced* (line 15), but also
primeval (line 13) and *silence* (line 17) depict the forest as an altogether inhospitable place. In Example (2), the contrast between the darkness of the forest
and the faint light of the colonizers' station is made explicit. The shadows of
the forest are slowly surrounding the station, the only place where the sunshine
still resists:

(2) The long shadows of the forest had slipped downhill while we talked, had
     gone far beyond the ruined hovel, beyond the symbolic row of stakes.
     All this was in the gloom, while we down there were yet in the sunshine,
     and the stretch of the river abreast of the clearing glittered in a still
     and dazzling splendour, with a murky and overshadowed bend above
     and below.

The third semantic field is related to the other two, as it combines with the idea of 'closedness' and 'darkness' to depict the forest as an immense place, almost shapeless, in which it is very easy to get lost. I label this semantic field 'immensity'. In the case of *forest*, it is instantiated by the words *deep* (line 20) and *depths* (line 22). It becomes more evident if we look at the concordance lines of *wilderness* (Figure 5.2). *Wilderness* occurs with *depths* (line 1); it is also an *immense* and *colossal* place (line 14), in which camps and stations are *lost* (line 15). In line with the 'closedness' semantic field identified in the concordance lines of *forest*, *wilderness* is described as a sentient being that surrounds and closes in whoever dares to challenge its impenetrableness: *closed* in line 13 and *surrounding* in line 17 (I return and expand on the agency of *wilderness* in Section 5.2.3). As with *forest*, *wilderness* is also described as an inhospitable and dark place. The 'darkness' semantic field is identifiable in the co-occurrence of words such as *desolate* (line 1), *mysterious* (line 2), *mystery* (line 10), *sorrowful* (line 14), *God-forsaken* (line 16), *vengeful* (line 19) and *brooding* (line 20).

Even though *jungle* occurs only 6 times in the text, it is equally possible to recognize a connection with *forest* and *wilderness*, for *jungle*, too, is described in terms of the three semantic fields identified. Consider Figure 5.3. As for the 'closedness' semantic field, the jungle is represented as an *impenetrable* (line 1)

```
 1  home--perhaps; setting his face towards the depths of the wilderness, towards his empty and desolate station. I did
 2          had closed round him--all that mysterious life of the wilderness that stirs in the forest, in the jungles, in the
 3   one would think, they were lugging, after a raid, into the wilderness for equitable division. It was an inextricable
 4             well equipped for a renewed encounter with the wilderness. 'Ah! I'll never, never meet such a man again.
 5      I tried to break the spell--the heavy, mute spell of the wilderness--that seemed to draw him to its pitiless breast
 6          himself, afterwards he arose and went out--and the wilderness without a sound took him into its bosom again.
 7   little touch of other things--the playful paw-strokes of the wilderness, the preliminary trifling before the more serious
 8           but this--ah--specimen, was impressively bald. The wilderness had patted him on the head, and, behold, it
 9   kept him unscathed. He surely wanted nothing from the wilderness but space to breathe in and to push on
10          which went rotten, and made the mystery of the wilderness stink in my nostrils. Phoo! I can sniff it now. I
11   It made me hold my breath in expectation of hearing the wilderness burst into a prodigious peal of laughter that
12      but I will wring your heart yet!' he cried at the invisible wilderness. "We broke down--as I had expected--and had
13   a few days the Eldorado Expedition went into the patient wilderness, that closed upon it as the sea closes over a
14      suddenly upon the whole sorrowful land, the immense wilderness, the colossal body of the fecund and
15   no going ashore. Here and there a military camp lost in a wilderness, like a needle in a bundle of hay--cold, fog,
16          clerks to levy toll in what looked like a God-forsaken wilderness, with a tin shed and a flag-pole lost in it;
17      anything so unreal in my life. And outside, the silent wilderness surrounding this cleared speck on the earth
18           noise. But his soul was mad. Being alone in the wilderness, it had looked within itself, and, by heavens! I
19   conquering darkness. It was a moment of triumph for the wilderness, an invading and vengeful rush which, it
20          She stood looking at us without a stir, and like the wilderness itself, with an air of brooding over an
21   have at least a choice of nightmares. "I had turned to the wilderness really, not to Mr. Kurtz, who, I was ready to
22          came to him at last--only at the very last. But the wilderness had found him out early, and had taken on
```

Figure 5.2 *Concordance lines of* wilderness

1	be if we attempted to move. Still, I had also judged the jungle of both banks quite impenetrable--and yet eyes
2	his talk of chains and purchases, made me forget the jungle and the pilgrims in a delicious sensation of having
3	you that never, never before, did this land, this river, this jungle, the very arch of this blazing sky, appear to me so
4	aspect of monotonous grimness. The edge of a colossal jungle, so dark-green as to be almost black, fringed with
5	of the towering multitude of trees, of the immense matted jungle, with the blazing little ball of the sun hanging over
6	large holes in the peaked roof gaped black from afar; the jungle and the woods made a background. There was no

Figure 5.3 *Concordance lines of* jungle

place closed in its *edge* (line 4); as for the 'immensity' semantic field, the jungle is *colossal* (line 4) and *immense* (line 5); finally, as for the 'darkness' semantic field, the jungle is described as *dark* and *black* (line 4).

These three semantic fields are not simply shared by *forest*, *wilderness* and *jungle*. The pervasiveness of this specific fictional representation is further confirmed by the fact that the semantic preferences are also realized by forms of the same lemmas or even identical words. *Depths* occurs with *forest* and *wilderness*; both occur with forms of the lemma SURROUND (*surrounded* and *surrounding*); *impenetrable* occurs with *jungle* and *forest*. Both *wilderness* and *jungle* are *immense* and *colossal*, while *jungle* and *forest* are *dark*. This reiteration of lexical choices in relation to Africa strengthens the connection of the three words and suggests that they participate together in the construction of a unified fictional entity. For ease of reference, the label 'place of darkness' is adopted to define the fictional representation of the African jungle resulting from the three semantic preferences, even though this name does not cover all the nuances expressed by the individual semantic fields ('darkness', 'closedness' and 'immensity'). The name for the label 'place of darkness' is suggested by Marlow himself: at the beginning of the book, he recognizes that Africa, once a blank space on the world map, still unexplored, now is instead 'a place of darkness' (Conrad [1902] 1994: 12).

As further evidence of the specificity of this fictional representation, the reference corpora are queried to check whether *forest*, *wilderness* and *jungle* co-occur with the same words discussed earlier in a similar span of 5:5. This test is not meant to prove that these co-occurrences in *HoD* represent statistically significant collocations, or that their collocational strength is stronger in *HoD* than in the two reference corpora. As explained in Chapter 3, the analysis in this and in the following chapter does not focus on the quantitative aspects of the lexical item. I argued that a strictly quantitative approach would cut out linguistic features that, despite their low frequency of occurrence, can still contribute distinctively to the construction of the two major themes under analysis. In this specific case, the words that form part of the 'darkness', 'closedness' and 'immens-ity' semantic preferences would hardly be considered statistical collocations. If Mutual Information (MI) were used as a statistical test, for example, these words would have most likely been excluded, because they occur only a few times in the whole text. In fact, given that MI tends to assign high scores to words with relatively low frequency (Baker 2006: 102), a frequency cut-off point is generally used to reduce this drawback (Xiao and McEnery 2006: 105); even a frequency cut-off point as low as 3 would have excluded most of the items that form part of the semantic fields. However, there is no frequency threshold for a word to be part of a semantic field, therefore semantic preferences and prosodies allow me to account for the cumulative effect of items whose frequency is not necessarily high.

Thus, the terms 'collocation' and 'collocate' are used here in a non-statistical sense or, in McEnery and Hardie's (2012: 126) words, as 'collocation-via-concordance', that is, collocations identified by eye through the analysis of concordance lines without statistical significance testing. Checking whether *forest*, *wilderness* and *jungle* occur with the same words in CC and RC, although without statistical support, is equally relevant, as it can shed light on how text-specific this representation of the jungle is. Consider Tables 5.1 to 5.3, where a grey cell is used to indicate when the co-occurrence of *forest*,

Table 5.1 *Comparison of the collocates of* forest

Collocates of *forest*	CC	RC
border	No	No
closed	Yes	No
dark	Yes	Yes
deep	Yes	Yes
depths	No	No
edge	Yes	Yes
fence	No	No
gloomy	Yes	No
impenetrable	Yes	No
limit	Yes	No
primeval	Yes	No
shadows	Yes	Yes
side	Yes	Yes
silence	Yes	Yes
spectrally	No	No
surrounded	No	No

Table 5.2 *Comparison of the collocates of* jungle

Collocates of *jungle*	CC	RC
colossal	No	No
impenetrable	No	No
edge	No	No
immense	No	No
dark	Yes	No
black	No	Yes

Table 5.3 *Comparison of the collocates of* wilderness

Collocates of *wilderness*	CC	RC
surrounding	Yes	No
God-forsaken	No	No
invisible	No	No
colossal	No	No
sorrowful	No	No
mysterious	No	No
closed	No	No
depths	No	No
immense	Yes	No
mystery	No	No
lost	Yes	No

wilderness and *jungle* with a word from the three semantic fields does not appear in the relative reference corpus. The three tables show that, in most cases, *forest*, *wilderness* and *jungle* do not occur with the words creating the 'place of darkness' representation in the reference corpora. The only exception is in Table 5.1, where the majority of the collocates appear in a 5:5 span from *forest* in CC. This indicates that Conrad uses the same words to describe forests also in his other works. However, apart from that, Tables 5.1 to 5.3 suggest that the 'closedness', 'darkness' and 'immensity' semantic preferences are text-specific, that they are more typical of the fictional representation of the African jungle in *HoD* than of Conrad's fictional language or the general literary language of the period.

5.2.2 The fictional representation of *darkness*

The fourth item of the 'Africa words' is *darkness*. Similarly to *wilderness*, *darkness* is a polysemous thematic signal keyword that carries both a figurative and a concrete meaning. Literary critics have interpreted the darkness as either connoting 'the unknown, the evil in humanity, the hidden self and the negation at the back of all things' (Goonetilleke 1999: 39) or simply referring to the heart of the African jungle. This polysemous nature has also been recognized from a linguistic point of view. Turci's (2007) analysis of *dark** (*dark*, *darkness*, *darker* and *darkly*) identifies six different aspects of *HoD* to which *dark** refers: 'European people', 'African people', 'Kurtz and/or Kurtz character merging with African landscape', 'Kurtz's African mistress', 'European places' and 'Africa and the Congo'. Turci (2007: 109) shows that, among these, *dark** refers most commonly to Kurtz, to European places and to Africa and the Congo, confirming that *dark** can equally relate to different aspects of the short novel.

The direct connection with the African landscape that Turci (2007) points out is further confirmed by the present analysis. *Darkness* in fact shares the very same 'place of darkness' representation as the other 'Africa words'. Consider Figure 5.4, which shows all of the 25 concordance lines of *darkness*. *Darkness*, too, co-occurs with the 'closedness' semantic field. The darkness is *impenetrable* (lines 12, 25 and 25) and described in terms of something you go in or

```
1    arms over the glitter of the infernal stream, the stream of darkness. She said suddenly very low, 'He died as he
2       to the lurking death, to the hidden evil, to the profound darkness of its heart. It was so startling that I leaped to
3       mind with its hint of danger that seemed, in the starred darkness, real enough to make me get up for the purpose
4       even to know you are being assaulted by the powers of darkness. I take it, no fool ever made a bargain for his
5       was to know what he belonged to, how many powers of darkness claimed him for their own. That was the
6    return. We penetrated deeper and deeper into the heart of darkness. It was very quiet there. At night sometimes the
7       died I have had no one--no one--to--to--' "I listened. The darkness deepened. I was not even sure whether he had
8          enough to penetrate all the hearts that beat in the darkness. He had summed up--he had judged. 'The
9    with an unearthly glow in the darkness, in the triumphant darkness from which I could not have defended her--from
10      saving illusion that shone with an unearthly glow in the darkness, in the triumphant darkness from which I could
11      in his time, perhaps. They were men enough to face the darkness. And perhaps he was cheered by keeping his
12      earth, the unseen presence of victorious corruption, the darkness of an impenetrable night.... The Russian tapped
13   far away there I thought of these two, guarding the door of Darkness, knitting black wool as for a warm pall, one
14          it last as long as the old earth keeps rolling! But darkness was here yesterday. Imagine the feelings of a
15          like the beating of a heart--the heart of a conquering darkness. It was a moment of triumph for the wilderness,
16   a voice speaking from beyond the threshold of an eternal darkness. 'But you have heard him! You know!' she cried.
17   going at it blind--as is very proper for those who tackle a darkness. The conquest of the earth, which mostly
18   smile of his, as though it had been a door opening into a darkness he had in his keeping. You fancied you had
19      to hide in the magnificent folds of eloquence the barren darkness of his heart. Oh, he struggled! he struggled! The
20      cottons, beads, and brass-wire set into the depths of darkness, and in return came a precious trickle of ivory.
21   smoke. "The brown current ran swiftly out of the heart of darkness, bearing us down towards the sea with twice
22   a boy to dream gloriously over. It had become a place of darkness. But there was in it one river especially, a
23          sky--seemed to lead into the heart of an immense darkness. arkness.
24      or the deceitful flow from the heart of an impenetrable darkness. "The other shoe went flying unto the devil-god
25      of my ideas. It's a duty.' "His was an impenetrable darkness. I looked at him as you peer down at a man
```

Figure 5.4 *Concordance lines of* darkness

out of: *door* (lines 13 and 18), *threshold* (line 16) and *opening* (line 18). The concordance lines also show the presence of the 'immensity' semantic field. *Darkness* co-occurs with words such as *profound* (line 2) and *immense* (line 23), but also *deeper* (line 6), *deepened* (line 7) and *depths* (line 20). It is also possible to identify the 'darkness' semantic field, as conveyed by items such as *infernal* (line 1), *evil* (line 2), *assaulted* (line 4), *unearthly* (line 10) and *corruption* (line 12) (in line 22, Africa is directly referred to as *a place of darkness*). What is more, the three semantic fields include again many of the exact same words and lemma forms used with *wilderness*, *jungle* and *forest*. *Darkness*, *forest* and *jungle* are *impenetrable* (among the most frequent collocates); *jungle*, *wilderness* and *darkness* are *immense*; forms of the lemma DEEP co-occur with *darkness* (*deeper*, *depths*, *deepened*), *forest* (*deep*, *depths*) and *wilderness* (*depths*).

Differently from *forest*, *jungle* and *wilderness*, the majority of the collocates of *darkness* do not seem to be typical of *HoD* (see Table 5.4). *Darkness* co-occurs with the same words also in CC and in RC, suggesting that relations such as *darkness-impenetrable*, *darkness-depths* and *darkness-profound* are perhaps not text-specific. However, more than the specificity of these collocations, what is relevant for the study of the fictional representation is the fact that *darkness* is described in similar terms as *forest*, *jungle* and *wilderness*. My analysis shows that a link exists between *darkness* on the one hand and *forest*, *wilderness* and

Table 5.4 *Comparison of the collocates of* darkness

Collocates of *darkness*	CC	RC
deepened	Yes	Yes
impenetrable	Yes	Yes
deeper	Yes	Yes
threshold	Yes	No
infernal	No	No
evil	No	Yes
unearthly	No	No
opening	No	Yes
door	Yes	Yes
depths	Yes	Yes
profound	Yes	Yes
immense	Yes	Yes
assaulted	No	No
corruption	No	No

jungle on the other. This link strengthens the relation between the metaphorical understanding of *darkness* and the actual depiction of Africa.

Overall, all four 'Africa words' show the same lexico-semantic patterns. These patterns represent a fundamental aspect of the way the African jungle is depicted in *HoD*. When *forest, wilderness, jungle* and *darkness* occur, the reader encounters the same 'place of darkness' fictional representation, enacted through the use of the same words, lemma forms and semantic fields. This repetition of semantically related vocabulary to refer to the same aspect of the fictional world throughout the text makes the depiction of the African jungle cohesive. A network is therefore established: the occurrences of the 'Africa words' are connected across the text by the repetition of their shared semantic preferences. '[T]he use of a lexical item recalls [through lexical chains] the sense of an earlier one' (Baker 2011: 211), creating in this way a thick cohesive network. This, as a result, builds up a unified and consistent fictional entity.

5.2.3 Africa as a metaphorical place

As shown in the previous sections, the use of *forest, wilderness* and *jungle* on the one hand, and *darkness* on the other, are interrelated. Their shared textual behaviour enacts a unified and cohesive representation of the African jungle in which the depiction of the physical place is linked to the figurative meaning of *darkness* and *wilderness*. These linguistic features construct the African jungle as a 'place of darkness'. It is dark and inhospitable (the 'darkness' semantic field, e.g. *dark, gloomy, shadows, black, desolate, mysterious, mystery, sorrowful, silent, spectrally*), immense and with blurred boundaries (the 'immensity' semantic field, e.g. *immense, colossal, deep, depths, lost*) but at the same time it is still a place closed in itself, unwelcoming to external intrusion (the 'closedness' semantic field, e.g. *edge, border, fence, impenetrable, surrounded, closed*). Ultimately, what these consistent lexico-semantic patterns enact is a symbolic and metaphorical representation of the African jungle, rather than a geographical or descriptive one.

In Section 4.4 we saw that Conrad's writing has been considered vague and indefinite. Leavis (1973: 180) has famously argued that Conrad 'mak[es] a virtue out of not knowing what he means', while Stubbs (2005: 8) has pointed out that *HoD* is full of 'examples of this vagueness about places, times, and people'. As far as places are concerned, the keyword categorization showed that common place nouns are much more frequent than proper place names. As a matter of fact, Congo is never named in the book, while the noun *Africa* appears only once, in the passage where Marlow refers to it as 'a place of darkness'. Apart from that, there is no other clearly defined geographical reference to the country. This lack of a concrete geographical focus is in agreement with what the analysis of the fictional representation of the African jungle has shown so far. The way in which the jungle is referred to shifts the depiction of the continent from a physical description to a figurative representation, contributing further to the overall feeling of vagueness. Challenging any attempt of spatialization and geographical contextualization, Conrad delivers a fictional representation of the jungle that turns Africa into a metaphorical space, into a symbol of indefiniteness and blankness.[1]

Brooker and Thacker (2005a: 4–5) recognize this practice of viewing material places only through the lens of aesthetic metaphors as typical of literary modernism. Many other critics have identified a shift from a geographical into a symbolic space in the construction of Africa in *HoD*. Hegglund (2005: 43) argues that Africa in Conrad is transmuted from referent to signifier, from content to form, in a way that separates the idea of Africa from its material reality. The result of this process is a homogenising abstraction that deprives the continent of its cultural–historical variety. This shapeless abstraction, according to Hegglund (2005), is emphasized through contrast, especially when Africa is used as a term of comparison to set against any number of (Western) symbols and values (Hegglund 2005: 48). In a similar way, Achebe (1990: 3) states that Africa in *HoD* ceases to be an actual place in order to become a symbolic place, 'the other world', the antithesis of Europe. In this symbolic form, functioning almost just as a setting and backdrop, it loses its human and cultural factors. Goonetilleke (1999: 42–3) also points out that, rather than being the practical description of an expedition, the journey into Congo becomes a symbolic journey into the darkness of man's unconsciousness, whereas Levenson (2009: 185) underlines that, as many other modernist writers, Conrad sets aside the wider context of the living culture, selecting instead only some aesthetic images of Africa. Finally, Hampson (2005: 56) compares *HoD* with Conrad's notes and diary from his journey to Congo to emphasize how the Africa depicted in *HoD* resists all attempts of mapping its space.

The textual patterns that I identified enact exactly this function: they construct a fictional representation of the African jungle that is more figurative than descriptive. The shared lexico-semantic features across all four 'Africa words' make the representation of Africa cohesive and persistent throughout the text. Finally, Africa ceases to be a geographical place and becomes instead a blank, empty space, a 'place of darkness': the stylistic features identified are the lexical tools through which this representation is instantiated.

5.3 The fictional representation of the African jungle as a personified entity

The patterns of the 'Africa words' enact an additional aspect of the fictional representation of the African jungle, besides its depiction as a 'place of darkness': the personification of the forest, by attributing to it agency and cognitive abilities. 'Personification' (or, sometimes, 'prosopopoeia') is defined as a figure of speech involving the attribution of human features to inanimate objects, animate non-human beings or abstract entities (see Wales 2011 or Mortara Garavelli 2010). It is an 'ontological metaphor' (Dancygier and Sweetser 2014: 62), in the sense that it alters the ontological status of an entity, often shifting it from inanimate to animate. Personification is commonly used in literary language to add vividness to a rhetorical discourse (Wales 2011: 314) and to represent figuratively the way an inanimate or abstract entity affects the speaker (Dancygier and Sweetser 2014: 63). Instances of personification have already been recognized in Conrad's work and in *HoD* in particular. Miller (2006), for instance, identifies prosopopoeia as one of most ostentatious literary features of *HoD*. Present even in the title, where a heart is ascribed to the darkness, personification is a key element in 'naming by indirection what Conrad calls, in a misleading and inadequate metaphor, "the darkness" or "the wilderness"' (Miller 2006: 467).

Out of the four 'Africa words', it is *forest* and *wilderness* that markedly show this tendency, identifiable in many of their concordance lines (see Figure 5.5). At times, *forest* and *wilderness* are depicted as animate entities able to move physically, as opposed to inanimate and immovable places. Their movements are actively produced, and not just the passive consequence of an external factor. *Forest* and *wilderness* are indeed given active agency through functioning as the actor of material clauses. For example, the forest *stood up* in line 1, or *stepped across* in line 3. Similarly, the wilderness in line 4 *had patted* Kurtz on his head, while in line 7 it *closed upon* the Eldorado Expedition. Other times, *wilderness* and *forest* seem to possess their own will and cognitive skills. In line 3 the forest *leisurely* steps across the steamer to *bar the way for our return*. Here an intention is recognizable behind the action of the forest, which acts as moved by leisure. This 'thoughtful' attitude is distinguishable also in the use of the adjective *pensive*,

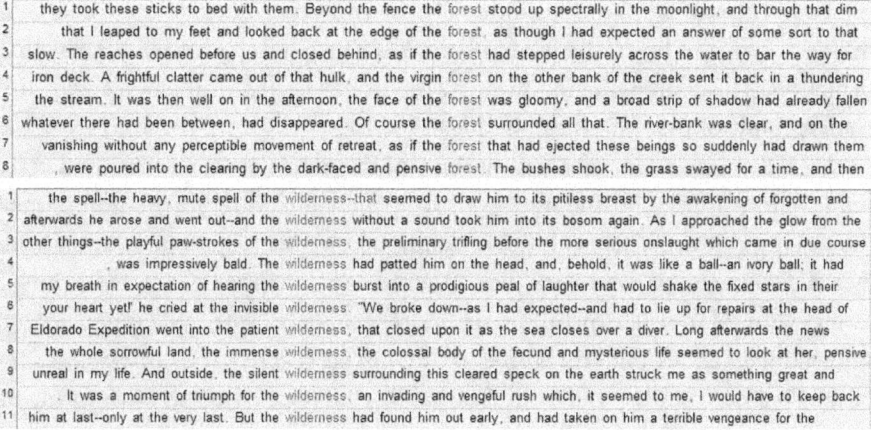

1	they took these sticks to bed with them. Beyond the fence the forest stood up spectrally in the moonlight, and through that dim
2	that I leaped to my feet and looked back at the edge of the forest, as though I had expected an answer of some sort to that
3	slow. The reaches opened before us and closed behind, as if the forest had stepped leisurely across the water to bar the way for
4	iron deck. A frightful clatter came out of that hulk, and the virgin forest on the other bank of the creek sent it back in a thundering
5	the stream. It was then well on in the afternoon, the face of the forest was gloomy, and a broad strip of shadow had already fallen
6	whatever there had been between, had disappeared. Of course the forest surrounded all that. The river-bank was clear, and on the
7	vanishing without any perceptible movement of retreat, as if the forest that had ejected these beings so suddenly had drawn them
8	, were poured into the clearing by the dark-faced and pensive forest. The bushes shook, the grass swayed for a time, and then

1	the spell--the heavy, mute spell of the wilderness--that seemed to draw him to its pitiless breast by the awakening of forgotten and
2	afterwards he arose and went out--and the wilderness without a sound took him into its bosom again. As I approached the glow from the
3	other things--the playful paw-strokes of the wilderness, the preliminary trifling before the more serious onslaught which came in due course
4	, was impressively bald. The wilderness had patted him on the head, and, behold, it was like a ball--an ivory ball; it had
5	my breath in expectation of hearing the wilderness burst into a prodigious peal of laughter that would shake the fixed stars in their
6	your heart yet!' he cried at the invisible wilderness. "We broke down--as I had expected--and had to lie up for repairs at the head of
7	Eldorado Expedition went into the patient wilderness, that closed upon it as the sea closes over a diver. Long afterwards the news
8	the whole sorrowful land, the immense wilderness, the colossal body of the fecund and mysterious life seemed to look at her, pensive
9	unreal in my life. And outside, the silent wilderness surrounding this cleared speck on the earth struck me as something great and
10	, It was a moment of triumph for the wilderness, an invading and vengeful rush which, it seemed to me, I would have to keep back
11	him at last--only at the very last. But the wilderness had found him out early, and had taken on him a terrible vengeance for the

Figure 5.5 *Concordance lines of* forest *and* wilderness: *Personification*

used with both *forest* (line 8) and *wilderness* (line 8) that, as physical spaces, are not expected to have the ability to think. However, both Marlow and Kurtz seem to have this expectation, as they verbally interact with the African jungle. In line 2, Marlow expects the forest to give him some sort of *answer* for his actions, whereas in line 6 Kurtz speaks out loud to the *invisible wilderness*. At times the wilderness seems even to be on the verge of interacting back, as in line 5, where the wilderness *burst into a prodigious peal of laughter*. Laughing can be seen as a behavioural process that typically pertains to humans (Halliday and Matthiessen 2004: 248). Its use in relation to the wilderness contributes to confer to it human traits. This is equally true for those cases in which *forest* and *wilderness* are involved in mental processes. In a clause of mental process, 'there is always one participant who is human' or, more precisely, a 'being "endowed with consciousness"' (Halliday and Matthiessen 2004: 201). Yet the entity endowed with consciousness in these examples is not human, but rather inanimate, that is, the wilderness. In line 8, the wilderness seems *to look at* Kurtz's assumed mistress, in a *pensive* way; in line 11, it *found out* Kurtz's *fantastic invasion* and takes vengeance on him.

The personifying tendency is instantiated not only through assigning human actions and behaviours to the African jungle, as seen so far, but also through the attribution of descriptive features and traits that are more animal- or human-like than specific to inanimate entities. An example of an animal attribute is recognizable in line 3, where *wilderness* appears to possess paws. However, more pervasive than the beastly representation is the depiction of the African forest as a woman. Apart from the ungendered *face* that co-occurs twice with *forest*, in lines 5 and 8, the forest is described as a *virgin* in line 4. The word *virgin*, although gender-neutral by definition, is commonly associated with the female gender, as its occurrences in RC show.[2] Additionally, a *breast* is attributed to the wilderness in line 1, while in line 2 the wilderness takes Kurtz into its *bosom*. Finally, this depiction is also strengthened through the use of *fecund* in reference with the colossal body of the wilderness, in line 8.

Overall, both actions and descriptions of the jungle as an animate and conscious entity ascribe hostile intentions to its personified representation, rather than benign ones. When the forest stands up, it does it *spectrally* (line 1); its face is *gloomy* (line 5) and *dark* (line 8). Its actions seem to be directed at interfering with Marlow's expedition or, more generally, with all human intrusions altogether. As underlined before, the forest *leisurely* tries to *bar the way* of the steamer (line 3), and both *forest* and *wilderness* co-occur with forms of the lemma SURROUND (*surrounded* in line 6 of *forest*; *surrounding* in line 9 of *wilderness*), which conveys the idea of an intentional effort to isolate intruders. The wilderness seems to laugh at Kurtz (line 5) when he dares to challenge its dominion, and then takes a *terrible vengeance* (line 11, but also *vengeful* in line 10) on him for his imprudence. Generally speaking, this matches the 'place of darkness' fictional representation, especially in its most obscure traits (the 'darkness' and 'closedness' semantic preferences).

Those described so far are the main trends of the personifying tendency in the context of *wilderness* and *forest*, as extracted from their concordance lines. Consider Example (3) now to see how the personification trope is developed in longer passages.

(3)   The wilderness had patted him on the head, and, behold, it was like a ball – an ivory ball; it had caressed him, and – lo! – he had withered; it had taken him, loved him, embraced him, got into his veins, consumed his flesh, and sealed his soul to its own by the inconceivable ceremonies of some devilish initiation.

In this extract, which provides extended context for line 4 of the concordance lines of *wilderness* (Figure 5.4), the metaphor of the wilderness as a woman is developed further. The image is that of a seductive yet dangerous partner who bewitches Kurtz, luring him into its *devilish initiation*. The lexical choices depict an almost physical encounter between lovers, whereby a personified wilderness caresses, embraces and finally loves Kurtz, although at the same time it consumes his flesh and withers his scalp, sealing his soul to its own. This relation between the wilderness and its feminine embodiment is made most explicitly when Marlow meets Kurtz's African mistress. Consider the extract in Example (4):

(4)   And in the hush that had fallen suddenly upon the whole sorrowful land, the immense wilderness, the colossal body of the fecund and mysterious

life seemed to look at her, pensive, as though it had been looking at the image of its own tenebrous and passionate soul.

From this passage (the extended context for line 8 of the concordance lines of *wilderness* in Figure 4.5) it is clear that not only the wilderness has *its own tenebrous and passionate soul*, but also that this soul finds its physical embodiment in an African woman. In fact, immediately before these lines, the African woman is described as *savage and superb, wild-eyed and magnificent; there was something ominous and stately in her deliberate progress*, a description that would work similarly well for the African jungle as it is fictionally represented in *HoD*.

5.4 The fictional representation of the African jungle in translation

The previous sections show how the 'Africa words' develop recurrent lexico-semantic patterns which build the 'where' of *HoD*. The lexical and semantic features identified transmute the real and geographical identity of Africa into a figurative representation. This representation reflects the sociocultural context it originates from: it is hardly a neutral depiction, but rather mirrors historical values and cultural prejudices. Therefore, these patterns have a double value: first, they are an integral part of the style of the text; second, they possess critical relevance, because they play a key role in the interpretation of the novel. This section examines whether and how these patterns have been reproduced in translation. It argues that their alteration can affect both the style of the text and its interpretation.

I start by comparing the TTs, in order to study whether or not an alteration of such patterns took place in translation. Building on the findings of the analysis of the ST, this section discusses the effects of translation on the fictional representation of the African jungle. In particular, Section 5.4.1 compares the representation of the jungle as 'a place of darkness' across the TTs, while Section 5.4.2 concentrates on the representation of the jungle as a personified entity in translation. This analysis shows that the alteration of the lexico-semantic patterns affects the cohesion of the translations, with consequences on the potential interpretation of text; in other words, this section illustrates the effects of alterations at the micro (textual) level on the macro (interpretational) level.

5.4.1 The representation of the jungle as a 'place of darkness' in translation

This analysis follows the methodology used for the study of the ST: it starts from a concordance analysis of the 'Africa words' to check whether their translation reproduces the semantic preferences identified in the original. The comparison begins with *forest* and *jungle*, because these items have a direct Italian equivalent, *foresta* and *giungla* respectively, used by all the TTs. Tables 5.5 and 5.6 collect the words forming part of the three semantic fields ('closedness', 'darkness', 'immensity') in the translations, in a span of 5:5. The tables show that the semantic preferences are maintained in all four of the TTs. It is in fact possible to identify the words that create the dominant semantic fields in the original. *Foresta* and *giungla* occur with words conveying the idea of darkness: for example, *cupo* (gloomy[3]), *fosco* (dull, dim), *buio* (dark), *ombre* (shadows), *nere* (black), *mistero* (mystery) and *spettrale* (spectral); with words conveying the idea of a closed and inaccessible place: for example, *impenetrabile* (impenetrable), *margine* (margin), *circondata* (surrounded) and *limite* (limit); and with words conveying the idea of a place which is difficult to circumscribe due to its immensity and blurred boundaries: for example, *profondità* (depth), *immense* (immense), *colossale* (colossal) and *intrico* (tangle).

Moving on to *wilderness* and *darkness*, the analysis becomes less straightforward. These two words do not have a direct, one-to-one Italian equivalent, as

Table 5.5 *Collocates of* foresta *belonging to the three semantic fields*[*]

Translation S, *foresta*

ciglio (4), profondità (2), abbracciò, cinto, circondato, cupo, dentro, deserta, fosca, impenetrabile, lati, limite, misteriosamente, ombre, oscurità, pensosa, silenzio, spettrale, tenebroso, tetra.

Translation B, *foresta*

margine (4), buia, circondata, circondato, cupo, deserta, entrata, impenetrabile, incupiva, mistero, ombre, profonda, profondità, selvaggi, selvaggia, silenzio, solitario, spettrale.

Translation G, *foresta*

ciglio (3), lato (2), profondità (2), abbracciava, circondata, circondava, cupo, dentro, espulso, immenso, impassibile, intrico, limitare, margine, muraglia, neri, ombre, oscura, oscurità, selvaggia, silenzio, spettrale, tetro, usciva.

Translation M, *foresta*

cupo (2), margine (2), orlo (2), profondo (2), silenzio (2), abbracciava, circondata, circondato, confuse, espulso, groviglio, impassibile, impenetrabile, lato, limite, limiti, nera, neri, ombre, parete, profondità, scuro, selvatica, silenzio, spaventoso, spettrale.

*Frequency, when ≥ 2, in brackets

Table 5.6 *Collocates of* giungla *belonging to the three semantic fields*[*]

Translation S, *giungla*

ciglio, colossale, cupo, immensa, misteriosamente, nere.

Translation B *giungla*

intrico (2), margine (2), fosco, immensa, immenso, invisibile, maledetta, muraglia, nere, profondità, selvaggi, usciva.

Translation G, *giungla*

colossale, immenso, impenetrabile, intrico, neri, selvaggi.

Translation M, *giungla*

colossale, immenso, impenetrabile, intrico, neri, orlo.

* Frequency, when ≥ 2, in brackets

in the case of *jungle* and *forest*. *Darkness* can have many different translations in Italian, depending on the context, whereas *wilderness* does not have a direct equivalent at all. The translators have to substitute or paraphrase it accordingly. Therefore, to compare these 'Africa words' in translation, we need first to identify how they have been translated in each TT, by comparing the original text to the Italian versions. The outcome of this comparison is summarized in Table 5.7.

Translation S adopts 12 different translations for *wilderness* and 5 for *darkness*; Translation B, 12 for *wilderness* and 3 for *darkness*; Translation G translates *wilderness* and *darkness* in 2 and 5 different ways respectively, while Translation M uses 6 for *wilderness* and 2 for *darkness*. Once these translations have been identified, it is possible to analyse their concordance lines so as to check whether the dominant semantic fields are also maintained in Italian. Consider Table 5.8 and Table 5.9, which list the 'closedness', 'darkness' and 'immensity' words that occur with the Italian translations of *wilderness* and *darkness* in a span of 5:5.

All four TTs maintain the semantic fields identified in the original, both in relation to *wilderness* and *darkness*. The Italian versions of *wilderness* and *darkness* equally co-occur with terms conveying the idea of 'closedness': for example, *racchiudeva* (enclosed), *richiuse* (closed), *circondava* (surrounded), *impenetrabile* (impenetrable), *porta* (door) and *soglia* (threshold); with terms conveying the idea of 'darkness': for example, *misteriosamente* (mysteriously), *silenziosa* (silent), *dolente* (sorrowful), *mistero* (mystery), *occulta* (occult), *pericolo* (danger) and *nera* (black); and with words conveying the idea of 'immensity': for example, *perduto* (lost), *colossale* (colossal), *enorme* (enormous), *profondità* (depths), *immensa* (immense), *sperduto* (lost) and *profonda* (profound).

Table 5.7 *Translations of* wilderness *and* darkness *for each TT**

	wilderness	darkness
Translation S	terra selvaggia (wild land) (6) immensità selvaggia (wild immensity) (3) mondo selvaggio (wild world) (2) solitudine selvaggia (wild solitude) (2) terra vergine (virgin land) (2) deserto vegetale (vegetation desert) foresta vergine (virgin forest) profondità selvaggia (wild depth) selvaggi recessi (wild recesses) selvatica vita (wild life) solitudine (solitude) terra (land) **Total:** 12 translations	tenebra (darkness; sing.) (17) tenebre (darkness; plur.) (5) oscurità (darkness, obscurity) tenebrosa aridità (dark aridity) tenebrosi (dark; adj.) **Total:** 5 translations
Translation B	terra selvaggia (wild land) (8) distesa desolata (desolate expanse) (4) desolazione (desolation) distesa selvaggia (wild expanse) foresta (forest) giungla (jungle) natura selvaggia (wild nature) plaga selvaggia (wild region) selva (woods) solitudine selvaggia (wild solitude) solitudini selvage (wild solitudes) terra desolata (desolate land) **Total:** 12 translations	tenebra (darkness; sing.) (20) tenebre (darkness; plur.) (4) buio (dark) **Total:** 3 translations
Translation G	landa selvaggia (wild land) (13) selva selvaggia (wild woods) (9) **Total:** 2 translations	tenebra (darkness; sing.) (16) tenebre (darkness; plur.) (5) oscurità (darkness, obscurity) (2) profondità tenebrosa (dark depth) sterilità tenebrosa (dark sterility) **Total:** 5 translations
Translation M	terra selvaggia (wild land) (17) immensità selvaggia (wild immensity) natura selvaggia (wild nature) regione selvaggia (wild region) vita misteriosa e selvatica (wild and mysterious life) zona selvaggia (wild zone) **Total:** 6 translations	tenebre (darkness; plur.) (14) tenebra (darkness; sing.) (11) **Total:** 2 translations

*Frequency, when ≥ 2, in brackets

Table 5.8 *Collocates of the translations of* wilderness *belonging to the three semantic fields**

Translation S, Italian translations of *wilderness*

abbandonata, attorno, misteriosamente, mistero, muta, muto, racchiudeva, richiuse, perduto, silenziosa, sola, vuota.

Translation B, Italian translations of *wilderness*

abbandonata, addentrava, chiuse, circondava, colossale, desolata, dolente, enorme, greve, immensa, misteriosa, mistero, muto, profondità, riaccolse, silente, sola, sperduto, vuoto.

Translation G, Italian translations of *wilderness*

silenziosa (2), circondava, colossale, dimenticata, greve, immensa, insondabile, isolamento, misteriosa, mistero, muto, profondità, richiuse, sperduto, vuota.

Translation M, Italian translations of *wilderness*

chiusa, circondava, desolata, dimenticata, mistero, muto, perduto, profondità, richiuse, silenziosa, vuota.

*Frequency, when ≥ 2, in brackets

Table 5.9 *Collocates of the translations of* darkness *belonging to the three semantic fields**

Translation S, Italian translations of *darkness*

impenetrabile (2), imperscrutabile, inabissava, occulta, pericolo, porta, profonda, profondamente, profondo, soglia, spiraglio.

Translation B, Italian translations of *darkness*

impenetrabile (3), aperta, immensa, nera, pericolo, porta, profonda, profondità, soglia.

Translation G, Italian translations of *darkness*

impenetrabile (3), circondava, immensa, invisibile, nascosto, profonda, socchiuso, soglia.

Translation M, Italian translations of *darkness*

impenetrabile (2), porta (2), aperta, immensa, impenetrabili, infittivano, invisibile, nascosto, nera, profonda, profondità.

*Frequency, when ≥ 2, in brackets

Considering also the collocates of *foresta* and *giungla*, it can be noted that the repetition of the exact same terms and forms of the same lemmas across the 'Africa words' is a feature of the Italian semantic fields as well. In Translation S, *mistero/misteriosamente* (mystery/mysteriously), *silenzio/silenziosa* (silence/silent), *impenetrabile* (impenetrable), *ciglio* (edge), *cupo* (gloomy) and *profonda/profondamente/profondo* (deep/deeply/deep) are shared by two or more 'Africa words'. In Translation B, *silente/silenzio* (silent/silence), *immensa/immenso* (immense), *selvaggi* (wild), *circondava/circondata/circondato* (surrounding/surrounded/

surrounded), *impenetrabile* (impenetrable), *nera/nere* (black), *profondità/profonda* (deepth/deep) and *mistero/misteriosa/misteriosamente* (mystery/mysterious/mysteriously) are shared by two or more 'Africa words'. In Translation G, *silenziosa/silenzio* (silent/silence), *circondava/circondata* (surrounding/surrounded), *immensa/immenso* (immense), *profondità/profonda* (depths/deep), *impenetrabile* (impenetrable), *intrico* (tangle), *neri* (black), *selvaggia/selvaggi* (wild) and *colossale* (colossal) are shared by two or more 'Africa words'. Finally, in Translation M, *nera/neri* (black), *circondava/circondata/circondato* (surrounding/surrounded/surrounded), *silenziosa/silenzio* (silent/silence), *impenetrabile/impenetrabili* (impenetrable), *immensa/immenso* (immense) and *profondità/profonda/profondo* (depths/deep) are shared by two or more 'Africa words'.

Summing up, the Italian translations of *forest, wilderness, jungle* and *darkness* establish equivalent lexico-semantic patterns as in the original, enacting a comparable local textual function. Generally speaking, the fictional representation of the African jungle as a 'place of darkness' is identifiable in all four TTs. However, what is irremediably altered in the translations is the lexical cohesion these patterns establish in the original.

5.4.2 Lexical cohesion in the translations

Section 5.2 argued that the persistent use of the 'closedness', 'darkness' and 'immensity' semantic fields with all four of the 'Africa words' establishes a lexical network that makes the fictional representation of the African jungle cohesive. The previous section showed that the TTs reproduce the semantic preferences of the original, keeping the network between the Italian 'Africa words' unaltered. However, in all four TTs, *wilderness* and *darkness* are translated in multiple ways: this section discusses how this choice affects the lexical cohesion of the TTs.

Even though the semantic fields are there, the lexical network that connects them to the 'Africa words' is less tight, because in the TTs the 'Africa words' are more numerous than in the original. The use of multiple translations for the same ST item affects the cohesive network and dilutes the lexico-semantic pattern which, in the ST, is based on fewer items: the translations insert different terms where in the original there was identical repetition. Consider the case of *wilderness*, for instance. *Wilderness* is the 'Africa word' that has been translated in the most different ways, so it lends itself to explaining the effect on the cohesion in the TTs. In the ST, every time *wilderness* occurs, the reader finds in its surrounding context similar words and semantic fields which, reiterated throughout the whole text, enact a cohesive and consistent image of the wilderness. Example (5) exemplifies this phenomenon: six random sentences in which *wilderness* occurs are gathered and put together one after the other, in the order they appear in the text. The node word is in bold while the 'closedness', 'darkness' and 'immensity' words are in italics. Every time *wilderness* occurs, the semantic preference is reiterated and a new tile is added to the overall mosaic to create a cohesive fictional representation.

(5)   Land in a swamp, march through the woods, and in some inland post feel the savagery, the utter *savagery*, had *closed* round him – all that *mysterious* life of the **wilderness** that stirs in the forest, in the jungles, in the hearts of wild men. [. . .] And *outside*, the *silent* **wilderness** *surrounding* this cleared speck on the earth struck me as something great and invincible, like *evil* or truth, waiting patiently for the passing away of this fantastic invasion. [. . .] In a few days the Eldorado Expedition went into the patient **wilderness**, that *closed* upon it as the sea closes over a diver. [. . .] And, after all, they did not eat each other before my face: they had brought along a provision of hippo-meat which went rotten, and made the *mystery* of the **wilderness** stink in my nostrils. [. . .] But the **wilderness** had found him out early, and had taken on him a *terrible vengeance* for the fantastic invasion. [. . .] And in the hush that had fallen suddenly upon the whole *sorrowful* land, the *immense* **wilderness**, the *colossal* body of the fecund and *mysterious* life seemed to look at her, pensive, as though it had been looking at the image of its own *tenebrous* and passionate soul.

In the first sentence, *closed* and *mysterious* occur in relation to *wilderness*. In the second sentence, *wilderness* co-occurs with *outside* and *surrounding*, building on the occurrence of *closed* in the previous sentence. Later in the novel, the reader finds *wilderness* co-occurring with *closed* again, in the third sentence. *Mystery*, in the fourth sentence, recalls the previous use of *mysterious*, while a verbatim repetition of *mysterious* reappears in the sixth sentence. Each instantiation of the semantic fields builds on the previous uses and reinforces the link that connects the semantic preferences to *wilderness*. This lexical network, spread consistently throughout the text, establishes a cohesive representation of the wilderness.

In translation, the link that connects one occurrence of *wilderness* to the other is interrupted because the term has been rendered into different items. Even though the semantic fields are there, they are not tied together since the reiterated node word which acts as the spine of the lexical network is missing. Example (5S) shows the same sentences in Example (5) from Translation S, selected because its wide range of different translations of *wilderness* is exemplificatory.

(5S)   Sbarcare in un pantano, marciare attraverso i boschi, e in qualche posto
avanzato dell'interno sentire che la natura *selvaggia*, tutto quel che si
può dare di più *selvaggio* s'è *richiuso* attorno a lui; tutta quella **selvatica
vita** che si agita *misteriosamente* nella giungla, nella foresta, nel cuore
dei barbari. [. . .] E, al di *fuori*, quella *silenziosa* **immensità selvaggia**
che *racchiudeva* quel minuscolo spiazzo sulla terra m'appariva non so
che di grande e d'invincibile, come il *male* o il vero, pazientemente in
attesa della fine di quella grottesca invasione. [. . .] Di lì a pochi giorni
la «Spedizione Eldorado» s'inabissò in quel paziente **deserto vegetale**,
che si *richiuse* su di lei come il mare sopra un palombaro. [. . .]
E poi, dopo tutto, non si mangiarono mai l'un l'altro in mia presenza.
S'eran portata seco una provvista di carne d'ippopotamo che finì per
imputridire, e mi rese sensibile il *mistero* di quella **terra vergine** in un
fetore che mi empiva le narici. [. . .] Ma quella **terra selvaggia** lo aveva
capito assai presto, e aveva preso su di lui una *tremenda vendetta* per
tutta quella grottesca invasione. [. . .] E nel silenzio che era subitamente
caduto su tutta quella *accorata* contrada, l'**immensità selvaggia**, il
corpo *colossale* di quella vita feconda e *misteriosa* pareva la guardasse,
intenta, quasi contemplando l'immagine della propria anima, *tenebrosa*
e appassionata.

(Disembarking in a morass, marching through the woods, and in some
place inland feeling that the *wild* nature, all that can be most *wild*, has
closed round him; all that **wild life** that stirs *mysteriously* in the jungle, in
the forest, in the heart of the barbarians. [. . .] And, *outside*, that *silent* **wild
immensity** that *closed* that minuscule open space on the earth appeared to
me as something great and invincible, like *evil* or truth, waiting patiently
for the end of that grotesque invasion. [. . .] In a few days the 'Eldorado
Expedition' sank into that patient **vegetation desert**, that *closed* upon her
as the sea upon a diver. [. . .] And then, after all, they never ate each other
in my presence. They had brought with them a provision of hippo-meat
which ended up rotting, and made me sensitive to the *mystery* of that
virgin land with a fetor that filled my nostrils. [. . .] But that **wild land**
had understood it very soon, and had taken on him a *terrible vengeance*
for all that grotesque invasion. [. . .] And in the *silence* that had fallen
suddenly upon that earnest region, the **wild immensity**, the *colossal* body
of that fecund and *mysterious* life seemed to look at her, intent, as though
staring at the image of her own souls, tenebrous and passionate.)

Although the semantic preference is identifiable, the link between one instantiation and the next is looser, as the semantic fields refer, in this specific example, to
five different node words. In the first sentence of Example (5S), *misteriosamente*
(mysteriously) and *richiuso* (closed) occur in the context of *selvatica vita* (wild
life). In the third sentence, *richiuse* (closed) occurs again, recalling the previous
use of *richiuso* (closed). However, this time *richiuse* (closed) refers to *deserto vegetale* (vegetation desert), and not to *selvatica vita* (wild life). Similarly, the occurrences of *mistero* (mystery) in the fourth sentence and *misteriosa* (mysterious)
in the sixth sentence do not build on each other as in the original, because in the
TT the link that relates them is missing. *Mistero* (mystery) and *misteriosa* (mysterious) refer to two different nodes, *terra vergine* (virgin land) and *immensità
selvaggia* (wild immensity). The lexical network is therefore interrupted.

Baker (2011: 215) acknowledges that, when there is a lack of ready equivalents, subtle or even major changes are sometimes inevitable in translation. If
these changes affect the cohesion of the text, Baker (2011) suggests substituting
the lexical chain of the ST with a different but equivalent chain in the TT, as
long as lexical cohesion is established. On the contrary, what the translator must
always avoid is 'the extreme case of producing what appears to be a random collection of items which do not add up to recognizable lexical chains that make
sense in a given context' (Baker 2011: 216). This is what seems to be happening
in Translation S, where the lexical chain is interrupted and substituted by a 'collection of items' (the different translations of *wilderness*) that 'do not add up'
to the same 'recognizable lexical chains' as in the original, where there is the
repetition of the core word *wilderness*. The lexical chain that links the instantiations of the semantic preferences is directly established only when *wilderness*
is translated with the same expression, for instance, *immensità selvaggia* ('wild
immensity') in Example (5S). As a result, the cohesion of the representation of
the wilderness in the TT is altered.

Another consequence of translating *wilderness* with multiple terms, which
equally affects the lexical cohesion of the TTs, is the loss of emphasis: the TT
items (the Italian translations of *wilderness*) do not carry the same emphasis
that the ST item (*wilderness*) carries. This loss of emphasis is due to the strategy that is mostly adopted to translate *wilderness* in Italian, namely, paraphrasing. Paraphrasing has the advantage of achieving a high level of precision
in conveying the semantic meaning of the original item. However, it has the
disadvantage of filling a one-item slot with a longer multi-item expression
(Baker 2011: 41). The most common way the noun *wilderness* is translated in
the TTs is by paraphrasing it with the construction 'noun + adjective', as in

terra selvaggia (wild land) or *natura selvaggia* (wild nature). *Selvaggio/selvaggia* (wild) is the most common adjective used in this construction, which carries most of the semantic meaning of *wilderness*. As a result, the emphasis that *wilderness* carries as a one-item noun is spread over two elements, a newly introduced noun and an adjective post- or pre-modifying it. This strategy alters the role *wilderness* plays in establishing cohesion. Although the semantic meaning of *wilderness* is to some extent reproduced by *selvaggio/selvaggia* (wild), 'expressive, evoked or any kind of associative meaning[s]' (Baker 2011: 41) cannot be equally maintained through paraphrasing. These meanings are 'associated only with stable lexical items which have a history of recurrence in specific contexts' (Baker 2011: 41). In the ST, *wilderness* does have such a 'history of recurrence in specific contexts', that is, its semantic preferences, in corpus linguistics terms. *Wilderness* co-occurs recurrently within the same specific semantic fields. The relation between the core *wilderness* and its contexts of occurrence provides *wilderness* with extra meanings, in addition to the semantic one: the expressive, evoked and associative meanings that Baker (2011: 41) refers to. Paraphrasing disrupts the relation between the core and its contexts of occurrence, because it substitutes a stable lexical item in the ST (*wilderness*) with multiple items that do not recur consistently enough in TTs. Some instances of this phenomenon can be found in Example (6) and Example (7):

(6)   But the *wilderness* had found him out early, and had taken on him a terrible vengeance for the fantastic invasion.

(6S)   Ma quella *terra selvaggia* lo aveva capito assai presto, e aveva preso su di lui una tremenda vendetta per tutta quella grottesca invasione.
(But that *wild land* had understood him very early, and had taken on him a tremendous vengeance for all that grotesque invasion.)

(7)   And outside, the silent *wilderness* surrounding this cleared speck on the earth struck me as something great and invincible, like evil or truth, waiting patiently for the passing away of this fantastic invasion.

(7B)   E fuori, la silente *distesa desolata* che circondava questo bruscolo disboscato sulla terra mi colpiva come qualcosa di grande e invincibile, come il male o la verità, pazientemente in attesa che scomparisse questa fantastica invasione.
(And outside, the silent *desolate expanse* that surrounded this cleared speck on the earth struck me as something great and invincible, like evil or truth, waiting patiently for this fantastic invasion to disappear.)

In Examples (6S) and (7B) the emphasis of *wilderness* is shifted to the noun *terra* (land) and *distesa* (expanse) respectively, introduced anew by the translators. In the case of Example (6S), although the semantic meaning of *wilderness* is maintained by the post-modifying adjective *selvaggia* ('wild'), the emphasis that *wilderness* carries in the ST is shifted onto a TT item, *terra* (land), which does not have the same 'history of recurrence in specific contexts' (Baker 2011: 41) as *wilderness* does in the ST. In the case of Example (7B), the semantic meaning of *wilderness* is lost altogether, since the adjective post-modifying *distesa* (expanse) has a completely different semantic meaning from *wilderness*, namely, *desolata* (desolate). As a result, the emphasis that the noun *wilderness* carries as a subject is moved to a TT item which has a different semantic meaning and interpretational implications. Overall, the nouns introduced by the translators can be regarded as hyponyms of the original item: *terra* (land) and *distesa* (expanse) can be seen as more specific terms than *wilderness*. This alteration narrows down the metaphorical and symbolic implications of the vaguer term *wilderness*, through an Italian translation that is more concrete and precise in conveying the idea of an actual place, instead of a figurative space, a metaphor, as it happens in the original. This is a significant alteration, considering that *HoD* plays repeatedly with the idea of vagueness.

These two types of alterations (disruption of the cohesive network and loss of emphasis) affect the patterns that the 'Africa words' create in the original. In turn, the lexical cohesion they establish is affected too. These alterations do not involve *forest* and *jungle*, as these two words have a direct Italian equivalent with which they have been consistently translated. However, I showed that the fictional representation of the African jungle hinges on the interrelation of all four 'Africa words' together. Therefore, even the alterations involving only *wilderness* and *darkness* can have a major impact on the overall depiction of the jungle. The interpretational implications that the depiction of the African jungle raises in the ST may be different in the TTs, as a consequence of the alterations at the level of consistency and cohesion. As Baker (2011: 219) suggests, different cohesive networks that do not match the networks created in the ST '[may] not trigger the same kinds of association in the mind of the target reader'. In other words, the target reader could perceive the theme 'Africa and its representation' differently from the source reader, because the construction of the African jungle in the translation is different from that of the original.

Before moving to the next section, it is important to mention that the alterations discussed in this section affect the translations to different extents. Translation S is the TT with the highest number of different variations for *wilderness* and *darkness*, therefore this is the Italian version in which the depiction of the jungle is most altered. At the other end of the scale, there is Translation G which, although presents five different translations of *darkness*, translates *wilderness* with only two variants. In this case, keeping the same terms throughout the text helps to establish a lexical network which is more similar to that of the ST compared to the other translations. In Translation G, the semantic preferences are established around only two variants instead of twelve, as in the case of Translation S.

5.4.3 Personification in translation

Section 5.3 argued that the African jungle is personified in *HoD* and showed which linguistic patterns enact this personification. *Forest* and *wilderness* have been shown to operate as active agents that perform physical actions, possess cognitive functions and display a malevolent disposition towards external intruders. This malicious characterization is also manifested in terms of a seductive yet dangerous woman, charming and wicked at the same time. Building on the discussion of the translation of *forest* and *wilderness*, this section extends the comparison of the TTs by investigating the personification tendency, looking at whether and how it has been maintained in translation.

Figure 5.6 shows the Italian concordance lines of *foresta*, the same concordance lines of *forest* shown in Figure 5.5. Overall, all four TTs maintain the personification associated with *foresta* (forest), mainly as a result of the literal translation of Conrad's lexical choices. For example, the forest is *vergine* (virgin), it has a *volto cupo* (dark face) – apart from Translation B where *il volto si incupiva* (the face darkened) – and *pensoso* (pensive), and it is expected to give a *risposta* (answer) to Marlow in all four of the TTs. However, in other cases the translators level out the personification, replacing some of Conrad's lexical choices with items that fit more standardly the description of a geographical landscape. This is the case of *the forest stood up* (line 1 in Figure 5.5). In Translations S, M and G, it becomes *la foresta si ergeva* (the forest rose) and in Translation B it becomes *la foresta si dispiegava* (the forest spread). Similarly, in the case of *the forest surrounded all that* (line 6 in Figure 5.5), *foresta* (forest) loses its role as the subject of the sentence in three out of four TTs, becoming instead the agent of a passive construction. In Translations S, B and M, *the forest surrounded all that* becomes *tutto ciò era, naturalmente, circondato dalla foresta* (all of that was, naturally, surrounded by the forest), *il tutto era circondato dalla foresta* (all of that was surrounded by the forest) and *tutto questo era circondato dalla foresta* (all of this was surrounded by the forest), respectively. The forest is deprived of its active agency, while the impression that it is performing a physical action is toned down, in accordance with a more

Translation S

1	davvero che se le portassero in letto. Di là dallo steccato la foresta s'ergeva spettrale nel chiaro di luna, e attraverso al
2	alcun movimento di ritirata, non altrimenti che se la foresta, la quale aveva buttato fuori quelle creature tanto
3	innanzi a noi, e si chiudeva alle nostre spalle, come se la foresta avesse tranquillamente attraversato le acque dall'una
4	selvaggi, si rovesciarono nella radura fuori da quella foresta fosca e pensosa. I cespugli si agitarono, l'erba
5	Un frastuono tremendo usciva fuori da quella carcassa, e la foresta vergine dall'altra parte della cala lo rifrangeva in un
6	io balzai in piedi e mi volsi a guardare verso il limite della foresta, come se m'aspettassi un qualche segno di risposta
7	era scomparsa. Tutto ciò era, naturalmente, circondato dalla foresta. Di sotto alla casa la ripa era parimenti sgombra, e
8	al fiume. Il pomeriggio era già alquanto inoltrato, il volto della foresta era cupo, e un'ampia striscia d'ombra era già scesa

Translation B

1	davanti a noi per chiudersi alle nostre spalle come se la foresta fosse entrata nell'acqua a passi indolenti per
2	Penso davvero che se li portassero a letto. Oltre il recinto la foresta si dispiegava spettrale al chiaro di luna, e attraverso
3	ferro. Un clangore spaventoso si levò da quello scafo, e la foresta vergine, sulla riva opposta della caletta, lo rimandò
4	senza alcun percepibile movimento di ritirata, come se la foresta, che così all'improvviso aveva eruttato quegli esseri,
5	che balzai in piedi e mi voltai a guardare il margine della foresta, quasi che mi fossi atteso una risposta qualsiasi a
6	erano scomparse. Naturalmente, il tutto era circondato dalla foresta. La riva era disboscata, e ai bordi dell'acqua vidi un
7	sulla corrente. Era ormai pomeriggio inoltrato, il volto della foresta s'incupiva e una larga striscia d'ombra era già
8	selvaggi, si riversarono dalla facciata buia e triste della foresta sulla radura. I cespugli si agitavano, l'erba ondeggiò

Translation M

1	di ferro. Dallo scafo si alzò un frastuono spaventoso e la foresta vergine sull'altra riva dell'insenatura lo rimandò come
2	portassero a letto con loro quei bastoni. Oltre lo steccato la foresta si ergeva spettrale al chiaro di luna e attraverso la
3	rigido sulla corrente. Era ormai pomeriggio inoltrato, la foresta aveva un volto cupo e un'ampia striscia d'ombra era
4	senza alcun percettibile movimento di ritirata, come se la foresta che aveva espulso quegli esseri all'improvviso, li
5	diretta al cuore stesso della terra; e come per incanto, la foresta dal volto scuro e pensoso riversò nella radura fiumi
6	davanti a noi e si richiudevano alle nostre spalle come se la foresta attraversasse con tutto comodo l'acqua per
7	scomparse. Naturalmente tutto questo era circondato dalla foresta. La sponda del fiume era sgombra, e presso
8	balzai in piedi per guardare, alle mie spalle, il margine della foresta, come se mi aspettassi una risposta qualunque a

Translation G

1	a noi e si richiudevano al nostro passaggio, come se la foresta, pigra e tranquilla, avesse scavalcato l'acqua per
2	se lo portassero a letto, quell'arnese. Oltre la staccionata la foresta si ergeva spettrale al chiaro di luna, e attraverso il
3	smantellato uscì uno spaventoso rumore di ferraglia che la foresta vergine, dall'altro lato dell'insenatura, rimandò come
4	senza alcun percettibile movimento di ritirata, come se la foresta che aveva espulso quelle creature così
5	esserci in mezzo a loro, erano sparite. Naturalmente la foresta circondava tutto, ma la riva era sgombra e sul
6	che balzai in piedi e mi voltai a guardare il ciglio della foresta, quasi mi aspettassi una qualche risposta a quel
7	rigido di traverso. Nel pomeriggio ormai inoltrato, il volto della foresta appariva cupo, e sull'acqua era già scesa una larga
8	feroci e movimenti selvaggi, si riversò nella radura dalla foresta dal volto scuro e pensoso. La boscaglia fremette,

Figure 5.6 *Concordance lines of* foresta: *Personification*

standardized representation of the African jungle as an inanimate entity. On the contrary, Translation G maintains the active construction with *foresta* as subject: *la foresta circondava tutto* (the forest surrounded all that).

With regard to *wilderness*, the lack of a one-to-one equivalent in Italian adds a further level of complexity to the analysis. Consider Figure 5.7, which shows the different translations of *wilderness* in the same concordance lines shown in Figure 5.5. The Italian translations of *wilderness* maintain overall the personifying tendency. For instance, in all four TTs, the wilderness has paws, *zampate* (blow with a paw) and laughs: *prodigiosa risata* (prodigious laugh), line 9 in Translation S; *enorme risata* (enormous laugh), line 9 in Translation B; *formidabile risata* (formidable laugh), line 11 in Translation M; and *fragorosa risata* (uproarious laugh), line 11 in Translation G. The wilderness also seems to be looking at Kurtz's mistress: *pareva la guardasse* (seemed that it looked at her), line 5 in Translation S; *pareva guardarla* (appeared to look at her), line 6 in Translation B; *sembrava [. . .] la guardasse* (seemed that it looked at her), line 1 in Translation M; and *sembrava pensosamente guardarla* (seemed it was looking at her pensive), line 2 in Translation G. The attribution of a breast, bosom and fecundity to the wilderness is also maintained in all the TTs: *breast* in line 1 of Figure 5.5 becomes *seno* (bosom) in Translations S and B, *petto* (breast) in Translation M, but *cuore* (heart) in Translation G; *bosom* in line 2 of Figure 5.5 becomes *seno* (bosom) in Translations S, B and M and *grembo* (lap, womb) in Translation G; finally, *fecund* in line 8 of Figure 5.5 is translated as *feconda* (fecund) in all four TTs.

Translation S

```
 1 | giorni la «Spedizione Eldorado» s'inabissò in quel paziente deserto vegetale. che si richiuse su di lei come il mare sopra un palombaro. Dopo molto
 2 | Cercai di rompere l'incanto — il greve e muto incanto della foresta vergine — che pareva se lo attirasse al seno, risvegliando in lui certi istinti brutali e
 3 | di tanto irreale in vita mia. E, al di fuori, quella silenziosa immensità selvaggia che racchiudeva quel minuscolo spiazzo sulla terra m'appariva non so che
 4 | di riaversi: finalmente s'alzò e se n'andò via, e quella muta immensità selvaggia lo accolse di nuovo nel suo seno. Uscendo dall'oscurità, m'andavo
 5 | era subitamente caduto su tutta quella accorata contrada, l'immensità selvaggia, il corpo colossale di quella vita feconda e misteriosa pareva la guardasse
 6 | modo di strapparti il cuore», egli gridò verso quell' invisibile mondo selvaggio. Un bel giorno la macchina s'arrestò — come avevo pur previsto — e ci
 7 | tenebra vittoriosa. Era un momento di trionfo per quella terra selvaggia una irruzione veemente e vendicatrice che, a quanto mi sembrava, mi sarebbe
 8 | da ultimo: proprio solo da ultimo, però. Ma quella terra selvaggia lo aveva capito assai presto, e aveva preso su di lui una tremenda vendetta per
 9 | senso volerlo il respiro nell'attesa di udir scoppiare quella terra selvaggia in una prodigiosa risata che avrebbe fatto tremare le stelle nelle loro sedi. Ogni
10 | esemplare era di una calvizie impressionante. Quella terra selvaggia gli aveva dato un buffetto sul capo: ed eccola di colpo, la sua testa simile a
11 | di questo o di quell'altro — scherzose zampate di quella terra selvaggia. frigoli preliminari di quel più serio assalto che venne poi a suo tempo. Dunque,
```

Translation B

```
 1 | di più irreale in vita mia. E fuori, la silente distesa desolata che circondava questo bruscolo disboscato sulla terra mi colpiva
 2 | Spedizione Eldorado si addentrava nella paziente distesa desolata. che si chiuse su di essa come il mare su di un tuffatore. Molto
 3 | di riprendersi: poi si alzò e se ne andò e la distesa desolata senza un suono lo riaccolse nel suo seno. Mentre dal buio mi
 4 | ma saprò ancora strapparti il cuore!», gridò alla giungla invisibile. — Come avevo previsto, andammo in avaria e si dovette stare
 5 | esemplare era calvo da fare impressione. Quella terra selvaggia gli aveva dato un colpetto sulla testa e, guardate, era diventata come
 6 | su tutta quella plaga dolente, l'immensa terra selvaggia, il corpo colossale di quella vita feconda e misteriosa pareva guardarla,
 7 | o un po' di qualcos'altro, giocose zampate della terra selvaggia, il trascurabile annuncio del più serio attacco che arrivò a suo tempo.
 8 | l'incantesimo — il greve, muto sortilegio della terra selvaggia, — che sembrava lo attraesse nel suo seno spietato risvegliando istinti
 9 | tenere col fiato in sospeso aspettando di udire la terra selvaggia scoppiare in una enorme risata che avrebbe scosso le stelle fisse
10 | vincitrice. Fu un momento di trionfo per la terra selvaggia. un'irruzione dilagante e vendicativa che, mi parve, avrei dovuto
11 | sia arrivata alla fine, proprio solo alla fine. Ma la terra selvaggia lo aveva scoperto presto. e si era presa su di lui una terribile
```

Translation M

```
 1 | silenzio che era caduto improvviso su quella terra addolorata, sull'immensità selvaggia, sembrava che quel corpo colossale dalla vita misteriosa e feconda la guardasse
 2 | che cercava di riprendersi; quindi si alzò e se ne andò — e la natura selvaggia se lo riprese in seno senza il minimo rumore. Mentre dal buio mi avvicinavo al fuoco.
 3 | fine debba averne avuto coscienza — soltanto alla fine. Quella terra selvaggia. però. l'aveva scoperto presto, e si era vendicata su di lui in modo terribile della
 4 | di qualche altro malessere — zampate giocose di quella terra selvaggia, avvisaglie dell'assalto più serio che sarebbe arrivato a suo tempo. Sì, li osservavo come
 5 | l'incantesimo — il pesante, muto incantesimo di quella terra selvaggia — che sembrava attirarlo al suo petto impetoso risvegliando dimenticati istinti brutali.
 6 | giorni dopo la Spedizione Eldorado se ne andò nella paziente terra selvaggia e questa si richiuse su di essa come il mare si richiude su di un tuffatore. Molto tempo
 7 | "Oh, ma ti strapperò ugualmente il cuore!» gridò all'invisibile terra selvaggia «Avemmo un'avaria — come avevo previsto — dovemmo ancorarci alla punta di un'isola per
 8 | — ah — esemplare era calvo in modo impressionante. La terra selvaggia gli aveva accarezzato la testa ed eccolo lì; calvo come una palla — una palla d'avorio; lo
 9 | Non ho mai visto nulla di tanto irreale nella mia vita. E fuori, la terra selvaggia che circondava quella minuscola radura mi pareva grande e invincibile quanto
10 | cuore di una tenebra vittoriosa. Fu un attimo di trionfo per la terra selvaggia, un'irruzione pervasiva e vendicatrice che, mi parve, avrei dovuto respingere da solo per la
11 | tutto gli apparteneva. Io trattenevo il fiato in attesa di udire la terra selvaggia scoppiare in una formidabile risata che avrebbe scosso le stelle fisse dalla loro sede. Gli
```

Translation G

```
 1 | fi a pochi giorni la Spedizione Eldorado si inoltrò nella paziente landa selvaggia. che si richiuse su di lei come fa il mare sopra uno che si tuffa. Dopo molto tempo
 2 | E nell'improvviso silenzio caduto su quella terra afflitta. l'immensa landa selvaggia, quel corpo colossale di vita feconda e misteriosa sembrava pensosamente guardarla
 3 | visto niente di tanto irreale nella mia vita. E intorno. la silenziosa landa selvaggia che circondava quel pezzetto disboscato di terra, mi colpiva come qualcosa di
 4 | di riprendersi: finalmente si alzò e se ne andò, e la silenziosa landa selvaggia se lo riprese in grembo. «Mentre mi avvicinavo al bagliore proveniente dall'oscurità,
 5 | o un leggero attacco di altre cose: le zampate scherzose della landa selvaggia le iniziali schermaglie che precedono l'assalto più serio che venne poi a tempo
 6 | ehm... questo esemplare era di una calvizie impressionante. La selva selvaggia gli aveva dato un buffetto sulla testa, ed ecco, era diventata come una palla: una
 7 | "Oh, ma te lo strapperò il cuore, vedrai!», gridò all'invisibile selva selvaggia. «Ci fu un'avaria - come me lo aspettavo - e dovemmo fermarci sulla punta di
 8 | di rompere l'incantesimo — il greve, muto incantesimo della selva selvaggia - che sembrava volerlo attrarre nel suo cuore impetoso risvegliando istinti brutali e
 9 | il cuore di una tenebra vittoriosa. Fu un momento di trionfo per la selva selvaggia. un'incursione invadente e vendicativa che a me sembrava di dover respingere da
10 | che ne sia reso conto alla fine, quasi all'ultimo istante. Ma la selva selvaggia lo aveva scovato subito. e si era presa una terribile vendetta su di lui per quella
11 | ." Era tutto suo. E io trattenevo il fiato aspettandomi di udire la selva selvaggia scoppiare in una fragorosa risata che avrebbe scosso le stelle fisse sul loro asse.
```

Figure 5.7 *Concordance lines of the translations of* wilderness: *Personification*

Summing up, the African jungle is a personified entity in all four TTs, as seen in the concordance lines of both *foresta* and the Italian translations of *wilderness*. It performs behavioural and mental processes, laughing, looking and finding out: *lo aveva capito* (had understood it), line 8 in Translation S; *lo aveva scoperto* (had found it out), line 11 in Translation B; *l'aveva scoperto* (had found it out), line 3 in Translation M; and *lo aveva scovato* (had tracked it down), line 10 in Translation G. Similarly, it performs material processes, for example, patting Kurtz on his head: *gli aveva dato un buffetto sul capo* (had flicked him on his head), line 10 in Translation S; *gli aveva dato un colpetto sulla testa* (had given him a small stroke on his head), line 5 in Translation B; *gli aveva accarezzato la testa* (had caressed his head), line 8 in Translation M; and *gli aveva dato un buffetto sulla testa* (had flicked him on his head), line 6 in Translation G. The reference to the beastly representation is maintained, as well as the feminine embodiment.

However, the instantiations of the personifying tendency do not always refer to the same lexical item. Often, they refer to the multiple translations of *wilderness*. Translating *wilderness* with multiple and unrelated items has an effect also on the personification. In the case of Translation S, the personification refers to five different lexical items: *deserto vegetale* (vegetation desert), *foresta vergine* (virgin forest), *immensità selvaggia* (wild immensity), *mondo selvaggio* (wild world) and *terra selvaggia* (wild land). It refers to three items in the case of Translation B – *distesa desolata* (desolate expanse), *giungla* (jungle), *terra selvaggia* (wild land) – and in the case of Translation M – *immensità selvaggia* (wild immensity), *natura selvaggia* (wild nature), *terra selvaggia* (wild land). Finally, it refers to two items in the case of Translation G: *landa selvaggia* (wild land) and *selva selvaggia* (wild woods). This alteration potentially affects the identification of the personification as referring always to the same fictional entity, with consequences for the overall cohesion of the fictional representation. This happens to different extents in the different TTs. The effect on the cohesion is stronger in the case of Translation S, where the lexical network is spread over five different items, while it is moderate in Translations B and M, and weak in Translation G, where *wilderness* is consistently translated with only two different items.

The effects on the personification deriving from translating *wilderness* with multiple items can be clearly seen if we compare the translations of the two extracts in Examples (3) and (4) shown previously in Section 5.3. Consider how they have been translated in Translation M:

(3M)   La *terra selvaggia* gli aveva accarezzato la testa ed eccolo lì, calvo come una palla – una palla d'avorio; lo aveva sfiorato e – guarda – era appassito; se l'era preso, l'aveva amato, abbracciato, gli era entrata nelle vene, aveva consumato la sua carne e sigillato la sua anima alla propria attraverso gli inimmaginabili cerimoniali di qualche iniziazione diabolica.

(The *wild land* had caressed his head and here he is, bald like a ball – an ivory ball; it had touched him lightly and – look – he had withered; it had taken him, had loved him, hugged, it had got into his veins, had consumed his flesh and sealed his soul to its own by the unimaginable ceremonies of some devilish initiation.)

(4M) E nel silenzio che era caduto improvviso su quella terra addolorata, sull'*immensità selvaggia*, sembrava che quel corpo colossale dalla vita misteriosa e feconda la guardasse, pensoso, come se stesse osservando l'immagine della propria anima tenebrosa e appassionata.

(And in the silence that had fallen suddenly on that sorrowful land, on the *wild immensity*, it seemed that that colossal body of fecund and mysterious life looked at her, pensive, as if it was observing the image of its own tenebrous and passionate soul.)

Example (3M) reproduces faithfully the personification of the African jungle as a seductive yet diabolic female entity, translating literally the lexical items that convey the trope. The extract depicts the *terra selvaggia* (wild land) seducing and bewitching Kurtz, luring him so as to get into his veins, to tie him to itself by *inimmaginabili cerimoniali* (unimaginable ceremonies). The *terra selvaggia* (wild land) touches Kurtz lightly, caresses him, takes him, loves him, hugs him; yet, at the same time, it withers his scalp and consumes his flesh – it seals his soul to its own. As a result, the *terra selvaggia* (wild land), an inanimate entity, is ascribed with human behaviours and cognitive skills. However, such a reference is missed later in the text, as in Example (4M) the personification has a different referent, namely, *immensità selvaggia* (wild immensity). In this case, the direct parallelism, the embodiment of the wilderness in the figure of Kurtz's African mistress, remains an independent instance, instead of one of a series of related personification tropes referring to *wilderness* throughout the text. Overall, the repetition of this phenomenon in various parts of the TTs affects the cohesion of the fictional representation of the African jungle as a personified entity.

5.4.4 Shifts and manipulation

This analysis showed that, even though the lexico-semantic patterns identified in the ST are maintained in the TTs, the cohesion of the African jungle as fictionally represented in *HoD* is altered in translation. The TTs reproduce the original semantic preferences but use multiple translations for *wilderness* and *darkness*, with a consequent disruption of the link between the semantic fields and the items they refer to. As a result, the textual depiction of the African jungle as a 'place of darkness' and as a personified entity is different from that of the original, and this difference may 'not trigger the same kinds of [interpretative] association[s] in the mind of the target reader' (Baker 2011: 219). Could this be labelled as manipulation?

Chapter 1 argued that manipulation is a fuzzy concept, but scholars usually agree on a number of features that define it. Manipulation is said to affect mainly literary translation, as literature is more likely to be manipulated and to manipulate given its cultural and ideological implications (Dukāte 2009: 151). In this respect, the alterations identified in this chapter fit this description, as they take place in the context of literary translation. Manipulation is also and most typically considered to be motivated and, in the majority of cases, this motivation is cultural, political or ideological (Dukāte 2009: 46). According to the 'manipulation school' (cf. Section 1.7), the translator manipulates the text in accordance with or in opposition to a cultural trend, a critical interpretation or an ideology, for instance. From this point of view, the findings of this chapter do not match the definition of manipulation as ideologically motivated. On the contrary, the alterations seem to be the result of linguistic differences between English and Italian. The lack of a direct one-to-one equivalent for *wilderness* and *darkness* forces the translators to make a choice on how to translate these items. Whereas with *darkness* they have to pick an option from a range of several translation equivalents, with *wilderness* there is no equivalent at all, so the translators have to replace the term and/or paraphrase it. In translation studies literature, this phenomenon has more commonly been defined as a 'shift', rather than manipulation.

Shifts can be defined as deviations between the ST and the TT that can take place 'at such linguistic levels as graphology, phonology, grammar, and lexis' (Venuti 2004: 148). They occur when there is a 'departure from formal correspondence' (Catford 1965: 73), that is, when a target language category or item does not 'occupy, as nearly as possible, the "same" place in the economy of the target language as the given source language category [or item] occupies in the source language' (Catford 1965: 32). Toury (2004: 208) distinguishes between obligatory and non-obligatory shifts. Obligatory shifts are linguistically motivated, while non-obligatory shifts can be due to the translator's literary, ideological or cultural considerations (cf. also Dukāte 2009: 52). According to van den Broeck (2014), only optional shifts can be studied as indicators of the 'translator's preoccupation with creating an "acceptable" target text, i.e. a text conforming to the norms of the target system' (van den Broeck 2014: 57).

This understanding of the difference between obligatory and non-obligatory shifts is in line with the general understanding of the difference between shift and manipulation. Obligatory shifts are not manipulation, because they are caused by linguistic constraints and therefore they are not ideologically motivated. Non-obligatory shifts can instead be the result of the translator's choice, can be motivated and, as such, they can indicate manipulation. However, Dukāte (2009) argues that manipulation can also be unconscious and not intentionally motivated by the translator, for example, as a result of 'the workings of human psyche' or of errors and mistakes (Dukāte 2009: 87). Linguistic and factual mistakes or ignorance on the part of the translator, although unintentional, can have manipulative effects. Dukāte (2009: 115) names this type of manipulation 'text-internal translational manipulation as unconscious distortion' and defines it as a 'manipulation due to the translator's lack of professionalism, and is manifested as errors, which seriously mislead the reader and distort the original text'.

The choice of translating *wilderness* and *darkness* with multiple terms, instead of using the same item, can be considered an error on part of the translators: they failed to recognize the importance of the reiteration, the function of the lexico-semantic patterns as a key device to make the fictional representation of the African jungle cohesive. Given the absence of an ideological motivation, this alteration could be easily dismissed as an example of linguistic shift. However, in line with Dukāte's (2009) definition of manipulation as unconscious distortion, I want to argue that this shift produces manipulative effects. If these alterations are seen in terms of the effect they produce on the target readership, as opposed to the reason why they were introduced in the first place, then it does not make any difference whether they are motivated or simply due to misrecognition. In both cases, they produce a distortion of the original text, from the point of view of the target reader. Without realising it, the translators modified a formal feature that is linked to a major theme in *HoD*. As a consequence, the way the reader perceives this theme can be affected. Whether the translators made this by mistake or by following a personal agenda, the effect would not be different for the target reader. In fact, as Dukāte (2009: 88) explains, 'an error or several errors can have a cumulative manipulative effect and as a result the text may seem to be factually, linguistically or ideologically manipulated'.

I would argue that the way manipulation has been generally regarded neglects the manipulative effects that even unconscious and/or unmotivated linguistic shifts can have. The outcome of this analysis suggests that manipulation can occur more elusively than is usually thought. Manipulative effects like the one discussed here may even be more common than what is usually defined as manipulation in translation studies research. This is simply because linguistic shifts occur in all sorts of translations, at different levels. Chapter 1 raised the question whether manipulation mainly occurs in contexts in which the balance of power between source culture and target culture is so uneven that a manipulative phenomenon is almost unavoidable (see Munday 2008 or Tymoczko 2010), as the literature on the topic seems to imply. My findings seem to suggest an alternative view: manipulative effects resulting from linguistic shifts can play an equally relevant role in altering the TTs as ideologically and/or politically motivated alterations do. Finally, the use of corpus methodologies to study manipulation allowed me to gain a linguistic close-up view of the phenomenon, showing concretely how lexical alterations can have manipulative effects, even when they are just the result of mere mistakes or misrecognitions.

5.5 Conclusion

This chapter demonstrated that the items resulting from the keyword analysis and categorization in Chapter 4 can be successfully analysed to establish a link between textual patterns and the fictional world. The study of the 'Africa words' showed how their use in *HoD* is interconnected to construct a cohesive fictional representation of the African jungle. The four words share the same semantic preferences and co-occur with related vocabulary: I argued that these lexico-semantic patterns (and the local textual function they jointly enact) are central to the interpretation of the theme 'Africa and its representation'. The chapter linked quantitative and qualitative analyses, showing both how the patterns develop throughout the entire text and how they are instantiated in individual textual extracts. This double perspective enhanced the understanding of the role that the lexical level of *HoD* plays in building the fictional world and triggering thematic concerns. I provided a detailed account of the precise stylistic tools that instantiate the fictional representation of the jungle as 'a place of darkness' and as a personified entity. These new insights into Conrad's writing were backed by the discussion of more traditional literary criticism.

The comparison of the TTs showed the effects of translation on the representation of the jungle. The analysis indicated that all four TTs maintain the dominant semantic fields identified in the original, probably as a result of a literal translation of Conrad's lexical choices. However, I argued that translating *wilderness* and *darkness* with multiple items disrupt the cohesive network that the original establishes, with a consequence on the overall cohesion of the TTs. In translation, the cohesion of the fictional representation of the African jungle is altered compared with the original; therefore, the jungle – its connection with *wilderness* and *darkness* – may be perceived less as a unitary fictional entity. The comparison also suggested that shifts and misrecognitions on the part of the translators can have manipulative effects. The corpus approach proved to be useful in illuminating this outcome, as it enabled me to look closely at the relation existing between alterations at the linguistic level and manipulations at the interpretative level.

'Black Things': The Fictional Representation of the African Natives

6.1 Introduction

This chapter examines how the African natives are linguistically represented in *HoD* and its four Italian translations. The investigation is based on the outcome of the keyword analysis (Chapter 4) and concentrates on the 'African words' (*nigger/niggers, negro, savage/savages, native/natives* and *black/blacks*).

This chapter is divided into two main parts. The first part (Section 6.2) focuses on the analysis of *HoD*. It begins, in Section 6.2.1, by investigating the usage of the 'African words' in the ST and compares their frequency in the reference corpora. It aims to test whether the frequency of the 'African words' in *HoD* is statistically deviant (Leech and Short 2007) compared with their frequency in CC and RC. Section 6.2.2 carries out a concordance analysis in order to identify the semantic preferences and prosodies of the items under investigation. It shows that the 'African words' and their lexico-semantic patterns play a central role in defining how the natives are represented in *HoD*. Specifically, it argues that these lexico-semantic patterns build up a dehumanizing fictional representation of the Africans (Section 6.2.3).

The second part of the chapter (Section 6.3) focuses on the analysis of the four Italian translations. To begin, Section 6.3.1 identifies, compares and discusses the translations of the 'African words'. Sections 6.3.1.1 to 6.3.1.5 concentrate on each 'African word' across the TTs, examining whether the translators' lexical choices produce a shift in the TT. In particular, these sections focus on those shifts that can intensify or mitigate the potential racist implications of the ST word. Section 6.3.2 discusses the general tendencies resulting from the individual yet repeated shifts, analysing their effect on the overall fictional representation of the Africans. It then investigates whether the TTs reproduce equivalent semantic preferences and prosodies as those identified in the ST, carrying out a concordance analysis of the Italian 'African words' (Section 6.3.3). Finally, Section 6.4 closes the chapter with a discussion of the findings.

6.2 The representation of the Africans in *Heart of Darkness*

Chapter 2 introduced 'race and racism' as a major theme in *HoD*, as well as one of the most debated issues by literary critics. I argued that the way the Africans are depicted in the text is central to the critical discussion of this theme. This section analyses the representation of the natives, through the examination of the 'African words'. First, it focuses on their specific use in *HoD* and the patterns they enact in context. Then, it discusses how the fictional construction of the Africans is related to the theme 'race and racism', linking the findings of the linguistic investigation to the literary debate.

6.2.1 Frequency comparison of the 'African words'

The analysis of the fictional representation of the Africans starts with a frequency comparison that aims to verify whether there is a deviance in the use of the 'African words' compared with their frequency in the reference corpora. Table 6.1 shows both raw and normalized frequencies in *HoD*, CC and RC. A log-likelihood test[1] is used to check whether the differences in frequency are statistically significant (*p*-value threshold = 0.0001). When statistically significant, the respective cell in the table is shaded in grey.

The frequencies in Table 6.1 refer to the total occurrences of the 'African words' in *HoD* and in the reference corpora, as opposed to the occurrences of the 'African words' referring specifically to the natives. This distinction concerns mainly *black*, as this word has a wider range of meanings compared to the other 'African words' and is used in ways other than referring to black people. *Black* is the most frequent item among the 'African words', occurring 42 times in *HoD*, but is used to refer to the Africans in 22 cases. With regard to the other 'African words', the distinction has minimal effect. *Savage* and *native* can be used as adjectives and can refer to something/someone other than the Africans, but this happens only a few times in *HoD* (cf. Section 6.2.2). *Blacks*, *savages* and *natives* are nouns and as such their range of use is restricted compared with the adjectival forms: they always refer to the Africans, except one occurrence of *savages*. Finally, *nigger*, *niggers* and *negro* are relevant in all cases because they

Table 6.1 *Frequency of the 'African words' in* HoD *and in the reference corpora*

	HoD		CC		LL HoD vs CC	RC		LL HoD vs RC
	Raw	Norm.*	Raw	Norm.	(*p* < 0.0001)	Raw	Norm.	(*p* < 0.0001)
nigger	5	0.13	43	0.02		12	0	
niggers	5	0.13	17	0.01		3	0	
Total	10	0.26	60	0.03	**21.63**	15	0	**60.52**
savage	13	0.33	152	0.09		145	0.03	
savages	9	0.23	35	0.02		41	0.01	
Total	22	0.56	187	0.11	**35.68**	186	0.04	**69.55**
negro	3	0.08	25	0.01	4.96	11	0	13.82
black	42	1.07	1,188	0.68		1,673	0.39	
blacks	1	0.02	5	0		5	0	
Total	43	1.10	1,193	0.68	8.08	1,678	0.40	**32.36**
native	2	0.05	140	0.08		199	0.05	
natives	5	0.13	43	0.02		49	0.01	
Total	7	0.18	183	0.10	1.63	248	0.06	6.14

*Normalization per 1,000 words

always refer to the Africans. The reason for not taking this distinction into consideration in Table 6.1 is that it would be very difficult and time-consuming to disambiguate the occurrences of *black* in the reference corpora. Even with the help of a part-of-speech tagger that distinguishes between nouns and adjectives, the results would still need to be checked manually in order to identify the occurrences that refer specifically to black people. This would involve analysing a very large number of concordance lines, given that *black* occurs more than 1,100 and 1,600 times in CC and RC, respectively.

With this in mind, Table 6.1 shows that all the normalized values are higher in *HoD* than in the reference corpora, although not all the differences are statistically significant. Starting from *nigger/niggers*, their frequency difference is significant: these items are used about 8 times more frequently in *HoD* than in CC and over 80 times more frequently than in RC. Similarly, a significant difference exists for *savage/savages*, used considerably more in *HoD* compared with both CC and RC. In contrast, the difference in the frequency of *black/blacks* is significant only when compared with that in the RC, but not when compared with CC. However, this is likely a result of the fact that the frequency count does not distinguish between *black/blacks* referring to black people and other uses of the words. Finally, there is no statistical significance in the frequency difference of *negro* and in the frequency difference of *native/natives*. In light of this, it can be said that a deviance exists in the use of *nigger/niggers* and *savage/savages* in *HoD*, compared with the two reference corpora, while the occurrence of *native/natives* and *negro* is in line with their expected frequency.

6.2.2　The 'African words' in context

Assigning prominence or literary relevance to a statistical deviance involves the identification of an 'artistically coherent pattern of choice' aimed at a 'particular literary end' (Leech and Short 2007: 40). This process goes beyond the identification of the deviance and requires the study of the deviant feature in its context. In this section, I carry out a concordance analysis of the 'African words', looking for the patterns they establish. Moreover, the concordance analysis allows me to identify and remove the occurrences that do not refer specifically to the Africans. Table 6.2 shows the outcome of this disambiguation, reporting the frequencies of only those cases in which the words do refer to the natives. This procedure has also enabled a further level of discrimination in the analysis. When used as an adjective, these terms can refer either to the Africans or to someone/something else. When referring to the Africans, these adjectives are still relevant to this study, while when referring to someone/something else they are not. It is therefore important to account for the former and exclude the latter. The concordance analysis made this distinction clear, showing when the 'African words' are used directly to refer to the natives and when they are instead used to refer to them indirectly, that is, as an attribute. For instance, in Example (1) *savage* is directly used as a noun to refer to a native:

(1)　And between whiles I had to look after the *savage* who was fireman. He was an improved specimen; he could fire up a vertical boiler.

Whereas, in Example (2) *black* is used as an adjective pre-modifying a noun that is not included in the 'African words' (*figure*). Although indirectly, *black* still refers to an African, as an attribute that specifies their physical appearance.

(2)　A *black* figure stood up, strode on long *black* legs, waving long *black* arms, across the glow.

The result of this analysis is summarized in Table 6.2. The table shows that, in the vast majority of cases, the 'African words' do refer to the natives, especially when they are used as nouns. *Savage* is mostly used as an attribute for the natives, while in 6 cases it does not refer to the natives at all (cf. Table 6.1). The only

Table 6.2 *Frequency of the 'African words' in* HoD *referring to the natives*

'African words'	Nouns	Attributes
nigger	5	0
niggers	5	0
savage	3	4
savages	8	0
negro	3	0
black	2	20
blacks	1	0
native	1	0
natives	5	0

item whose frequency displays a clear drop is, as expected, *black*. There are only 2 instances where it is used as a noun for a black person, while the remaining 20 occurrences are indirect references. Taking into consideration the use of the 'African words' as nouns to indicate directly a native (that is, excluding the attribute uses), a tendency can be identified: the African natives that populate the book's pages are more frequently called *nigger/niggers, negro* or *savage/savages* than *black/blacks* or *native/natives*.

With the non-relevant uses of the 'African words' removed, the remaining instances are examined in order to delineate their semantic and pragmatic profile. Similar to what I showed with the 'Africa words' (cf. Chapter 5), the concordance analysis of the 'African words' highlights the presence of four repeated semantic preferences, shared by all the items in the group. I call the first semantic field 'physicality'; see Figure 6.1. The 'physicality' semantic field includes body part words, such as *feet* (line 1), *body* (line 2) and *shoulder* (line 4), and also items referring more generally to the bodily appearance of the natives. In the sample of concordance lines in Figure 6.1, these are represented by *overfed* (line 3), *footsore* (line 5) and *broad-chested* (line 6).

The second semantic field is labelled 'collectives' as it includes collective nouns used to refer to the African natives as a homogeneous group, as opposed to different individuals. This is illustrated in Figure 6.2 with the words *crowd* (lines 2 and 6), *band* (line 3), *strings* (line 4) and *lot* (line 5).

The third semantic field is called 'incomprehensibility'. This field collects words referring to the sounds produced by the natives, perceived by the non-natives as non-language and incomprehensible. For example, in Figure 6.3, this field is represented by *groaned* (line 2), *moaned* (line 3), *yells* (line 4) and *howling* (line 6). This field also includes terms that indicate directly this lack of

1	was in a muddle--heads, things, buildings. Strings of dusty niggers with splay feet arrived and departed; a stream of
2	any road or any upkeep, unless the body of a middle-aged negro, with a bullet-hole in the forehead, upon which I
3	uncivil. He was quiet. He allowed his 'boy'--an overfed young negro from the coast--to treat the white men, under his very
4	to fasten them with. And every week the messenger, a long negro, letter-bag on shoulder and staff in hand, left our
5	impressed pilgrims. A quarrelsome band of footsore sulky niggers trod on the heels of the donkey; a lot of tents,
6	to their satisfaction. Their headman, a young, broad-chested black, severely draped in dark-blue fringed cloths, with

Figure 6.1 *'Physicality' semantic field*

2	his self-respect in some way. Therefore he whacked the old nigger mercilessly, while a big crowd of his people watched
3	impressed pilgrims. A quarrelsome band of footsore sulky niggers trod on the heels of the donkey; a lot of tents,
4	was in a muddle--heads, things, buildings. Strings of dusty niggers with splay feet arrived and departed; a stream of
5	had cleared out a long time ago. Well, if a lot of mysterious niggers armed with all kinds of fearful weapons suddenly
6	, and almost at the same time I noticed that the crowd of savages was vanishing without any perceptible movement

Figure 6.2 *'Collectives' semantic field*

2	of hissing; steam ascended in the moonlight, the beaten nigger groaned somewhere. 'What a row the brute makes!'
3	greatness, the amazing reality of its concealed life. The hurt nigger moaned feebly somewhere near by, and then
4	rush walls, of peaked grass-roofs, a burst of yells, a whirl of black limbs, a mass of hands clapping of feet stamping, of
5	foliage. The steamer toiled along slowly on the edge of a black and incomprehensible frenzy. The prehistoric man
6	, even such as I had noticed in the howling sorrow of these savages in the bush. I couldn't have felt more of lonely

Figure 6.3 *'Incomprehensibility' semantic field*

4	, even such as I had noticed in the howling sorrow of these savages in the bush. I couldn't have felt more of lonely
5	of noise and smoke when I made a dash at the wheel. The fool-nigger had dropped everything, to throw the shutter open
6	of hissing; steam ascended in the moonlight, the beaten nigger groaned somewhere. 'What a row the brute makes!'
7	glance, with that complete, deathlike indifference of unhappy savages. Behind this raw matter one of the reclaimed, the
8	his self-respect in some way. Therefore he whacked the old nigger mercilessly, while a big crowd of his people watched

Figure 6.4 *'General negative' semantic field*

comprehension between the colonizers and the natives, for instance, *incomprehensible* in line 5.

Finally, the largest semantic field, 'general negative' (Figure 6.4), gathers a wide variety of words that have negative implications. It includes terms referring to specific negative actions (*whacked* and *beaten*, lines 8 and 6, respectively), negative descriptions (*unhappy* and *fool*, lines 7 and 5) and also words indicating negative states or feelings (*indifference* and *sorrow*, lines 7 and 4).

Table 6.3 collects all the collocates of *nigger/niggers*, *savage/savages*, *negro*, *native/natives* and *black/blacks* in a span of 5:5 that form part of the 'physicality', 'collectives', 'incomprehensibility' and 'general negative' semantic fields.

In addition to the four shared semantic preferences, another pattern emerges from the concordance analysis, related to *black*. As indicated in Table 6.2, *black* is used only twice as a noun to refer to a black person, while in the majority of cases (20 occurrences) it refers to the natives indirectly, as an attribute. Specifically, *black* often occurs in the construction '*black*[ADJ] + common

Table 6.3 *Collocates of the 'African words' belonging to the four semantic fields*

'Physicality'
feet, footsore, old, body, middle-aged, overfed, young, long, shoulder, head, broad-chested, athletic, neck, necked, limbs, hands, legs, arms, eyelids, wild-eyed, face, bones.

'Collectives'
crowd (2), strings, lot, band, camp, picket, tribe, file.

'Incomprehensibility'
howling, mysterious, groaned, row, moaned, yells, incomprehensible, frenzy.

'General negative'
beaten (2), hate (2), suppression (2), unrestrained, grief, sorrow, deathlike, indifference, unhappy, death, dusty, quarrelsome, sulky, hurt, fool, whacked, mercilessly, enemies, scuffle, insolent, disease, listlessly, starvation.

*Frequency, when ≥ 2, in brackets.

noun', such as *black figure* in Example (2). Figure 6.5 shows all 20 occurrences of *black* as an attribute. It can be noted that *black* does not co-occur only with words that are usually employed to indicate men or women, as in *black men* (line 1), *black fellows* (lines 2, 8 and 12) and *black people* (lines 4 and 9). Rather, it occurs more frequently with abstract terms, for example, *figure/figures* (lines 3 and 14), or even with items that can hardly be considered synonyms of *men*, *fellows* or *people*: *whirl of black limbs* (line 5), *black things* (line 7), *black bones* (line 10), *black shadows* (line 11) and *black shapes* (line 13). This pattern is also observed by Kujawska-Lis (2008), though her study does not provide any quantification to support the claim. Kujawska-Lis (2008: 168) hypothesizes that Conrad might have preferred to use a vocabulary that emphasized clearly the belonging to the native race, such as *nigger* and *negro*, limiting the use of *black* to 'metaphorical' meanings, as in the constructions shown in Figure 6.5.

Overall, the textual behaviour of the 'African words' is, in some respects, similar to that of the 'Africa words' (cf. Section 5.2.3). In this case too, when the reader comes across *nigger/niggers*, *savage/savages*, *negro*, *native/natives* and *black/blacks*, they often find these words within the same semantic fields in their contexts of occurrence. This repeated lexico-semantic pattern, when maintained throughout the whole text, establishes a persistent fictional representation. The depiction of the Africans emphasizes their body and bodily appearance, rather than what they think or feel; there is a tendency to refer to them as a homogeneous and undistinguished group, rather than as individuals; they are represented as producing unintelligible noises that are impossible to comprehend; finally, they are associated with negative and unpleasant situations or states of

1	"A slight clinking behind me made me turn my head. Six blackADJ] men advanced in a file, toiling up the path.
2	the contrast of expressions of the white men and of the blackADJ] fellows of our crew, who were as much
3	out suddenly, and we went outside. The moon had risen. BlackADJ] figures strolled about listlessly, pouring water
4	scene of inhabited devastation. A lot of people, mostly blackADJ] and naked, moved about like ants. A jetty
5	walls, of peaked grass-roofs, a burst of yells, a whirl of blackADJ] limbs, a mass of hands clapping of feet
6	deliberately to the first I had seen--and there it was, blackADJ], dried, sunken, with closed eyelids--a head
7	blue space, sparkling with dew and starlight, in which blackADJ] things stood very still. I thought I could see a
8	discretion with great gravity. 'I have a canoe and three blackADJ] fellows waiting not very far. I am off. Could you
9	path was steep. A horn tooted to the right, and I saw the blackADJ] people run. A heavy and dull detonation shook
10	Then, glancing down, I saw a face near my hand. The blackADJ] bones reclined at full length with one shoulder
11	not criminals, they were nothing earthly now--nothing but blackADJ] shadows of disease and starvation, lying
12	one a momentary contact with reality. It was paddled by blackADJ] fellows. You could see from afar the white of
13	of the launched earth had suddenly become audible. "BlackADJ] shapes crouched, lay, sat between the trees
14	We were within thirty yards from the nearest fire. A blackADJ] figure stood up, strode on long blackADJ] legs,
15	foliage. The steamer toiled along slowly on the edge of a blackADJ] and incomprehensible frenzy. The prehistoric
16	stood up, strode on long blackADJ] legs, waving long blackADJ] arms, across the glow. It had horns--antelope
17	nearest fire. A blackADJ] figure stood up, strode on long blackADJ] legs, waving long blackADJ] arms, across the
18	and faces. Suddenly the manager's boy put his insolent blackADJ] head in the doorway, and said in a tone of
19	idea at all connected with it? It looked startling round his blackADJ] neck, this bit of white thread from beyond the
20	not hear, he frowned heavily, and that frown gave to his blackADJ] death-mask an inconceivably sombre, brooding,

Figure 6.5 *Concordance lines of* black *used as an adjective*

mind. These semantic preferences, and the resulting negative semantic prosody, build a dehumanizing fictional representation of the African natives, which closely mirrors Achebe's (1990) interpretation.

6.2.3 Dehumanization in the fictional representation of the natives

In Chapter 2, I argued that one of the key points on which Achebe's (1990) criticism hinges is the way African natives are portrayed in *HoD*. The passages in which they appear are, according to this critic, the 'most revealing' (Achebe 1990: 5) of Conrad's racist attitude. Natives' descriptions emphasize the physicality of their appearance, and never reveal their inner thoughts or psychology; descriptions in which they are not 'just limbs or rolling eyes' are in fact rare (Achebe 1990: 6). They are deprived of human expression and language altogether (Achebe 1990: 8), babbling and grunting frenziedly even among themselves. They disappear, from the general picture, as human factor and are reduced to the role of props (Achebe 1990: 12). In the final analysis, Achebe (1990: 12) claims that Africans are dehumanized in the text and that *HoD* is a novel that celebrates this dehumanization.

The question of dehumanization has been touched upon by many other scholars, who agree and disagree on this issue similarly to the way critics agreed and disagreed with Achebe's (1990) overall argument. For example, prior to Achebe's

(1990) public lecture, Curle (1914) praises Conrad's skills in representing non-European people as neither dehumanized nor Europeanized (Curle 1914: 121, cf. Chapter 2 for more details). Hawkins (2006), in contrast, agrees with Achebe (1990) and recognizes dehumanization in *HoD*. The dehumanizing tendencies he identifies (Hawkins 2006: 366) are also very similar to those pointed out by Achebe (1990): none of the natives have a proper name; none of them are given more than one paragraph (apart from Kurtz's assumed African mistress); and there is no representation of their thoughts or points of view, partly because they never speak, apart from four pidgin sentences in the whole text. Lawtoo (2012) also identifies the presence of dehumanization in the representation of the natives, although the way he points it out is less straightforward. He simply maintains that the text oscillates continuously back and forth 'between racist injunctions that dehumanize racial others and repeated attempts to nuance such racist distinctions' (Lawtoo 2012: 248).

The semantic preferences and prosody discussed in the previous section instantiate linguistically that dehumanizing process Achebe (1990), Hawkins (2006) and Lawtoo (2012) recognize. What is more, the semantic fields identified match quite accurately what the critics referred to when breaking down the dehumanization into specific tendencies or attitudes. The 'physicality' semantic field reflects the representative focus on the Africans' bodily appearance and materiality as opposed to their consciousness. An instance of this tendency is provided in Example (2) (included also in Figure 6.5, line 14), where the description returns insistently to the native's black limbs (*black legs, black arms*), stressing his physical appearance. This fictional representation is enacted so pervasively throughout the text that it is possible to identify further instantiations also in extracts other than those taken into account with the concordance analysis. Instances of dehumanization (or the emphasis on physical description, as in this case) are recognizable also where the natives are referred to in terms other than the 'African words' or in portions of the text longer than the 5:5 span accounted for in the creation of the semantic fields. Consider Example (3).

(3)   Then, glancing down, I saw a *face* near my hand. The *black bones* reclined at full length with one *shoulder* against the tree, and slowly the *eyelids* rose and the sunken *eyes* looked up at me, enormous and vacant, a kind of blind, white flicker in the depths of the *orbs*, which died out slowly.

For the identification of the 'physicality', 'collectives', 'incomprehensibility' and 'general negative' semantic fields, a span of 5:5 was adopted, that is, only words that occurred within the limit of five words to the left and five words to the right of the core were counted. In the case of Example (3), only *face* and *bones* were included in the 'physicality' semantic field, as they occur in a span of 5:5 from *black*. However, the stress on the bodily description is not limited to these two items. Extending the analysis to the whole passage, it can be noted that all of the references to the African are related to a part of his body – besides *face* and *bones*, there is also *shoulder, eyelids, eyes* and *orbs*. This extract also evokes the familiar metaphor associated with the eyes, 'the eyes are the mirror of the soul', in order to subvert it and to intensify the focus on the body. The eyes are usually seen as providing access beyond the exterior appearance of an individual to the inner self and spirit. In Example (3), Marlow looks at the African's face but, when the eyelids slowly rise, he only sees an enormous, blinding void, as if there is nothing to grasp inside that bodily shell, as if there is no soul inside to be mirrored in the orbs of that figure.

In Vermeule's (2010) definition of 'mind blindness' – one of the commonest tropes of dehumanization – the deprivation of mind takes centre stage: 'the point is to deny other people the perspective of rational agency by turning them into animals, machines, or anything without a mind' (Vermeule 2010: 195). The emphasis on the 'limbs or rolling eyes' (Achebe 1990: 6) subordinates the mind of the natives to their physical appearance, or even denies its presence altogether. This effect is corroborated by the natives' lack of language, as pointed out by Achebe (1990: 8) and Hawkins (2006: 366), and as reflected by the 'incomprehensibility' semantic field. The present analysis shows that the Africans, rather than speaking, moan (Figure 6.3, line 3), yell (line 4), frenzy (line 5) or howl (line 6). Depriving the natives of language not only undermines their cognitive ability, but questions their very humanity by implying that they are closer to howling and frenzied beasts than people.

Again, this tendency is easily recognizable in extended contexts, within passages that were not looked at through the concordance analysis, because no 'African word' appears in them. For instance, Example (4) is taken from the final part of the text: Marlow, after having taken Kurtz on board, is sailing out of the station, while a group of natives stare puzzled at the steamer.

(4)   When we came abreast again, they faced the river, stamped their feet, nodded their horned heads, swayed their scarlet bodies; [. . .] they *shouted* periodically together strings of *amazing words* that resembled *no sounds of human language*; and the deep *murmurs* of the crowd, interrupted suddenly, were like the responses of some *satanic litany*. [. . .] There was an eddy in the mass of human bodies, and the woman

with helmeted head and tawny cheeks rushed out to the very brink of
the stream. She put out her hands, *shouted* something, and all that wild
mob took up the *shout* in a *roaring chorus* of *articulated, rapid, breathless
utterance.*
'Do you understand this?' I asked.

'Do you understand this?' (Conrad [1902] 1994: 96), a bewildered Marlow
asks Kurtz, after witnessing what seems to him to be an incomprehensible
frenzy. The way Marlow describes it in Example (4) makes it clear: these shouts
resemble *no sounds of human language.* In just a few lines, this passage gathers
many items that would fit perfectly the 'incomprehensibility' semantic field.
The natives *shouted* and produced *murmurs*, as well as *a roaring chorus* of
amazing words and *breathless utterances* that for Marlow and his crew sound
almost like a *satanic litany.* This proves further that the tendencies unveiled
by the concordance analysis are used pervasively throughout the text, and not
just in the short contexts of the concordance lines. What is more, this extract
shows how the various aspects of the fictional representation, the four semantic preferences, interact and co-occur. The 'physicality' semantic field and its
focus on the bodily appearance are also clearly notable in Example (4). The
fictional representation of the natives stresses again their physical exteriority
– their *bodies*, stamping *feet* and *horned heads*; and in the case of the woman,
her *head*, *cheeks* and *hands*.

The extract in Example (4) shows also another one of the tendencies signalled
by the critics as contributing to the dehumanization, and similarly represented
by one of the semantic fields identified: the tendency to refer to the Africans
as a homogeneous group instead of individuals, instantiated by the 'collectives'
field. The natives are referred to as *crowd*, *mass* and *wild mob* in Example (4).
Hawkins's (2006: 366) observation that no native is referred to with a proper
noun is related to this, as proper nouns signal individuality and uniqueness; on
the contrary, this uniqueness is lost in a collective noun, which merges together
differences and individualities until they are homogenously flat. Example
(5) shows another instance of this process in a passage not accounted for in the
concordance analysis as, again, no 'African words' occur in it.

(5)   When next day we left at noon, the *crowd*, of whose presence behind the
      curtain of trees I had been acutely conscious all the time, flowed out of the
      woods again, filled the clearing, covered the slope with a *mass* of naked,
      breathing, quivering, bronze bodies.

Crowd and *mass* are the collective nouns used in this extract to refer to the natives. The image conveyed in Example (5) is that of a homogeneous fluid that pours out of the forest, with lexical choices such as *flowed, filled* and *covered* enacting this image. This indistinct and indistinguishable *crowd* fills the slope with *a mass of naked, breathing, quivering, bronze bodies*, recalling again the emphasis on the natives' physicality.

Finally, the 'general negative' semantic field does not represent directly any of the observations made by the critics. There is no specific tendency or aspect of the dehumanization that mirrors it, in contrast to the other three fields that instead seem to be direct linguistic instantiations of the dehumanizing attitudes identified by Achebe (1990) and Hawkins (2006). Nevertheless, the 'general negative' field acts as the adhesive for the other tendencies. It is the largest field and is widely spread across the whole text, sometimes occurring simultaneously with the other fields. This strengthens the negative semantic prosody that the 'African words' – or the overall fictional representation of the Africans in general – possess.

According to Vermeule (2010), mind blindness, or dehumanization in general, is a tool of emotional dominance, common in the context of war or oppression where opposing groups of people demonize each other. Moral conventions and social behaviours are valid and shared within one group, but tend to be overlooked or totally negated to the opposing group. When dehumanization takes place, 'the members of the hated countergroup do not count as human, and therefore moral rules do not apply to them' (Vermeule 2010: 195). This could happen for many reasons: from the intellectual stimulation that this process might encompass to the need to show what an individual is really like by comparing them to something other than human. However, Vermeule (2010: 200) asserts that the most important reason why dehumanization happens is to 'assert mastery over the other person'. In fact, shifting the ontological status of a person from a civilized and rational human being to a brute, animal or machine facilitates that process of moral justification necessary to perpetrate domination. This is especially true in the context of colonial domination, where the motif of the 'civilising mission' was the constant hypocrisy which legitimated seeing 'those who have a different complexion or slightly flatter noses than ourselves' (Conrad [1902] 1994: 10) as 'sullen peoples, half devil and half child' (Kipling [1899] 2013: 111) in need of guidance and authority. In light of this, the dehumanizing representation of the African natives in *HoD* can be seen as a reflection of that 'emotional dominance' that the colonizers impose on the colonized. Its linguistic instantiation – the semantic preferences and prosody – echoes that socioculturally established and generally accepted vision of the non-European other as intellectually inferior and emotionally unstable, driven by instinct rather than reason and underdeveloped on a scale of assumed civilization.

6.3 The comparison of the translations

This section compares the TTs on the basis of the findings of the ST analysis. First, Section 6.3.1 studies the translators' lexical choices to translate each of the 'African words'. Second, Section 6.3.2 takes into account all the lexical choices together in order to analyse whether they constitute an overall tendency in the TTs. Finally, Section 6.3.3 examines the semantic preferences and prosody of the Italian 'African words' and compares them with the ones in the original. The overarching aim of Section 6.3 is to study the consequences of the TT textual alterations on the fictional representation of the African natives, and how these can affect the theme 'race and racism'.

The comparison between the ST and the TTs revolves around the identification of shifts in the translators' lexical choices, that is, whether the translators opted for a word other than the closest equivalent to translate the 'African words'. For example, the direct equivalent of *nigger* in Italian is *negro*. A shift would occur if a word other than *negro* (nigger) is used to translate *nigger*, like *nero* (black). When repeated, shifts like this can be indicative of manipulative phenomena, therefore they are relevant to study translation manipulation. This approach, based on the analysis of shifts, has been followed by other studies with similar aims. For instance, in Section 4.5.2, I discussed a study by Kujawska-Lis (2008: 167) in which she looks at shifts in the translation of *HoD* into Polish. She focuses on terms that can be related to the accusation of racism, for example, *black*, *savage*, *nigger* and *negro*. She compares two Polish translations to test whether Achebe's (1990) criticisms affected the translators' lexical choices. Kujawska-Lis (2008: 169) shows that, in the early translation, *nigger* is translated with the Polish *Murzyn*, which simply describes a person of black African race. However, in the modern translation, *nigger* is translated with its Polish equivalent, *czarnuch*. She argues that, in the case of the early translation, a neutral target language term (*Murzyn*) is used to replace an abusive ST item (*nigger*), while in the case of the modern translation, the abusive word is translated with its similarly abusive Polish equivalent (*czarnuch*): these choices are seen as having the potential to affect the perception of the text as racist at the lexical level (Kujawska-Lis 2008: 169).

A similar method is adopted by Trupej (2012) in a comparative study of the translation of *nigger* in two Slovenian versions of Mark Twain's *Adventures of Huckleberry Finn*, one from 1948 and the other from 1962. Trupej (2012: 93) examines shifts in the translation of *nigger* and discusses the effects they have on the construction of characters and plot in the TTs. The 1948 translation displays numerous instances of translational shifts, as the terms chosen to translate *nigger* intensify the racist discourse (Trupej 2012: 98). *Nigger* is replaced with items such as *prekleti črni ubijalec* (damned black killer), *smrdljiva črna drhal* (stinking black rabble) or *črni malopridneži* (black good-for-nothing). In other cases, the personal pronoun *he* is replaced by *zamorec*, the Slovenian equivalent of *nigger* (Trupej 2012: 98). Trupej (2012: 99) defines these shifts as 'explicit intensifications of racist discourse' and argues that, as a consequence of them, both positive and negative characters appear more racist in translation. On the other hand, in the 1962 TT, *nigger* is often omitted, replaced by a personal pronoun, or by *črnec*, the Slovenian neutral term for black person (Trupej 2012: 101). Trupej (2012: 102) considers these shifts as 'less severe' lexical choices that 'significantly reduce the severity of the racism displayed in the novel'.

Another example of this methodology is provided by Mouka et al. (2015), who employ corpus tools to explore shifts in the context of racist discourse in film translation. Except for their use of corpora, Mouka et al.'s (2015) approach is similar to Kujawska-Lis's (2008) and Trupej's (2012): they compare the ST with the TTs in order to identify shifts, which are then classified as neutral transfer, over-toning or under-toning, depending on the translators' lexical choices (Mouka et al. 2015). Corpus tools are used to retrieve the examples of racist discourse from the films analysed, while reference corpora are employed to help interpret how racist markers are used in the cross-linguistic contexts. Their analysis focuses on five films (*Do the Right Thing, American History X, Monster's Ball, Crash* and *This is England*) and their Spanish and Greek translations. Some of the shifts they discuss are related to the word *nigger*. For example, they look at a passage from *American History X, We'll let the niggers, kikes and spics grab for their piece of the pie* and its Spanish translation, *Dejemos que negros y latinos se llevan su parte* (Let the blacks and Latinos get their part). They mark the use of *nigger* in the original as 'highly negative' (Mouka et al. 2015: 60), while considering *negros* (blacks) a shift that neutralizes the derogatory connotation of the original utterance. Evaluating all the shifts in a similar fashion, they conclude that the general tendency in their data is to mitigate or omit racial slurs, although some instances of over-toning are identified as well (Mouka et al. 2015: 63).

In line with these studies, I compare *HoD* with the four TTs to identify shifts in the translation of the 'African words'. When a shift is recognized, it is assessed whether it intensifies or mitigates the potential racist implications of the original ST item. In order to help me assess whether a shift can affect the potential racist implication of the Italian direct equivalent of the 'African words', additional corpus evidence is employed, in the form of the Italian reference corpus itTenTen (Jakubíček et al. 2013, cf. Section 3.3.2). itTenTen is used to check the contexts in which the 'African words' occur in Italian, so as to provide a better understanding of the potential racist implications of the Italian 'African words'.

6.3.1 The 'African words' in translation

To start with, I compare the ST and the TTs in order to identify the translations of the 'African words'. Only the items referring to the Africans have been taken into consideration (those counted in Table 6.2), independent of whether they are used as a noun to refer directly to a native or as an adjective, used as an attribute. The Italian translations of the 'African words' are shown in Table 6.4. The following sections focus on each of them individually.

6.3.1.1 *Nigger/niggers*

Starting with *nigger/niggers*, all TTs but Translation G opt for its direct Italian equivalent, *negro/negri* (nigger/niggers). In the case of Translation G, a shift is recognizable, for the ST item is replaced with *nero/neri* (black/blacks). In line with Kujawska-Lis (2008), Trupej (2012) and Mouka et al. (2015), I consider translating *nigger/niggers* with *nero/neri* (black/blacks) a shift that mitigates the potential racist implications of the original term. *Nigger* has been considered 'the most socially consequential racial insult' (Kennedy 2002: 32). As a result of its ties with the practice of slavery, *nigger* has been perceived as a 'highly offensive racial insult' since 1800 (Hughes 2006: 327). The salience of its social consequences when used as an ethnical slur is witnessed by the fact that *nigger* figures in the reports of the US Supreme Court in episodes concerning racially motivated violence or arson since 1871 (Kennedy 2002: 33). In 1899, when *HoD* was first published, *nigger* was already changing from 'only mildly insulting' to a stigmatizing term, a 'genuin[e] taboo' (Hughes 2006: 25). *Nero* (black), on the other hand, is considered in contemporary Italian to be a neutral term, the

Table 6.4 *'African words" and their frequency in the TTs*

HoD		Trans. S		Trans. B		Trans. M		Trans. G	
nigger	5	negro	5	negro	5	negro	5	nero	5
niggers	5	negri	5	negri	5	negri	5	neri	5
savage	7	selvaggio	7	selvaggio	6	selvaggio	7	selvaggio	7
				indigeno	1				
savages	8	selvaggi	8	selvaggi	7	selvaggi	8	selvaggi	8
				indigeni	1				
negro	3	negro	3	negro	2	negro	2	nero	3
				giovane di colore	1	negretto	1		
native	1	indigene	1	indigene	1	indigena	1	indigene	1
natives	5	indigeni	5	indigeni	5	indigeni	5	indigeni	5
black	22	nera/e/i/o/issime	14	nera/o/e/i	16	nera/e/i/o	17	neri/e/a/o	22
		negro/i	7	negro/i	5	negro/i	5		
				giovane di colore	1				
blacks	1	negri	1	negri	1	negri	1	neri	1
Total	57		56		57		57		57

*negro/negri (nigger/niggers), selvaggio/selvaggi (savage/savages), indigeno/indigena/indigeni/indigene (native/natives), nero/nera/neri/nere/nerissime (black/blacks/very black), negretto (little nigger), giovane di colore (young person of colour).

choice of which is strongly preferred to *negro* (nigger) when used to refer to a black person (*Vocabolario Treccani* 2015, www.treccani.it/vocabolario).

Examining the usage of the two Italian words in the itTenTen corpus, there are noticeable differences. First, *negro* (nigger) occurs as a noun 4,655 times (1.51 times per million words, pmw), while *nero* (black) occurs as a noun 13,500 times (4.39 pmw): the latter is much more frequently used than the former. Second, *negro* (nigger) and *nero* (black) display very different collocational relationships. Collocations are calculated setting a span of 5:5 and a minimum frequency of 5, using three different statistics: MI, log-likelihood and logDice. See Figure 6.6 for a comparison of the collocations of *negro* (nigger) and *nero* (black) as nouns. Excluding proper names (those with the first letter capitalized), the vast majority of the collocates of *negro* (nigger) suggest that this word is used derogatively. It occurs frequently with a wide range of insults, from homophobic and sexist (*frocio*, faggot; *finocchio*, queer; *troia*, bitch) to general ones (*sporco*, dirty; *coglione*, asshole; *lurido*, filthy; *bastardo*, bastard). The left-side table also includes *merda* (shit), which refers to the phrase *negro di merda* (literally 'nigger

	Frequency	MI	log likelihood	logDice		Frequency	MI	log likelihood	logDice
P | N negro	142	14.035	2,486.949	8.827	P | N seppia	497	15.067	9,484.793	9.921
P | N Babo	52	16.825	1,119.194	8.427	P | N Avola	132	13.406	2,196.853	8.054
P | N sporco	265	12.914	4,232.776	8.311	P | N affitti	135	11.410	1,868.458	7.478
P | N Sporco	35	16.025	711.446	7.841	P | N bianco	1,002	10.336	12,437.414	7.432
P | N Hoango	16	17.842	370.329	6.802	P | N ft	75	13.522	1,260.296	7.361
P | N Carmaux	18	13.482	300.802	6.694	P | N vestita	125	11.072	1,671.088	7.259
P | N zingaro	24	12.338	362.821	6.671	P | N Donne	252	10.467	3,159.379	7.255
P | N nigger	15	15.807	300.076	6.670	P | N avola	55	15.405	1,075.971	7.030
P | N merda	137	11.137	1,845.788	6.645	P | N vestite	72	11.529	1,008.068	6.952
P | N frocio	20	12.664	311.409	6.614	P | N corvino	51	15.074	972.081	6.916
P | N blanco	14	15.309	270.034	6.554	P | N vestito	192	10.023	2,287.845	6.823
P | N schiavo	45	11.298	615.421	6.484	P | N grigio	155	10.118	1,866.822	6.809
P | N ebreo	65	10.976	860.209	6.357	P | N illustraz	42	15.358	818.579	6.647
P | N terrone	15	12.757	235.492	6.335	P | N marrone	59	10.237	719.952	6.294
P | N abbronzato	16	12.121	237.013	6.221	P | N scuro	87	9.581	982.594	6.177
P | N schiaccio	11	13.609	185.761	6.105	P | N vestiti	138	9.323	1,509.791	6.174
P | N Emmanuel	17	11.519	237.608	6.037	P | N rosso	346	9.058	3,663.945	6.134
P | N Negro	16	11.465	225.987	6.033	P | N emersione	44	9.941	518.812	5.927
P | N scappato	23	11.061	306.880	6.000	P | N ontano	26	13.199	424.898	5.914
P | N bovero	9	18.256	214.957	5.979	P | N t.e	24	15.829	485.404	5.854
P | N puzzi	9	13.637	152.336	5.847	P | N seppie	28	11.398	386.835	5.854
P | N Narciso	14	11.381	192.999	5.819	P | N dissolvenza	26	12.111	385.079	5.843
P | N spiritual	9	13.118	145.814	5.792	P | N nero	372	8.736	3,773.920	5.843
P | N coglione	21	10.674	268.916	5.709	P | N risotto	35	10.098	420.277	5.786
P | N spirituals	7	14.407	126.049	5.558	P | N lutto	57	9.242	616.873	5.740
P | N negri	14	10.740	180.537	5.510	P | N spaghetti	39	9.725	448.154	5.735
P | N amburghese	7	13.545	117.585	5.508	P | N israeliane	36	9.883	421.562	5.732
P | N fuggiasco	8	12.197	119.346	5.503	P | N tavv	22	13.181	358.943	5.682
P | N mulatto	7	13.441	116.564	5.499	P | N Attiva	25	10.753	322.932	5.608
P | N negra	8	12.006	117.214	5.464	P | N Colore	30	9.971	354.940	5.597
P | N Atufal	6	17.919	139.656	5.395	P | N lucente	24	10.538	302.830	5.517
P | N Bernard-Marie	6	16.305	124.392	5.385	P | N tinge	22	10.685	282.095	5.445
P | N Scontro	9	11.229	122.154	5.369	P | N intenso	97	8.526	953.877	5.435
P | N grido	49	9.882	573.971	5.364	P | N tagliolini	19	11.953	277.215	5.415
P | N erculeo	6	14.842	111.735	5.359	P | N Belgrado	30	9.281	326.237	5.327
P | N Balotelli	17	10.086	203.820	5.215	P | N blu	125	8.321	1,193.960	5.319
P | N indio	7	11.558	98.203	5.212	P | N giallo	95	8.390	916.256	5.317
P | N dispregiativo	7	11.545	98.084	5.209	P | N lucido	36	8.994	377.165	5.317
P | N troia	10	10.618	127.249	5.209	P | N argento	83	8.396	801.240	5.287
P | N seminaba	5	18.849	125.645	5.135	P | N colore	248	8.110	2,298.785	5.219
P | N Zumbon	5	17.486	112.750	5.132	P | N manodopera	38	8.707	383.043	5.185
P | N veluto	5	17.197	110.438	5.131	P | N vestirsi	21	9.638	238.729	5.140
P | N Masserelli	5	15.984	101.304	5.122	P | N sfumature	44	8.566	431.301	5.133
P | N semen	5	15.486	97.704	5.115	P | N tonalità	33	8.742	334.240	5.122
P | N gridandogli	5	14.156	88.270	5.082	P | N xilografie	15	12.215	224.346	5.111
P | N lurido	6	11.700	85.360	5.071	P | N sottopagati	16	11.048	213.242	5.106
P | N m.	49	9.509	548.650	5.031	P | N Troia	23	9.285	250.227	5.105
P | N bastardo	12	10.066	143.518	5.027	P | N inchiostro	31	8.762	314.813	5.092
P | N xxxxxxxxxx	5	13.125	81.049	5.027	P | N lavoretti	17	10.332	209.627	5.077
P | N finocchio	8	10.423	99.640	4.946	P | N tavole	57	8.183	533.320	5.004

Figure 6.6 *Collocates of* negro *(left side) and* nero *(right side)*

of shit'), *schiavo* (slave) and *puzzi* (you smell). *Negro* (nigger) seems also to be related to other ethnical/racial slurs: it occurs with *zingaro* (gypsy), *ebreo* (Jew) and *terrone* (derogatory term for a southern Italian).

In contrast, *nero* (black) does not seem to be used in similar contexts. The collocates in the right-side table refer mainly to the semantic field of colours (*bianco*, white; *grigio*, grey; *marrone*, brown; *rosso*, red; *colore*, colour; *giallo*, yellow; *blu*, blue; *argento*, silver), clothes (*vestita/vestite/vestito/vestiti*, dressed/ dress/dresses), and art/photography (*dissolvenza*, fade-out; *sfumature*, hues; *tonalità*, shades; *xilografie*, xylographies; *inchiostro*, ink; *tavole*, figures). These collocates reflect the wider variety of uses of *nero* (black) as a noun, rather than indicating that it is used as a neutral word to refer to a black person. In this respect, using corpus evidence to support the difference of usage between *negro* (nigger) and *nero* (black) has some limitations. As acknowledged by Mouka et al. (2015: 64), reference corpora do not always provide evidence for ambiguous terms such as *nero* (black); for their analysis, the examination of the item in its specific contexts of use may be more revealing. Yet, the comparison of *negro* (nigger) and *nero* (black) in itTenTen has been very insightful, as it has shown that *negro* (nigger) is used in very derogatory contexts while *nero* (black) is not. This corpus evidence can therefore be considered to further support the argument that the translation shift from *nigger* to *nero* (black) mitigates the potential racist implications of the ST word.

6.3.1.2 *Savage/savages*

Savage and *savages* are translated into their direct Italian equivalents (*selvaggio* and *selvaggi*) in all four TTs, apart from one case for each item in Translation B, where *savage* is substituted for *indigeno* (native) and *savages* for *indigeni* (natives). According to Hughes (2006: 147), general terms like *savage* can reflect the prejudicial superiority of the 'home' culture over the assumed savagery of outsiders. Similarly, *native* can be seen – especially in the context of colonialism – as a label that generalizes and homogenizes the colonized other, independently from their specific identity and nationality, as opposed to *European*, for example (Hughes 2006: 148). Therefore, both can have derogatory implications, depending on their context of usage, in English as well as in Italian.

Using itTenTen to check whether there are marked differences in the usage of *selvaggio* (savages) and *indigeno* (native) provides little evidence of distinct contexts of use. Therefore, it seems safe to assume that, although replacing *savage/savages* with *indigeno/indigeni* (native/natives) can be considered a shift, it is not relevant for this analysis, because my aim is to examine shifts that have the potential to alter the racist implications of the ST. Moreover, this shift occurs only once in Translation B and, as I argued in Chapter 3, a lexical feature contributes to a style only when it is a repeated choice. A choice in isolation, on the other hand, can be stylistically meaningful per se, but it is the patterns of repeated choices that develop the style of a text (Leech and Short 2007: 34).

6.3.1.3 *Negro*

With *negro*, the translators adopt different strategies. As with *wilderness* and *darkness*, this ST term does not have a direct equivalent in Italian,[2] therefore the translators are faced with a choice to make. Translation S replaces it with the Italian *negro* (nigger) for all 3 occurrences. Translation B uses *negro* (nigger) twice and *giovane di colore* (young person of colour) for the remaining one. Translation M adopts *negro* (nigger) twice and *negretto* (little nigger) once. Finally, consistently with its previous choice, Translation G opts for *nero* (black) to replace the ST *negro*.

As in the case of *nigger*, the English term *negro* is stigmatized by its relation with slavery (Hughes 2006: 327). Especially with a lower *n*, as it is used in *HoD*, *negro* has been 'furiously objected' to by black people (Kennedy 2002: 114). Today, it is regarded as outdated and offensive (*Oxford English Dictionary* 2015, www.oed.com), although until the mid-twentieth century it was recorded in dictionaries as the anthropological designation for '[a] member of a dark-skinned group of peoples originally native to sub-Saharan Africa; a person of black African origin or descent' (*Oxford English Dictionary* 2015). Coeval dictionaries focus on its almost 'technical' use. *Lloyd's Encyclopædic Dictionary* (1895) marks it as an anthropology jargon for '[t]he distinctly dark, as opposed to the fair, yellow, and brown varieties of mankind'; *The Chambers English Dictionary* (1905) defines it as 'one of the black-skinned woolly-haired race in the Soudan and central parts of Africa [...]'; whereas *A New English Dictionary on Historical Principles* (1888–1928) defines it as '[a]n individual (esp. a male) belonging to the African race of mankind, which is distinguished by a black skin, black woolly hair, flat nose and thick protruding lips'.

Translating the ST item *negro* with the Italian *negro* (nigger) or *negretto* (little nigger) can and cannot be seen as a shift that affects the racist implications of the original term. On the one hand, if *negro* (Eng) is considered to be as imbued with racist implications as *nigger* is, then replacing *negro* (Eng) with the Italian term *negro* (nigger) would not create much of a shift from the point of view of the racist discourse. Alternatively, if *negro* (Eng) is considered to have been used in its anthropological sense, then replacing it with the slur *negro* (nigger) does make a difference. However, the two scenarios are most probably intertwined: even if *negro* (Eng) is used in its technical acceptation, this does not automatically exclude that fact that the word can nevertheless have racist implications. Therefore, the boundaries between the two possibilities are fuzzy.

In contrast, translating *negro* (Eng) with *giovane di colore* (young person of colour) and *nero* (black) represents a shift that alters the racist implications of the original term. The use of *nero* (black) was already discussed in Section

6.3.1.1. Replacing *negro* (Eng) with *nero* (black) can have an effect similar to substituting *nigger* with *nero* (black) (cf. Section 6.3.1.1). Analogously, translating *negro* (Eng) with *giovane di colore* (young person of colour) can be seen as mitigating the racist implications of the ST term. *Giovane di colore* (young person of colour) occurs 143 times in itTenTen (0.05 pmw), less frequently than both *negro* (nigger) and *nero* (black). Looking at its collocates (Figure 6.7), they do not seem to indicate usage in negative contexts, although they are mostly function words and as such they are not very revealing. If the item had occurred more frequently, its description could have been more reliable. A similar limitation is pointed out by Mouka et al. (2015: 64), who note that low frequency affects the usefulness of their reference corpus in showing the usage of a term.

6.3.1.4 *Native/natives*

With *native* and *natives*, all of the four TTs translate them with their Italian equivalent *indigeno* and *indigeni*, therefore no shifts occur in the case of this 'African word'.

6.3.1.5 *Black/blacks*

Despite the availability of a straightforward Italian equivalent, *black/blacks* is translated in different ways in the TTs. Translation S uses *nero/neri/nere/nera/nerissime* (black, singular and plural, masculine and feminine and superlative form) 14 times, omits *black* once, and replaces it with *negro/negri* (nigger/niggers) 8 times. Translation B translates *black/blacks* into *nero/neri/nere/nera* (black, singular and plural, masculine and feminine) 16 times, into *negro/negri* (nigger/niggers) 6 times and once using *giovane di colore* (young person of colour). Translation M uses *nero/neri/nere/nera* (black, singular and plural, masculine and feminine) 17 times and *negro/negri* (nigger/niggers) 6 times. Finally, Translation G is the only TT that avoids using *negro* (nigger), adhering to the Italian equivalent *nero/neri/nere/nera* (black, singular and plural, masculine and feminine) and remaining consistent with the strategy adopted so far.

In line with the discussion in Section 6.3.1.1, the translation of *black/blacks* with *negro/negri* (nigger/niggers) is considered a shift that intensifies the potential racist implications of the ST item. The classification of the shift is less clear in the case of *black* translated with *giovane di colore* (young person of colour) in Translation B. Based on the corpus evidence available and their dictionary meaning (cf. Section 6.3.1.1 and Section 6.3.1.3), I do not consider this shift as markedly changing the potential racist implications of the ST item.

	Frequency	MI	log likelihood	logDice
P | N un	89	6.077	645.548	-3.282
P | N fa	6	5.881	37.371	-3.478
P | N era	5	5.116	25.915	-4.243
P | N ad	9	5.031	45.862	-4.328
P | N una	23	4.678	108.577	-4.681
P | N ll	6	4.131	23.271	-5.228
P | N a	26	4.022	100.647	-5.337
P | N che	37	4.018	146.025	-5.341
P | N il	32	4.013	124.904	-5.346
P | N con	14	3.976	52.195	-5.383
P | N in	25	3.898	92.539	-5.461
P | N da	11	3.870	39.270	-5.489
P | N gli	5	3.847	17.516	-5.512
P | N	6	3.800	20.689	-5.559
P | N ,	87	3.572	331.744	-5.787
P | N al	7	3.488	21.389	-5.871
P | N si	9	3.428	26.922	-5.931
P | N :	9	3.425	26.887	-5.934
P | N di	52	3.412	170.059	-5.946
P | N .	46	3.408	148.007	-5.951
P | N '	5	3.270	13.843	-6.089
P | N del	13	3.255	36.372	-6.104
P | N è	12	3.231	33.142	-6.128
P | N i	8	3.158	21.177	-6.201
P | N e	25	2.932	61.729	-6.427
P | N)	6	2.803	13.221	-6.556
P | N (	5	2.693	10.337	-6.666
P | N "	8	2.672	16.474	-6.687
P | N non	6	2.534	11.327	-6.825
P | N la	10	2.311	16.530	-7.048
P | N per	7	2.256	11.044	-7.103

Figure 6.7 *Collocates of* persona di colore

6.3.2 Tendencies in the translation of the 'African words'

The previous section compared the translation of each 'African word' across the TTs, identifying shifts that have the potential to affect the racist implications that these terms may carry. This section looks instead at all the 'African words' at once, for each TT, in order to examine whether the individual strategies adopted for the single words create a wider and consistent tendency. Table 6.5 shows the frequency of the translations of the 'African words' for each TT. The TTs are searched for the Italian 'African words' on the basis of the translations listed in Table 6.4. For example, *negro* (nigger) is counted throughout the TTs and all the occurrences are reported, inclusive of those translating a ST word different from *nigger*.

Table 6.5 clearly shows the overall tendencies in the translation of the 'African words'. Translations S, B and M have a high frequency of *negro* (nigger), higher than the ST (*nigger* and *niggers* occur 10 times in the original). Not only do these TTs consistently use *negro* (nigger) in all of the cases in which *nigger* is used in the ST, but they also translate other words into *negro* (nigger). The previous section (cf. Table 6.4) showed that it is mostly *negro* (Eng) and *black* that have been translated into *negro* (nigger). *Nero* (black), in its various forms, occurs less frequently in these three TTs than in the ST (*black/blacks* occurs 23 times in the original). When reiterated, this lexical choice becomes a tendency that can affect the potential racist implications of the ST, intensifying them in translation. In these three TTs, the Africans are more frequently referred to as *negri* (niggers) than *neri* (blacks), compared with the original.

A diachronic distinction needs to be made, though, as there is a sixty-year gap between Translation S and Translations B and M. The use and potential racist implications of *negro* (nigger) may have changed in these sixty years. Further research supported by evidence from an Italian historical corpus is needed to prove this hypothesis. However, in the absence of this evidence (an Italian historical corpus is not available at the time of writing), it could be assumed that the use and potential racist implications of *nigger* in *HoD* (1902) are closer to the use and potential racist implications of *negro* (nigger) in Translation S (1928) than in Translation B (1989) and Translation M (1990). I therefore suggest that the shifts in Translations B and M can be seen as more marked than those in Translation S.

I discuss now some textual extracts and their translations, in order to demonstrate the effects of these shifts. Consider Example (6), which shows the translation of *negro* (Eng) with *negro* (nigger).

Table 6.5 *Frequency of the translations of the 'African words' in each TT*

	Translation S	Translation B	Translation M	Translation G
negro	24	18	19	0
selvaggio	17	17	19	19
indigeno	8	10	7	7
giovane di colore	0	2	0	0
nero	15	16	17	36

*Frequency counts include the frequency of each different form (singular, plural, masculine, feminine and superlative).

(6)   And every week the messenger, a lone *negro*, letter-bag on shoulder and
        staff in hand, left our station for the coast.

(6B)   E ogni settimana il cursore, un *negro* solitario, sacco della posta in spalla
        e bastone in mano, lasciava la nostra stazione diretto alla costa.
        (And every week the courier, a lone *nigger*, letter-bag on shoulder and
        staff in hand, left our station for the coast.)

(6M)   E ogni settimana il corriere, un *negro* solitario con il sacco della posta
        sulle spalle e il bastone in mano, partiva dalla stazione diretto alla costa.
        (And every week the courier, a lone *nigger* with the post-bag on shoulder
        and the staff in hand, departed from the station for the coast.)

In the ST, *a lone negro* works in apposition with the subject of the sentence, *the
messenger*. If *negro* (Eng) is considered in its anthropological sense (cf. Section
6.3.1.3), then Translation B and Translation M can be seen as intensifying the
potential racist implications of the original term. However, if *negro* (Eng) is
regarded as having similar racist implications as *negro* (nigger), then no marked
alteration occurs in this case.

In contrast, a marked shift occurs when *black* is translated with *negro* (nigger), as in Example (7):

(7)   An athletic *black* belonging to some coast tribe and educated by my poor
        predecessor, was the helmsman.

(7B)   Timoniere era un *negro* atletico venuto da qualche tribù della costa, e
        addestrato dal mio sventurato predecessore.
        (The helmsman was an athletic *nigger* come from some coast tribe, and
        trained by my unfortunate predecessor.)

(7M)   Un *negro* atletico di qualche tribù della costa, istruito dal mio povero
        predecessore, era il timoniere.
        (An athletic *nigger* of some coast tribe, instructed by my poor
        predecessor, was the helmsman.)

The shift here is more evident than in Example (6). The substitution of *an athletic
black* in the original with *un negro atletico* (an athletic nigger) in the two TTs intensifies (or even adds altogether) the potential racist implications of the ST item. In
the case of Translation B, in Example (7B), the shift is paralleled by another lexical
choice: the translation of *educated* with *addestrato* (trained). *Addestrare* (to train)
is commonly used in relation to animals, for instance in the context of animals
trained for the circus or trained pets. *Educated*, in the original, does not refer to
these contexts, being instead related with intellectual knowledge and schooling.

As far as Translation G is concerned, an opposite tendency compared with Translations S, B and M is observable. As shown in Table 6.5, Translation G replaces every occurrence of *nigger, niggers* and even *negro* with *nero* (black). *Negro* (nigger) does not occur at all in Translation G, while the various forms of *nero* (black) occur much more frequently than in the original: 36 vs. 23. This consistent lexical choice produces a tendency that mitigates the potential racist implications of the ST. In Translation G, the African natives are always referred to as *neri* (blacks) rather than *negri* (niggers). See Examples (8) and (9):

(8)   A *nigger* was being beaten near by. They said he had caused the fire in some way;

(8G) Non lontano da lì, stavano bastonando un *nero*. Dicevano che in un modo o nell'altro, era stato lui a provocare l'incendio;
(Not far away from there, they were beating a *black man*. They said that in one way or the other, he had caused the fire;)

(9)   And every week the messenger, a lone negro, letter-bag on shoulder and staff in hand, left our station for the coast.

(9G) E ogni settimana, il messaggero della nostra stazione, un *nero* solitario, sacco postale in spalla e bastone in mano, partiva per la costa.
(And every week, the messenger of our station, a lone *black man*, post-bag on shoulder and staff in hand, departed for the coast.)

In Example (8), *nigger* is replaced with *nero* (black): this choice mitigates the racist discourse. The syntactic structure of the sentence is modified too. In the ST, the sentence is in passive form and its object, *a nigger*, is placed in the initial position, carrying the emphasis that this position possesses. In contrast, in Example (8G) the sentence has been converted into an active form: *un nero* (a black man) remains the object of the sentence but the initial position is occupied by the implied subject, *loro* (they). In this case, the emphasis of the violent action of beating someone is put on the perpetrators of such action, namely, the whites. Example (9) reports the same extract used in Example (7) to illustrate the different strategy adopted by Translator G compared with the other TTs. Whereas the other translators use the term *negro* (nigger) to translate *negro* (Eng), Translation G employs *black* (nero), toning down the potential racist implications of the ST item.

The other shifts described in Section 6.3.1, related to the translation of *savage/savages* and *native/natives*, do not occur as frequently as those described so far; therefore they cannot be considered as general tendencies. Specifically, the shift from *savage* and *savages* to *indigeno* and *indigeni* (native and natives) occurs only once in Translation B, as well as the translation of *negro* (Eng) with *giovane di colore* (young person of colour) in the same TT. As for the other occurrence of *giovane di colore* (young person of colour) in Translation B, it is used as a translation of *black*: I argued in Section 6.3.1.5 that this does not represent a marked shift in terms of alterations at the level of potential racist discourse.

Overall, Translation G displays a tendency to mitigate as far as possible the use of potential racist discourse, from a lexical point of view. In this respect, the shifts in Translation G can be seen as producing a manipulative effect that alters the fictional representation of the African natives in comparison to the original. In contrast, Translation B and Translation M show a tendency to maintain or even intensify the potential racist implications of the ST. These shifts too can be considered to enact a manipulative effect, as they alter – in an opposite way compared with Translation G – the depiction of the Africans. The TT reader is more likely to recognize a racist discourse at the lexical level in Translation B and Translation M than in Translation G. Translation S can be seen as the least manipulative, if the diachronic dimension is taken into account. Even though this translation repeatedly uses *negro* and *negri* (nigger and niggers), I suggestd that the potential racist implications of these terms are equivalent to those of the ST words, therefore this translation choice does not produce a shift as marked as in the other TTs. Again, evidence from Italian historical corpora would be needed to test this hypothesis and check whether the use of *negro* (nigger) at the time is comparable to the use of *nigger* in the original.[3]

It is worth pointing out that the manipulation described in this section seems to be of a different nature from that discussed in Section 5.4.4. In Chapter 5, I argued that manipulation takes place as a result of unconscious alterations of the lexico-semantic patterns of the original, whereas in this case the manipulation seems to be intentional. In Chapter 2, I outlined the debate on whether *HoD* is a racist text or not, which emerged as a consequence of Achebe's (1990) influential lecture. I explained that, before Achebe's (1990) accusation, the issue of race and racism was practically absent from any literary criticism, whereas today the theme is virtually unavoidable. The influence of this debate seems to be reflected in the finding of this analysis, especially in the lexical choices of Translations M, B and G. The translation of the 'African words' in these TTs seems to respond to the debate, as each of the translators alters the fictional representation of the Africans, in terms of how the natives are referred to in the text. This outcome shows once more that translation is a social artefact that responds to the historical and cultural milieu in which it occurs. As such, it is never a transparent replica of its original, but rather a rewriting that follows dominating canons and norms as much as questioning them. Ultimately, translation enacts a process of production, rather than of reproduction.

6.3.3 Semantic preferences and prosody in translation

The previous sections concentrated on the translations of the 'African words' across the TTs and discussed the effects of the translators' lexical choices on the fictional representation of the Africans in *HoD*. This section examines whether the semantic preferences and prosody identified in the ST have been reproduced in the TTs. I carry out a concordance analysis on the translation of the 'African words' (*negro, selvaggio, indigeno, giovane di colore* and *nero*, in all their different forms) to study whether they enact equivalent local textual functions to those identified in the ST.

The concordance analysis shows that the 'African words' in all of the TTs have the same semantic preferences recognized in the ST. Analysing their collocates in a span of 5:5, it is possible to identify the semantic preferences observed in the original: 'physicality', 'collectives', 'incomprehensibility' and 'general negative'. This means that in the TTs as well, the fictional representation of the Africans is built up around these four aspects. Tables 6.6 to 6.9 display the words forming part of each of the semantic preferences for the four TTs. In addition to the preferences, the tables also show that all the TTs maintain the use of *nero* (black) as an adjective pre-modifying a metaphorical reference to an African, in which the head of the phrase is not a synonym of man or woman. In the TTs too, *nero* (black) co-occurs with items such as *ombra* (shadow), *cose* (things), *forme* (shapes) and *figure* (figures).

Tables 6.6 to 6.9 show that, in the TTs as well, the 'African words' co-occur with the 'physicality', 'collectives', 'incomprehensibility' and 'general negative' semantic fields. In other words, the TTs maintain equivalent semantic preferences as those in the original. This implies that all of the Italian versions have equivalent linguistic features to enact a dehumanizing, negative semantic prosody. In translation too, the Africans are described mainly in terms of their bodily appearance, neglecting altogether their thoughts and feelings; natives are referred to as indistinct masses, rather than people with their own individuality; they do not communicate in a way that is comprehensible to the colonizers; finally, the Africans are frequently related to negative contexts and situations.

The reproduction in translation of the semantic preferences and prosodies of the 'African words' mirrors what was identified in Chapter 5: the fact that the semantic preferences of the 'Africa words' are similarly maintained in the TTs. In the previous chapter, I argued that, despite the reproduction of the semantic preferences, translating *wilderness* and *darkness* with multiple terms disrupts the cohesive network that exists between the semantic

Table 6.6 *Semantic fields of the 'African words' in Translation S*

Semantic fields	Words
Physicality	nutrito, piedoni, petto, schiena, corpo, ispalla, ignuda, eretta, testa (2), palpebre, gambe, membra, collo, volto, spalla, atletico.
Collectives	ciurma, file, torma, turba, folla (3), fila, campo.
Incomprehensibility	misteriosi, lamentando, gemere, baccano, tumulto, ululati, incomprensibile.
General negative	povero, bastonato (3), idiota, solitario, ferito, polverosi, litigiosa, immusoniti, zoppicanti, lamentando, legnò, servitorello, spietatamente, afflizione, soppressione, indifferenza, morte (2), tumulto, rimpianto, angosciosi, mortale, infelici, odiare, odiarli, cattivi, paura, baruffa, nemici, insolente, immobilità, malattia, svogliatamente.
black [ADJ]	figura nera (2), forme nere (2), nere figure, neri simulacri, cosi neri, carcame nero.

*Frequency, when ≥ 2, in brackets.

Table 6.7 *Semantic fields of the 'African words' in Translation B*

Semantic fields	Words
Physicality	teste, piedi (2), nuda, palpebre, testa (2), ossa, membra, mani, braccia, gambe, collo, petto, pasciuto, atletico.
Collectives	tribù, file, picchetto, banda, masnada, folla, fila, accampamento, torma, massa, turbinio.
Incomprehensibility	gemeva (2), ululato, tumulto, incomprensibile, frenesia, grida.
General negative	pestò, picchiavano, picchiato, gemeva, battuto, solitario, scimunito, impolverati, rissosa, ingrugniti, doloranti, misteriosi, cadavere, doloroso, mortale, infelici, spiacevole, angoscia, morte (2), soppressione (2), indifferenza, rimpianto, odiare, odiarli, rissa, paura, incomprensibile, insolente, indolenti, malattia, inedia, immobilità.
black [ADJ]	figura nera, nere figure, nere ombre, forme nere, cosi neri.

*Frequency, when ≥ 2, in brackets.

fields and the 'Africa words'. The findings in this chapter suggest a similar disruption. Altering the 'African words' in translation has consequences for the TTs, even though the original semantic preferences are there. This is the case for Translation G, where contrasting tendencies regarding the representation of the Africans coexist. On the one hand, Translation G mitigates the potential racist implications of the ST at the lexical level. On the other, it maintains the dehumanizing, negative semantic prosody produced by the semantic fields. These two aspects, which are aligned in the original, are in

Table 6.8 *Semantic fields of the 'African words' in Translation M**

Semantic fields	Words
'Physicality'	atletico, teste, musi, nuda, robusto, testa (2), palpebre, membra, mani, ossa, braccia, gambe, collo, petto, narici.
'Collectives'	picchetto, fila, mucchio, file, frotta, tribù, folla, accampamento.
'Incomprehensibility'	gemeva, lamentava, urlo, grida, frenesia, imperscrutabile, confuse.
'General negative'	bastonando, bastonato (3), lamentava, gemeva, bastonò, misteriosi, terribili, litigiosa, solitario, idiota, povero, cadavere, dolore, morte (2), soppressione (2), indifferenza, rimpianto, odiare, odiarli, straziato, mortale, infelici, nemici, zuffa, temeva, avvilito, malattia, inedia, insolente, svogliatamente.
black [ADJ]	figura nera (2), ombre nere, forme nere (2), figure nere.

*Frequency, when ≥ 2, in brackets.

Table 6.9 *Semantic fields of the 'African words' in Translation G**

Semantic fields	Words
'Physicality'	occhi, supernutrito, atletico, nudi, testa (2), ossatura, gambe, braccia, membra, mani, piedi (2), corpo, spalla, collo, torace.
'Collectives'	folla, campo, file, picchetto, fila, banda (2).
'Incomprehensibility'	ululato, incomprensibile, frenesia, grida, gemeva, lamentava.
'General negative'	angoscioso, mortale, infelici, odiare, odiarli, morte (2), pena, indifferenza, rimpianto, nemici, paura, impietriti, deficiente, insolente, apatiche, impolverati, misteriosi, litigiosa, immusoliti, doloranti, solitario, malattia, fame, servitore, pietà, bastonando, picchiato, gemeva, bastonato, lamentava, bastonò.
black [ADJ]	ombra nera, sagoma nera, ombre nere, nere ombre, cose nere, forme nere.

*Frequency, when ≥ 2, in brackets.

contrast in Translation G, as shown in the comparison of the following textual extracts.

The reproduction of the semantic preferences in Translation B and Translation M is not in contrast with the strategy adopted to deal with the 'African words'. The increased frequency of *negro* (nigger) parallels the reproduction of semantic fields that trigger a dehumanizing representation of the Africans. See Example (10): the 'African word' is in bold; the items belonging to the semantic fields, in italic.

(10)   It was paddled by **black** *fellows*. You could see from afar the white of
their *eyeballs* glistening. They *shouted, sang*; their *bodies* streamed with
perspiration; they had *faces* like *grotesque* masks – these *chaps*; but they
had *bone, muscle*, a wild vitality, an intense energy of movement, that
was as natural and true as the surf long their coast.

(10B)   C'erano dei **negri** alla pagaia. A distanza si vedeva risplendere il bianco
dei loro *occhi. Gridavano, cantavano*, grondavano sudore per tutto il
corpo; avevano *facce* simili a maschere *grottesche*, quei *tipi*; ma avevano
ossa, muscoli, una selvaggia vitalità, un'intensa energia di movimento,
naturale e vera come la risacca lungo la loro costa.
(There were some **niggers** at the paddle. From afar you could see the
white of their *eyes* glistering. They *shouted, sang*, dripped with sweat
all over their *body*; they had *faces* like *grotesque* masks, those *types*; but
they had *bone, muscle*, a wild vitality, an intense energy of movement,
as natural and true as the surf long their coast.)

(10M)   Alle pagaie stavano dei **negri**. Di lontano si vedeva brillare il bianco
dei loro *occhi. Gridavano, cantavano*; i *corpi* grondanti di sudore; quella
gente aveva *facce* come maschere *grottesche*; ma aveva *ossa, muscoli*,
una vitalità selvaggia, un'intensa energia nel movimento, naturale e
autentica quanto la risacca lungo la loro costa.
(At the paddles there were some **niggers**. From afar you could see the
white of their *eyes* sparkling. They *shouted, sang*; their *body* dripping
sweat; those *people* had *faces* like *grotesque* masks; but they had *bone,
muscles*, a wild vitality, an intense energy of movement, as natural and
authentic as the surf long their cost.)

Section 6.3.1 explained that Translation B and Translation M use *negro/negri*
(nigger/niggers) when the original employs a different term, an instance of
which is shown in Example (10). In this passage, *black fellows* is translated,
in both cases, as *negri* (niggers), in this way intensifying the potential racist
implications of the item, compared with the ST. This lexical choice does not
clash with the reproduction of the semantic preferences of the 'African words'
as, generally speaking, they both tend towards a negative representation of the
Africans. In Example (10) it is possible to note the dominating presence of the
'physicality' semantic field (*eyeballs, bodies, faces, bone, muscle*), as well as the
'incomprehensibility' (*shouted, sang*), the 'collectives' (*chaps*) and the 'general
negative' (*grotesque*) ones. Both Translations B and M translate these terms

literally, maintaining the semantic preferences and prosody. Finally, the use of a potentially racist term (*negri*, niggers) matches the dehumanizing depiction of the paddlers.

In contrast, Translation G mitigates the potential racist implications of the 'African words'. However, this tendency does not match the reproduction of the semantic fields, which instead can have dehumanizing implications. Translation G applies this toning-down strategy only with the most obvious reflections of the racist discourse, namely, the words *nigger*, *niggers* and *negro*. On the other hand, the dehumanizing representation built up by the semantic preferences is not altered, even though this contrasts with the attempt to remove any potential racist inference from the ST. Consider Examples (11) and (12):

(11) *Strings* of *dusty* **niggers** with splay *feet* arrived and departed;
(11G) *File* di **neri** *impolverati* e con i *piedi* piatti che arrivavano e ripartivano;
         (*Strings* of **blacks**, *dusty* and with splay *feet*, that arrived and departed;)
(12) A *quarrelsome band* of *footsore sulky* **niggers** trod on the heels of the donkey;
(12G) Una *banda litigiosa* di **neri** *immusoniti* e coi *piedi doloranti* tallonava l'asino;
         (A *quarrelsome band* of *sulky* and *footsore* **blacks** heeled the donkey;)

In both examples, the potential racist discourse enacted by the use of *niggers* is mitigated in translation, as the translator replaces it with *neri* (blacks). In this respect, Examples (11G) and (12G) are less likely to trigger racist implications than Examples (11) and (12). However, the semantic preferences of the 'African words' are maintained, as well as the resulting dehumanization: the 'physicality' (*feet, foot*), 'collectives' (*strings, band*) and 'general negative' (*dusty, quarrelsome, footsore, sulky*) semantic fields are reproduced. Thus, when compared with the ST, Translation G shows the presence of contrasting tendencies in relation to the fictional representation of the Africans, a phenomenon that does not occur in the original.

6.4 Conclusion

This chapter described and discussed the stylistic tools with which the fictional representation of the Africans is constructed. In particular, this investigation demonstrated the role that specific textual patterns play in establishing this representation. I argued that the semantic preferences and prosody identified dehumanize the Africans in the text. This analysis not only offered linguistic evidence to support what critics have previously hinted at when referring to the way *HoD* depicts the natives, but it also offered original knowledge concerning the appreciation of *HoD*, providing new insight into how this dehumanizing process is actually enacted, which specific lexical features it encompasses, which semantic fields convey the dehumanization and how they relate to each other. Therefore, this chapter contributed new material to the discussion about race and racism in *HoD*.

From a translational perspective, this chapter discussed different and, at times, contrasting tendencies in dealing with the construction of the natives in the TTs. First, I showed how some of the translators' lexical choices intensify the potential racist implications of the ST. This happens when *black* and *blacks* are translated with *negro* and *negri* (nigger and niggers). Other choices instead mitigate these implications, that is, when *nigger*, *niggers* or *negro* are translated with *nero* (black). I argued that these shifts manipulate this specific aspect of the text, with consequences on the reception of the theme 'race and racism' in the target context. Second, I discussed how the reproduction of equivalent semantic preferences and prosody can be in contrast with the way the 'African words' have been translated. This is the case in Translation G, where contrasting tendencies in the depiction of the Africans coexist. Overall, the analysis of the translations showed how alterations at the micro-linguistic level can have effects at the macro-textual, interpretational level.

This chapter is related to the previous one in the discussion of translation manipulation. The analyses in Chapter 5 and Chapter 6 illustrated different types of translational shifts. In the previous chapter, I argued that the shifts identified are the result of the lack of a translation equivalent and are therefore obligatory. Most of the shifts identified in this chapter are non-obligatory, as an equivalent is available. As I demonstrated, both shifts can create manipulative effects: this provides further evidence that, independently from their intentionality or motivation, both types of shifts have the same potential to manipulate the TT.

Finally, before moving on to the next chapter, it is worth pointing out another parallelism existing between the two analyses. Chapter 5 showed that Translation G is the TT that displays a different strategy in dealing with the fictional representation of the African jungle compared with the other TTs. In contrast, Translations S, B and M show a more similar behaviour in the translation of *wilderness* and *darkness*. The analysis reported in this chapter pointed to a comparable picture. Translations S, B and M show equivalent tendencies in dealing with the 'African words'. In particular, Translation B and Translation M share this tendency even more closely, given the similarity of the sociocultural contexts in which the translation practice took place. In contrast, Translation G again displays an independent behaviour, differing markedly from the strategies adopted by the other TTs. This outcome is paralleled and further explored in the next chapter.

Applying PCA to the Study of Literary Translation

7.1 Introduction

This chapter employs principal component analysis (PCA) to compare the TTs and the ST. PCA uses the frequency patterns of such a large portion of the total number of tokens in the texts that, statistically speaking, the analysis can be said to approximate comparison at the level of whole texts. This analysis aims to compensate the comparison of the translations with a perspective which has not been taken into account so far. It offers a contrastive view of the TTs based on their overall degree of difference, rather than focusing on specific stylistic features. In addition, this chapter also seeks to provide a bird's-eye-view framework to interpret the local differences identified in the previous chapters, as the TTs' alterations discussed in Chapters 5 and 6 can be related to the overall picture of the texts' relation that PCA offers. This twofold perspective offers a more nuanced understanding of how the ST and the TTs relate to each other, combining different levels of analysis.

The input of PCA is parallel lists: Section 7.2 introduces parallel wordlists and parallel word-sequence lists, explaining how they were obtained and how they are used here. Once parallel lists are obtained, the comparison of the TTs is established in two different ways. First, Section 7.3 uses the frequency patterns of the most frequent words in the TTs to calculate their overall degree of difference. Second, Section 7.4 repeats the analysis using the most frequent sequences: two-word sequences in Section 7.4.1 and three-word sequences in Section 7.4.2. Section 7.5 discusses the results of the two comparisons and relates the findings to each other. Finally, Section 7.6 provides some concluding remarks.

7.2 Parallel word- and word-sequence lists

PCA is a statistical method that converts the observations of a large number of variables into a smaller number of values, that is, principal components. The principal components are defined so as to account for as much variance in the data as possible. It is therefore a procedure that facilitates the handling of a large quantity of data by 'compressing' it into a more manageable format. In computational stylistics/stylometry, PCA is usually used to obtain a measure of difference across texts or corpora based on the performance of a given number of variables (see Section 3.4.4). Most commonly, these variables are the most frequent words (MFWs) or most frequent sequences (MFSs) in the texts under analysis. PCA uses the frequency patterns of these MFWs/MFSs to provide a statistical approximation of the overall degree of similarity of a number of texts. The more similar the patterns are across texts, the more likely the relation of similarity between these texts; the more different the patterns are, the higher their 'degree of unlikeliness' (Burrows 2002b). The frequency patterns necessary for the calculation are provided in the form of parallel lists: wordlists when using MFWs as variables, and word-sequence lists when using MFSs. A parallel list includes the frequency list of all the words/word sequences in a corpus, plus individual frequency lists for each text in the said corpus (Hoover 2015). The corpus word/word-sequence list is sorted by decreasing frequency, while the text lists are not; rather, they follow the order set by the corpus list. See an extract of a parallel wordlist in Table 7.1.

The first column lists the words in the corpus of the TTs in descending order of frequency. The other columns are not sorted by frequency: the frequency of *che* in Translation S, for instance, is higher than the frequency of *e*, yet *che* comes after *e*. The order that the translation columns follow is dictated by the corpus wordlist (the first column). The numbers represent the relative frequency of each word in the translations. All the frequency entries are normalized so that they are comparable across texts of different sizes: the entry represents the word frequency expressed as a percentage of the total number of running words in that translation. Parallel word-sequence lists work in a similar way to parallel wordlists: they have the same ordering and format of a parallel wordlist, conveying the same frequency information on word sequences, instead of individual words. Parallel lists are generated with the tool *Intelligent Archive 2.0* (www.newcastle.edu.au/research-and-innovation/centre/education-arts/cllc/intelligent-archive), introduced in Section 3.4.5.

Table 7.1 *Sample of TTs parallel wordlist*

Word	Translation B	Translation G	Translation M	Translation S
di	3.722262	3.747468	3.7493248	4.31183
e	2.5530899	2.451566	2.5526743	2.3329823
che	2.2031336	2.581416	2.3419774	2.4215162
un	2.394019	2.236015	2.2879524	2.1941998
a	1.861131	1.6335117	1.7531065	1.9908116
la	1.7047112	1.9087934	1.815235	1.4572167
il	1.7153159	1.7399886	1.7693139	1.368683
non	1.4820117	1.6023477	1.5045921	1.6366769
in	1.4475464	1.324469	1.3641275	1.3734686
una	1.2858242	1.225783	1.212858	1.3447549
era	1.227498	1.3192749	1.2533766	1.1078675
per	1.0498688	1.0284111	0.97244734	1.0432619
si	0.9570773	1.0647691	1.0075635	0.7106623
con	0.9623797	0.8310393	0.86169636	0.74416155
mi	0.80330867	0.84662133	0.86439764	0.81355286
l'	0.7184708	0.8388303	0.8725014	0.64127105
le	0.6521912	0.69599545	0.6293895	0.5958078
come	0.7317267	0.6258765	0.645597	0.5503446
da	0.60181874	0.61548847	0.5645597	0.5766654
[...]	[...]	[...]	[...]	[...]

Before starting the comparison, it is important to specify that Italian words with apostrophes are considered as autonomous tokens in this study, instead of parts of the items with which they occur. For example, *l'albero* (the tree) counts as two separate tokens: *l'* and *albero* (in fact, *l'* appears on its own in the parallel wordlist in Table 7.1). Apostrophes are commonly used in Italian. One of their main uses is to indicate the dropping of a vowel at the end of a word, when such a word precedes another word starting with a vowel. For example, *lo* (the) before *albero* (tree) becomes *l'albero* (the tree). Elided words are generally very common function words (such as *l'*, definite article, and *d'*, preposition), whose frequency is much higher than that of the word they occur with (often content words). Considering an elided word and the word it occurs with as a single token would mean substantially affecting the frequency of the elided function word. The total frequency of the elided word would then be split into the several occurrences of the other content words with which it occurs. For instance, *l'albero* (the tree), *l'orologio* (the watch) and *l'occhio* (the eye) would be counted as three separate types in the case that elided words were considered part of the word they occur with. In contrast, when considering them individually, we would have four types: *l'* occurring 3 times and the other three nouns each occurring once. Tognini-Bonelli (2001: 138) adopts the same distinction in her study of *in case of* and its Italian translation *nel caso di*. She considers the elided form of the preposition *dell'* as independent from the word it follows. Laviosa (personal communication) agrees with Tognini-Bonelli (2001) and suggests that words with apostrophes should be counted separately.

7.3 Comparing the TTs using MFWs

In this section, I analyse the overall degree of similarity between the translations based on the frequency patterns of a number of MFWs. But how many MFWs to take into account? There is no general agreement on this number and different studies have used different pools. For example, McKenna et al. (1999) use 99, 61 and 65 MFWs, Burrows (2002b) uses 20, Burrows (2002a) adopts multiple pools (150, 120, 100, 80, 60 and 40), Grabowski (2012, 2013) uses 2,000 and 1,000, respectively and Rybicki et al. (2014) employ 1,000 MFWs. According to Hoover (2002), when multivariate analyses are applied to authorship attribution, small numbers of MFWs are ineffective in clustering texts accurately, while increasing the number of MFWs increases the accuracy of the attribution. However, once a maximum accuracy is reached, increasing further the number of MFWs reduces accuracy. Using different pools of MFWs ranging from 20 to 500, Hoover (2002: 159–60) shows that the accuracy of a cluster analysis increases with the rise of MFWs. But once 88 per cent of accuracy is reached with 300 MFWs, accuracy decreases as more MFWs are added. An explanation for this may be that very large pools of MFWs lead to the increase of the number of words that are unattested in some of the texts (Hoover 2002: 160). The larger the number of words taken into account, the larger the proportion of words that appear only in some texts but not in the others. This increase in the number of unattested words could affect the accuracy of the analysis.

Despite the different nature of his study (comparison of translations as opposed to authorship attribution), Rybicki (2006) reaches similar conclusions as Hoover (2002). He also tries various numbers of MFWs (30, 100, 200 and 250) and finds that smaller numbers do not produce results as consistent as those obtained with 250 MFWs (Rybicki 2006: 93). An analogous method based on multiple preliminary tests is used by Rybicki and Heydel (2013: 711): their analysis is performed with different ranges of MFWs (from 100 to 1,000) and then the individual results are combined in order to produce the most consistent outcome. In the specific case of PCA, Hoover (2015) advocates a similar approach: starting with a large number of MFWs and then decreasing the number gradually: 'what you are looking for, and what you will usually find, is a series of analyses at some points that are very similar [. . .]. These are the most reliable results' (Hoover 2015: online).

This book follows Rybicki's (2006) and Hoover's (2002, 2015) approach, consisting of carrying out preliminary analyses with different numbers of MFWs to identify similar results. Specifically, I run tests ranging from 1,000 to 50 MFWs, removing fifty words for each new test and comparing the results. The results were almost identical in the 800–250 range, while before and after that range (from 50 to 200 and from 850 to 1,000) the outcome of PCA changed considerably between one pool of MFWs and the next. This finding is in line with Rybicki's (2006) and Hoover's (2002, 2015) considerations: too small numbers of MFWs did not provide as consistent results as larger numbers; however, with too many words, results were not consistent again. I therefore decided to use 250 MFWs for the final analysis, as this is a manageable number when it comes to analyse more qualitatively individual words in order to see how they discriminate one translation from the other.

Figure 7.1 shows the plot representing the overall degree of similarity between the TTs, based on the frequency patterns of the 250 MFWs. As mentioned before, PCA is a procedure of dimension reduction and Figure 7.1 is the visual representation of this reduction: PCA concentrates high-dimensional information (the frequency patterns of 250 words across four different texts) into a low-dimensional space, a 2D graph. The two axes are the two principal components that account for most of the variance across the data. The numbers in parenthesis indicate the percentage of the variance explained by each component (first and second dimensions): 51.96 per cent for the first and 25.36 per cent for the second. The dots stand for the TTs; the variation between them is represented by their distance: the closer the translations are to each other, the more similar they are; the further away they are, the more variance there is among them.

The first component, the horizontal axis, always accounts for more variance than the second component, the vertical axis, meaning that the distance between the TTs on the x axis represents stronger variation than the distance on the y axis. A first look at Figure 7.1 immediately shows that the greatest variance is that existing between Translation S and Translations B, M and G. The first explanation for this that comes to mind is the temporal distance between them;

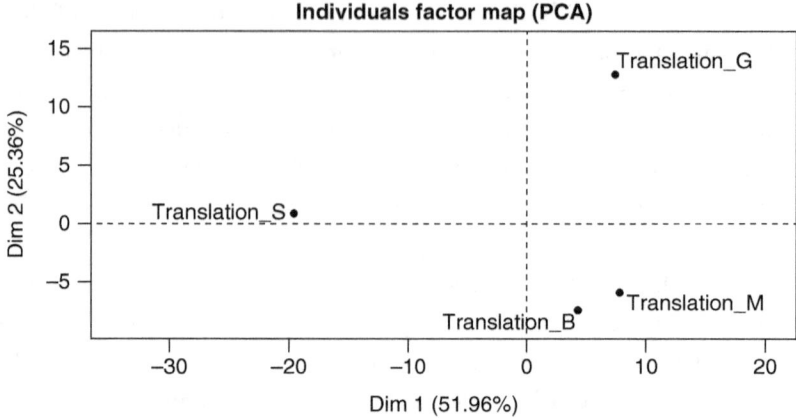

Figure 7.1 *Translation plot based on the 250 MFWs of the TTs*

there is a 62-year gap between the two sets. However, this does not mean that the contemporary TTs are similar to each other. On the contrary, Translation B and M form a close pair, while Translation G stands on its own. There is no temporal gap between them, therefore their variance must be due to some other factors. The closeness between Translation B and Translation M, and their distance from Translation G, is more probably due to the translations' individual styles.

This result is in line with the findings of the previous chapters. Both the study of the fictional representation of the African jungle and that of the fictional representation of the African natives showed an analogous picture: Translations B and M display similarities in respect to the translational issues discussed in Chapters 5 and 6, as opposed to Translation G, which shows a different tendency. As explained in Section 3.4.4, the analysis in Chapters 5 and 6 and the analysis in the present chapter are based on very different approaches. These three chapters adopt different methodologies and examine different textual features, that is, low-frequency content words in the case of Chapters 5 and 6, and function words plus high-frequency content words in the case of this chapter. Nonetheless, a parallelism between the findings is noticeable.

To help explain the variance between the TTs pointed out by Figure 7.1, a graphical output that plots the individual MFWs, instead of the translations, can be generated. This word plot, as shown in Figure 7.2, displays how the MFWs define the variance represented by the two components. Each MFW is represented as a vector pointing away from the centre. The angle of the vector in relation to the axes represents the correlation between that word and the components. The more a vector is aligned with the horizontal axis, the more it is related to the first component and less to the second; the more it is aligned vertically, the more it relates to the second and less to the first. Given that we know, from Table 7.1, that the first component represents most strongly the variance between Translation S and Translations B, M and G, we can look at the vectors that point in opposite – or almost opposite – directions on the horizontal axis to identify the words whose frequency patterns most distinguish Translation S from the contemporary TTs (a larger version of this and the following word plots is provided in Appendix 2).

Figure 7.2 confirms the interpretation according to which the variance between Translation S and Translations B, M and G is due to their temporal distance. Translation S differs from the contemporary TTs for the use of archaic or dated forms that are not commonly adopted in (literary) Italian today. For example, among the strongest discriminators of Translation S (the words at the left-hand side of the graph, aligned with the horizontal axis) are: *m'*, *s'* and *d'*. *M'* and *s'* are the elided forms of the object personal pronouns *mi* and *si* (first person singular and reflexive third person singular, respectively), while *d'* is (in most of cases) the elided form of the preposition *di* (of/at/in). These elided forms sound dated today and their use is currently decreasing in written language. The fact that they appear as what discriminates Translation S from the contemporary TTs is a confirmation of this tendency. Examples (1) to (3) show instances in which Translation S uses *m'*, *s'* and *d'*, while the other TTs opt for the forms *mi*, *si* and *di* in the same ST sentence.

(1S)   Ripresi a camminare lungo Fleet Street, ma non mi riuscì di liberarmi di quell'idea. Il serpent *m'aveva* affascinato.
(I started walking again along Fleet Street, but I couldn't get rid of that idea. The snake had charmed me.)

(1B)   Continuai a camminare per Fleet Street, ma non riuscivo a liberarmi da questa idea. Il serpent *mi aveva* incantato.
(I kept walking along Fleet Street, but I couldn't get rid of this idea. The snake had charmed me.)

(2S)   Tutte le navi *s'assomigliano*, e il mare è sempre quello.
(All ships look alike, and the sea is always the same.)

(2M)   Le navi *si assomigliano* tutte e il mare è sempre lo stesso.
(All ships look alike and the sea is always the same.)

(3S)   Sogni *d'uomini*, sementi di comunità novelle, germi di imperi.
(Dreams of men, seeds of new communities, germs of empires.)

(3B)   Sogni *di uomini*, semi di comunità, germi di imperi!
(Dreams of men, seeds of communities, germs of empires!)

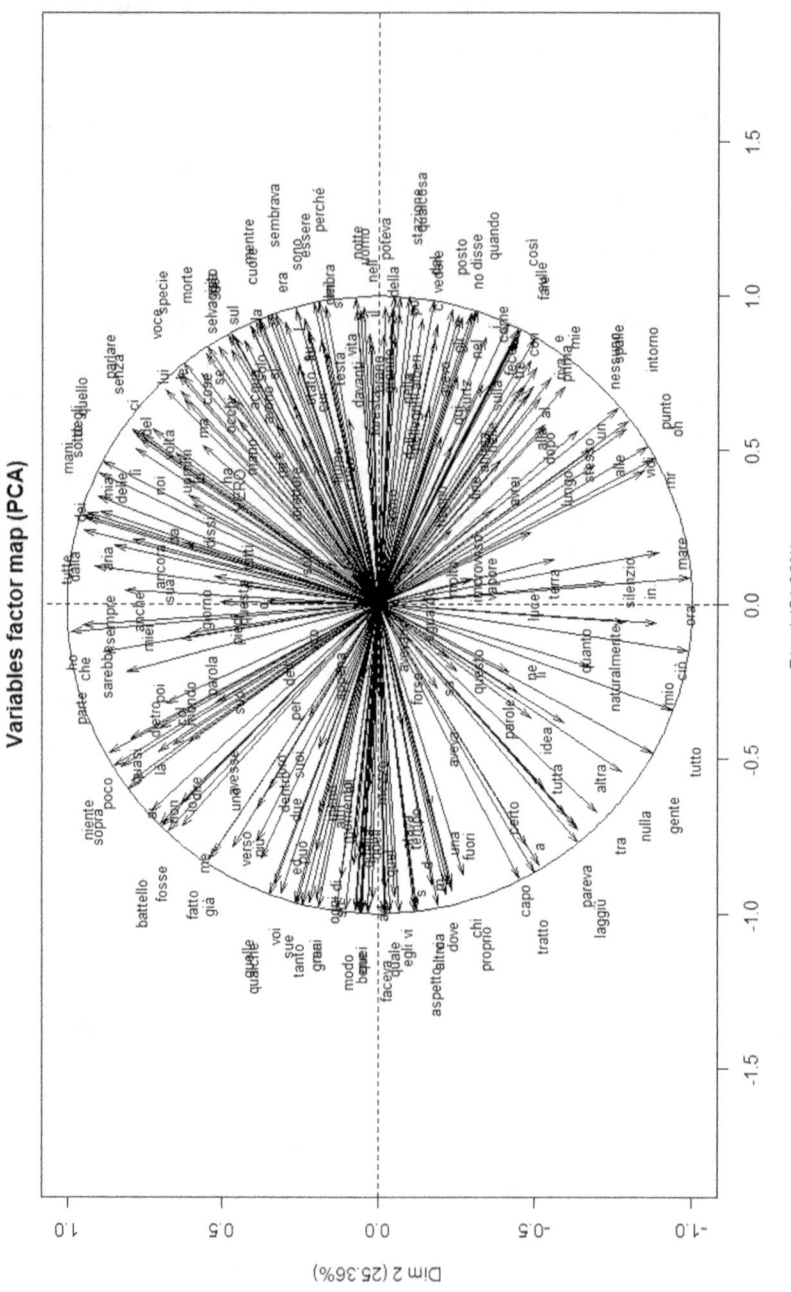

Figure 7.2 *Word plot based on the 250 MFWs of the TTs*

Other examples of dated forms among the discriminators of Translation S are *ed*, *ad* and *egli*. *Ed* (and) and *ad* (at/in/to) are the euphonic forms of *e* and *a*. The addition of a euphonic -*d* is nowadays avoided in literary language, while it is kept in the case of fixed expressions (e.g. *ad un tratto*, all of the sudden) or when *e* or *a* are followed by a word starting with the same vowel (*e*- or *a*-). It is often the case that, whereas Translation S uses *ed*, the other TTs use alternative constructions to avoid the use of the euphonic -*d*. For instance, Translation S translates *He scrambled to his feet exclaiming* as *Saltò in piedi d'un balzo, ed esclamò* (He jumped on his feet and exclaimed), while all the other translations keep the gerund form *esclamando* (exclaiming) to avoid the conjunction *ed*: *Egli si tirò su in piedi esclamando* (Translation B), *Balzò subito in piedi esclamando* (Translation G) and *Si rialzò in piedi esclamando* (Translation M).

Egli is a dated form of the third person masculine singular pronoun (he), the use of which has dramatically dropped both in written and spoken language. This decrease in use is confirmed by the fact that *egli* is predominantly used by Translation S, whereas the other TTs either omit the pronoun altogether or use the alternative form *lui* (he) instead. For example, *He had come out for a moment, he said* becomes *Era uscito per un momento, egli mi disse* (He had come out for a moment, he told me) in Translation S, but *Era usicto un momento, disse* (He had come out for a moment, [he] said) in Translations B and G and *Era uscito un attimo, disse* (He had come out for a moment, [he] said) in Translation M.

Egli is not the only pronoun among the discriminators of Translation S. Also *voi* (you, subject personal pronoun second person plural) and *vi* (direct object pronoun second person plural or reflexive pronoun second person plural) contribute to distinguish Translation S from the other TTs. These items also mark the temporal distance between the texts, for in Translation S *voi* and *vi* are used as courtesy forms to address people in formal situations. This practice was particularly widespread at the time Translation S was written, during the fascist regime, when the use of *voi*, as opposed to *lei*, was eagerly fostered (Ajello 2008). Today, also as a reaction against the regime imposition, *lei* (she) is very much preferred to *voi* as a courtesy form, and is used much more widely. All the TTs apart from Translation S use *lei* as a polite form to address people in formal contexts, as indicated by the fact that *lei* appears on the right-hand side of the plot, only slightly angled in relation to the horizontal axis: *lei* is a discriminator that distinguishes the contemporary TTs from Translation S. An example of this tendency can be seen in the translation of *I wouldn't be talking like this with you*, which becomes *non starei qui a parlare a questo modo con voi* (I wouldn't be here talking with you in this way) in Translation S, but *non starei qui a parlare con lei in questo modo* in Translation B, *non parlerei così con lei* in Translation G and *non sarei qui a parlarle così* in Translation M.

The differences between Translation S and the other TTs do not seem to be limited to the influence of the temporal gap though, since there are other discriminators that cannot be related to diachronic changes. In particular, the use of deixis seems to be another factor that contributes to the variance between Translation S and the contemporary TTs. Different types of deictics appear among the discriminators of Translation S. An example is a group of demonstrative deictics: *quell, quel, quella, quelle* and *quei* (that and those, masculine and feminine). Their presence in the left-hand side of the plot signals a higher frequency of use of this grammatical class in Translation S compared with the other translations. Translation S often introduces this type of deictics where there is none in the ST, or replaces a definite article with one of them. This tendency cannot be identified in the other TTs, and seems to be characteristic of Translation S only. Consider Example (4):

(4)   Two youths with foolish and cheery countenances were being piloted over, and she threw at them the same quick glance of unconcerned wisdom. [. . .] She seemed uncanny and fateful.

(4S)   Due giovinotti dall'aspetto idiota e ridente venivano pilotati dall'altra parte in quel momento, e colei gettò su di loro quello stesso rapido sguardo di sapienza indifferente. [. . .] Quella donna aveva un'apparenza misteriosa e fatale.

(Two youths with an idiotic and smiling appearance were being piloted to the other side at that moment, and she threw at them that same quick glance of indifferent wisdom. [. . .] That woman had a mysterious and fatal appearance.)

(4B)   Due giovani dall'aria gaia e melensa venivano pilotati innanzi, e lei gli lanciò la stessa rapida occhiata di saggezza impassibile. [. . .] La donna aveva un qualcosa di arcano e fatale.

(Two youths with a gay and cheerful look were piloted forward, and she threw at them the same quick gaze of impassive wisdom. [. . .] The woman had an arcane and fatal look about her.)

In just a couple of sentences, Translation S adds three demonstrative deictics. The first instance is in the construction *in quel momento* (at that moment), which is not there in the ST. In the second instance, *the* in *the same quick glance* is replaced by *quello* (that) in *quello stesso rapido sguardo* (that same quick glance). Finally, another *quella* is added in the last sentence, where *She seemed* becomes *Quella donna aveva* (That woman had). These changes do not occur in the contemporary TTs, as exemplified in Example (4B) which shows Translation B reproducing more faithfully the linguistic choices of the ST.

In addition to demonstratives, another type of deictics that is correlated to Translation S is person deictics: the aforementioned *egli, m', s', voi* and *vi*, but also *io* (I), *me* (object personal pronoun first person singular), *suoi* (his) and *sue* (her). Contrary to English, subject pronouns are not obligatory in Italian, and are often dropped. Keeping them is a marked choice that usually signals some sort of emphasis. For instance, in the case of *Afterwards nobody seemed to trouble much about Fresleven's remains, till I got out and stepped into his shoes*, all TTs decide to keep *I*, as it emphasizes the fact that only the *io* (I), the narrator, troubles about Fresleven's remains; Example (5) shows how this sentence has been translated in Translation M:

(5M)   In seguito nessuno sembrò darsi gran pena per i resti mortali di Fresleven, finché non saltai fuori io a prenderne il posto.
(Afterwards nobody seemed to care too much about Fresleven's mortal remains, till I got out to take his place.)

Even though *I* is in the original, its translation in Example (5) gives a special emphasis to the action of the narrator, which is not present in the ST. The prominence of person deictics in Translation S means that this special emphasis exemplified in Example (5M) is more often added in Translation S compared with the other TTs. One of these cases is shown in Example (6):

(6)   He alluded constantly to Europe, to the people I was supposed to know there [. . .].
(6S)   Alludeva a ogni momento all'Europa, alle persone che egli supponseva io conoscessi lassù [. . .].
([He] alluded all the time to Europe, to the people he supposed I knew there [. . .].)
(6B)   Alludeva continuamente all'Europa, alle persone che supponeva dovessi conoscere là [. . .].
([He] alluded continuously to Europe, to the people [he] supposed [I] knew there [. . .].)

Translation S keeps both *io* (I) and *egli* (he) in Example (6S), although they are not needed and as such they represent a marked choice. In contrast, Translation

B, in Example (6B), omits both personal pronouns, reproducing the unmarked use of pronouns in the English counterpart.

The last type of deictics observable among the discriminators of Translation S is spatial deictics, such as *là* (there) and *laggiù* (down there). The vectors that represent these MFWs in Figure 7.2 are not as aligned with the horizontal axis as other MFWs, meaning that their contribution to the variance is less prominent than some of the other discriminators discussed earlier. In fact, checking the frequency of *là* and *laggiù*, it can be noted that they are only slightly more frequent in Translation S than in the other TTs. Yet, they contribute together with the other discriminators to characterize the use of deixis in Translation S. Generally speaking, the function of deictics is that of defining specific elements of the fictional world that are being referred to. Demonstrative deictics refer to the degree of proximity to the speaker/writer or, in our case, the narrator (Halliday and Matthiessen 2004: 314), person deictics contribute to establish the focalization from which we experience the narrative, while spatial deictic devices help to set the spatial coordinates of what is being narrated (Wales 2011: 107). The overall increase of this class of elements in Translation S can be seen as emphasizing the personal involvement of the narrator, compared with the other TTs, highlighting his presence at the centre of what is being told. In Translation S, we are reminded more often that we are experiencing the story through the eyes of Marlow, as his point of view is more markedly emphasized in the narrative. The personal, spatial and temporal coordinates of his narration are more prominent in Translation S than in the other TTs.

The first component does not describe much of the variance between the contemporary translations, which are all close to each other on the *x* axis (cf. Figure 7.1). However, Translations B and M are quite distant from Translation G on the *y* axis, meaning that their variance is better described by the second component. As mentioned earlier, given that there is no temporal gap between the contemporary TTs, it can be assumed that the variance between these translations is more likely to indicate idiosyncratic preferences. Looking at the discriminators on the vertical axis, it is possible to group together MFWs that belong to the same grammatical category or word class. For example, *ho* (have, first person singular) and *ha* (has) are strongly correlated to Translation G, suggesting that this translation makes greater use of the 'passato prossimo' tense (roughly comparable to English present perfect) compared with the other two contemporary translations. A look at the concordance lines of these items confirms this hypothesis: *ho* and *ha* are used more frequently as auxiliaries for the 'passato prossimo' tense in Translation G than in Translations B and M. Consider Example (7):

(7)   [...] yet to understand the effect of it on me you ought to know how
      I got out there, what I saw, how I went up that river to the place where
      I first met the poor chap.

(7G) Però, per capire l'effetto prodotto su di me, bisogna che sappiate come
      sono giunto fin là, cosa ho visto, e come ho risalito quel fiume fino al
      luogo in cui per la prima volta ho incontrato quel poveraccio.
      (But, to understand the effect produced on me, you need to know how
      I've got out there, what I've seen, and how I've gone up to that river
      where I've first met that poor chap.)

(7M) [...] eppure per comprendere l'effetto che ebbe su di me, dovete sapere
      come finii laggiù, che cosa vidi e come risalii quel fiume fino al punto in
      cui incontrai per la prima volta quel poveraccio.
      ([...] yet to understand the effect that it had on me, you have to know
      how I ended down there, what I saw and how I went up that river to the
      place where I first met that poor chap.)

In this illustrative case, Translation G translates the simple past verbs in the ST
with 'passato prossimo' verbs. *I saw*, *I went up* and *I first met* become *ho visto*
(I've seen), *ho risalito* (I've gone up) and *per la prima volta ho incontrato* (I've
first met), respectively. *I got out there* too is translated with a 'passato prossimo'
tense, *sono giunto fin là* (I've got up there): even though this time the auxiliary
verb is different – *essere* (to be) instead of *avere* (to have) – the tendency exemplified is the same. In contrast, Translation M in Example (7M) (and Translation
B) uses the 'passato remoto' tense, which is closer to the English simple past. *I got
out*, *I saw*, *I went up* and *I first met* are translated with *finii laggiù* (I ended down
there), *vidi* (I saw), *risalii* (I went up) and *incontrai* (I met).

Another example of groups of grammatically related words that characterize
one or the other translation is prepositions. Translation G appears to prefer the
prepositions *dei* and its various forms *dei, delle, del, dell* and *degli* (of the), *su*
and *sul* (on/above/up/etc.) and *sopra* (on top of/on/upon/atop), whereas *sulla*
and *sulle* (on/above/up/etc.) are more strongly correlated to Translations B and
M. For example, *over a man's head* is translated with *sulla testa di uno* (over
someone's head) and *sulla testa di un uomo* (over a man's head) in Translations
B and M respectively, while Translation G uses *sopra la testa di un uomo* (over
a man's head).

In Chapter 3, I argued that function words can be seen as the markers of the
relationships that words establish with each other in a text. As such,
function words are also the markers of everything these relationships entail

(McKenna et al. 1999: 152). The use of specific function words – for example, prepositions or auxiliary verbs – leads to the use of specific phrase and sentence constructions, for instance, prepositional phrases. The fact that different forms of the same function word all relate to the same TT (or pair, in the case of Translations B and M) does not simply indicate that they are used more frequently by one translator compared with the others. This distinctive use of words belonging to the same grammatical category or class can result in a distinctive use of a given construction: rather than simply signalling that *sopra* or *ho* are frequently used in Translation G, they can suggest that specific prepositional phrases or tense forms are more prominent in one translation compared with the others.

7.4 Comparing the TTs using MFSs

This section compares the TTs by investigating their overall variance based on the frequency patterns of their MFSs. Shifting the focus from single words to word sequences widens the perspective on the TTs' relation, allowing me to encompass more complex lexico-grammatical structures. For the sake of clarity, 'word sequence' is simply defined as a sequence of continuous words. The MFSs used in this section are two-word and three-word sequences. Two- and three-word sequences are also used by Barlow (2013) in his multifunctional analysis of the spoken output of six White House press secretaries. Conversely, Hoover (2002) uses only two-word sequences and ignores longer sequences. Hoover (2002: 162) claims that three-word (or longer) sequences do not occur frequently enough to be worth investigating. To bear this out, he carries out a cluster analysis with 40 three-word MFSs, proving that only in six out of seventeen cases the author is attributed correctly. However, this study does not aim to attribute authorship. In line with Barlow (2013), I use two-word (Section 7.4.1) and three-word sequences (Section 7.4.2), and show that in both cases the analyses provide relevant results, as they are consistent with what has been obtained using MFWs.

As for the previous analysis, I carried out preliminary tests with different pools of MFSs in order to identify the number of MFSs that works better for this study. Working with two-word MFSs, PCA produced similar results from 1,000 to 350. From 300 to 150 MFSs, the outcomes of the tests started to change slightly, while 100 and 50 produced very different results to the previous ones. In accordance with the criteria adopted in the previous section, 350 is the number of two-word MFSs used. With respect to three-word sequences, the results were basically the same from 1,000 to 100, changing only when 50 MFSs were used. For the sake of consistency, 350 is the number of three-word MFSs taken in consideration.

7.4.1 Comparing the frequency patterns of two-word MFSs

To start with, the TTs are compared using 350 two-word MFSs as variables. The result, displayed in Figure 7.3, shows an unequivocal similarity with what has been obtained using MFWs. Again, the distance between Translation S and the contemporary translations represents the strongest variance between the texts, while Translations B, M and G cluster quite close together on the horizontal axis. The variance among the contemporary TTs is represented by their distance along the vertical axis: Translation B and Translation M are next to each other, while Translation G appears in the top-right quadrant of the graph. Overall, the relation among the TTs is unaltered.

A look at the vectors in the word plot (Figure 7.4) suggests that, this time, the temporal gap is not the strongest discriminating factor. Examining the MFSs that contribute most to the variance represented by the first component, it can be noted that dated and archaic forms are not as predominant as they were in Figure 7.2. Only *s'era* (reflexive third person pronoun + was) and *d'un* (of a/of an) can be recognized as referring back to the 'old-fashioned' MFWs identified in the previous section, that is, *s'* and *d'*. The un-elided form *si era* appears at the opposite side of the plot as a strong discriminator of the contemporary

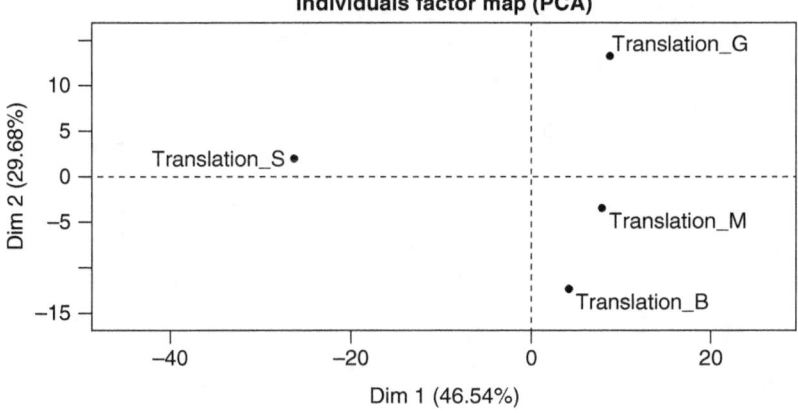

Figure 7.3 *Translation plot based on the 350 two-word MFSs of the TTs*

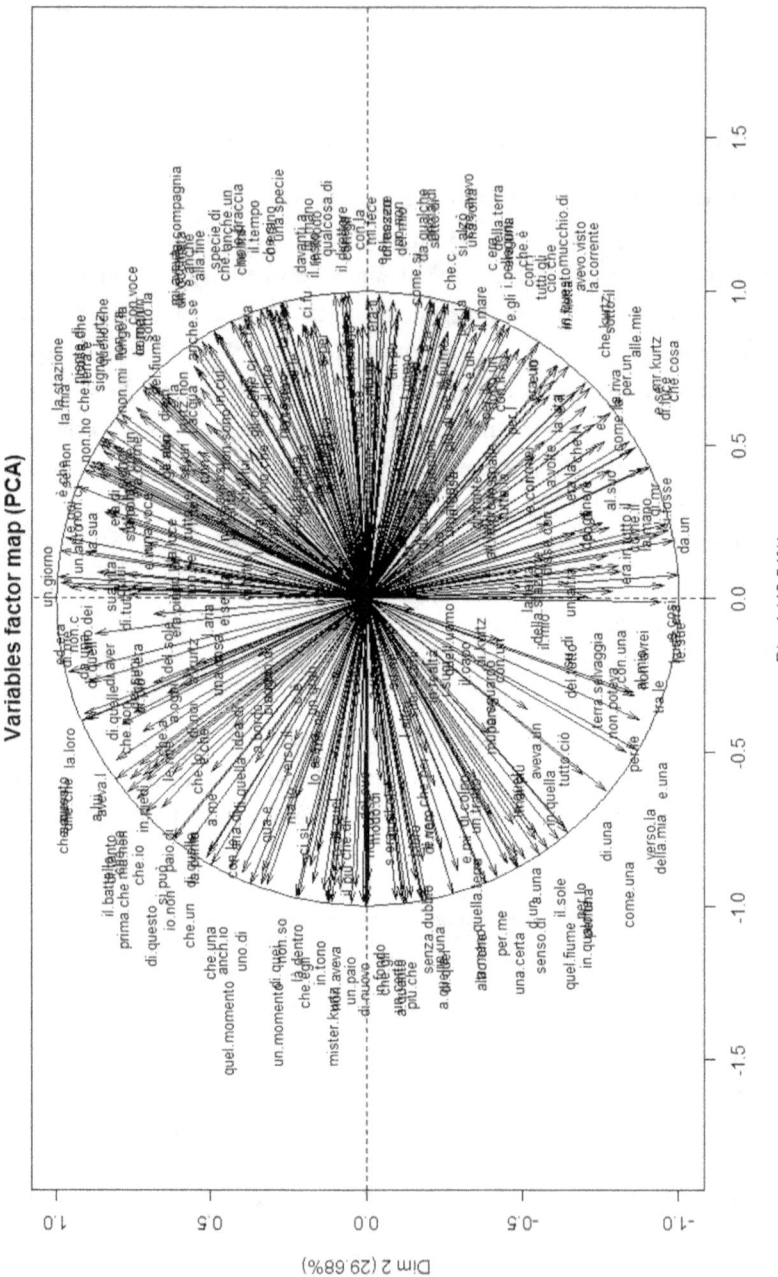

Figure 7.4 *Word plot based on the 350 two-word MFSs of the TTs*

translations. Thus, if we looked at Figure 7.4 only, it would be very difficult to guess that Translation S is 62 years older than the other TTs without already being aware of the temporal gap. On the other hand, there is an abundance of MFSs referring back to the MFWs not linked to the temporal gap, especially deictics. There are many MFSs with person deictics: *io non* (I do/did not), *a me* (to me), *anch'io* (me too), *ma io* (but I), *che egli* (that he), *s'era* (reflexive third person pronoun + was), *del suo* (of his), *che gli* (that + indirect object third person pronoun), *e mi* (and + indirect object first person pronoun), *mi parve* (seemed to me), *per me* (for me) and so on. There are also MFSs with determiner deictics (*quel momento*, that moment; *di quella*, of that; *di quei*, of those; *a quel*, at that; *a quella*, to that; *di quel*, of that; etc.), and a few with spatial deictics, such as *qua e* (here and) and *là dentro* (there inside). In addition to these returning groups, there is a new group emerging, that of MFSs related to time expressions: *quel momento* (that moment), *un momento* (a moment), *un tratto* (a sudden), *di colpo* (suddenly) and *un certo* (at a given). They are all part of longer time adverbial phrases, for example, *in quel momento* (at that moment), *ad un certo punto* (all of the sudden), *ad un tratto* (suddenly). For example, in translating *At eight or nine, perhaps, it lifted as a shutter lifts*, only Translation S adds the time adverbial *d'un tratto*, while the other TTs do not. Thus the ST sentence becomes *Potevano essere le otto o le nove all'incirca, quando essa si alzò d'un tratto, al modo di una saracinesca* (It was about eight or nine, when it lifted suddenly as a shutter lifts) in Translation S, but *Alle otto, o forse alle nove, si alzò come una serranda* (At eight, or maybe at nine, it lifted as a shutter) in Translation B. This group of temporal expressions adds up to the other deictics in emphasizing the spatial-temporal coordinates of the narrative in Translation S, to a greater extent than the contemporary TTs. Overall, the first component's discriminators confirm that the use of deixis is a major factor in differentiating the TTs.

In the case of the second component, it is again possible to observe MFSs related to the MFWs discussed in the previous section. This supports the hypothesis that the differences identified refer to idiosyncratic preferences of the contemporary TTs. Among Translation G's discriminators, there are *non ho* (I have not) and *l'ho* (I have + object third person pronoun), both of them mostly used in 'passato prossimo' verb phrases, such as *non ho ancora visto* (I haven't see yet) or *ve l'ho detto* (I have told you). The various forms of the preposition *dei* in relation to Translation G are here identifiable in the MFSs *dei suoi* (of his), *uno dei* (one of) and *del fiume* (of the river), whereas the preposition *su* appears in the MFSs *su un* (on a) and *sul ponte* (on the bridge). An interesting new addition to the discriminators of Translations B and M that emerges as a result of using two-word sequences instead of individual words is *terra selvaggia* (wild land). This MFS is particularly relevant because it links directly the outcomes of PCA to the analysis of the fictional representation of the African jungle. In fact, *terra selvaggia* is the translation of *wilderness* most frequently used by both Translation M and Translation B, as opposed to Translation G that instead uses *landa selvaggia* (wild land) most of the time. Finally, another minor stylistic difference that distinguishes Translation G from Translations B and M is the way they refer to Kurtz. Translations B and M use the English loan word *mr*, while Translation G opts for the Italian *signor* (mister). This is mirrored in the presence of sequences such as *di mr* (of mr) and *mr Kurtz* (mr Kurtz) at the bottom of the plot, and *signor Kurtz* (mister Kurtz) and *il signor* (mister) at the top.

7.4.2 Comparing the frequency patterns of three-word MFSs

Switching from two-word to three-word MFSs (Figure 7.5) does not change the overall picture. Translation S is in the left-hand side of the plot, far away from the other three TTs. In the right-hand side, Translations M and B cluster close together, separated on the vertical axis from Translation G.

The word plot of the individual sequences (Figure 7.6) confirms what has been noted in the two-word MFS analysis. As far as the first component is concerned, the variance due to the temporal gap is hardly recognizable in the discriminators of Translation S. Only *che egli non* (that he does/did not) stands out as related to the MFWs discussed in respect to out-dated forms. However, many of the three-word sequences link back to the other MFWs and two-word

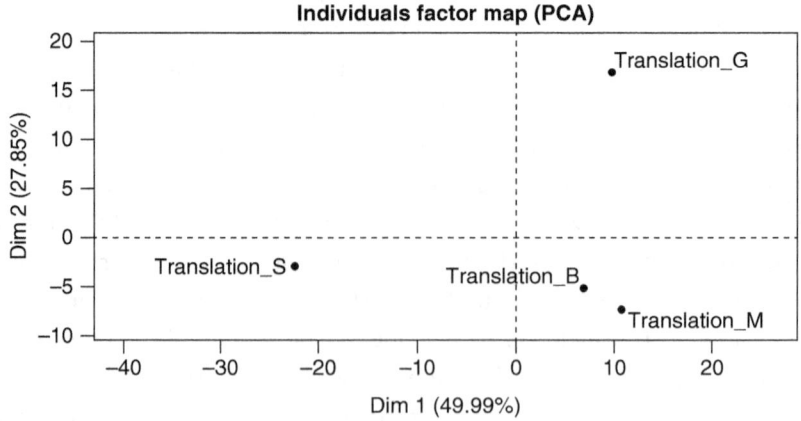

Figure 7.5 *Translation plot based on the 350 three-word MFSs of the TTs*

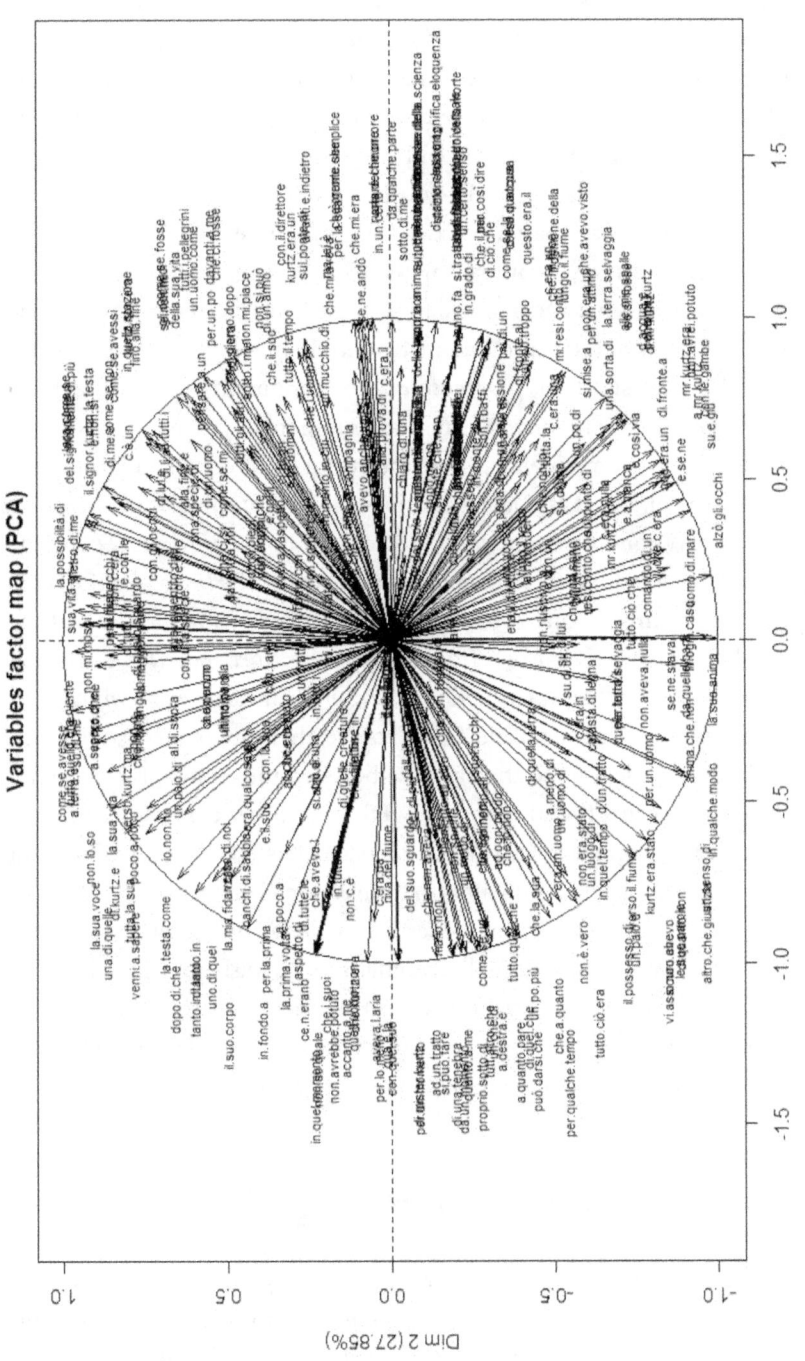

Figure 7.6 *Word plot based on the 350 three-word MFSs of the TTs*

MFSs discussed previously. For example, there are MFSs with demonstrative deictics (*con quel suo*, with that [. . .] of his; *in quel momento*, in that moment; *di quelle creature*, of those creatures; *quell'uomo non*, that man does/did not; *di quel che*, of that which; *di quella terra*, of that land), some with person deictics (*che i suoi*, that his; *ma io non*, but not me; *quanto a me*, as far as I'm concerned; *che io non*, that I do/did not; *i suoi occhi*, his eyes; *accanto a me*, next to me) and one with spatial deictics (*qua e là*, here and there). There are also time adverbial phrases, confirming the key role these expressions play in defining the variance between Translation S and the contemporary translations: *in quel momento* (at that moment), *per un momento* (for a moment), *ad un tratto* (all of the sudden), *momento all'altro* (moment to the other), *d'un tratto* (suddenly), *da un momento* (from one moment).

As for the second component, among the vectors that contribute to the variance on the vertical axis it is equally possible to identify three-word MFSs that build on the MFWs and two-words MFSs discussed in the previous sections. On the top half of the plot there are *su di me* (on me), *il signor Kurtz* (mister Kurtz) and *del signor Kurtz* (of mister Kurtz), which correlate strongly with Translation G. On the bottom half, there is *a mr Kurtz* (to mr Kurtz), *mr Kurtz non* (mr Kurtz does/ did not), *di mr Kurtz* (of mr Kurtz) and *mr Kurtz era* (mr Kurtz was), which correlate strongly with Translations B and M. Of course, there are other discriminators that contribute considerably to the variance between the contemporary translations. However, it seems that three-word MFSs offer fewer chances to group the vectors together into grammatically or semantically related categories. For example, among the strongest discriminators of Translation G are *verso di me* (towards me), *c'era niente* (there was anything), *a terra e* (on land and), *ai miei occhi* (at my eyes), whereas among the strongest discriminators of Translations B and M are *in ogni caso* (in any case), *la sua anima* (his soul) and *alzò gli occhi* (lifted his eyes). Their frequency patterns contribute individually to differentiate the translations, but they can hardly be interpreted as signalling a more general tendency.

7.5 Relations between the findings

The results of PCA with different variables show a high degree of consistency. There are two main outcomes that return consistently throughout the three analyses. The first one is the overall degree of similarity/difference between the TTs. Independently on whether the comparison was based on the frequency patterns of MFWs, two-word or three-words MFSs, the result was always the same. The highest level of variance is that between Translation S and Translations

B, M and G, whereas, among the latter, Translation G differs the most from Translations B and M. The lowest degree of variance is that between Translation B and Translation M. The fact that each successive analysis confirmed the outcome of the previous one brings support to the general relationship between the TTs pointed out in this chapter.

The second main outcome that recurs in all three stages of the analysis is the interrelated nature of the MFWs and MFSs that discriminate each translation. Using single words as variables shows that the temporal gap existing between Translation S and the contemporary translations is not the only source of variance. In addition to dated forms, Translation S differs also in the use of deixis, especially demonstrative, person and spatial deictic devices. The contemporary translations differ in terms of preferences for specific linguistic features, such as verbs or prepositions. The fact that the MFWs could be grouped into categories – for example, auxiliary verbs (*ho* and *ha*), different forms of the same preposition (*dei, delle, degli* or *sulla, sulle*), or demonstrative deictics (*quell, quel, quella, quelle*, etc.) – suggests that the preference is not for the individual words, but rather for a grammatical class or structure, for example, the use of 'passato prossimo' verbal tense or specific prepositional phrases. This is further supported by the results of PCA using MFSs as variables, which show that some of the two-word and three-word sequences that discriminate a given translation contain the MFWs that were previously related to that same TT. Thus, some of the MFSs that strongly correlated to Translation S contain deictics, whereas the MFS discriminators of the contemporary TTs contain prepositions.

This continuity in the results can be seen as an indication that the difference between the TTs, as it is pointed out by PCA, is the result of idiosyncratic preferences for formal features, rather than for individual words. Function words – most of the MFWs taken into account – function as building agents for the structuring of sentences; they establish those relationships among content words which help the text to convey meaning. Compared with single MFWs, two-word and three-word MFSs are one step ahead in the process of constructing the text, the latter just adding one level more to the former. For example, *io* (I), *io non* (I do/did not) and *che io non* (that I do/did not) are three successive steps in the construction of the same structure. The consistency in the findings mirrors the consistency in the choices of the translators, suggesting that MFW, two-word MFS and three-word MFS analyses refer to the same idiosyncratic preferences in using specific lexico-grammatical tools at distinct levels of development. As a result of these choices, the TTs can have different 'stylistic overtones' (McKenna et al. 1999) compared with one another. For instance, the high frequency of deictic devices in Translation S can result in a style that emphasizes the focalization of the narrative. Similarly, the prepositional phrases that characterize the contemporary TTs can mark a more descriptive or reflective tendency in writing (cf. McKenna et al. 1999: 152). Ultimately, it is these ideolectal differences and their effect on the style of the translations that mostly distinguish the TTs from each other at a textual level.

7.6 Conclusion

This chapter compared the translations as whole texts, using PCA to provide a statistical measure of their overall variance, based on the frequency patterns of items which have not been taken into account in the previous chapters. The occurrence of these items is so common that it is unlikely they are consciously regulated by authors: they have in fact been seen as 'authorial wordprints' (Hoover 2002) or 'stylistic signature' (Burrows 2002a) and, as such, considered author- and text-specific. PCA pointed out that Translation S is very different from the contemporary TTs; that Translation G is the least similar among the contemporary translations; and finally, that Translations M and B are very similar to each other. By highlighting how the TTs compare with each other when examined as whole texts, this investigation provided an answer to the fourth research question.

The approach adopted in Chapters 5 and 6 and the approach used in this chapter both prioritize lexis. Yet, the range of lexis analysed differs completely. Chapters 5 and 6 focused on the semantic level. The items examined were mostly low-frequency content words, and the analysis was centred on their semantic preferences and semantic prosodies. In contrast, this chapter focused on high-frequency items, mainly function words. Function words are the connectors between content words, so their study here emphasized the structures they establish between content words. I argued that differences in the frequency patterns of content words across texts can indicate preferences for a given grammatical or formal structure. In this way, this chapter did not only show the overall relationship between the translations, but also shed some light on stylistic tendencies that can explain the variance between the TTs. Yet, despite the differences of approaches and linguistic levels taken into account by this and the previous chapters, a link between the outcomes emerged. The results of this chapter are in line with the findings of the previous chapters: the similarity between Translations M and B, and their difference from Translation G mirrors the differences identified in Chapters 5 and 6, namely, the diverse tendencies the translations display in the way they deal with the fictional representation of the African jungle and the African natives. The two levels – the content level and the structural level – seem to match coherently, suggesting their interplay. Deepening the investigation of the extent to which these two levels interact could be the aim of a new methodological circle. As explained in Chapter 3, this chapter represents the last step of a methodological circle that could, potentially, be repeated. PCA moved the perspective of the analysis from the study of individual features to the whole texts. Building on the findings of this chapter, a new cycle could be started, so as to explore more qualitatively, for example, the idiosyncratic preferences emerged in the PCA analysis and study how they interact with the semantic level of the texts.

Conclusions

8.1 Introduction

This chapter provides a concluding discussion of the contributions and implications of this book. Section 8.2 discusses the major findings that emerged from this study, while Section 8.3 suggests some directions for expanding further this and similar projects.

8.2 Major findings

Three major findings emerged from this study: the role of textual patterns as building blocks of the fictional world, the effect of translation on the relation between textual patterns and the fictional world, and the link between the comparison at the level of individual features and that at the level of whole texts. Sections 8.2.1, 8.2.2 and 8.2.3 discuss these points, respectively.

8.2.1 Textual patterns as building blocks of the fictional world

This book argued that textual patterns can function as building blocks of fictional worlds in literature. It foregrounded the role of specific patterns in constructing the fictional representation of the African jungle and of the African natives, both quantitatively and qualitatively. The identification of these patterns started with a keyword analysis. In corpus linguistics, keyword analysis is commonly used to commence a study by identifying a pool of items to examine in detail, items that are characteristic of the text/corpus under investigation and easily manageable in terms of quantity. In this respect, this book is not an exception; however, I also showed that keyword analysis can be employed to establish a connection between the lexical level of a text and its themes. Although individual keywords can hardly account for a theme in a book as complex as *HoD*, I showed that groups of keywords offer a different picture. Groups of semantically and thematically related words are able to establish a link between a given theme and the lexical level of the text.

Generally speaking, keywords are considered to be particularly effective in signalling what a text is about (Scott 2016a). However, I argued that to establish the link between themes and lexis the simple identification of 'aboutness' keywords is not enough. A more fine-grained discrimination is necessary, such as that provided by a categorization model that takes into account the role that keywords can play in building the fictional world and conveying thematic concerns. For this study, this model was provided by Mahlberg and McIntryre's (2011) fictional world signal and thematic signal keywords. Groups of keywords categorized according to this model are able to establish a link with specific aspects of the text, such as its characters, its setting, its atmosphere and its themes. The resulting 'Africa words' and 'African words' include fictional world signal keywords, thematic signal keywords and thematically related words. The study of these items was a well-grounded way to examine how major themes in *HoD* are connected to the linguistic level of the short novel.

The patterns that the 'Africa words' and the 'African words' establish function as building blocks of the fictional world, because they linguistically construct the representation of the jungle and of the natives in the text. This study identified three main patterns associated with the items in the two groups: lexical repetition, semantic preferences and semantic prosody. Their persistent co-occurrence shapes the depiction of these fictional entities, defining them as discussed in Chapters 5 and 6, and as summarized in Table 8.1.

The consistency of these patterns ensures that every time the reader comes across one of the 'Africa words' or 'African words', they find them associated with the features summarized in Table 8.1. Occurrence after occurrence, these

Table 8.1 *Summary of the representation of the jungle and of the natives*

African jungle	African natives
Personified	Dehumanized
Metaphorical representation	Physical representation
Shapeless place	Represented as groups rather than individuals
Impenetrable place	Incomprehensible to the colonizers
Dark place	Related to negative states or situations

features literally build up the representation of the fictional world throughout the text – the patterns are indeed building blocks.

The implications of this specific textual representation go beyond the construction of the fictional world. The fictional world, in turn, is related to the text's literary themes. Throughout Chapters 2, 4, 5 and 6, it was shown how the depiction of the African jungle relates to the theme 'Africa and its representation', while the depiction of the African natives is linked to the theme 'race and racism'. A postcolonial reading of *HoD* emphasizes the way Africa and Africans are represented because such representations can be regarded as indicative of Conrad's ideologies and attitudes towards the colonial enterprise. Africa is in a dialogic opposition to the Western world, and through this dialogue issues of imperialistic power and domination can be analysed. Moreover, given its popularity, *HoD* has contributed significantly to shape the reception of Africa, both in literature and in popular culture. Similarly, Achebe's (1990) criticism, and the critical debate that he generated, considers the way Africans are represented in *HoD* as central to the discussion about race and racism. Therefore, when we look at how Africa and Africans are described in *HoD*, we are not only looking into the settings and characters of the novel, but we are also considering how these aspects of the fictional world reflect more complex issues.

Given the close connection between the fictional world and the major themes of *HoD*, I argued that the patterns that this book identified have a double role. Not only do they function as building blocks of the fictional world, but they also contribute to the two major themes. The persistent use of repeated vocabulary and semantic fields throughout the text establish a lexical network that makes the fictional representation of the jungle and of the natives cohesive. This notion of the cohesive network can also be applied to the themes: the consistent use of the same fictional representation throughout the text establishes a thematic network that contributes to the overall process of theme construction. In a sense, the textual patterns are building blocks of both the fictional world and of the major themes.

This twofold function reflects the two perspectives that this book took into account: the text-based and the reader-based perspectives. On the one hand, I provided insight into the distinctive linguistic features that characterize *HoD* as an artistic work, compared with other texts. The analyses in Chapters 5 and 6, for example, build on the outcome of the keyword analysis in Chapter 4: keywords are automatically identified on the basis of their unusual frequency. Examining them enabled me to provide insight into the intrinsic linguistic features of *HoD*. On the other hand, these text-based features were discussed in light of reader-based perspectives. Whereas keywords are statistically defined on the basis of textual features – their frequency compared with a reference corpus – the categories I used to group them reflect instead how the critics understand the text, thus following criteria that are not necessarily text-based. The 'Africa words' and 'African words' emerged as relevant items for the study of *HoD*'s major themes; these themes, in turn, mirror a shared and consolidated interpretation of the text, that of the literary criticism. The conjunction of these two perspectives is in line with the very nature and aim of corpus stylistics: relating linguistic description to literary appreciation.

This study also showed that discursive constructions can be identified and studied in literature. Corpus methods have frequently been employed in critical discourse analysis to investigate the linguistic representation of different social and cultural groups, such as refugees and asylum seekers (Gabrielatos and Baker 2008), suffragettes and suffragists (Gupta 2015) and Muslims (Baker et al. 2013). These studies have shown that corpus approaches can uncover ideologies and stances as they are reflected by discursive representations (Gabrielatos and Baker 2008: 6). However, research in this field is mainly focused on language in the media. A similar approach can be applied in literary studies, because all literary texts are tied to a particular social context. Analysing the linguistic representation of characters or groups in a fictional text thus provides insight into larger social discourses. This is the case for the representation of Africa and Africans in *HoD* that, although specific to a given text, establishes links with a wider historical context.

8.2.2 Textual patterns and the fictional world in translation

One of the main arguments of this book is that texts are organized on the basis of word relations. Meaning emerges from the relationship between words, rather than from their use in isolation (Sinclair 1991, 2004). Similarly, text cohesion is established through grammatical and lexical networks (Halliday and Hasan 1976). These relations and networks are as important in translation as they are in the original. This study showed that the discrepancies produced by translating are not simply the result of shifts at the level of the individual word, but are rather the consequences of the individual shifts on word relations.

Both Chapter 5 and Chapter 6 showed how the translators maintain the semantic preferences/prosody identified in the original, reproducing equivalent semantic fields. However, the relation between the fields and the 'Africa/African words' is altered. Translating *wilderness* and *darkness* with multiple terms significantly affects the network existing between the fictional entity and its textual representation. Similarly, replacing all the uses of *nigger/niggers* and *negro* with *nero/neri* (black/blacks) creates a mismatch between the way black people are described (semantic fields) and the way they are referred to ('African words'), a mismatch that is not present in the original. Thus, discrepancies in the word relations result in discrepancies in the fictional representations.

Given the link between linguistic features and literary themes, I argued that alterations to the fictional world have the potential to affect how these themes are perceived within the target culture. If the description of Africa and black people is key to our understanding of how *HoD* engages with issues of colonial power and race, then it is not surprising that the way we perceive these issues can change if the descriptions of Africa and Africans themselves are altered. My analysis foregrounded how alterations to the micro-level of individual textual features can affect the macro-level of the text, its interpretational implications (cf. Munday 2008). In this respect, such alterations can be said to have manipulative effects.

Chapter 1 discussed the concept of translation manipulation, outlining the criteria in accordance to which it is usually defined in translation studies research. The outcomes of Chapters 5 and 6 suggested a rethinking of the phenomenon, as its usual definition may be too restrictive, particularly the view that manipulation is always intentional and that it always has an ideological motivation. I agreed with Dukāte (2009) in recognizing the existence of both intentional and unintentional manipulation. More importantly, I supported this view by providing a comparison of two different types of shift, namely, obligatory and non-obligatory (Toury 2004). In Chapter 5, I discussed obligatory shifts, resulting from the lack of a direct equivalent: *wilderness* does not have an equivalent in Italian, while *darkness* has several equivalents, depending on the context. In Chapter 6, I examined non-obligatory shifts, that is, those which are not due to a lack of an equivalent, but rather to the choice of the translator. It was suggested, for example, that translating *nigger* with *nero* (black) or *black* with *negro* (nigger) are non-obligatory shifts, given that both ST terms have a direct Italian equivalent. This study showed that the two different shifts can have equally manipulative effects on the TT, independent of whether they were intentional or unintentional. From an 'effect-oriented perspective', both shifts have the potential to produce the effect that is usually attributed to manipulation: misleading the reader and distorting the original text.

8.2.3 Different levels of comparison

The approach to the study of literary translation adopted by this book is based on the comparison between the ST and the TT. I suggested a method that establishes a comparison from two distinct but interrelated perspectives. In Chapters 5 and 6, comparison was established on the basis of individual linguistic features, whereas in Chapter 7 *HoD* and its translations were compared as whole texts. These two different approaches shed light on different aspects of the texts: the semantic level of content words and the structural level of function words, respectively. Yet, despite the diverse approaches and items taken into account, the two methodological perspectives match in their results.

Chapters 5 and 6 focused on how the patterns of low-frequency, yet thematically relevant, content words are reproduced in translation. Both analyses showed that Translation G is distinct from the other TTs, while the other translations share similar tendencies. Specifically, Translation G is the TT least affected by the loss of lexical cohesion, as it uses only two different terms to translate *wilderness*. It is also the only translation that consistently mitigates the potential racist implications of the ST's lexical choices. In contrast, Translations M, B and S use a large range of items for *wilderness*, and maintain or intensify the potential racist implications of the original. These differences can be seen as more marked within the contemporary translations, given that they are products of the same sociocultural context, unlike Translation S. A similar picture was obtained in Chapter 7. With PCA, the comparison of the TTs was established on a wider ground, covering the majority of the tokens in the texts, including all of the most frequent function words. On this basis, the same relations are once again observable: Translation G is the most different TT among the contemporary ones; Translations B and M are very similar to each other; Translation S stands out for its diachronic distance. Thus, the two levels of comparison support each other, leading to the same unvarying picture. This convergent picture aligns with the view of a text as a complex unit in which different constituents interact cooperatively in order to construct a cohesive whole. The compatibility of the results would suggest that the two comparisons – one focused on the content level, based on low-frequency content words; the other focused on the structural level, based on high-frequency function words – do not represent independent views, but rather different, yet interacting, textual levels.

8.3 Mixing approaches

This book deliberately adopted a textual approach, in the sense that it focused mainly on the qualitative analysis of textual patterns and their relation to the fictional world. Because of this relation, it was argued that the translation alterations to the patterns have the potential to trigger discrepancies in the way both the fictional world and the themes are perceived by the target reader. This question could be approached from the reader's point of view, and the potential discrepancies in the perception of the TT could be tested by drawing on data collections for reader-response analysis. For example, questionnaires and interviews with readers would provide direct insight into the effects of the linguistic alterations. The response of source language readers to a given extract from the ST can be compared with the target language readers' response to the same extract in the TT, so as to test whether the translator's alterations manipulate the perception of the extract. Specifically, the reader's perception of the fictional representation of Africa and of the natives in the ST can be compared with the reader's perception of the same elements in the TTs. If readers were provided with a series of extracts focusing on the wilderness, would they perceive *wilderness* as a cohesive fictional entity with a defined textual representation in the ST? In turn, would target language readers miss the cohesive network in the TT as a result of the multiple terms used to translate *wilderness*? Moreover, would the reader's response to a translation where the natives are described mainly in terms of *negro/negri* (nigger/niggers) be different from the response to a translation where all the potentially racist terms have been replaced by *nero/neri* (black/blacks)? If so, would this difference have an effect on the perception of the other aspects of the fictional representation, that is, the semantic preferences and prosody?

In addition to offline studies involving interviews and questionnaires, online psycholinguistic experiments could be carried out. Seeking support from psycholinguistics can shed some light on the psychological reality of the patterns identified and the cumulative effects they create through reading. For example, Mahlberg et al. (2014) use eye-tracking to investigate how body part clusters are read in Dickens's work. They relate reading times to readers' awareness of body part clusters, aiming to understand what effects such clusters can have on the understanding of characters. Similarly, eye-tracking could be used to compare the reading times of the patterns across the ST and TTs, or across different translations. The pattern alterations introduced by translating can be used to explain potential differences in reading times. The development of this line of enquiry would contribute to the study of the effects of manipulation on the target reader in a more empirical fashion, allowing the researcher to relate specific textual alterations with potential interpretative implications.

An additional proposal for further development would be to shift the focus of the analysis from the ST to the TTs. Chapters 1 and 3 explained that this book concentrates on the study of Conrad's style in translation, rather than on the translators' style. However, building on the analysis of the original's style, it could be possible to examine the style of the individual translators, too. Baker (2000) maintains that if we wish to argue convincingly that translation is not simply a reproductive activity, but that it also involves creativity, then we need to pay more attention to the style of the translators and study it independently from the ST. Excluding the ST completely, however, could be counterproductive in some cases, because it is sometimes virtually impossible to separate out neatly the translator's own stylistic features from the intrinsic features of the ST. Huang and Chu (2014) and Huang (2015) suggest taking both perspectives into account, as at times a feature of the TT can be the result of both the translator's individual style and the influence of the ST and/or source language. This book already offered insights into the style of *HoD* and how the translators dealt with it; a further development of the present project would build on these findings to improve the understanding of the translators' style. Combining the two perspectives – the study of the original author's style in translation and the study of the translators' style – would provide a more nuanced picture of the relation between style and translation.

To undertake this advanced line of research, however, additional reference corpora would be needed. Both Baker (2000) and Saldanha (2011a) explain that, in order to define a linguistic feature as a translator's style, such a feature should be identifiable across a range of TTs by the same translator and distinguishable from the style of other translators. Reference corpora of translated texts are notoriously more difficult to build, given that translations in digital format are less available than original texts. This is also due to copyright restrictions, since translations are usually protected by copyrights even when the original work is in the public domain. If more of such translated literature corpora were available, it would be possible to compare the TTs on the basis of their own specific features, as opposed to how the TTs reproduced a specific feature of the ST. For example, carrying out a keyword analysis of the TTs would emphasize those items that characterize each translation. These items can then be compared with the original, in order to examine whether they have been triggered by ST features or represent the actual stylistic idiosyncrasies of the translators.

Appendix 1

Texts in the Reference Corpora

Reference corpus (RC)

1887 – *Little Novels*. Collins, W.

1889 – *The Legacy of Cain*. Collins, W.

1889 – *The Master of Ballantrae*. Stevenson, R. L.

1893 – *Catriona*. Stevenson, R. L.

1894 – *Life's Little Ironies*. Hardy, T.

1894 – *The Jungle Book*. Kipling, R.

1894 – *The People of the Mist*. Haggard, H. R.

1895 – *Jude the Obscure*. Hardy, T.

1895 – *The Amazing Marriage*. Meredith, G.

1896 – *The Island of Doctor Moreau*. Wells, H. G.

1896 – *The London Pride*. Braddon, M. E.

1898 – *The War of the Worlds*. Wells, H. G.

1901 – *Kim*. Kipling, R.

1902 – *The Hound of the Baskervilles*. Conan Doyle, A.

1904 – *Henry Brocken*. De la Mare, W.

1905 – *Ayesha: The Return of She*. Haggard, H. R.

1905 – *The Marriage of William Ashe*. Ward, H.

1905 – *Where Angels Fear to Tread*. Forster, E. M.

1906 – *The Fifth Queen*. Madox Ford, F.

1906 – *The Man of Property*. Galsworthy, J.

1908 – *A Room with a View*. Forster, E. M.

1908 – *The Old Wives' Tales*. Bennett, A.

1910 – *Celt and Saxon*. Meredith, G.

1910 – *Clayhanger*. Bennett, A.

1910 – *The Return*. De la Mare, W.

1911 – *In a German Pension*. Mansfield, K.

1911 – *The Case of Richard Meynell*. Ward, H.

1913 – *Sons and Lovers*. Lawrance, D. H.

1914 – *Innocent, Her Fancy and His Fact*. Corelli, M.

1915 – *The Good Soldier*. Madox Ford, F.

1915 – *The Valley of Fear*. Conan Doyle, A.

1918 – *The Clue of the Twisted Candle*. Wallace, E.

1919 – *Night and Day*. Woolf, V.

1920 – *The Mysterious Affair at Style*. Christie, A.

1920 – *Women in Love*. Lawrence, D. H.

1921 – *Bones in London*. Wallace, E.

1921 – *Crome Yellow*. Huxley, A.

1921 – *The Secret Power*. Corelli, M.

1921 – *To Let*. Galsworthy, J.

1922 – *Jacob's Room*. Woolf, V.

1922 – *The Garden Party and Other Stories*. Mansfield, K.

1922 – *The Secret Adversary*. Christie, A.

Conrad corpus (CC)

1985 – *Almayer's Folly*

1896 – *An Outcast of the Islands*

1897 – *The Nigger of the 'Narcissus'*

1898 – *Tales of Unrest*

1898 – *Youth*

1900 – *Lord Jim*

1901 – *Amy Foster*

1901 – *Falk*

1902 – *The End of the Tether*

1902 – *To-morrow*

1902 – *Typhoon*

1904 – *Nostromo*

1907 – *The Secret Agent*

1908 – *A Set of Six*

1911 – *Under Western Eyes*

1912 – *'Twixt Land and Sea*

1913 – *Change*
1915 – *Victory*
1915 – *Within the Tides*
1917 – *The Shadow Line*
1919 – *The Arrow of Gold*
1920 – *The Rescue*
1925 – *Tales of Hearsay*

Appendix 2

Larger Word Plots

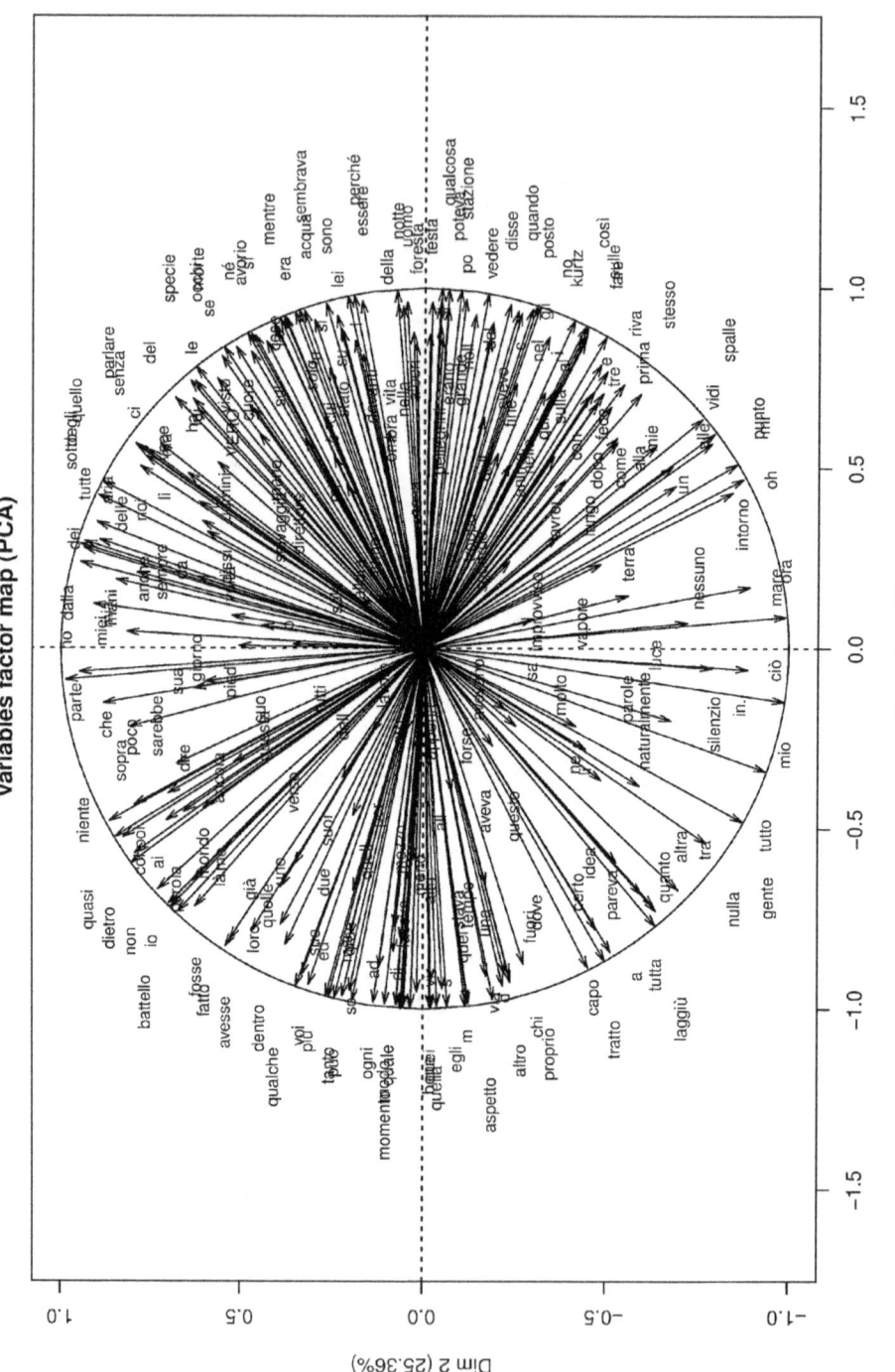

Figure A2.1 *Larger word plot based on the 250 MFWs of the TTs*

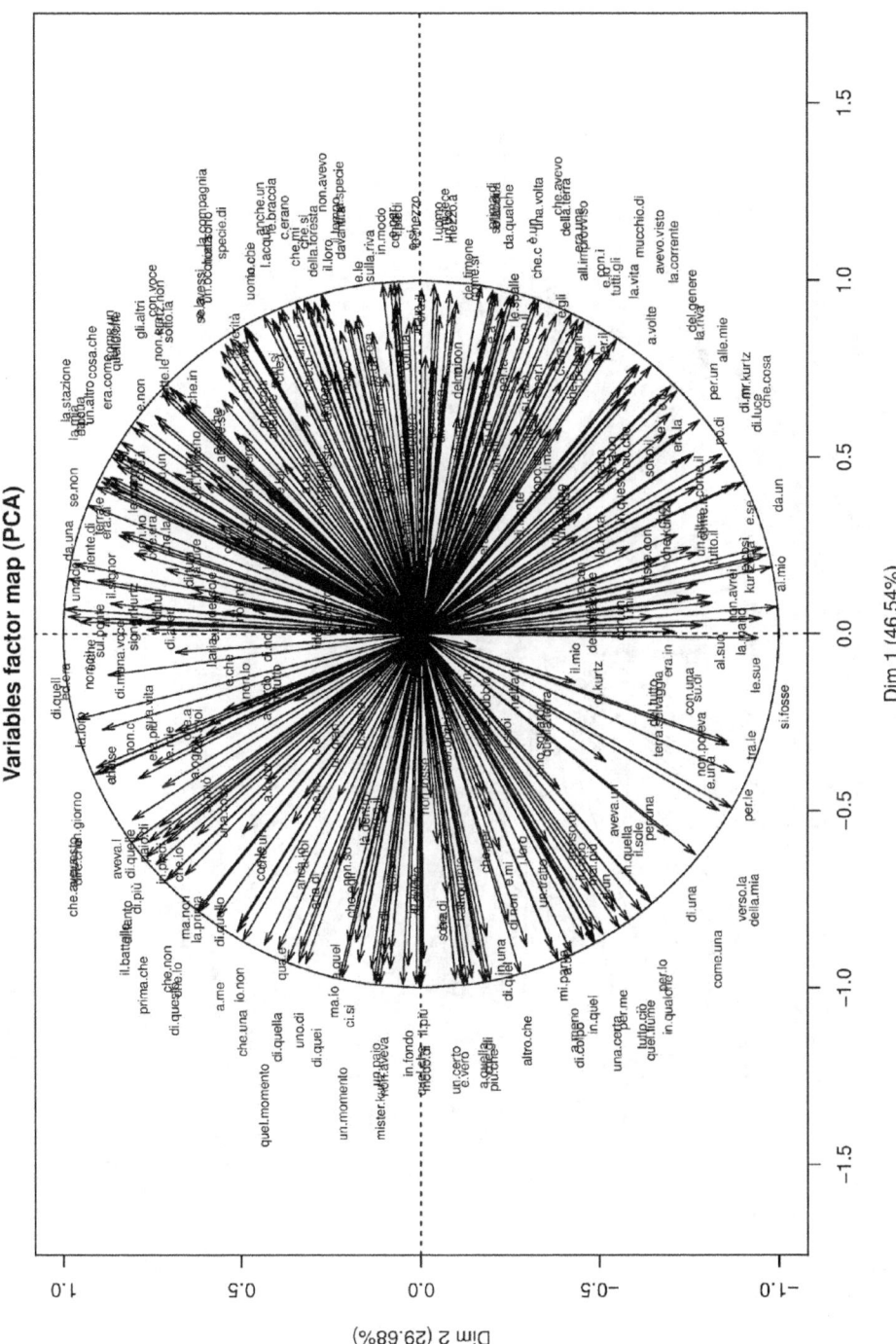

Figure A2.2 *Larger word plot based on the 350 two-word MFSs of the TTs*

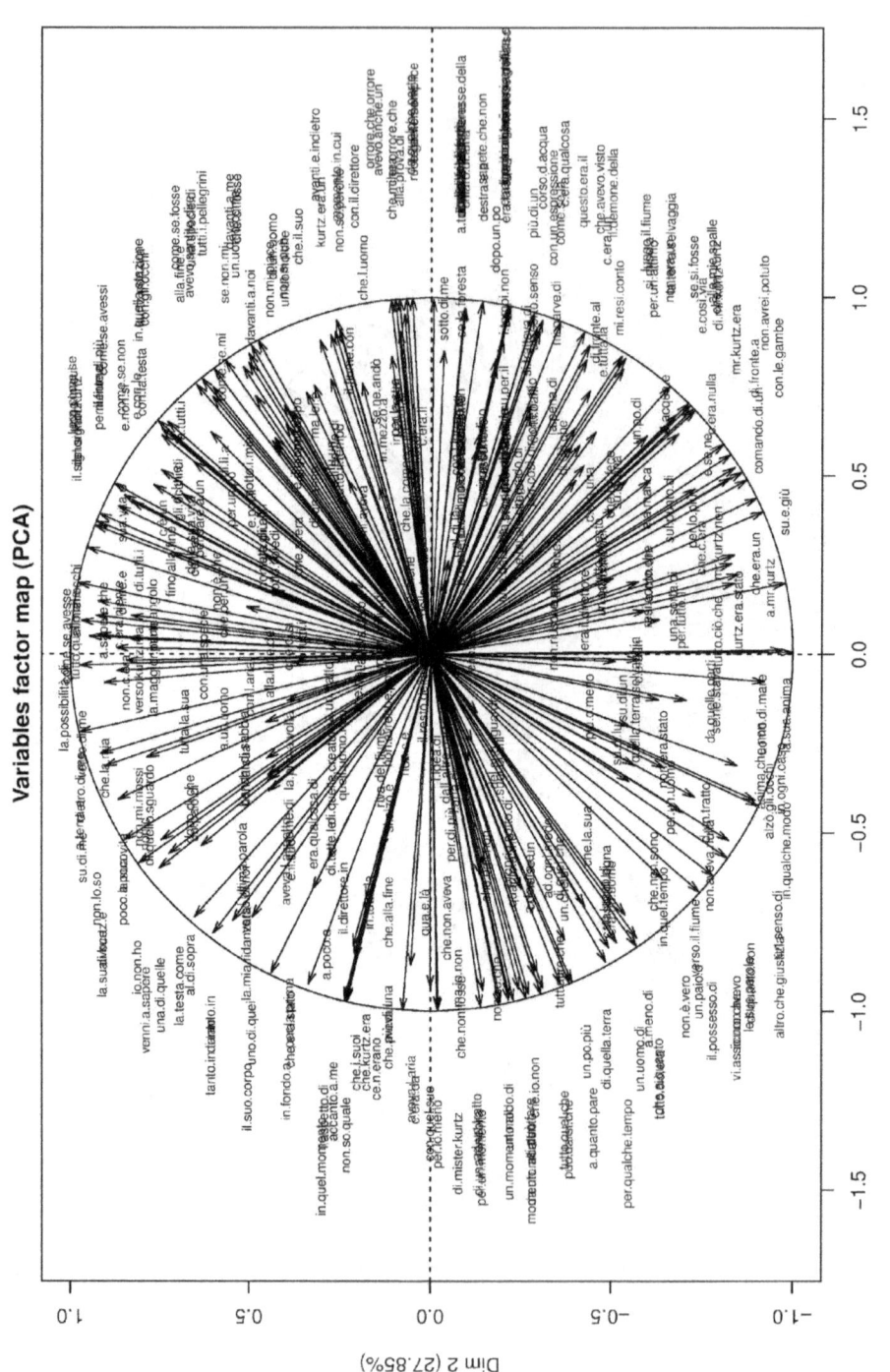

Figure A2.3 *Larger word plot based on the 350 three-word MFSs of the TTs*

Notes

Chapter 1

1 Cf. Maczewski (1996) for another corpus study of Woolf's *The Waves* in French and German, especially to notice the sensible development of the field in these ten years.

Chapter 4

1 Scott's (2016a) three types of keywords are in fact just meant to describe the most common kinds of keywords, rather than offering a classification model.

Chapter 5

1 Some readers might be interested to learn that this figurative rather than concrete representation of the African jungle was not the result of a lack of knowledge of Africa on the part of Conrad. Decades of expertise as professional seafarer and his personal experience in the very place he describes in *HoD* gave him first-hand knowledge of both Congo and how to geographically situate this place. Hampson (2005) suggests that Conrad was surely at ease with maps and mapping, with geographical and spatial coordinates. This is further confirmed by Conrad's *Congo Diary*, in which his observations of the landscape and of the route followed during the journey reveal unquestionably his trained eye and professional skills (Hampson 2005: 57). Conrad also exaggerates, historically speaking, the primitiveness and isolation of his fictional Congo by predating it (O'Prey 1983: 15). In reality, the country was much less underdeveloped in 1890 than the way Conrad portrays it (Goonetilleke 1999: 10).

2 In RC, *virgin* occurs 65 times. In the majority of these cases, the word refers to the female gender: either to the Virgin Mary (23 times) or more generally to a woman (23 times). It directly refers to a man only in 3 cases. In CC, *virgin* occurs 8 times: 7

times it refers to *forest, forests* and *woods* and in one case it is used to describe the intelligence of a woman.

3 The back-translations into English are always as literal as possible, as opposed to 'literary' translations.

Chapter 6

1 The log-likelihood calculator is available at http://ucrel.lancs.ac.uk/llwizard.html.

2 To be precise, there are words to translate *negro* in its meaning 'member of the Negroid race', for example *negroide* or *negride*. However, they are much more technical and jargonistic than the English equivalent. In fact, in itTenTen (3 billion words), *negroide* occurs 103 times (0.03 pmw) while *negride* only twice (0.00 pmw), compared to *negro* (nigger) and *nero* (nero) that occur 4,655 (1.51 pmw) and 13,500 (4.39 pmw) respectively.

3 As an additional note, it is worth mentioning that a coeval Italian dictionary (*Vocabolario Italiano della Lingua Parlata* 1921) does not list as a meaning of *nero* (black) its use as a noun to refer to a black person. This may offer an explanation why *negro* (nigger) is used instead of *nero* (black).

References

Achebe, C. (1990). An image of Africa: Racism in Conrad's *Heart of Darkness*. In *Hopes and Impediments: Selected Essays* (pp. 1–20). New York, NY: Anchor Books. (Original work published 1988)

Ajello, N. (2008, January 27). La guerra dei pronomi nell'Italia in orbace. *La Repubblica*. Retrieved from http://ricerca.repubblica.it/repubblica/archivio/repubblica/2008/01/27/la-guerra-dei-pronomi-nell-italia-in.html (last accessed July 2017).

Allington, D. (2006). First steps towards a rhetorical psychology of literary interpretation. *Journal of Literary Semantics*, 35(2), 123–44.

Arrojo, R. (1998). The revision of the traditional gap between theory & practice & the empowerment of translation in postmodern times. *The Translator*, 4(1), 25–48.

Bachmann, I. (2011). Civil partnership – 'gay marriage in all but name': A corpus-driven analysis of discourses of same-sex relationships in the UK Parliament. *Corpora*, 6(1), 77–105.

Baker, M. (1993). Corpus linguistics and translation studies: Implications and applications. In M. Baker, G. Francis & E. Tognini-Bonelli (Eds.), *Text and Technology: In Honour of John Sinclair* (pp. 233–50). Amsterdam: John Benjamins.

Baker, M. (1996). Corpus-based translation studies: The challenges that lie ahead. In H. Someres (Ed.), *Terminology, LSP and Translation Studies in Language Engineering: In Honour of Juan C. Sager* (pp. 175–86). Amsterdam: John Benjamins.

Baker, M. (1999). The role of corpora in investigating the linguistic behaviour of professional translators. *International Journal of Corpus Linguistics*, 4(2), 281–98.

Baker, M. (2000). Towards a methodology for investigating the style of a literary translator. *Target*, 12(2), 241–66.

Baker, M. (2004). A corpus-based view of similarity and difference in translation. *International Journal of Corpus Linguistics*, 9(2), 167-93.

Baker, M. (2011). *In Other Words: A Coursebook on Translation* (2nd ed.). London: Routledge.

Baker, P. (2006). *Using Corpora in Discourse Analysis*. London: Continuum.

Baker, P. (2010). *Sociolinguistics and Corpus Linguistics*. Edinburgh: Edinburgh University Press.

Baker, P., Gabrielatos, C., Khosravinik, M., Krzyzanowski, M., McEnery, T., & Wodak, R. (2008). A useful methodological synergy? Combining critical discourse analysis and corpus linguistics to examine discourse of refugees and asylum seekers in the UK press. *Discourse & Society*, 19(3), 273–306.

Baker, P., Gabrielatos, C., & McEnery, T. (2013). Sketching Muslims: A corpus-driven analysis of representations around the word 'Muslim' in the British Press 1998–2009. *Applied Linguistics*, 34(3), 255–78.

Barlow, M. (2013). Individual differences and usage-based grammar. *International Journal of Corpus Linguistics, 18*(4), 443–78.

Baroni, M., & Bernardini, S. (2003). A preliminary analysis of collocational differences in monolingual comparable corpora. In D. Archer, P. Rayson, A. Wilson & T. McEnery (Eds.), *Proceedings of the Corpus Linguistics 2003 Conference* (pp. 1–10). Lancaster: UCREL, Lancaster University.

Bassnett, S. (2007). Culture and translation. In P. Kuhiwczak & K. Littau (Eds.), *A Companion to Translation Studies* (pp. 13–23). Clevedon: Multilingual Matters.

Bassnett, S., & Lefevere, A. (1990). *Constructing Cultures: Essays on Literary Translation.* Clevedon: Multilingual Matters.

Bednarek, M. (2008). Semantic preference and semantic prosody re-examined. *Corpus Linguistics and Linguistic Theory, 4*(2), 119–39.

Berman, A. (1990). La retraducion come espace de la traducion. *Palimpsestes, 4*(1), 1–7.

Bernardini, S. (2007). Collocations in translated language: Combining parallel, comparable and reference corpora. In M. Davies, P. Rayson, S. Hunston & P. Danielsson (Eds.), *Proceedings of the Corpus Linguistics 2007 Conference* (pp. 1–16). Birmingham: University of Birmingham.

Biber, D. (1988). *Variation across Speech and Writing.* Cambridge: Cambridge University Press.

Binongo, J. N. G., & Smith, M. W. A. (1999). The application of principal component analysis to stylometry. *Literary and Stylistic Computing, 14*(4), 445–65.

Blum-Kulka. (1986). Shifts of cohesion and coherence in translation. In J. House & S. Blum-Kulka (Eds.), *Interlingual and Intercultural Communication: Discourse and Cognition in Translation and Second Language Acquisition Studies* (pp. 17–36). Tübingen: Gunter Narr Verlag Tübingen.

Boase-Beier, J. (2004). Saying what someone else meant: Style, relevance and translation. *International Journal of Applied Linguistics, 14*(2), 276–87.

Bosseaux, C. (2004). Translating point of view: A corpus-based study. *Language Matters: Studies in the Language of Africa, 35*(1), 259–74.

Bosseaux, C. (2006). Who's afraid of Virginia's *you*: A corpus-based study of the French translations of *The Waves. Meta: Journal des Traducteurs/Meta: Translators' Journal, 51*(3), 599–610.

Brantlinger, P. (1985). *Heart of Darkness*: Anti-imperialism, racism, or impressionism? *Criticism, 27*(4), 363–85.

Brooker, P., & Thacker, A. (2005a). Introduction: Locating the modern. In P. Brooker & A. Thacker (Eds.), *Geographies of Modernism: Literatures, Cultures, Spaces* (pp. 1–5). London: Routledge.

Brooker, P., & Thacker, A. (Eds.) (2005b). *Geographies of Modernism: Literatures, Cultures, Spaces.* London: Routledge.

Burrows, J. (1987). *Computation into Criticism: A Study of Jane Austen's Novels and an Experiment in Method.* Oxford: Clarendon.

Burrows, J. (2002a). 'Delta': A measure of stylistic difference and a guide to likely authorship. *Literary and Linguistic Computing, 17*(3), 267–87.

Burrows, J. (2002b). The Englishing of Juvenal: Computational stylistics and translated texts. *Style*, *36*(4), 677–750.

Carter, R. (2004). *Language and Creativity: The Art of Common Talk*. London: Routledge.

Catford, J. C. (1965). *A Linguistic Theory of Translation: An Essay in Applied Linguistics*. Oxford: Oxford University Press.

Čermáková, A. (2015). Repetition in John Irving's novel *A Widow for One Year*: A corpus stylistics approach to literary translation. *International Journal of Corpus Linguistics*, *20*(3), 355–77.

Čermáková, A., & Fárová, L. (2010). Keywords in Harry Potter and their Czech and Finnish translation equivalents. In F. Čermák, A. Klégr & P. Corness (Eds.), *InterCorp: Exploring a Multilingual Corpus. Studie z korpusové lingvistiky, svazek 13* (pp. 177–88). Prague: Nakladatelství Lidové noviny/Ústav českého národního korpusu.

Cheng, W. (2009). Describing the extended meanings of lexical cohesion in a corpus of SARS spoken discourse. In J. Flowerdew & M. Mahlberg (Eds.), *Lexical Cohesion and Corpus Linguistics* (pp. 65–83). Amsterdam: John Benjamins.

Childs, P., & Fowler, R. (2006). *The Routledge Dictionary of Literary Terms*. London: Routledge.

Ciompi, F. (2005). Under Italian eyes: Conrad's critical reception in Italy. In M. Curreli (Ed.), *The Ugo Mursia Lectures: Papers from the International Conrad Conference, University of Pisa (September 16th–18th 2004)* (pp. 123–38). Pisa: Edizioni ETS.

Clark, H. H., & Clark, E. V. (1977). Memory for prose. In *Psychology and Language: An Introduction to Psycholinguistics* (pp. 133–73). New York, NY: Harcourt Brace Jovanovich.

Coats, J. M. (2013). Unreliable heterodiegesis and scientific racism in Conrad's *Secret Agent*. *Modernism/Modernity*, *20*(4), 645–65.

Conrad, J. (1950). Preface. In *The Nigger of the 'Narcissus' and Typhoon & Other Stories* (pp. vii–xii). London: Dent. (Original work published in 1897)

Conrad, J. (1994). *Heart of Darkness*. London: Penguin. (Original work published 1902)

Craig, H. (2008). 'Speak, that I may see thee': Shakespeare characters and common words. In P. Holland (Ed.), *Shakespeare Survey Online: Shakespeare, Sound and Screen, 61* (pp. 281–88). Cambridge: Cambridge University Press.

Craig, H. (2015). Intelligent Archive [Computer software]. Newcastle: University of Newcastle.

Cuddon, J. A. (1979). *A Dictionary of Literary Terms*. London: Penguin.

Culpeper, J. (2002a). A cognitive stylistic approach to characterisation. In E. Semino & J. Culpeper (Eds.), *Cognitive Stylistics: Language and Cognition in Text Analysis* (pp. 251–77). Amsterdam: John Benjamins.

Culpeper, J. (2002b). Computers, language and characterisation: An analysis of six characters in *Romeo and Juliet*. In U. Melander-Marttala, C. Ostman & M. Kyoto (Eds.), *Conversation in Life and Literature: Papers from the ASLA Symposium* (pp. 11–30). Uppsala: Universitetstryckeriet.

Culpeper, J. (2009). Keyness: Words, parts-of-speech and semantic categories in the character-talk of Shakespeare's *Romeo and Juliet. International Journal of Corpus Linguistics, 14*(1), 29–59.

Curle, R. (1914). *Joseph Conrad: A Study.* London: Kegan Paul, Trench, Trübner.

Curreli, M. (2009). *Le Traduzioni di Conrad in Italia.* Pisa: Edizioni ETS.

Dancygier, B., & Sweetser, E. (2014). *Figurative Language.* Cambridge: Cambridge University Press.

Diaz-Cintas, J. (2013). Subtitling: Theory, practice and research. In C. Millán & F. Bartrina (Eds.), *The Routledge Handbook of Translation Studies* (pp. 273–87). London: Routledge.

Dixon, P., Bortolussi, M., Twilley, L. C., & Leung, A. (1993). Literary processing and interpretation: Towards empirical foundations. *Poetics, 22*(1), 5–33.

Dukāte, A. (2009). *Translation, Manipulation and Interpreting.* Frankfurt: Peter Lang.

Egbert, J. (2012). Style in nineteenth century fiction: A multi-dimensional analysis. *Scientific Study of Literature, 2*(2), 167–98.

Even-Zohar, I. (1990). Polysystem studies. *Poetics Today, 11*(1), 1–268.

Firth, J. R. (1957). *Papers in Linguistics, 1934–1951.* London: Oxford University Press.

Fischer-Starcke, B. (2009). Keywords and frequent phrases of Jane Austen's *Pride and Prejudice. International Journal of Corpus Linguistics, 14*(4), 492–523.

Fischer-Starcke, B. (2010). *Corpus Linguistics in Literary Analysis: Jane Austen and her Contemporaries.* London: Continuum.

Fish, S. E. (1979). What is stylistics and why are they saying such terrible things about it? Part II. *Boundary 2, 8*(1), 129–46.

Fish, S. E. (1980). What is stylistics and why are they saying such terrible things about it? In *Is There a Text in This Class? The Authority of Interpretative Communities* (pp. 68–96). Cambridge, MA: Harvard University Press.

Flowerdew, J., & Mahlberg, M. (Eds.) (2009). *Lexical Cohesion and Corpus Linguistics.* Amsterdam: John Benjamins.

Fowler, R. (1966). Linguistic theory and the study of literature. In R. Fowler (Ed.), *Essays on Style and Language: Linguistic and Critical Approaches to Literary Style* (pp. 1–28). London: Routledge & K. Paul.

Gabrielatos, C., & Baker, P. (2008). Fleeing, sneaking, flooding: A corpus analysis of discoursive constructions of refugees and asylum seekers in the UK press, 1996–2005. *Journal of English Linguistics, 36*(1), 5–38.

GoGwilt, C. (2005). The interior: Benjaminian arcades, Conradian passages, and the 'impasse' of Jean Rhys. In P. Brooker & A. Thacker (Eds.), *Geographies of Modernism: Literatures, Cultures, Spaces* (pp. 65–75). London: Routledge.

Goonetilleke, D. C. R. A. (1999). Introduction. In D. C. R. A. Goonetilleke (Ed.), *Heart of Darkness* (pp. 9–48). Peterborough: Broadview.

Grabowski, Ł. (2012). Between stability and variability. A corpus-driven study of translation universals: The case of Polish translations of *Lolita*. In E. Piechurska-Kuciel & L. Piasecka (Eds.), *Variability and Stability in Foreign and Second Language Learning Contexts* (pp. 2–24). Newcastle upon Tyne: Cambridge Scholars.

Grabowski, Ł. (2013). Interfacing corpus linguistics and computational stylistics: Translation universals in translational literary Polish. *International Journal of Corpus Linguistics*, *18*(2), 254–80.

Granger, S., Lerot, J., & Petch-Tyson, S. (2003). *Corpus-based Approaches to Contrastive Linguistics and Translation Studies*. Amsterdam: Rodopi.

Gries, S. Th. (2010). Corpus linguistics and theoretical linguistics: A love–hate relationship? Not necessarily ... *International Journal of Corpus Linguistics*, *15*(3), 327–43.

Guerard, A. J. (1966). The journey within. In *Conrad the Novelist* (pp. 1–59). Cambridge, MA: Harvard University Press.

Gupta, K. (2015). *Representation of the British Suffrage Movement*. London: Bloomsbury.

Halliday, M. A. K. (1971). Linguistic function and literary style: An enquiry into the language of William Golding's *The Inheritors*. In S. Chatman (Ed.), *Literary Style: A Symposium* (pp. 330–68). New York, NY: Oxford University Press.

Halliday, M. A. K., & Hasan, R. (1976). *Cohesion in English*. London: Longman.

Halliday, M. A. K., & Matthiessen, C. (2004). *An Introduction to Functional Grammar – Third Edition*. London: Arnold. (Original work published 1985)

Hampson, R. (2005). Spatial stories: Joseph Conrad and James Joyce. In P. Brooker & A. Thacker (Eds.), *Geographies of Modernism: Literatures, Cultures, Spaces* (pp. 54–64). London: Routledge.

Hawkins, H. (2006). *Heart of Darkness* and racism. In P. B. Armstrong (Ed.), *Heart of Darkness* (pp. 365–75). New York, NY: Norton.

Hegglund, J. (2005). Modernism, Africa and the myth of continents. In P. Brooker & A. Thacker (Eds.), *Geographies of Modernism: Literatures, Cultures, Spaces* (pp. 43–53). London: Routledge.

Hermans, T. (1999). *Translation in Systems: Descriptive and System-Oriented Approaches Explained*. Manchester: St. Jerome.

Hermans, T. (2014a). Introduction: Translation studies and a new paradigm. In T. Hermans (Ed.), *The Manipulation of Literature: Studies in Literary Translations* (pp. 7–15). London: Routledge. (Original work published in 1985)

Hermans, T. (Ed.) (2014b). *The Manipulation of Literature: Studies in Literary Translations*. London: Routledge. (Original work published in 1985)

Ho, Y. (2011). *Corpus Stylistics in Principles and Practice: A Sylistic Exploration of John Fowles' The Magus*. London: Continuum.

Hoey, M. (1991). *Patterns of Lexis in Text*. London: Oxford University Press.

Holmes, J. S. (2004). The name and nature of translation studies. In L. Venuti (Ed.), *The Translation Studies Reader – Second Edition* (pp. 180–92). London: Routledge. (Original work published 1972)

Hoover, D. L. (2002). Frequent word sequences and statistical stylistics. *Literary and Linguistic Computing*, *17*(2), 157–80.

Hoover, D. L. (2012). The Parallel Wordlist Spreadsheet. Retrieved from https://files. nyu.edu/dh3/public/TheParallelWordlistSpreadsheet.html (last accessed July 2016).

Hoover, D. L. (2015). Cluster Analysis, Principal Component Analysis (PCA), and T-testing in Minitab. Retrieved from https://files.nyu.edu/dh3/public/The%20Excel%20Text-Analysis%20Pages.html (last accessed July 2016).

Hori, M. (2004). *Investigating Dickens' Style: A Collocational Analysis*. Basingstoke: Palgrave Macmillan.

Huang, L. (2015). *Style in Translation: A Corpus-based Perspective*. Heidelberg: Springer.

Huang, L., & Chu, C. (2014). Translator's style or translational style? A corpus-based study of style in translated Chinese novels. *Asia Pacific Translation and Intercultural Studies, 1* (2), 122–41.

Hughes, G. (2006). *Encyclopedia of Swearing: The Social History of Oaths, Profanity, Foul Language, and Ethnic Slurs in the English-Speaking World*. Armonk, NY: M. E. Sharpe.

Hung, J.-J., Bingenheimer, M., & Wiles, S. (2010). Quantitative evidence for a hypothesis regarding the attribution of early Buddhist translations. *Literary and Linguistic Computing, 25*(1), 119–34.

Hunston, S. (2010). How can a corpus be used to explore patterns? In A. O'Keeffe & M. McCarthy (Eds.), *The Routledge Handbook of Corpus Linguistics* (pp. 152–66). New York, NY: Routledge.

Jakobson, R. (1960). Closing statement: Linguistics and poetics. In T. A. Sebeok (Ed.), *Style in Language* (pp. 350–77). Cambridge, MA: MIT Press.

Jakubíček, M., Kilgarriff, A., Kovář, V., Rychlý, P., & Suchomel, V. (2013). The TenTen corpus family. In A. Hardie & R. Love (Eds.), *Corpus Linguistics 2013 Abstract Book* (pp. 125–27). Lancaster: UCREL, Lancaster University.

Jarosz, L. (1992). Constructing the dark continent: Metaphor as geographic representation of Africa. *Geografiska Annaler. Series B, Human Geography, 74*(2), 105–15.

Jeffries, L., & McIntyre, D. (2010). *Stylistics*. Cambridge: Cambridge University Press.

Johansson, S. (2003). Contrastive linguistics and corpora. In S. Granger, J. Lerot & S. Petch-Tyson (Eds.), *Corpus-based Approaches to Contrastive Linguistics and Translation Studies* (pp. 31–44). Amsterdam: Rodopi.

Kennedy, R. (2002). *Nigger: The Strange Career of a Troublesome Word*. New York, NY: Pantheon Books.

Kenny, D. (2001). *Lexis and Creativity in Translation: A Corpus-based Study*. Manchester: St. Jerome.

Kenny, D. (2008). Equivalence. In M. Baker & G. Saldanha (Eds.), *Routledge Encyclopedia of Translation Studies* (pp. 96–9). New York, NY: Routledge.

Kilgarriff, A., Baisa, V., Bušta, J., Jakubíček, M., Kovář, V., Michelfeit, J., Rychlý, P., & Suchomel, V. (2014). The Sketch Engine: Ten years on. *Lexicography, 1*(1): 7–36.

Kipling, R. (2013). The white man's burden. In T. Pinney (Ed.), *100 Poems Old and New: Rudyard Kipling* (pp. 111–13). Cambridge: Cambridge University Press. (Original work published 1899)

Knowles, O. (2009a). Critical responses: 1925–1950. In A. H. Simmons (Ed.), *Conrad in Context* (pp. 67–74). London: Cambridge University Press.

Knowles, O. (2009b). Literary influences. In A. H. Simmons (Ed.), *Joseph Conrad in Context* (pp. 33–41). London: Cambridge University Press.

Krein-Kühle, M. (2002). Cohesion and coherence in technical translation: The case of demonstrative reference. In L. V. Vaerenbergh (Ed.), *Linguistics and Translation Studies. Translation Studies and Linguistics. Linguistica Antverpiensia* (pp. 41–53). Antwerpen: Hogeschool Antwerpen.

Kruger, A., Wallmach, K., & Munday, J. (Eds.). (2011). *Corpus-based Translation Studies: Research and Applications*. London: Bloomsbury.

Kujawska-Lis, E. (2008). Turning *Heart of Darkness* into a racist text: A comparison of two Polish translations. *Conradiana, 40*(2), 165–78.

Lambrou, M., & Stockwell, P. (Eds.) (2007). *Contemporary Stylistics*. London: Continuum.

Lavid, J., Arús, J., & Moratón, L. (2009). Comparison and translation: Towards a combined methodology for contrastive corpus studies. *International Journal of English Studies, 9*(3), 159–74.

Laviosa, S. (2002). *Corpus-based Translation Studies*. Amsterdam: Rodopi.

Laviosa, S. (2008). Corpus studies of translation universals: A critical appraisal. In A. Martelli & V. Pulcini (Eds.), *Investigating English with Corpora: Studies in Honour of Maria Teresa Prat* (pp. 223–38). Monza: Polimetrica.

Laviosa, S. (2013). Corpus-based translation studies: Where does it come from? Where is it going? In A. Kruger, K. Wallmach, & J. Munday (Eds.), *Corpus-based Translation Studies: Research and Applications* (pp. 13–32). London: Bloomsbury.

Lawtoo, N. (Ed.) (2012). *Conrad's Heart of Darkness and Contemporary Thought: Revisiting the Horror with Lacoue-Labarthe*. London: Bloomsbury.

Le, S., Josse, J., & Husson, F. (2008). FactoMineR: An R package for multivariate analysis. *Journal of Statistical Software, 25*(1), 1–18.

Leavis, F. R. (1973). Joseph Conrad. In *The Great Tradition. George Eliot, Henry James, Joseph Conrad* (pp. 173–226). London: Chatto & Windus. (Original work published 1948)

Leech, G. (1985). Stylistics. In T. A. van Dijk (Ed.), *Discourse and Literature. New Approaches to the Analysis of Literary Genres* (pp. 39–57). Amsterdam: John Benjamins.

Leech, G., & Short, M. (2007). *Style in Fiction: A Linguistic Introduction to English Fictional Prose*. Harlow: Pearson Education. (Original work published 1981)

Lefevere, A. (1992). *Translation, Rewriting, and the Manipulation of Literary Fame*. London: Routledge.

Lefevere, A. (2014). Why waste our time on rewrites? The trouble with interpretation and the role of rewriting in an alternative paradigm. In T. Hermans (Ed.), *The Manipulation of Literature: Studies in Literary Translation* (pp. 215–43). New York, NY: Routledge. (Original work published 1985)

Levenson, M. (2009). Modernism. In A. H. Simmons (Ed.), *Joseph Conrad in Context* (pp. 179–86). London: Cambridge University Press.

Li, D., Zhang, C., & Liu, K. (2011). Translation style and ideology: A corpus-assisted analysis of two English translations of *Hongloumeng*. *Literary and Linguistic Computing, 26*(2), 153–66.

Louw, W. E. (1993). Irony in the text or insincerity in the writer? The diagnostic potential of semantic prosodies. In M. Baker, G. Francis & E. Tognini-Bonelli (Eds.), *Text and Technology: In Honour of John Sinclair* (pp. 157–74). Amsterdam: John Benjamins.

MacDonald, M., & Hunter, D. (2013). The discourse of Olympic security: London 2012. *Discourse & Society, 24*(1), 66–88.

Maczewski, J. M. (1996). Virginia Woolf's *The Waves* in French and German waters: A computer assisted study in literary translation. *Literary and Linguistic Computing, 11*(4), 175–86.

Mahlberg, M. (2005). *English General Nouns: A Corpus Theoretical Approach.* Amsterdam: John Benjamins.

Mahlberg, M. (2007a). A corpus stylistic perspective on Dickens's *Great Expectations*. In M. Lambrou & P. Stockwell (Eds.), *Contemporary Stylistics* (pp. 19–31). London: Continuum.

Mahlberg, M. (2007b). Corpora and translations studies: Textual function of lexis in *Bleak House* and in a translation of the novel into German. In V. Intonti, G. Todisco, & M. Gatto (Eds.), *La Traduzione. Lo Stato dell'Arte. Translation. The State of the Art.* (pp. 115–35). Ravenna: Longo.

Mahlberg, M. (2009). Lexical cohesion: Corpus linguistic theory and its application in English language teaching. In J. Flowerdew & M. Mahlberg (Eds.), *Lexical Cohesion and Corpus Linguistics* (pp. 103–22). Amsterdam: John Benjamins.

Mahlberg, M. (2012a). Corpus stylistics – Dickens, text-drivenness and the fictional world. In J. John (Ed.), *Dickens and Modernity* (pp. 94–114). Woodbridge: Boydell & Brewer.

Mahlberg, M. (2012b). The corpus stylistic analysis of fiction or the fiction of corpus stylistics? In M. Huber & J. Mukherjee (Eds.), *Corpus Linguistics and Variation in English: Theory and Description* (pp. 77–95). Amsterdam: Rodopi.

Mahlberg, M. (2013). *Corpus Stylistics and Dickens's Fiction.* New York, NY: Routledge.

Mahlberg, M., Conklin, K., & Bisson, M.-J. (2014). Reading Dickens's characters: Employing psycholinguistic methods to investigate the cognitive reality of patterns in texts. *Language and Literature, 23*(4), 369–88.

Mahlberg, M., & McIntyre, D. (2011). A case for corpus stylistics: Ian Fleming's *Casino Royale*. *English Text Construction, 4*(2), 204–27.

Mahlberg, M., & Smith, C. (2010). Corpus approaches to prose fiction: Civility and body language in *Pride and Prejudice*. In D. McIntyre & B. Busse (Eds.), *Language and Style* (pp. 449–67). Basingstoke: Palgrave Macmillan.

Mahlberg, M., & Smith, C. (2012). Dickens, the suspended quotation and the corpus. *Language and Literature, 21*(1), 51–65.

Mastropierro, L. (2015). *-ly* adverbs in Lovecraft's *At the Mountains of Madness* and in two Italian translations: A corpus stylistic approach to literary translation. In L. Pontrandolfo (Ed.), *Spazi della Memoria* (pp. 217–41). Bari: Edizioni dal Sud.

Mastropierro, L., & Mahlberg, M. (2017). Key words and translated cohesion in Lovecraft's *At the Mountains of Madness* and one of its Italian translations. *English Text Construction, 10*(1), 78–105.

McEnery, T. (2009). Keywords and moral panics: Mary Whitehouse and media censorship. In D. Archer (Ed.), *What's in a Word-list? Investigating Word Frequency and Keyword Extraction* (pp. 93–124). Farnham: Ashgate.

McEnery, T., & Hardie, A. (2012). *Corpus Linguistics*. Cambridge: Cambridge University Press.

McIntyre, D. (2012). Linguistics and literature: Stylistics as a tool for the literary critic. *SRC Working Papers, 1*, 1–11.

McIntyre, D. (2014). Characterisation. In P. Stockwell & S. Whiteley (Eds.), *The Cambridge Handbook of Stylistics* (pp. 149–64). Cambridge: Cambridge University Press.

McKenna, W., Burrows, J., & Antonia, A. (1999). Beckett's trilogy: Computational stylistics and the nature of translation. *Revue Informatique et Statistique dans les Sciences Humaines, 35*, 151–71. Retrieved from http://promethee.philo.ulg.ac.be/RISSHpdf/Annee1999/Articles/WMckennaetc.pdf (last accessed July 2017).

Miller, J. H. (2006). Should we read *Heart of Darkness*? In P. B. Armstrong (Ed.), *Heart of Darkness* (pp. 463–74). New York, NY: Norton.

Miller, J. H. (2012). Prologue: Revisiting '*Heart of Darkness* revisited' (in the company of Philippe Lacoue-Labarthe). In N. Lawtoo (Ed.), *Conrad's Heart of Darkness and Contemporary Thought: Revisiting the Horror with Lacoue-Labarthe* (pp. 17–35). London: Bloomsbury.

Mortara Gavarelli, B. (2010). *Manuale di Retorica*. Milano: Bompiani.

Mouka, E., Saridakis, I. E., & Fotopoulou, A. (2015). Racism goes to the movies: A corpus-driven study of cross-linguistic racist discourse annotation and translation analysis. In C. Fantinuoli & F. Zanettin (Eds.), *New Directions in Corpus-based Translation Studies* (pp. 35–69). Berlin: Language Science Press.

Munday, J. (2008). *Style and Ideology in Translation: Latin America Writing in English*. London: Routledge.

Munday, J. (2011). Looming large: A cross-linguistic analysis of semantic prosodies in comparable reference corpora. In A. Kruger, K. Wallmach & J. Munday (Eds.), *Corpus-based Translation Studies: Research and Applications* (pp. 169–86). London: Bloomsbury.

Murfin, R. C. (Ed.) (1989). *Heart of Darkness: A Case Study in Contemporary Criticism*. Boston, MA: Bedford Books.

Niland, R. (2009). Critical responses: 1950–1975. In A. H. Simmons (Ed.), *Joseph Conrad in Context* (pp. 75–82). Cambridge: Cambridge University Press.

Nida, E. A. (1964). *Toward a Science of Translating*. Leiden: Brill.

Oakes, M. P., & Ji, M. (Eds.) (2012). *Quantitative Methods in Corpus-based Translation Studies*. Amsterdam: Benjamins.

O'Halloran, K. (2007). The subconscious in James Joyce's *Eveline*: A corpus stylistic analysis that chews on the 'Fish hook'. *Language and Literature, 16*(3), 227–44.

Olohan, M. (2004). *Introducing Corpora in Translation Studies*. New York, NY: Routledge.

O'Prey, P. E. (1983). *Heart of Darkness*. London: Penguin Books.

Orpin, D. (2005). Corpus linguistics and critical discourse analysis. *International Journal of Corpus Linguistics, 10*(1), 37–61.

Oster, U., & van Lawick, H. (2008). Semantic preference and semantic prosody: A corpus-based analysis of translation-relevant aspects of the meaning of phraseological units. In B. L.-T. Thelen (Ed.), *Translation and Meaning VIII* (pp. 333–44). Maastricht: Hogeschool Maastricht, School of Translation and Interpreting.

Øverås, L. (1998). In search of the third code: An investigation of norms in literary translation. *Meta: Journal des Traducteurs/Meta: Translators' Journal, 43*(4), 557–70.

Pagano, A., Figueredo, G. P., & Lukin, A. (2016). Modelling proximity in a corpus of literary retranslations: A methodological proposal for clustering texts based on systemic-functional annotation of lexicogrammatical features. In M. Ji (Ed.), *Empirical Translation Studies: Interdisciplinary Methodologies Explored* (pp. 93–127). Sheffield: Equinox.

Parks, T. (2007). *Translating Style: A Literary Approach to Translation, a Translation Approach to Literature*. Manchester: St. Jerome.

Partington, A. (2004). 'Utterly content in each other's company': Semantic prosody and semantic preference. *International Journal of Corpus Linguistics, 9*(1), 131–56.

Peters, J. G. (Ed.) (2008). *Conrad in the Public Eye*. Amsterdam: Rodopi.

Purssell, A. (2009). Critical responses: 1975–2000. In A. H. Simmons (Ed.), *Joseph Conrad in Context* (pp. 83–90). Cambridge: Cambridge University Press.

R Core Team (2016). R: A language and environment for statistical computing [Computer software]. Vienna: R Foundation for Statistical Computing. Retrieved at www.R-project.org/ (last accessed July 2017).

Randall, J. H. (2008). Joseph Conrad: His outlook on life. In J. G. Peters (Ed.), *Conrad in the Public Eye* (pp. 108–23). Amsterdam: Rodopi. (Original work published 1925)

Rayson, P. (2008). From key words to key semantic domains. *International Journal of Corpus Linguistics, 13*(4), 519–49.

Redelinghuys, K., & Kruger, H. (2015). Using the features of translated language to investigate translation expertise: A corpus-based study. *International Journal of Corpus Linguistics, 20*(3), 293–325.

Rybicki, J. (2006). Burrowing into translation: Character idiolects in Henryk Sienkiewicz's Trilogy and its two English translations. *Literary and Linguistic Computing, 21*(1), 91–103.

Rybicki, J., & Heydel, M. (2013). The stylistics and stylometry of collaborative translation: Woolf's *Night and Day* in Polish. *Literary and Linguistic Computing, 28*(4), 708–17.

Rybicki, J., Hoover, D., & Kestemont, M. (2014). Collaborative authorship: Conrad, Ford and Rolling Delta. *Literary and Linguistic Computing, 29*(3), 422–31.

Said, E. W. (1994). *Culture and Imperialism*. London: Vintage.

Saldanha, G. (2008). Linguistic approaches. In M. Baker & G. Saldanha (Eds.), *Routledge Encyclopedia of Translation Studies* (2nd. ed.) (pp. 148–52). London: Routledge.

Saldanha, G. (2009). Principles of corpus linguistics and their application to translation studies research. *Revista Tradumàtica: Tecnologies de la Traducciò, 7*. Retrieved from http://webs2002.uab.es/tradumatica/revista/num2007/articles/2001/art.htm (last accessed July 2016).

Saldanha, G. (2011a). Translator style: Methodological considerations. *The Translator, 17*(1), 25–50.

Saldanha, G. (2011b). Style of translation: The use of foreign words in translations by Margaret Jull Costa and Peter Bush. In A. Kruger, K. Wallmach, & J. Munday (Eds.), *Corpus-based Translation Studies: Research and Applications* (pp. 237–58). London: Bloomsbury.

Saldanha, G. (2014). Style in, and of, translation. In S. Bermann & C. Porter (Eds.), *A Companion to Translation Studies* (pp. 95–106). West Sussex: Wiley-Blackwell.

Schäffner, C. (2008). Functionalist approaches. In M. Baker & G. Saldhana (Eds.), *Routledge Encyclopedia of Translation Studies* (pp. 115–21). New York, NY: Routledge.

Schjoldager, A. (1994). Interpreting research and the 'Manipulation School' of translation studies. *Hermes, Journal of Linguistics, 12*, 65–89.

Scott, M. (2016a). *WordSmith Tools Help*. Liverpool, UK: Lexical Analysis Software. Retrieved from http://www.lexically.net/downloads/version6/HTML/index. html?getting_started.htm (last accessed July 2017).

Scott, M. (2016b). *WordSmith Tools version 6* [Computer software]. Liverpool, UK: Lexical Analysis Software.

Segarra, S., Eisen, M., Egan, G., & Ribeiro, A. (2016). Attributing the authorship of the *Henry VI* plays by word adjacency. *Shakespeare Quarterly, 67*(2), 232–256

Senn, W. (1980). *Conrad's Narrative Voice: Stylistic Aspects of his Fiction*. Bern: Francke Verlag.

Simmons, A. H. (Ed.) (2009). *Joseph Conrad in Context*. Cambridge: Cambridge University Press.

Simpson, P. (2004). *Stylistics: A Resource Book for Students*. London: Routledge.

Sinclair, J. (1991). *Corpus, Concordance, Collocation*. Oxford: Oxford University Press.

Sinclair, J. (2003). *Reading Concordances: An Introduction*. London: Pearson Education.

Sinclair, J. (2004). *Trust the Text: Language, Corpus and Discourse*. London: Routledge.

Snell-Hornby, M. (1988). *Translation Studies: An Integrated Approach*. Amsterdam: John Benjamins.

Spitzer, L. (1962). Linguistics and literary history. In *Linguistics and Literary History* (pp. 1–39). New York, NY: Russell & Russell.

Starcke, B. (2006). The phraseology of Jane Austen's *Persuasion*: Phraseological units as carriers of meaning. *ICAME Journal, 30*, 87–104.

Stubbs, M. (2002). *Words and Phrases: Corpus Studies of Lexical Semantics*. Oxford: Blackwell.

Stubbs, M. (2005). Conrad in the computer: Examples of quantitative stylistic methods. *Language and Literature, 14*(1), 5–24.

Thacker, A. (2005). The idea of critical literary geography. *New Formations, 57*, 56–73.

Tognini-Bonelli, E. (2001). *Corpus Linguistics at Work*. Amsterdam: John Benjamins.

Toolan, M. (2008). Narrative progression in the short story: First steps in a corpus stylistic approach. *Narrative, 16*(2), 105–20.

Toury, G. (1995). *Descriptive Translation Studies – and Beyond*. Amsterdam: John Benjamins.

Toury, G. (2004). The nature and role of norms in translation. In L. Venuti (Ed.), *The Translation Studies Reader* (2nd. ed.) (pp. 205–18). New York, NY: Routledge.

Toury, G. (2014). A rationale for descriptive translation studies. In T. Hermans (Ed.), *The Manipulation of Literature: Studies in Literary Translation* (pp. 16–41). New York, NY: Routledge. (Original work published 1985)

Trebits, A. (2009). Conjunctive cohesion in English language EU documents: A corpus-based analysis and its implications. *English for Specific Purposes, 28*(3), 199–210.

Trupej, J. (2012). Translating racist discourse in Slovenia during the socialist period: Mark Twain's *Adventure of Huckleberry Finn*. In B. Fischer & M. N. Jensen (Eds.), *Translation and the Reconfiguration of Power Relations: Revisiting Role and Context of Translation and Interpreting* (pp. 91–107). Münster: Lit-Verlag.

Turci, M. (2007). The meaning of 'dark*' in Joseph Conrad's *Heart of Darkness*. In D. R. Miller & M. Turci (Eds.), *Language and Verbal Art Revisited: Linguistic Approaches to the Study of Literature* (pp. 97–114). London: Equinox.

Tymoczko, M. (1998). Computerized corpora and the future of translation studies. *Meta: Journal des Traducteurs/Meta: Translators' Journal, 43*(4), 652–60.

Tymoczko, M. (2010). *Translation, Resistance, Activism*. Amherst, MA: University of Massachusetts Press.

Ulrych, M., & Anselmi, S. (2008). Towards a corpus-based distinction between language-specific and universal features of mediated discourse. In A. Martelli & V. Pulcini (Eds.), *Investigating English with Corpora: Studies in Honour of Maria Teresa Prat* (pp. 257–73). Monza: Polimetrica.

van den Broeck, R. (2014). Second thoughts on translation criticism: A model of its analytic function. In T. Hermans (Ed.), *The Manipulation of Literature: Studies* in *Literary Translation* (pp. 54–62). New York, NY: Routledge. (Original work published 1985)

Vandevoorde, L., De Sutter, G., & Plevoets, K. (2016). On semantic differences between translated and non-translated Dutch. Using bidirectional parallel corpus data for measuring and visualizing distances between lexemes in the semantic field of inceptiveness. In M. Ji (Ed.), *Empirical Translation Studies: Interdisciplinary Methodologies Explored* (pp. 128–48). Sheffield: Equinox.

van Peer, W. (2002). Where do literary themes come from? In M. M. Louwerse & W. van Peer (Eds.), *Thematics: Interdisciplinary Studies* (pp. 253–63). Amsterdam: John Benjamins.

Venuti, L. (1996). Translation, heterogeneity, linguistics. *TTR: Traduction, Terminologie, Rédaction, 9*(1), 91–115.

Venuti, L. (Ed.) (2004). *The Translation Studies Reader* (2nd ed.). London: Routledge.

Venuti, L. (2008). *The Translator's Invisibility: A History of Translation* (2nd ed.). London: Routledge.

Vermeule, B. (2010). *Why Do We Care about Literary Characters?* Baltimore, MD: The Johns Hopkins University Press.

Wales, K. (2011). *A Dictionary of Stylistics*. Harlow: Pearson Education.

Wang, Q., & Li, D. (2012). Looking for translator's fingerprints: A corpus-based study on Chinese translation of *Ulysses. Literary and Linguistic Computing, 27*(1), 81–93.

Warren, M. (2009). Cohesive chains and speakers' choice of prominence. In J. Flowerdew & M. Mahlberg (Eds.), *Lexical Cohesion and Corpus Linguistics* (pp. 45–63). Amsterdam: John Benjamins.

Watt, I. (2006). Impressionism and symbolism in *Heart of Darkness*. In P. B. Armstrong (Ed.), *Heart of Darkness* (pp. 349–65). New York, NY: Norton.

Watts, C. E. (1990). *Heart of Darkness and Other Tales*. Oxford: Oxford University Press.

Waugh, A. (1919). *Tradition and Change: Studies in Contemporary Literature*. London: Chapman and Hall.

Winters, M. (2005). *A Corpus-based Study of Translator Style: Oeser's and Orth Guttmann's German Translations of F. Scott Fitzgerald's* The Beautiful and Damned (Unpublished doctoral dissertation). Dublin City University, Dublin, Irland.

Winters, M. (2007). F. Scott Fitzgerald's *Die Schönen und Verdammten*: A corpus-based study of speech-act report verbs as a feature of translators. *Meta: Journal des Traducteurs/Meta: Translators' Journal, 52*(3), 412–25.

Winters, M. (2010). From modal particles to point of view: A theoretical framework for the analysis of translator attitude. *Translation and Interpreting Studies, 5*(2), 163–85.

Xiao, R., & McEnery, T. (2006). Collocation, semantic prosody, and near synonymy: A cross-linguistic perspective. *Applied Linguistics, 27*(1), 103–29.

Youmans, G. (1990). Measuring lexical style and competence: The type-token vocabulary curve. *Style, 24*(4), 584–99.

Zins, H. (1982). *Joseph Conrad and Africa*. Nairobi: Kenya Literature Bureau.

Index